# Abandoned

## ALLISON BRENNAN

St. Martin's Paperbacks

This is a work of fiction. All of the characters, organizations, and events portrayed in this novel are either products of the author's imagination or are used fictitiously.

Published in the United States by St. Martin's Paperbacks, an imprint of St. Martin's Publishing Group.

ABANDONED

For information, address St. Martin's Publishing Group, 120 Broadway, New York, NY 10271.

www.stmartins.com

Library of Congress Catalog Card Number: 2018004423

ISBN: 978-1-250-16449-0

Our books may be purchased in bulk for promotional, educational, or business use. Please contact your local bookseller or the Macmillan Corporate and Premium Sales Department at 1-800-221-7945, ext. 5442, or by email at MacmillanSpecialMarkets@macmillan.com.

Printed in the United States of America

St. Martin's Press hardcover edition / August 2018
St. Martin's Paperbacks edition / October 2019

10  9  8  7  6  5  4  3  2

For those who step up

# Acknowledgments

When I decided to set this book on the Chesapeake Bay, I knew little of the area. I know much more thanks to Stacia Childers of the Eastern Shore Public Library, who freely answered my many questions. If I messed it up, that's on me.

Writers are a generous group. Two in particular helped this time around: the fabulous Marti Robb (who writes as Mariah Stewart), who gave me a wealth of information about the location and industries; and the wonderful Robin Burcell, retired cop and all-around great person, who always steps up to help fellow writers.

When I reached out to the Sisters in Crime group for help with sailing questions, several people offered their assistance—or the assistance of their family members! A special shout-out to Ken Littlefield and Terry Shames for going above and beyond in answering my questions—both the basic and the complex. While I hope I got everything right, don't hold any errors against them.

Wally Lind and his gang at the Crime Scene Writers group helped immensely by answering questions as broad as the condition of human remains after more than a decade; how the Coast Guard boards ships; and art theft. I don't know what I would do without this great group of people to help me!

Another shout-out to Lee Lofland and the Writers Police Academy. Lee is a selfless retired cop, who never says no to writers who need his guidance. He wants us to get it right.

And, as always, my deepest appreciation to the usual suspects: my agent, Dan Conaway; my editor, Kelley Ragland; the Minotaur team, especially Joe Brosnan, Maggie Callan, and Sarah Melnyk; my mom, who is my biggest cheerleader; and my husband, Dan, who never blinks when I suddenly say, "So I need a tasteless poison to mix into a mimosa . . ." And especially thanks to my kids who let me do my thing and love me anyway.

# Prologue

TWENTY-TWO YEARS AGO

Martha Revere couldn't leave without saying good-bye to Maxine. She was her daughter, after all.

But she had to get out of the house before her mother returned from whatever charity event she'd decided to grace with her presence. Eleanor Sterling Revere was psychic, Martha was certain of it. How else could she always know what Martha was doing? What her plans were? Especially before Martha herself had even figured everything out? Not to mention the stern judgment from on high, as if Eleanor were perfect, as if she were a god.

Just that morning, not even forty-eight hours after Martha came home, Eleanor confronted her.

*What are your plans, Martha?*

Like she needed to plan out her *life*. Eleanor had never done anything spontaneous, she had never understood Martha's need to go where her whims took her.

*Maxine needs stability. A good school, to learn proper manners, to attend university. Maxine must understand the benefits and responsibilities of being a Revere. You live like a nomad, Martha. You're raising a waif.*

Eleanor had been watching her closely—too closely—ever since she came home Thanksgiving morning with her beautiful daughter in tow. And then the clincher. While her father was bringing the car around this afternoon, Eleanor stood in the foyer, dressed impeccably, her hair done just right, her makeup perfectly applied, her clothes both fashionable and appropriate for a wealthy woman of her age.

*When you leave, Martha—and I know that is what you are planning, so don't lie to me—leave Maxine with me. She deserves better than what you are doing for her.*

How had she known that Martha never planned to stay? That leaving Maxine was always part of the plan?

For about two minutes, Martha decided to take Max with her, just to spite Eleanor. Serve her right. She never cared about Martha, yet seemed to care about the granddaughter she didn't know? Taking Max after introducing her to Eleanor would upset her mother, and that pleased Martha.

The two-minute mental debate ended. Max would ruin *everything*. All Martha wanted was a few months to have fun, and Max was *just* like Eleanor. She simply didn't know how to have fun.

Besides, as soon as Maxine acted up—and she would, because she didn't know how to keep her mouth shut, which was *almost* as bad as not knowing how to have fun—Eleanor would rue the day she told Martha to leave her. When Martha came back, Eleanor would insist she take Max, and Max would beg to leave. Because no way could anyone sane live under Eleanor's ridiculous rules and social mores.

Maxine was in the library. There were three "libraries" in the huge house—her father's cozy study that always smelled like bay rum and pipe tobacco; her mother's prim and stately sitting room where punishments were doled out; and here, the main library, with thousands of books no one ever read. And yet Maxine sat on the unblemished leather sofa, bare feet curled under her, reading a leather-bound book Martha doubted had been opened in a hundred years. She did a double take when she saw the title. *The Lion, the Witch and the Wardrobe*. Wasn't that a kid's book? Leave it to her mother to find the stuffiest edition of a child's book for her snooty library.

Max looked up from the book and stared at Martha with Eleanor's too-smart, all-knowing, dark blue eyes. The "I know you're going to leave" look. The look of disapproval. Disappointment. Judgment.

How on earth could a kid not yet ten have mastered the Eleanor Revere glare so quickly?

Martha straightened her spine. This was for the best. Ha! That sounded like something Eleanor would say.

*This is the second time I've caught you sneaking back into the house this week. You're grounded. Your father and I decided to take your car for a month. It is for the best. You need to learn responsibility and respect, Martha. To understand that you have a duty to family and community because you are a Revere.*

Eleanor never understood that Martha wasn't like them. She needed to be free, not living in the stuffy confines of *norms* and *responsibility* and *expectations*.

Why the hell should she have any *duty* to anyone but herself?

"Are you coming back?" Maxine asked in her quiet, too-regal voice.

"Of course, silly," Martha said. "I always do."

This time, however, she wasn't certain she *would* return. Or when. Maxine had been turning into her mother, even though Martha had done everything in her power to make sure Maxine didn't end up a Revere. Maybe genetics had more to do with personality than anyone thought.

"When?"

"I don't know. Why do I need to give you a schedule?

Look at this place. It's huge. It wasn't *all* bad growing up here. And there are books. You love books. You've been nagging me about school. Now you can go. See? Win-win."

Why Maxine wanted to go to school, Martha would never understand. She hated school, from day one when Sierra Noble pushed her off the swing and said that there were *rules* to the playground and Sierra *made* the rules. And the first rule was that she always got to swing first at recess.

Martha hated rules before Sierra, and she hated them twice as much after that little bitch.

Of course, Martha had gotten back at the whiny, self-absorbed bully. And it never came back on *her*. Because she was *that good*.

She almost smiled at the memory of Sierra crying her big brown eyes out. She'd waited years for her revenge, but it was *so* worth it.

*"But I didn't cheat!"*

*"We have solid evidence, Sierra. School policy dictates a zero on the final plus a three-day suspension. I'm sorry, Sierra, we certainly expected better of you."*

Martha had always been good at school—at least good enough to get by, manipulate the teachers, and make her parents happy. At least with grades. But that didn't mean that she enjoyed it, or found it at all necessary.

"Look, Maxie, I'll try to be back by your birthday, okay? That's only a few weeks away."

"Five weeks."

"Jeez, semantics! I have things I want to do, okay? And you can't come with me. You'll fit in perfectly here, you're exactly like my mother."

She hadn't meant to say that, or use that tone. Was the kid going to cry? God, she hated when Maxie cried, almost as much as she hated the look of disappointment on her face. Fortunately, she rarely cried.

"Why can't you let me live with my father? I've never even met him. It's not fair."

Fair? What about life was *fair*? "I told you, he's married and it's complicated. He doesn't want you. I wanted you, I kept you, I didn't get rid of you like everyone said I should have." She shouldn't have said that, either, but Maxine was making her feel guilty. The only other person who had ever made her feel guilty was her mother. She didn't like it, not one bit, so she pushed the guilt aside. It had become quite easy to do over the years.

"I don't want to fight, Maxie," Martha said. "You don't like Jimmy anyway."

"So you're leaving me here with people I don't know because you and Jimmy don't want me around to cramp your style."

"No." God, how did she do that? She was *nine years old.* How did she figure this stuff out?

And it was clear she didn't believe Martha anyway, so why even try?

"Life is meant to be *fun*," Martha said. "Life has plans, baby. Never forget that. I guarantee when I come back, you'll be *begging* me to take you away from this place and all the stupid rules. You will never want to be a Revere when you see what it really means. The formals. The charities. The smiling and being polite when all you want to do is go off with your friends but you *can't* because you have *responsibilities*. Then you'll *finally* understand and not judge me all the damn time. I really have to go now. Jimmy's waiting for me."

She hugged Maxine and pretended her daughter hugged her back. She didn't have time for this, she didn't want a confrontation with her mother. The only thing she kind of regretted was that she'd promised her dad that she'd go into the city with him and Maxine tomorrow afternoon like they used to do when she was a little girl. He would take her on the trolley car and they'd walk along the wharf and have fresh clam chowder soup in bread bowls at restaurants that Eleanor wouldn't walk by, let alone eat at.

Those were the best memories of her childhood.

But the guilt was fleeting. Guilt was a useless emotion, Martha told herself on the rare occasions it crept in. She'd send her dad a postcard, explain that she couldn't live with her mother, that she had things to do and he would understand.

At least, she convinced herself that her dad would understand.

"Good-bye for now!" Martha said with a bright smile. She walked right out the front door. No one else was in the house to stop her—it was the Saturday after Thanksgiving and Eleanor had given her staff the weekend off. No one else lived in the house. Martha didn't have to answer to anyone, not anymore. Not even her daughter.

A white Mercedes coupe had pulled in to the driveway and Brooks got out. She glared at him.

"Where are you going?" he demanded.

"None of your business."

"Where's your kid?"

"Reading."

"You have a lot to answer for, Martha."

She hated her brother. Hated him more than anyone else. He had made her life miserable growing up, and why her mother actually seemed to like him more, Martha would never understand. "Good-bye." She started to walk past him.

Brooks grabbed her arm and spun her around. "Don't you dare leave that bastard girl here."

Martha jerked her arm away from him. "Wait until you really get to know Maxine," she said with a sneer. "She'll hate you as much as I do."

"I will send her to boarding school."

Martha laughed. "Good luck with that. If Eleanor didn't send me, she's not going to send Max. Suck it up, Brooks. Your perfect life just got shaken and stirred."

"You'd better come back for her, Martha."

"Or what? You forget, I know every one of your secrets, and Mother may not like me, but she'll believe me. She'll believe everything."

Brooks reddened. He *should* be scared.

She walked away before her brother could get under her skin. She wished there was another way. Brooks might eat Max alive—he hated Martha enough to make the kid's life miserable.

But Max was a smart kid—really, for a not quite ten-year-old, she was smarter than most adults. Brooks might have met his match because he would underestimate her, and then *wham!* Martha almost wished she could be around to watch.

Unfortunately, it was clear from the minute they hooked up with Jimmy last month that Jimmy and Max were oil and water. Martha had given her daughter a decade of her time and attention—and truly, it was becoming more difficult. Max nearly blew their last gig, and that's when Jimmy convinced Martha that maybe it was time to let someone else in the family step up and watch her. He'd wanted to ship her off to her father, but Jimmy didn't know who Max's father was, and that was a secret Martha would take to the grave.

But there was more to family than a mother and father. The Reveres could take over raising Max, at least until Martha decided to come back for her. A month? Two? Six? Some day she'd come back. And Maxie would beg to leave.

*Take that, Mother.*

Jimmy was waiting for her at the end of the driveway in the BMW he'd rented. She climbed into the passenger seat and gave him a big, sloppy kiss. "I'm free!"

"Good." He sped much too fast out of the neighborhood, but Martha didn't care. She was *free*. Free, free, free! She should have done this a long time ago. She'd thought having a kid would be a lot more fun than it actually was. It wasn't like she'd planned to get pregnant, it just happened. Maybe it was just *that* kid. Maybe another wouldn't be so bad, a kid with Jimmy. And they could raise her—or him—to have *fun*.

Maxine was a kid and Martha gave her all the freedom she'd never had growing up. They traveled everywhere, all over the world! Maxine didn't even have to go to school. Martha had wanted to see the world when she was young enough to appreciate it, and she'd taken Maxine along for the ride. They'd been to every major museum in Europe and the States; they'd stayed in the nicest hotels and once spent the entire summer at a villa in France.

And all the little brat could do was make Martha feel inadequate.

"Where are we going?" she asked Jimmy.

"We have three days before we can go to the bank, but we have enough to get by until then. It's dreary here. Let's drive south. We have a lot of plans to make. A *lot* of plans. We're going to have fun, Martha. A Hawaiian adventure."

She laughed and rubbed Jimmy's thigh. Finally, she had her life back. The life she'd been searching for ever since she walked out of the house after her high school graduation, when she finally had partial control over her trust fund and an increase in her monthly allowance. And there was nothing that her parents could do about it because the trust was iron-clad.

Any residual guilt Martha had over leaving her daughter disappeared at the Atherton town limits. After all, she deserved a life, too.

# Chapter One

Maxine Revere had been an investigative reporter, in one capacity or another, for more than a decade. In the beginning, she had been the sole collector of information. She'd spent thousands of hours in libraries, interviewed hundreds of people, and traveled across the country to collect key pieces of intelligence to solve cold cases.

Now that she had a monthly cable crime show, had written four true crime books, and recently published her seventy-sixth article in a major trade magazine, she enjoyed the benefits of her success: a staff that was as good at research—and sometimes better—than she was; an assistant both smart and disciplined; and a real career that had garnered her both respect and animosity, praise and criticism.

She liked her job and she made a difference. Max solved cold cases that seemed unsolvable because of the limited resources of law enforcement. That, and her driving need to uncover the truth wherever it led.

Now, for the first time, she had a real chance of learning the truth about what had happened to her mother sixteen years ago. She might even find out why her mother left her in the first place to be raised by grandparents she had never known before that fateful Thanksgiving, only weeks before her tenth birthday.

The disappearance of her mother was personal, and she wasn't going to film a segment for "Maximum Exposure." She had no plans to write a book, an article, or even a blog about Martha Revere's life and presumed death. Max had the resources—namely, money—to investigate this case on her own, and could take the time to do it, even if it cost Max her career.

Some things were worth sacrificing everything. The truth—especially the truth about *her* life—was one of them.

Two months ago, she'd learned from a private investigator, Sean Rogan, that her mother had bought a car in Miami under a false identity, and that car had turned up abandoned in Northampton County, Virginia, three months later. Max hired the PI to dig deeper into the identity and the timeline of Martha Revere's whereabouts from when she left Max at her grandparents' house that Thanksgiving weekend, until she stopped sending Max postcards shortly after Max's sixteenth birthday.

It was difficult and tedious work for many reasons, the passage of time being an almost insurmountable factor. Martha left Max twenty-two years ago. All Max had— she'd turned copies over to Rogan—were sixteen postcards sent over a six-year period. Financial records were archived and not readily accessible. Someone with one false identity may have additional false identities. And the one thing that Max had learned after living with her mother for the first ten years of her life—Martha Revere was smart, unpredictable, and wild.

Rogan had made great headway, but he had a life and a business and had been unavailable for the last few weeks due to a major case he was working on. Max was antsy. She needed to get into the field and learn the truth. She already knew where Martha's car had been found, the name she had been using—that of her elderly aunt. She had basic information that Rogan had dug up, enough that she could go to Northampton herself and find more answers. And she'd filmed two shows for "Maximum Exposure" in the time it usually took her to do one—just in case the investigation took longer than she planned.

Her producer, Ben Lawson, wasn't happy that she was taking time off with no set return date. She recognized if she were any other person, she'd be fired or her series canceled. And maybe it would be. At this point, she didn't care. For the first time in her life, she had a *hint* about what happened to her mother, and enough clues to follow the bread crumbs. *This* was more important than anything else in her life. It was more important than her fledgling love life, more important than her career, more important than her family, who didn't want her digging into the past at all.

This was the most important investigation she'd ever undertaken.

On Saturday morning, she emailed Rogan and told him she was taking the information he'd gathered and would be leaving the following morning for Cape Haven, a small community in Northampton County. She had reserved a small beach house at a resort for the entire month of April, and she'd stay longer if necessary. She hadn't heard back from the PI, so she assumed he didn't have anything new to share with her.

She packed Saturday evening, then poured herself a glass of wine and made herself a chef's salad. She lived in a penthouse in Greenwich Village with a view of the Hudson River. She bought the place after she graduated from Columbia and renovated it to suit her needs and lifestyle. She had no plans to move. She traveled extensively, but this was her home. Maybe because she hadn't had a real home growing up. First, living like a nomad with her mother for nearly ten years, then living with her grandparents for the next nine years in their subdued mansion in a prestigious northern California zip code. Nothing had been *hers*. But this penthouse was all Max. Her space. A place for her things.

She didn't have much—not because she was a minimalist, but because she didn't see the need to accumulate stuff for the sake of having stuff. But she cherished what she did have. Art she bought because she liked it, not because it was valuable—though much of it was. Furniture that was both comfortable and aesthetically pleasing. A kitchen of state-of-the-art appliances, because she loved to cook when she had the time. An entire wall devoted to books because she loved reading. It was an eclectic collection. History, especially books that discussed how history was reflected in the art of the times; architecture because that, too, touched on both art and history; mysteries—give her a good puzzle to lose herself in, and she was happy for the night. Some books she felt she had to read because everyone else had read them. And many, many classics. And she'd always had a fondness for Louis L'Amour, because her grandfather had loved the writer of Westerns. When she bought the penthouse, her grandmother had sent her his entire collection with a note from her grandfather, who had died a few years before:

> *Dearest Maxine,*
> *I used to believe you indulged me when I would*
> *read you passages from some of my favorite*
> *L'Amour books, but you always listened and*
> *humored this old man. One day, I saw you reading*
> *The Sacketts by the fire, and realized you weren't*
> *simply appeasing me; you enjoyed the stories*

*as much as I did. I hope you have room for my
collection in your new home; there is no one else I
would want to have them.*
 *With love,*
 *Grandfather*

He'd died when she was fifteen, long before she bought
the penthouse. Her grandmother never told her about the
collection, so when she received them as she was settling
in to her home, she was touched. Reading her grandfather's letter, written before he passed, had been bittersweet.

She finished her salad, washed her plate, and poured
a second glass of wine. She sat in her reading corner and
reviewed her schedule for the week. She'd already set up
an appointment with the sheriff of Northampton County
to talk to him about the investigation into the disappearance of "D. Jane Sterling," the owner of the car that Max
was certain belonged to her mother.

Still, now that she had made the decision and planned
to leave tomorrow morning, she'd become apprehensive.
Her assistant, David Kane, would say that it was because
she was scared.

*"You have always lived in the shadow of your moth-
er's choices,"* David had told her when she began to pursue the information Rogan uncovered two months ago.
*"That the truth is so close terrifies you."*

*"I've never shied away from the truth."* His observa-
tions made Max more than a little irritated at him.

*"While I'll admit that Rogan is unusually gifted in his
field, you certainly could have found or paid to find the
same information he did."*

That was true, and it was something Max had been
thinking about a lot since she hired Rogan to dig deeper.

*"I'm putting it out there, Max. You have never backed down from a challenge—but with your mother's disappearance, you've never confronted it."*

Max trusted David more than anyone else in her life, and when he'd called her on her hypocrisy, she realized that he was right. First her mother lied to Max about her paternity, all the while leading a wild and carefree lifestyle before dumping her to live with her grandparents; then Martha disappeared off the face of the earth when Max was sixteen. Every decision her mother had made, both before and after that fateful Thanksgiving, had colored Max's life and every choice *she* made. She'd never lied to herself about any of it, because Max abhorred lies—especially to herself. But until David called her out, she didn't realize the deep truth: she *was* scared. She feared learning the whole truth about her mother because it would de facto change who Max was and how she viewed herself in the world.

Not knowing had driven her for years, and once the truth came to light, what would she do? Who would she be?

Fear was no excuse. Now, there was no turning back.

There was a knock at her door. That meant one of two people: her neighbor who owned the other top-floor penthouse, or David, who had a passkey to the building. He also had a key to her apartment, but he wouldn't use it except in an emergency.

She opened the door. David. "I wasn't expecting you."

"Rogan found something. He wants to talk to both of us."

In the past, Max would have been furious that the PI she hired had contacted her assistant instead of her. Though David had become more of a partner than an assistant, this was still a personal investigation, not affiliated in any way with NET, the cable television station that paid David's salary.

"I know," David said without her having to say anything.

"You don't."

"Let's go to your office."

"I've already packed." She sat down at the dining table and called Rogan from her cell phone, then put it on speaker.

"Rogan," a voice said.

"Sean, it's Maxine Revere and David Kane."

"Glad I caught you before you left."

"Bright and early tomorrow morning."

"I learned something last week and was trying to get more details before I called you, but since you're jumping now I thought you should know."

"I appreciate that."

"If any of my other feelers pan out, I'll let you know, but I have another job that will keep me busy for the rest of the week."

"You warned me you couldn't devote all your time to the project, so just tell me what you have and we'll go from there."

"Do you recall a man named James Truman? He went by the name Jimmy."

The past slapped Max in the face. She hadn't heard that name in a long, long time.

"Yes." She shook her head, trying to purge memories of the jerk. "He was one of my mother's many boyfriends."

"When you told me you were going to Northampton County to talk to the sheriff about the abandoned car, I revisited the list of Martha's known associates during the years between when she left you and when she disappeared.

Martha and Truman were very good at covering their tracks, but I found records in New York, Texas, Florida, Hawaii, Italy, and New Zealand that put them together. In fact, I may be going out on a limb here, but I think they were together the majority of those six years."

"My mother never stayed with one man longer than three or four months," Max said. "And that's stretching it."

"You created the timeline of her known locations based on where she withdrew her trust fund allowance. I took that and extrapolated. She was off the radar most of the time, but Jimmy Truman wasn't—until she disappeared."

"I don't see what you're getting at, Rogan." She was trying to wrap her head around the idea that her mother could have been committed to *anyone*.

"The FBI opened an investigation into James Truman ten years ago. I couldn't get much more than that except that it's linked to a case in Dallas at least sixteen years ago."

Sixteen years? That was the time her mother disappeared. "Was there an investigation into my mother, too?" She would be stunned—she would have known. She'd dated a federal agent on and off for nine years. Certainly *someone* would have made the connection, and she had never distanced herself from her mother. It was on her Web page, her biography, and she'd even touched on her childhood in articles she'd written. Yet the FBI had never interviewed her—or her grandparents, as far as she knew.

"No, not Martha Revere. If she had a really good fake identity—better than the Sterling identity—maybe they simply didn't know who she was."

David asked, "What was he being investigated for?"

"That I don't know. All I know was that it was opened out of the Norfolk regional FBI office and then attached to an older Dallas investigation. I don't even have an agent of record. I can dig deeper."

"I have contacts in the FBI," Max said. "I'll get it, if it's important."

"Like I said, I'm going to be out of pocket for the next week or two, but I put out a lot of feelers specifically following the money trail. Some of your information isn't accurate."

Max straightened her spine. "What?" Her family had thwarted her in the past, but something of this magnitude—falsifying bank records—that was beyond the pale.

"Most of the information I'm looking for isn't maintained for this long. But I confirmed that on at least three occasions, the money was transferred out of your mother's bank account to an offshore account. So the records are technically accurate, but your mother wasn't present to receive her funds."

Max's mother had never kept a bank account longer than a few months because she had once told Max that she didn't want Eleanor to know what she was doing or who she was doing it with. It made no sense then, and now Max wondered *why*. Was it just Martha's way of flipping the bird to her family? Or did she have another, more logical—more criminal—reason?

"Thank you," she said.

"I also have a request into the State Department for her passport travel records—I should say *you* made the request, you're next of kin. It's faster and easier that way, but I put myself down as the contact. If I hear anything, I'll call you."

David said, "I'll be in Miami following up on Martha's alias. Max is going to Virginia."

"Which brings me to the other information I learned about Truman. First, I believe he was using the alias J. J. Sterling in Miami, so David, you might want to follow up on that as well. He was born and raised in Virginia—in a small town called Cape Haven. It's less than fifteen miles from where Martha's car was found."

David stared at Max. "I should go with you."

"It's been sixteen years," Max said. "Truman isn't around, or if he is, he's not going to remember me. We need the information from Miami, and you're the only one I trust—other than me—to get it."

David didn't look happy, but Max wasn't worried about danger. Her mother had been missing for sixteen years. If it was foul play that didn't mean squat. Sixteen years was a long time.

"What else do you know about Truman?" David asked Rogan.

"He obtained a Virginia State driver's license when he was eighteen that has never been renewed. That doesn't mean anything—he could have gotten one in another state, and I have inquiries in the states I know he spent some time. His parents are deceased—his father died in a fishing boat accident when he was a teenager, and his mother, Emily, died of cancer ten years ago. He has a younger brother, Gabriel, a U.S. Navy veteran honorably discharged sixteen years ago in September. Gabriel Truman lives in the family home in Cape Haven and owns a charter boat business attached to a resort. He keeps a low profile—no personal social media profiles. His business is all business, no personal information other than basic. No criminal record."

Jimmy Truman. Max barely remembered him, but she hadn't liked him. *That* she hadn't forgotten.

"That's pretty extensive," David said.

"Not as much as I would have liked. I don't have a current photograph of Truman, for example, and no sign of him in the last ten years—which could mean he's dead or he has a solid new identity."

"What are you thinking in this?" David asked. "That

Jimmy Truman killed Martha? Is that why there's an investigation?"

"I couldn't say—only that the federal government doesn't generally open murder investigations," Sean said. "But again, you'll need to get the file from Norfolk or Dallas."

"I'll get it," Max said.

"If you need help, I can make calls."

"Like I said, I have my own FBI contacts. Sean, back up—you said you tracked him up until ten years ago? And nothing since?"

"I think I have. I uncovered two of his aliases—my guess is that he may have had more, and I'm working on it now that I know his pattern. He went under the name James Masters in Texas, and under the name J. J. Sterling in Florida. I have a list of your family members and have been running those names and variations in Texas, Florida, and New York—three of the places Martha seemed to return at least once a year."

What had Jimmy and her mother been up to? Nothing would surprise Max at this point.

That wasn't completely true. She'd be surprised if her mother was alive.

David asked, "Keep both of us in the loop if you learn anything else, Rogan."

Max was staring out the window and didn't realize that David had disconnected the call.

"Max?" It was a quiet inquiry from her partner and her friend. She and David had been through a lot together over the last two years. She'd faced several truths from her past with David by her side. But this one mystery haunted her.

"When I found out Martha was using Aunt Delia's identity, the truth didn't hit me."

"You lost me."

"Martha was involved in something illegal. It's the only explanation."

"She could have been in trouble, maybe dated the wrong guy. Like Jimmy Truman."

She glanced at David. "I met Jimmy. He and Martha hooked up a month before she left me with my grandparents. I didn't like him, my mother knew it. I thought she'd grow tired of him like she did every other guy she slept with. When she didn't come back for me, I determined that she much preferred her freedom to being saddled with a precocious child. I never thought she'd stayed with him."

"We don't know anything right now, not about their relationship or how close they were. Anything could have happened. He could have been blackmailing her, she could have been working with him, or maybe she was a victim."

She laughed humorlessly. "Martha Revere, the victim? No. She was never a victim, and if she was killed—by Jimmy or anyone else—she probably got into something she couldn't talk or buy her way out of. The people she liked to hang with weren't all saints. Maybe she got in over her head, or maybe she knew exactly what she was doing. Whatever *it* was."

"We'll find the answers."

Max had more answers now, in the two months that Rogan had been helping her, than she had in the twenty-two years since her mother left. But every answer led to more questions.

"Be careful with Gabriel Truman."

She turned and gave David a half smile. "You knew I'd reach out to him?"

"It would be my first play. But we don't know who he is, not really. So be cautious."

In the past, she would have given David a snippy

response—after all, she'd been an investigative reporter long before David was hired by NET to be her bodyguard, in far more dangerous areas than the Chesapeake Bay— but she'd learned that David's caution wasn't a criticism of her abilities, but came from his experience in security and their friendship.

"I'm going to do a little research locally, then reach out to him," she said. "And I'll proceed with caution, I promise."

"I can hop on a plane and be there in only a few hours," he said. "Just ask. And—as a reminder—if I don't hear from you, I'll show up anyway."

# Chapter Two

Max woke before dawn Tuesday morning, made coffee, and walked out onto the deck to watch the sunrise. She pulled the thick robe around her shoulders and put her arms on the railing as the first light cut along the Atlantic Ocean.

Bliss. Even better than yesterday.

She'd spent Sunday and yesterday, her first full day in Cape Haven, getting the lay of the land, but today she planned to dig in and focus on her agenda: the library, then meeting with the sheriff, and hopefully she'd find the first answer of many as to what happened to her mother sixteen years ago.

But now, in this moment, Max sipped her coffee and let her mind catch up with her body.

Max had leased a two bedroom, three-story beach cottage right on the water. It was large for one person, but she liked her space. Downstairs was a small living area, bedroom, and bath; the middle floor had a large great room with a kitchen, dining area, living area, and a den that she had turned into her office. A balcony with decking on all four sides gave her an amazing view. Upstairs was the master suite and a large bathroom that opened out to a hot tub and another smaller, private deck. Her first night here she'd sat outside until it grew too cold, just watching the boats come in and out of the harbor.

Northampton County comprised the southern half of the Eastern Shore of Virginia. It connected to the rest of Virginia via a bridge, and fishing and tourism were the two major industries—both of which had taken hits over the last two decades. Since it was a sparsely populated and close-knit community, Max had decided she needed to immerse herself for a few days as a "tourist." Familiarize herself with the town, talk to people, absorb the environment.

Okay, *tourist* wasn't the right word. She wasn't hiding her identity, for example. But for the first time since last year when she had gone to Lake Tahoe for a week with her now ex-boyfriend, she felt like she was on a real vacation. The private cottage she had in the lone Cape Haven resort gave her exactly what she needed: peace, quiet, and a private beach. She could sit on the deck and not see anyone.

But this wasn't really a vacation, and while soul-searching might be part of the journey considering she was looking for answers to her past, she would never forget the real reason she'd come to the Eastern Shore of Virginia: to find out what happened to her mother.

That her mother had abandoned her car here, of all places, seemed odd. True, it had the ocean that Martha Revere loved so much. Martha loved boats, preferably yachts owned by rich, sexy men. They'd once spent three weeks on a luxury liner with one of Martha's boyfriends when Max was eight. They'd taken a cruise to the Caribbean—not quite as fun because Max had *not* liked that boyfriend, a jerk who looked like he wanted to throw both her *and* her mother overboard.

Quaint and quiet towns were not Martha's style. The resort in Cape Haven was very loosely called a resort. When both the restaurant and room service shut down at ten on the weekend—and nine during the week—Max knew that her mother wouldn't have stayed here. She could have been just passing through. Norfolk was on the other side of the Chesapeake Bay Bridge-Tunnel.

Or, she could have been here because of Jimmy Truman.

Max had never understood her mother when she was a child who simply followed where her mom led. Now? Max had met women like Martha. Women who were innately selfish, but always felt they needed to be *with* a man. As if her self-worth was partially determined by her boyfriend. Martha wanted to be attached to someone, but she didn't cling. She dumped her boyfriends when it was no longer "fun." A narcissist? Perhaps. She seemed to like to cause conflict for the simple reason that conflict excited her.

Max recognized she was remembering her mother through glasses tinted by her youth and immaturity, a view obscured by deep anger and sorrow. Max never lied to herself, and accepted that her memories could be flawed. What was formed out of the emotions of being left behind—out of fear and rage she hadn't understood that young—was clouded by her decade-long pursuit of cold cases. Had those cases given her additional insight? Could she trust it? Or was that insight somehow slanted because of her past?

When she investigated cases involving people she didn't know, cases where she had no personal stake, hadn't known the victim, didn't know the families, her job was easier because she had no emotional connection.

It was much, much harder investigating a missing person that she knew. She'd done it before, her first case that led to her first book. Her best friend and roommate, Karen Richardson, had disappeared and was presumed dead during spring break in Miami when they were college seniors. Max had spent a year searching for answers. She knew in her heart that Karen was dead, that the guy she'd hooked up with had killed her. But there was no proof other than far too much blood at the scene for anyone to lose and still survive. Her body had never been found. Her killer had no alibi, but there was no physical evidence that pointed to him as the killer. He gloated and left the country because as a foreign national, there was no reason for the police to detain him.

Max had been emotionally involved, but she'd also been young. She wanted to believe she had gained a certain distance to assess things with clear impartiality, but too often in the last few months she'd found herself with the same feelings she'd been left with years ago, chief among them loneliness.

*You picked the wrong time to split with your boyfriend.*

Breaking it off with Nick, the detective she'd been dating for almost a year, had been easier than she thought—and harder to live with. She had cared for him, but she wasn't going to sit back and wait for him to get his life together. She recognized for the first time in her life that she deserved better than half a relationship, because that's what it had felt like with Nick. Sure, the sex had been great, the man could cook, and he quickly learned to accept her independence and career choices. She had thought that would be sufficient.

It wasn't. Nick had baggage with an ex-wife and kid, and chose to shut her out instead of including her. Maybe it was selfish of her to want to be included, if not in the decisions then at least in the conversation.

She'd decided that the split was for the best. She, too, had baggage. She hadn't realized until the last year that everything in her past had made her a better investigative reporter. Except that her past hung over her, a cloud dark enough to make Eeyore think he walked under a ray of sunshine. What had happened to her had made her stronger, but had also damaged everything in her life. Her relationships—romantic, personal, and professional— had been impacted. Her inability to trust, her way of keeping people at arm's length, and her drive to uncover the truth in everything had all come at a cost.

Max wasn't naïve enough to think that solving her mother's disappearance would brighten her life or change her in any fundamental way. She'd always told crime victims and survivors that she would uncover the truth, warts and all. Some people didn't want the truth, they wanted the facts to fit their own narrative. But some people truly wanted to know what happened to their loved one, the good and bad. They needed the truth so they could take the next step without darkness clouding their path. Max was good at uncovering the truth for others; now she had to learn her own truths.

When the sun breached the horizon, Max went back inside, prepared another cup of coffee in the Keurig, and reviewed her timeline. She'd spent most of yesterday converting the cottage's den into her office. A timeline had been tacked over two walls—the corner representing the Thanksgiving when her mother left her with her grandparents. One thing Rogan had been very good at was using Max's own childhood journals and her mother's trust fund records to create a timeline of where Martha had been prior to that Thanksgiving, and during the nearly six and a half years after, when her car was found abandoned and she stopped collecting her trust allowance. There were a few holes, but a timeline had emerged.

Max was a visual person. She liked to see everything at once, to recognize the patterns. Rogan had been correct in that there were a few places Martha returned to with regularity. Miami was one of her regular stopping points. So were New York, France, and cruises to St. Thomas or another Caribbean island. Did she have friends there? Had she felt comfortable? A sort of home base?

But the outliers were even more revealing.

Martha had spent three months in Hawaii right after she left Max, but had never returned. She had been with Jimmy Truman at the time. Max remembered vaguely spending time in Hawaii when she was very little, but she had no real recollection of it. The financial records indicated she'd been there with her mother the fall before she turned four.

Martha had spent several months in Dallas, Texas, two years later, and had never returned. There was no information as to whether Truman was there at the same time.

Martha had spent three months in Montreal two years after that, and again never returned—nor had she ever been there with Max. There was no indication as to whether Truman was with her.

And while Miami and other Florida cities had been a regular stop for Martha over the years, Miami had been the last place she'd been before she bought the car under the name D. Jane Sterling, drove to the Eastern Shore of Virginia, and disappeared.

Had she taken another false identity? Because she was in danger or trouble?

Max didn't see that. If Martha had voluntarily disappeared, she would have found a way to access her money. But her accounts had been untouched after April first of that year. She'd never been found—dead or alive—by law enforcement. Eleanor had hired a private investigator when Martha had been missing for seven years, to expedite the death certificate, but he hadn't found anything. Or so Eleanor claimed.

Maybe Rogan was just that much better. Or maybe Eleanor didn't want Martha to be found.

Eleanor resented Martha. Not because she left Max with her, but because of her wanton lifestyle and the continual slap in the face her behavior was to the family.

Eleanor admitted to Max—once—that she had the PI do the bare minimum necessary for the court to issue the death certificate.

*"Truly, Maxine, I don't want Martha back in my life, or in yours. I believe in my heart she is dead. How and why is irrelevant. When she returned with you, she gave your grandfather false hope—he always had a soft spot for Martha, always dismissed her selfish behavior as youth and a free spirit. When she left two days later without a good-bye, she killed that hope and he was never the same."*

While Eleanor could be difficult, Max respected her. But her grandfather was wholeheartedly different. He was a good man, successful and hard-working, with a kind soul and overwhelming love for his family. James Revere was the strong, silent type, a true patriarch whose death had hit everyone hard because he was the glue that had held the family together—even Eleanor's family, the Sterlings. And it was through her grandfather's eyes that Max had learned to love her grandmother.

Max was surprised when tears burned. She squeezed her eyes shut, took a deep breath, and refocused on her plans for the day.

Under the timeline headings were questions on sticky notes. And the most pressing question was about the police file of the abandoned car. And that was where she would start—after she did some legwork.

"May I get you anything else, Ms. Revere?"

Max glanced up. Mrs. Burg, the head librarian at the main Eastern Shore library in Accomac, had been extremely helpful. But some things Max had to do herself, like sitting at the microfiche machine reading old papers.

"I think I have everything," she said. "I sent some articles to print."

"I have them here." The trim, middle-aged woman smiled and handed Max a stack of paper clipped together. "Forty-seven pages, at twenty cents a page, is nine dollars and forty cents."

The staff had been helpful in providing her with the microfiche or hard copies of newspapers from the April that her mother's car had been found abandoned. But nothing in the newspapers gave her the answers she needed, just more questions.

Max started to collect the films and Mrs. Burg told her she would take care of it. "I hope you find out what happened to your mother," she said. "What an awful thing, not to know about your own family."

Max agreed with her grandmother that Martha was dead. But even though she'd been declared dead and her trust fund—and board seat—had converted to Max as her sole heir, Max wanted to see the proof.

"May I help you with anything else?" Mrs. Burg asked.

"I assume property records will be at the county office?"

"Yes, that is correct. Unless you're looking for historical documents. We have documents going back to the seventeen hundreds, particularly important for those studying genealogy and family history."

"I'm not interested in anything that far back, but thank you."

"If you need anything else, please call or come in. I'll be happy to help."

Max was about to leave, but she turned and said, "Actually, I need an obituary. I don't have the exact date, but the woman was Emily Truman, a resident of Cape Haven. She died about ten years ago."

"Emily?"

Mrs. Burg knew Emily Truman. This could be a problem.

*You should have assumed. This is a small community—
everyone probably knows everyone else.*

"You knew her?"

"Yes, she was a teacher at the high school. Both my
sons had her for English."

It was clear Mrs. Burg wanted to ask why Max was
interested, but as a librarian, she didn't—the professional
in her said it was none of her business, which Max used
now. She didn't want it getting around that she was looking into either of Truman's sons.

"Are the obituaries on microfiche?"

Mrs. Burg, who had been warm from the minute Max
walked in, turned a few degrees cooler. "Yes. I'm sure
you know how to look through the card index. I need to
help Mrs. Crabtree. Please excuse me."

She walked over to an older woman who didn't look
like she wanted or needed help. Max ignored the slight
and searched through the files.

It was difficult because she didn't have an exact date.
She asked for four tapes which covered a two-year period. It took her two hours to sort through the information, scanning every obituary, before she found Emily
Truman.

She printed it out because she didn't have time to read
in depth—she was already late to her appointment with
the sheriff. Mrs. Burg barely said two words to her as she
left, and Max wondered if her presence was going to get
around town sooner rather than later.

She really didn't want Gabriel Truman knowing she
was looking into his family, not before she told him herself. She might have to do that earlier than she'd planned.

# Chapter Three

Maxine Revere walked into the Northampton County Sheriff's Department Tuesday after lunch.

Northampton County, a thirty-five mile stretch along the southeastern shore of the Delmarva Peninsula—more popularly known as "The Shore"—boasted 12,000 residents, lots of water, farms, and fishing. The sheriff's department had a couple dozen sworn deputies and an elected sheriff, whom Max had opted to contact ahead of time and set up a formal meeting.

While she had no problem pushing the envelope—and pushing hard—working this cold case needed a bit more finesse. And she had no reason to believe that the sheriff wouldn't cooperate. After all, he didn't even have a dead body to go with the abandoned car.

"Maxine Revere here for Sheriff William Bartlett," she said to the civilian manning the main desk. Civilian because she didn't wear a uniform and appeared far too old to be a cop.

"Do you have an appointment?" the blue-haired woman asked.

"Yes. I'm a few minutes late—I called."

She smiled pleasantly. "Please have a seat. I'll see if the sheriff is ready."

Max opted to stand and walked over to the wall where there were photos of the different sheriffs—past and present. There was an old black-and-white turn-of-the-century photo of the sheriff at the time swearing in a deputy. She was antsy, practically nervous—and she didn't know exactly why. She was never nervous on an interview, never worried about ticking off the authorities, and she had no intention of playing hardball unless Bartlett put on the brakes. So far, his office had been accommodating and downright friendly, at least on the phone.

*Don't lie to yourself, Maxine. You damn well know why you're nervous.*

Truth. The truth about her mother was here, in Virginia, sixteen years after she fell off the face of the earth.

She might not get answers—what happened to her mother, why was she using Aunt Delia's name, why had she abandoned Max all those years ago—but Max should be able to prove that Martha was dead, one way or the other.

And damned if she would sit back and guess on the rest. She would exhaust every avenue to find out the *whys* and, if possible, the *who*. She was a crime reporter, after all, and if she couldn't ferret out the truth no one could.

Because she was damn good at her job.

"Ms. Revere?"

The voice was male, deep, and commanding. Max turned and faced Sheriff William Bartlett, full uniform, sans the hat. He was a large man in every sense of the word with dark graying hair and a thick mustache.

She extended her hand; he took it and didn't give her a lackluster shake. She liked him immediately. No-nonsense, with a sparkle in his eye. "Thank you for agreeing to meet with me."

"You want answers, and I hope to find them for you."

She'd told him on the phone about her search for her

mother. He also knew that she was a crime reporter with a cable show out of New York City, but unlike many in law enforcement, he didn't seem to hold that against her.

"Let's go to my office."

She followed him. It wasn't a large department—wouldn't need to be for the community—but people worked at desks and two deputies passed them on their way out. Bartlett exchanged a few words and she tried not to eavesdrop though that was difficult. There was a disturbance on Old Mill Road.

Even the names of the streets were quaint.

Bartlett's office was large, cluttered but clean, and opened into the main room. The door was propped open, and he didn't make a move to close it—seemed that he had a well-established open-door policy. Max didn't object.

"Where are you staying?" Bartlett asked.

"Cape Haven."

"At the new resort?"

"New?"

"Well, new by my standards. Caters to the golfers and the boaters. Owned by locals."

That she knew. Gabriel Truman and his cousin Brian Cooper owned and operated the resort.

"I have a cottage on the water, it's very nice."

"How long are you staying?"

"As long as it takes to get answers."

"Here's a copy of the report about Ms. Sterling's car."

She glanced through the report Bartlett handed her.

The sedan had been registered to D. Jane Sterling in Miami, Florida. Her mother had practically stolen her aunt's identity—Delia Jane Sterling was married to Max's great-uncle Archer, her grandmother's brother. Max had traveled home to California three weeks ago to celebrate Archer's eightieth birthday. She'd learned then that eighteen years ago—two years before the abandoned car—Aunt Delia had some odd details show up on her credit report, but their financial manager had taken care of the discrepancies. No one had suspected Martha was using the name. Now, so long after the fact, there were no records.

Well, no easily found records. Apparently Rogan was unusually smart and he'd dug up a few tidbits in financial archives that all pointed to Max's mother using the name of D. Jane Sterling for more than two years.

"We worked the case to the best of our ability," Bartlett was saying. "I wasn't sheriff then—I was still in the military."

"Career?"

He nodded. "Thirty years in the navy. Good life. Retired ten years ago and was talked into running for sheriff after my cousin died in office."

"I'm sorry. Was he killed on duty?"

"Nothing violent. Heart attack. Harvey had been having problems, was never one to talk about himself, not even to his doctor. Sixty-one, dropped dead in the middle of the office one afternoon." He shook his head. "I'd never been a cop, but we're a small county, I run a tight ship, and my staff is good."

"The investigator was Detective Marcel Lipsky," Max said, pointing to the typed name at the bottom of the initial report. "Is he still around?"

"He still owns his family home, a little place on the Maryland border. He left shortly after I came on board, took a position in Norfolk. More crime, more money. But he's still on the job, if that's what you mean."

She'd need to talk to Lipsky.

"When we spoke last month," Max said, "you indicated that no bodies had been found that matched my mother's description. How wide did you canvass?"

"The entire shore—two counties. No Jane Does at all. In fact, the only unidentified bodies we had in the last twenty years were two males in their twenties who were found a year apart on the seaside of the peninsula. They were unidentifiable—been buried for years—and we sent the bodies to the state lab. They have far more resources and so they handle any big cases."

"But not this missing person."

"Well, we didn't know anyone was missing at the time," Bartlett said.

Max didn't want to become irritated at Bartlett—he'd been more than cooperative since she reached out last month—but how could he think there was no one missing when they found an abandoned car?

"Detective Lipsky's report seems complete, but a bit too neat," Max said.

"Too neat?"

"According to his notes, he investigated the case as a missing person originally—the car was far off the beaten track, but there was no evidence that it had been in an accident. He couldn't find a record of Ms. Sterling in Virginia, traced her back to Miami where he contacted the local Miami police to follow up. Indicated that he spoke to a detective down there who confirmed that Sterling had an apartment in Miami, but that he hadn't been able to speak to her. Yet he didn't file a report with missing persons."

"You'll also note that Ms. Sterling had extensive debt and there was evidence of an identity theft scam at her apartment. Marcel concluded that she may have dumped her Sterling identity and taken a new one. No one came forward at the time asking about her or anyone who fit her description."

Max weighed how much she should tell Bartlett.

"I've been working with the Miami police on this.

Because she disappeared more than a decade ago, I assume her landlord had sold off her belongings." She'd spent weeks trying to track down the former landlords, but they'd had a property management company that had changed hands multiple times in the last sixteen years and there was no record of Martha's rental or what happened to her belongings. David was in Miami right now. Sixteen years was a long time, but he was tracking down people who lived in the apartment building at the same time as her mother.

"Do you have any proof that your mother was using this identity? Perhaps the cases aren't connected."

When she first talked to Rogan about the connection he'd made, she was certain it was a coincidence. Then he went through his methodology and showed her Sterling's driver's license. There was no doubt that it was her mother. She'd dyed her hair, but it was her. The eyes didn't lie. Neither did the birthday—she'd knocked three years off her age, but kept June tenth.

"My private investigator tracked down the original driver's license from Miami, it's definitely my mother."

Bartlett looked at his notes. "Martha Revere."

She nodded. "I've also learned that she was associated with James Truman, goes by Jimmy, a local resident from Northampton who also seems to have disappeared—albeit ten years ago, not sixteen."

The change on Bartlett's face was subtle, but Max always kept a close eye on the mannerisms and expressions of anyone she interviewed. She'd picked up on more truth—and lies—by paying attention.

But the sheriff didn't say anything. He was good.

"You know him." It wasn't a question.

"I know the family," he said. Nothing more.

"Did you know Jimmy's brother Gabriel from the navy?"

If he was surprised that she had the information about Gabriel Truman, he didn't let on.

"No. We never served together. But this is a small community. I know most everyone who has lived here a time."

She was certain he not only knew the Trumans, but knew them well—at least well enough to be talking to Gabriel after she left. She scrubbed the idea of playing incognito any longer.

"So you're familiar with Jimmy Truman's criminal record?"

Silence. "I wasn't the sheriff then."

That wasn't an answer. He damn well knew about Truman's record. Though Bartlett was older than both Truman brothers, and he hadn't been a cop at the time, he certainly knew the history. Small community, as he kept saying. Military man. Sheriff. Yeah, he knew everyone in the area, personally or by reputation. She might need his information or insight down the road—or his help—so she wasn't going to confront him about this now.

Instead, she said, "I appreciate the report." She held up her copy of the report. "I'm going to talk to Detective Lipsky, and then I may have additional questions."

"Like I said, I'm happy to help in any way I can. I wish I had more for you."

So did Max.

"One more question—the report says the car was taken to impound. Is it still there?"

"Sixteen years? I couldn't tell you—possibly, but it would have been stored outside, and any evidence inside the car would have been logged in a police storage locker. We don't have the storage here—not for something that old—but we share space with the state police."

A lot of legwork, Max thought, but she was in this for the long haul.

"Who would I speak with?"

Bartlett wrote on his tablet. "Let me follow up for you. I can get the information easily, though it may take them a day or two to track it down, especially if it's not logged in the computer. I'll call you."

He was being more than a little helpful now that she'd stopped talking about the Trumans.

"I appreciate your help, Sheriff."

"Call me Bill, please. We're not formal around here."

Max went to the public records office at the county seat. She had the address of the house Jimmy Truman had grown up in, thanks to Sean Rogan, and a copy of the deed that said it now belonged to Gabriel Truman. She checked the tax rolls—he was current on his property taxes. He'd taken out a small mortgage on the house ten years ago, shortly after his mother died. She also pulled his business records for the charter boat company and the resort. She searched for any business or property in the name of James or Jimmy Truman—or J. J. Sterling or Delia Sterling or Jane Sterling, to cover her bases. Nothing.

She'd have to go through Gabriel's business documents in more detail—she didn't have the time here nor did she want to draw attention to her activities. So she had everything she might need copied and took them with her.

None of this information probably mattered, but it was always best to know everything about everyone who might be connected to an investigation.

As she drove back to Cape Haven she needed to remember to think of Martha Revere's disappearance like a case—an investigation she had done hundreds of times over the last decade. She couldn't think of Martha as her mother, or that she had a personal stake in the outcome. She had to think as an outsider, at least *try* to be impartial. That Martha Revere hadn't abandoned *her,* she'd simply abandoned her daughter. That Martha Revere hadn't lived off her trust fund without any word to her family, that she hadn't been a selfish bitch who only thought about herself and her own wants and desires.

Max rubbed her eyes, then focused on the road. She *was* too close to this. Everything she felt as a child had returned two months ago when Rogan told her he'd found out Martha had been using the Sterling name. Then learning Saturday night that Jimmy had been using the name, too—that angered Max more than a little. That bastard— what had he been up to?

Max couldn't think of Martha as a victim, even if she had been murdered. Martha had never acted like a victim in anything. Once, when Max was six or seven, they'd stayed with one of Martha's boyfriends in Cabo for a few weeks. Martha and the jerk argued, and he backhanded her so hard she fell and hit her head on the coffee table. Bleeding and furious, Martha had attacked him—it was one of Max's most distinctive memories. He'd been stunned, and that bought Martha time. He was down and getting up, then she repeatedly kicked him in the groin. He was in tears and begging—trying to at least—when she walked out.

She'd almost forgotten Max that night. Max had been watching from the doorway. If Max hadn't ran and followed her mom, she couldn't honestly say that Martha would have come back for her.

Martha was no victim, and neither was Jimmy. So what had happened between them? Had they really been together for as long as six years after Martha left Max? Had Jimmy killed her? If so, why?

"Hello, Bill." Gabriel Truman was surprised that the sheriff had come all this way without a phone call. He opened the door and let the man in. "Is this official?"

Bill was still dressed in his uniform, and he took off his hat. "No, I'm heading home."

They both knew that Cape Haven was not on Bill's way home.

"I'll only keep you a moment," Bill added.

"It's fine—I'm just making dinner." He motioned for Bill to follow him to the back of the house.

Eve looked up from her homework. "Hi, Sheriff Bartlett," she said, then wrinkled her nose. "Do you understand rational equations? Dad says he does, but I don't understand *him*."

"Go," Gabriel said. "Watch that YouTube video I found. If you still don't get it, I'll find a different way to explain after dinner." He didn't know why Bill was here, but if he was making a house call, it wasn't good news. Eve didn't need to know who was in trouble or why. Maybe he sheltered her a bit too much, but after his childhood, he wanted to give Eve as much room to be a kid as possible, without the worries of an adult. She was already too smart and wise for her years—except for math.

Eve looked from Gabriel to Bill, then nodded. "Right. You want privacy. You could have just asked. Can I go to Shelley's? Please? I'll be home by seven, and I promise, this is the last homework I have tonight."

"Six thirty—that's when dinner will be ready," Gabriel said. Shelley lived a block and a half away.

"Not a minute later!" She jumped up and was halfway out the back door with a quick, "Thanks, Dad!"

Gabriel motioned for Bill to sit at the kitchen table. He stirred the clam chowder he was making, something easy that would be enough for several meals. He needed to make a salad, but that could wait. He sat across from Bill. "What's wrong?"

"Nothing, really, but your brother's name came up today, and I wanted to talk to you about it before the reporter found you."

His blood chilled. "Reporter?"

"Maxine Revere. She's following up on a car abandoned near here years ago, when you were still overseas. She believes it belonged to her mother."

Bill was talking, but Gabriel only partly heard him. *Revere.* Maxine Revere. Who was she? Why was she asking questions?

"What kind of reporter? What does she want with Jimmy?"

"She said she's not here as a reporter, she's here for personal reasons."

This could not be happening. "Personal?"

"Like I said, a car she believes belonged to her mother was found on a dirt road near Oyster Bay, past the Hendersons' farm."

"Her mother?" Gabriel's voice was quiet, he wasn't even certain he'd spoken, until Bill continued.

"It's debatable. The car was registered to D. Jane Sterling from Florida. Ms. Revere believes that was an alias for her mother, Martha Revere. According to her, her mother had been romantically involved with your brother way back when. Did you know her?"

"No," he said automatically. Was it a lie? Not really. Meeting a woman once didn't mean he *knew* her. "When did all this happen? With the car."

"Sixteen years ago, this month. I only know because I read the report. It was investigated by a detective who's now in Norfolk, and there was really nothing to investigate. No sign of foul play, not much of anything to go on. But because this Ms. Revere seemed interested in her mother's relationship with your brother, I didn't want you to be blindsided. Your brother caused you and your family a lot of heartache and pain."

"That's an understatement," Gabriel muttered. "You said this car wasn't even registered to this reporter's mother?"

"No, but she has compelling evidence that Sterling and her mother are one and the same. I don't think she'd be spending all this time here if she didn't have something to go on."

"All what time?"

"Said she's staying at your resort for the next month or so, until she finds out what happened to her mother."

"My resort?" Why would she pick Cape Haven? What did this damn reporter know about her mother and Jimmy? Was she looking to dig up dirt? Write a nasty little article for some personal vendetta?

"I don't think you have anything to worry about," Bill said cautiously.

Gabriel got up and stirred the soup again, then pulled the vegetables out of the drawer in the refrigerator and started making a salad. Bill was a cop. He might also be a friend, but he was a cop first, and Gabriel needed to figure out what he was going to do about this reporter—without Bill in the room. He needed to do something with his hands so he didn't lose his temper.

He said, "Anytime I hear Jimmy's name, I get angry all over again." That was the truth, and should mask his reaction. He hoped.

"That you and your brother came from the same parents is a mystery, that's for certain," Bill said. "But as you know, you're not your brother's keeper. He got himself into trouble time and time again. But you haven't seen him in years, he probably found some trouble he couldn't con his way out of."

Bill knew about the federal investigation into Jimmy's activities, and Gabriel had gone on record stating that he hadn't seen or heard from his brother since before he left the navy. The last time he'd seen him was at Christmas twenty years ago when they were both home at the same time.

Which was a lie, but one that Gabriel would never back away from. Ever. His brother was going to ruin his life, even now. All Gabriel had ever done was clean up after Jimmy until his brother stole nearly everything from his mother, forced her to go back to work to make ends meet. That was when Gabriel told him to leave and never come back.

But his mother had forgiven him. A mother's love, she said.

*He's my son, Gabriel. I can't turn my back on him. I know he has problems, but he's still my boy.*

Gabriel hadn't understood at the time. Now that he had Eve—maybe, he understood a little. *A very little.* Because Eve was all that was good in the world, and Jimmy was all that was evil. What if his mother couldn't see him for what he was because she loved him unconditionally?

*A mother's love . . .*

"I'll never forgive him for what he did to my mother," Gabriel said. The truth, and a truth that could explain his rage.

*If you only knew how cruel Jimmy really was . . .*

"Emily was a good woman," Bill said. "And she had you. She was proud of you, Gabriel. And don't think we all don't know that you gave up your career to take care of her in her last years."

"And I had Eve."

"She's a great kid, you've done a good job raising her."

"No complaints." He wanted this conversation over. Bill told him what he needed to know, and Gabriel would find out what this Maxine Revere was up to, find a way to make her to leave without learning anything about his family.

"I don't know that the reporter is going to find the answers that she's looking for," Bill said, "because there's really nothing to find." He pulled an envelope from his pocket. "Here's a copy of everything I gave her. You can see there wasn't much to go on then, and sixteen years later? But she's tenacious, and I wouldn't be surprised if she reached out to you."

"I'll tell her to take a hike," Gabriel said. "I'm not going to let her stir up this shit with Jimmy. He didn't just hurt my mother—he hurt a lot of people in Cape Haven."

"No argument here. If she oversteps, let me know and I'll have a talk with her."

"Thanks, Bill." But Gabriel would take care of his own problems. He always had.

He walked Bill to the door, waited until he drove off, then went back to the kitchen and stared at nothing in particular.

*Maxine Revere. Why the hell are you really here?*

# Chapter Four

"I love Hawaii." Martha leaned back on the chaise lounge by the pool. It had rained most of the morning, but she and Jimmy had slept in and now the warm, tropical afternoon caressed her skin, relaxing her like very little could.

Jimmy sipped his drink and lifted up his sunglasses to look at her. "Why haven't you been back? You talk about it all the time."

"It was *years* ago, and it's complicated."

"It's always complicated with you."

"Stop."

But she wasn't really angry with him. She was in heaven here, and they had had the *best* time. Two weeks at the most exclusive Waikiki resort.

Yet she was getting antsy, and as if Jimmy could sense her pending mood, he said, "I have a surprise."

"Oh?"

"Walter and Olivia invited us to their party tonight."

She almost jumped out of her chair. "What? How did you manage that? Those two are the most arrogant jerks I've ever met."

He laughed, and for a moment she wasn't certain he was laughing at her or at his own manipulation of Walter and Olivia Fielding.

"Darling, they will not know what hit them. I've primed Olivia, and she is ready to take the fall. Plus, I learned something else—they have a prenup."

"How did you get her to tell you that?"

"She didn't. I found it when I was over at the house yesterday."

Martha was always pleasantly surprised by how Jimmy got information. She stopped asking how because sometimes just having the information was far more fun than getting it.

"Sneaky," she said with a sly grin. "I like that."

"You did a terrific job convincing Olivia I have my own pot of gold. Subtle, smooth."

"That's me."

Olivia deserved it. She had made Martha's life hell in high school and Martha hated her. Olivia had no clue. She thought they were *friends*.

*You hurt me, I'll hurt you twice as hard.*

Best, Olivia would never know. She'd think Jimmy was scamming them both. It was a *perfect* game.

"Walter is leaving for a business trip tomorrow at noon—all I need is for you to do your thing. It'll be the tipping point. Then when I go over after he leaves, she'll be ripe and ready."

Martha wasn't a jealous woman. That Jimmy would not only seduce Olivia but have sex with the woman didn't bother her. Especially since in the nearly three months she'd been with Jimmy, she'd had more fun than she'd ever had in her life. He brought just as much money into their relationship as she had in her trust—he just had them work for it.

And working for it was *almost* as much fun as taking it out of her bank every month.

"You *must* tell me everything."

"You can watch the video, darling."

A thrill ran through her spine.

Jimmy leaned over. "You like the idea?"

She glanced at his swim trunks. "I see you like the idea, too. Of me watching or of you screwing Olivia?"

"It's always about you, baby. Let's go to the room."

"Now?"

"Unless you want me to take you here with an audience."

Another thrill ran through her and she laughed. They grabbed their things and ran down the path that led to their bungalow as fast as they could.

Jimmy stayed with Olivia all night. Martha woke early, antsy, and she didn't know why. Everything had gone perfectly at the party. She took Walter into his den—alone. Nothing happened, he'd simply helped her with an accounting "error" at her bank—one she'd created just for him to solve. Martha noticed that Olivia—much younger than her husband—couldn't keep her eyes off Jimmy. Who could? He was dashing, especially in the tuxedo he wore to this elite New Year's Eve party. Jimmy and Martha had a "quiet" fight that they made sure Olivia saw. And then after Jimmy confirmed Walter had been on the flight to Japan, he went over to the house ostensibly to find the purse Martha'd left behind "accidentally."

He'd called her once with a brief message.

*Game on.*

And she waited.

And waited.

She walked to the gift shop and bought Maxine a postcard. She hadn't called yesterday for her birthday—she wouldn't, either, because she didn't want to talk to her mother. She scribbled out a message and put the card aside—she'd have to get around to mailing it.

At noon, Martha was tired of waiting for Jimmy. She

ate in the bar, enjoyed a delicious Bloody Mary, then went to the spa and had the works—massage, facial, manicure, pedicure, and then splurged on a gorgeous, sexy white dress with a cascade of red flowers down one side. Shoes to match.

Jimmy found her in the bar talking to a tourist who was hitting on her. She wouldn't have *done* anything with the young, sexy college boy, but he sure was appreciative of her pampering herself.

Jimmy slid into the seat across from college boy and glared at him. The kid left with a mumbled apology and Martha laughed.

"Now who's jealous?" she teased.

"Game over," Jimmy said. He pulled a disk from his pocket. "Want to watch?"

She was tipsy and horny from flirting with College Boy and a little bit (tiny bit) jealous that Jimmy had been with Olivia all night and most of the day.

"Maybe."

"Oh, you do." He reached between her legs and grinned. "We're going to make a lot of money from this disk."

Revenge was definitely sweet, Martha thought as they went to their bungalow to watch Olivia and Jimmy's sex tape.

When it was done—and after Martha and Jimmy reenacted much of it—Martha laughed.

"I don't have the energy to move let alone laugh," Jimmy said.

"Revenge is sweet, baby. So very sweet."

Olivia would pay *anything* to keep her husband from seeing the sex tape. And the best thing? She'd never know Martha had set the whole plan in motion.

Maxine sat in the rose garden in the backyard, outside her grandmother's library. It was a small area of the yard—well, small compared to the two-acre, well-manicured spread behind the deceptively modest-looking house. From the outside, the house looked like an old one-story rambler. Inside, the five thousand square feet were spread elegantly and seamlessly back into the yard, providing many places to relax or hide. Designed by an apprentice of Frank Lloyd Wright, the house was timeless and fluid.

But Max much preferred the rose garden and koi pond and watching the fish swim around and around and around. Where she could sit mostly undisturbed and listen to the fountain rain water down onto the fish.

She stared at the postcard in her hands. A generic tourist picture of a beach in Hawaii.

Max had always loved the beach. Beaches, lakes, rivers . . . anyplace near water comforted her like nothing else, and she'd never really figured out why. That her mother sent her a beach photo—no matter how generic (and really, from Hawaii there probably weren't many postcard options that didn't include a beach)—gave her some peace. That her mother had listened to her, that she'd known her—at least enough of her that she remembered Max liked water.

She turned the card over.

*Hi, Maxie,*
*Happy birthday, baby girl! We're having the best*
*time. Jimmy and I have been living in this amaz-*
*ing beach house on Maui for the last two weeks,*
*after spending a month at a resort at Waikiki.*
*You'd love it. Too bad you and Jimmy are like oil*
*and water, we could have had a good thing going.*
*Life is meant to have fun! Are you having fun?*
*I am. We're leaving Hawaii soon. Don't know*
*where we're going yet, but that's the best part of*

*life! I can go anywhere. I'll call later and we can
chat.*
   *XOXO*
   *Martha*

The card was postmarked January nineteenth, nearly
three weeks after Max's December thirty-first birthday.
   She didn't care.
   *Yes, you do. You care because your mother left you
here with people you don't know and who don't know you
and she hasn't called or written in two months.*
   She hated her mother.
   *If you hated her you wouldn't care. You're mad, you're
upset, you're a big baby. Grow up, Max. You're ten years
old now. Grow up and realize that your mother is never
coming back. She's having too much fun.*
   She folded the postcard and put it in the pocket of her
jeans. It was cold, but the damp chill made her feel something. She'd been so out of sorts over the last two months
that she didn't know what to do. Eleanor wanted her to
go to school, but Max refused. Ironic, perhaps, because
she'd been begging her mom to settle down so she could
go to school. Once, she'd even asked her to send her to a
boarding school. Martha thought was the stupidest thing
Max had ever said.
   *"You read better than most adults, you read what you
want to know. School is boring. Trust me on that, you are
too smart for school."*
   Max had been pretty certain that when Martha got
tired of Jimmy she'd come back and get her.
   But she was still with him. For Martha, three months
with one guy was an eternity.
   The French doors opened and Eleanor walked into the
garden. Unconsciously, Max straightened her spine. The
horrific stories her mother had told her about being raised

in this house, the strict rules and cruelty, had seeped in. Eleanor Revere was a forbidding woman who looked like she could be the evil sister of the Queen of England. Regal, perfectly dressed, face done just so. She hadn't left the house today, but she still had put on makeup and jewelry and styled her hair. Max called her Grandmother, but most of their conversations were perfunctory. Eleanor telling her what she should do or say or what she should wear, and Max thinking that she was just as awful as her mother had always said. Why did Eleanor care if she wore jeans or read a book in her pajamas? Why did she have to get dressed to leave her bedroom?

Other times, Eleanor told Max about family history, about responsibility and school and college and ideas for the future. Then, Max was riveted. When Max met her great-grandmother, Genevieve Sterling, everything changed—but Max didn't accept it, not then. Grandmother Genie, as she wanted to be called, was nothing like Max thought she would be as a wealthy matriarch of the family. She had a contagious laugh, eyes that sparkled with happiness that seemed to come from within, and she insisted that Max come to her house every week for tea and sandwiches so they could get to know each other. Just Max, without anyone else.

Max was already looking forward to her next lunch with Grandmother Genie.

Mostly, however, Max appreciated that Eleanor talked to her like an adult. She never once talked down to her. She never once complained that Max had been left for her to take care of. She never once acted like she didn't want her. She expected a lot . . . some things that Max had a hard time living up to . . . but she told her from the beginning that she was a Revere, that being a Revere meant something, and she expected Max to act like a Revere.

Though Max had once complained to Grandmother

Genie about the strict rules of the house, she secretly liked knowing exactly what was expected of her. There were no surprises. After living the first ten years of her life never knowing what to expect—or even where they'd be living week to week—the stability comforted her.

She felt safe. She could relax in her room, not fear that she'd have to leave everything at a moment's notice because her mother wanted to visit friends in Vail or fly to Switzerland for a festival or New York for a new art exhibit.

For the first time, Max felt like she had a home, even if the people she lived with were strangers.

"May I sit with you?" Eleanor asked.

She shrugged.

"Did you lose your voice?"

"What?"

"If you can speak, speak."

"Yeah, you can sit."

"When someone asks you a question, even as simple as an invitation to sit, shrugging an answer is rude."

Max didn't say anything. She felt small inside. Eleanor had that effect. That nothing Max said or did would be good enough for her. Maybe Eleanor looked at Max and saw Martha. If that were the case, Max would never make Eleanor happy.

Or was that her mother's twisted stories clouding her judgment?

Eleanor frowned and sat in the chair across from Max. There was a small table out here that Eleanor had said she liked to drink tea on warm afternoons, but it had been too cold this winter. Max didn't mind the cold. Or the heat. Temperature never bothered her.

Eleanor wore a warm coat and still looked like she was shaking from the chill.

"What did your mother have to say?"

"It was a postcard—didn't you read it?"

"The postcard was addressed to you. It would have been rude and disrespectful for me to read it."

Martha lied so easily all the time that Max didn't always know whether she could believe people, but she believed Eleanor. In fact, even though she was only ten, Max had gotten pretty good at knowing when people were lying. Maybe after living with a liar for so long she'd developed skills without even trying.

Max took the postcard out of her pocket and slid it over to her grandmother.

Eleanor picked it up, read it, handed it back to Max.

"You know this Jimmy?"

"Her boyfriend of the month. Only, he's lasted three months. He didn't like me."

"I see."

"No, you really don't. My mom will get tired of Jimmy. She gets bored easily. Then she'll come back."

Her voice cracked. Even as she said it, she didn't believe it. She didn't believe that Martha would come back for her, even after she left Jimmy.

"If your mother walked through that door this afternoon, would you want to leave with her?"

"She's my mother."

"That wasn't my question."

Max's lip trembled. She hated to cry, and she'd gotten really good at holding back her emotions. Her mother didn't like it when she got upset; Martha always said Max made her feel guilty, that guilt was a useless emotion.

Quietly, Max said, "I don't know."

Eleanor didn't say anything for a long minute. Somehow, the silence didn't bother Max. They both looked at the rosebushes, trimmed and flowerless because it was January. "The garden," Eleanor said after a time, "is truly beautiful in the spring."

"I saw pictures."

"I'd like you to go to school."

Max didn't know what to say. They'd had this conversation twice over the last month, when it was clear that Martha wasn't coming back anytime soon. Even Grandmother Genie brought it up at their last lunch.

"Do you want to go to school?"

Max shrugged.

"Maxine, I will try to be understanding because you weren't raised with manners, but you'll need to take correction. Shrugging is not an acceptable method of communication. I will not tolerate it."

"I'm sorry."

Eleanor frowned and Max didn't know what she'd done.

"What did I do now?" Max said, irritated.

"Do not say you're sorry, Maxine. First, you have nothing to be sorry about at this point. You are barely ten years old. A child. None of this—none of what your mother has chosen to do—is your fault. Second, if you ever say I'm sorry, you had better mean those exact words and truly have something you feel remorse for."

That sunk in. It made sense. "Okay."

"You're highly intelligent, Maxine. William is only a month younger than you and he's in the fourth grade. While I suspect you will test high in reading—I don't remember fourth-graders reading Charles Dickens—your math skills are atrocious. Whatever you're struggling in, I'll hire a tutor. William has friends, he'll make sure you fit in and have a place."

Max wasn't worried about school. She'd been reading since she was four and figured she could learn anything that was written down.

"I don't think William likes me."

"William is family." As if that was an answer to her unsaid question.

Max was worried about the family. How could she ever live up to Eleanor Revere's high expectations? According to her mother, they were impossible to meet. Her cousin William looked at her like she was an alien, and William's father, Uncle Brooks, hated her. It was clear as day, and she knew her mother felt the same way about him. What had happened between her mother and her uncle that they not only disliked each other, but Brooks didn't like Max, either? She'd never done anything to him. She hadn't even known him until two months ago.

They sat in silence for a while longer, and surprisingly, Max was comfortable in the quiet. Eleanor was everything her mother had said . . . and nothing like it at all. Maybe she was missing something. Or maybe, she should form her own judgment about Eleanor Revere. Try to start with a clean slate.

"What are the rules?" Max asked.

"I don't understand what you mean."

"My mother said you had a lot of rules. I don't want to break them."

Eleanor didn't say anything for a long time. "Your mother and I had a difference of opinion as to what constituted rules. I will tell you what I expect from you, which is what I expected from my three children, and what I expect from my other grandchildren. First, respect. Respect your grandfather, respect me, respect your teachers, and yourself. If you have no respect for yourself, you can't possibly show it to others. Second, honesty. I expect you to always tell me the truth, even when it's inconvenient. Honesty builds integrity, which is an essential character trait for a Revere."

"Did you know my mother had me?"

"Yes, but not because she told me."

Max frowned. She had no idea what Eleanor meant.

Eleanor continued. "I heard about you when you were three from a friend who saw your mother at a resort in Florida. I have tried to reach out to Martha over the years, but she doesn't make it easy to find her. And—I can be proud. Too proud, my James tells me. I didn't try as hard as I should have."

"We moved a lot," Max whispered.

Take the money and run, Max thought. Withdraw her trust fund allowance on the first of every month and go someplace new.

*Where should we go now, Maxie? Maine! I've never been to Maine. Well, once when I was sixteen with my friend Ginger, but that was forever ago. We'll rent a house on the beach and eat lobster every night.*

"If Martha returns, you don't have to leave with her."

"She's my mother," Max repeated because she didn't know what to say.

There was something in Eleanor's expression that Max couldn't read. She said, "You're my granddaughter. This will always be your home."

Max didn't know what she should say. She stared at the postcard.

"You are a Revere. You come from a strong, independent family on both sides, Maxine. It's time for you to take your place. If Martha returns, you'll make the right choice."

"Which is?"

"You'll know." Eleanor rose, a bit stiffly. Max got up as well and they walked inside. She was as tall as Eleanor, and felt awkward. She'd grown several inches over the last year and was gangly. All arms and legs and red hair—hair that no one else in the family had. If she didn't have Eleanor's eyes, she might doubt that she was her mother's daughter.

"My mother isn't coming back," Max said. She knew it when Martha left with Jimmy. Saying it out loud was both upsetting and maybe a bit cathartic. As if she'd been holding on to a secret that was now free. How could she be both happy and sad? How could she miss her mother and be happy she had a home?

Happy? She'd never really been happy. And that was why she and Martha didn't get along. Martha was carefree, wild, laughing, always happy. Max lived in fear of the unknown. Where they would be living, what would happen when the money ran out for the month, whether what Martha told her was the truth or another lie. A lie not designed to reassure Max, but to make her stop asking questions.

"All right," Eleanor said.

"I miss her."

"She's your mother. You should miss her."

Max bit her lip. "If she comes back and I decide I want to stay, would you make me leave with her if she wanted to take me?"

"Make you leave?"

Max nodded. Then remembered that Eleanor liked verbal answers. "Yes." Her voice cracked.

Eleanor took both of her hands into hers. Her skin was cold and thin and her hands smaller than Max's. "You are a Revere. You are my granddaughter. You have a home here for as long as you want."

"What if my mother makes a scene?" Martha was very good at that.

"If you tell me you want to stay here, I will fight for you. My daughter knows I will win. I always do."

She said it with such assurance and confidence that

Max believed her. She believed that Eleanor would protect her. That she would give her a real home.

"You're cold," Max said.

"I feel the chill more than I did in my youth," she said with a small, regal smile. "I'd like to take you to the school tomorrow for an interview with the principal, and then you'll start on Monday."

"I didn't say yes."

"You don't want to go to school?"

"I do, but—" How could she explain what she was thinking? What she was feeling? Everything was new, and not like the changes she had growing up with Martha.

Eleanor looked at her. "Why are you scared?"

"I'm not," she said quickly.

But she was. How had her grandmother known she was terrified? She'd never been to school, she'd never interacted with kids her own age, over and above playing in hotel pools and arcades. She'd never had a friend her own age. She'd never really had a friend *ever.*

She didn't know what to expect.

"You are a strong girl, Maxine. I am a very good judge of character, and when you walked into my life Thanksgiving morning, I said to James, 'She is our granddaughter.' I hope as you adjust to living in our house that when your mother returns, you will choose to stay."

"And if I don't?"

"As I said, you are strong and intelligent. You will make the right choice."

As it was, Martha never returned and Max never had to make the choice. She and Eleanor didn't always agree—and they argued quite extensively as Max grew up—but Max still thought of Atherton as her home, Eleanor as her grandmother, and herself as a Revere.

# Chapter Five

Late Tuesday afternoon Max reached the area on the far Eastern Shore, near Oyster Bay, where her mother's car had been abandoned. Though the police file was thin, the map and photos helped.

It was close to six and the light was rapidly fading. Not to mention she was on a dirt road deep in what she would call a swamp, but she supposed others might call it something else.

There were three houses along this road, all large spreads far from one another. One was clearly farmland with extensive fields growing a crop Max couldn't identify. The second house, which was on a point surrounded on three sides by water, had a long paved driveway. The third house was the farthest back and she could barely make out the roof. It, too, might be ag land, but again, research was her friend. Max made a note of each address. She would have to check to see who owned the property sixteen years ago. Had Martha been out here to meet someone? Or was this simply a convenient place for a killer to dump her car?

Now that the sun was setting, it was getting chilly and Max pulled a jacket over her thin twin-set blue sweater. She slipped out of her sandals and into boots. They didn't match her slacks, but no way would she be able to get through this rocky, damp terrain liberally dotted with prickly shrubs, not in Jimmy Choo flats.

She figured she'd have thirty minutes tops to inspect the area before the light disappeared, and even then she was pushing it. She should return in the morning. But now that she was here, she didn't want to leave.

The car had been discovered north of the three properties, where the road was barely a road and clearly leading to a dead end. Had Martha gotten lost? Attempted to turn around and became stuck? Why hadn't her body been found? Had someone killed her elsewhere and disposed of the car here, hoping no one would uncover it? Had Martha herself dumped her own car and used another car and another identity because she was in trouble? Running from Jimmy Truman? Or had she gotten involved with someone else?

Sixteen years was a long time, especially on the Eastern Shore where the water, wind, and hurricanes could change the landscape quite substantially over the years. Max wasn't a hundred percent positive she was in the right location, but she had to be close.

She looked at the photos in the police file, then inspected the terrain. There were sand dunes that had changed over time, but for as far as she could see there were dunes mixed with shrubs and tall grasses. She couldn't see the water, but she could smell the salt air and a slightly rotting fishy smell. The estuary that made up the entire eastern side of the peninsula had that same pervasive undercurrent. It was less prevalent on the Chesapeake Bay side.

To the east were numerous bays, inlets, and nature preserves, but if Max had read her maps correctly, no one lived out there. Some of the islands would come and go with the tides or seasons. Some could be visited during the day, some were restricted use.

She heard no traffic, no voices, no machinery. During harvest season there would be tractors and other heavy-duty machines, but today, at dusk, only nature spoke. The birds were few and far between, likely nesting for the night. One of the things she'd enjoyed yesterday when she walked through the small town of Cape Haven was the variety of birds everywhere. They would be even more plentiful here, another reason to visit earlier in the day.

When she closed her eyes, slowed her breathing, she could hear the water beyond the dunes, the gentle waves of the bay. Some animals scurrying in the bushes, most likely rabbits and smaller rodents.

Max opened her eyes and took several photos of the area. She could compare them in greater detail on her computer with the crime scene photos.

But one thing was abundantly clear to Max. There was no logical reason for her mother to have been parked here, at the end of a dirt road.

By the time Max arrived back at her beach house, showered and changed, and walked to the restaurant, it was eight thirty and the dinner rush—such as it was so early in the season—was over. There were only a half-dozen occupied tables, and Max suspected they were locals more than tourists. She'd talked to the concierge at the resort—a knowledgeable older gentleman named Reginald Cruthers who'd once run a fishing trawler until an accident took his arm. He was chatty, which was good for Max because she'd learned a lot of tidbits which may or may not be valuable down the road. One fact: the resort was only a third full, though they had reservations starting early May that would bring them to near capacity by Memorial Day. Then they were booked through Labor Day, which had been a common occurrence since their renovation and expansion a decade ago.

Max sat in the bar. They didn't serve dinner in the bar, but she'd looked at the menu last night and she would be just as happy with their crab cakes appetizer and a glass of wine. Her wine was served almost immediately, and while she waited on the crab cakes she opened her iPad and logged into her email.

Nothing from Rogan, but she wasn't expecting anything new. David had told her more about what Rogan and his wife, an FBI agent, had been doing over the last few weeks, and Max was surprised Rogan had any time to work on her case. She was pleasantly surprised by his professionalism—when they first met in January, she hadn't liked him. He was arrogant and acted like a bully. Other than his good looks, she couldn't imagine what his wife saw in him.

As she got to know him, she realized that while she was correct in her assessment of his arrogance, he *was* intelligent and resourceful. He wasn't so much a bully as protective of his wife—who didn't need protecting, Max mused, though Agent Rogan didn't seem to mind her husband's he-man attitude. And the way he looked at his wife . . . well, Max realized that even her snap judgments could be wrong on occasion.

An email from Ben with questions. Very straightforward and he didn't attempt to guilt her about her prolonged trip. She answered them all, and agreed to a conference call with him and the marketing team for later in the week.

The email from David was by far the most interesting in her in-box.

*Max—*
*When Martha cleared out of her apartment, she put everything in a storage unit and paid for a*

*year. When the unit was in default, they sold off
the items. The storage facility has the same owner
and I'm going to talk to them—they may remember
something unusual that was sold, or there may be
a record of the items.*

*I talked to Miami PD. A case this old they
don't mind talking, but they couldn't find much.
I'm meeting with the retired detective who worked
the case sixteen years ago. The file stated that
Northampton County Sheriff's Department
was investigating a car abandoned in their
jurisdiction, registered to D. Jane Sterling of
Miami, Florida. They determined that she'd moved
out of her apartment—though she didn't give
notice—and that there was no sign of foul play.
There may be nothing here—and after all this
time I'm not confident the detective will remember
anything useful, if at all.*

*But because I played nice with the police,
they gave me a rap sheet on James Truman.
He'd been arrested twice in Miami, charges
dropped. Both more than ten years ago. Once
for possession of narcotics, once for driving
a stolen vehicle. Don't know why they were
dropped. He was wanted for questioning in a
fraud investigation, however, but the warrant
expired when the statute of limitations was up—
again, more than ten years ago. They didn't have
his possible alias of J. J. Sterling, but feel that
after all this time there isn't anything they can
do, so have no plan to reach out to neighboring
jurisdictions. The retired detective may have
more information.*

*There is nothing on Martha Revere or D. Jane*

*Sterling or Delia Sterling in the Miami criminal database.*

*Call me tonight and let me know what you learned.*

*—DK*

Max didn't hold out hope that there would be anything left from a storage unit abandoned sixteen years ago, but if any of the belongings could be found, she put her money on her partner to locate them.

She responded to his email that she'd call later because her crab cakes had arrived.

She had just finished her meal and was still hungry. She ordered a second glass of wine and crab cakes to go—she was the last person in the restaurant, other than the staff. A tall, blond man with thinning hair walked in and approached her. He smiled.

"Ms. Revere?"

She nodded, sipped her wine, and assessed him. He dressed like many in the area—jeans, a cable-knit sweater, and loafers. He looked like he would be comfortable relaxing on a yacht or working on one.

"I'm Brian Cooper, co-owner of Havenly. May I sit down?"

"Of course."

He pulled out a chair. "I should have tracked you down when you first checked in. We get our fair share of celebrities, but they're regulars. I don't believe you've been here before."

"I'm hardly a celebrity."

He laughed. The bartender walked over with a glass of scotch for Cooper. "For us, you are. I wanted to introduce myself, thank you for choosing our resort. Extended vacation?"

He must have looked at her record and noticed she'd

reserved the cottage for the entire month of April. She didn't know if she would be staying that long, but she wanted the option.

"Business and pleasure."

"If there's anything I can do to make the pleasure part of your stay more enjoyable, please let me know. We're very happy to have you here with us."

"Thank you, I will."

He smiled, picked up his drink, and walked over to the bartender where he gestured to the bottles and asked a question Max couldn't hear.

Max didn't consider herself a celebrity, but now that her cable show had been running for more than two years, she didn't have the anonymity she'd once had. Now people often went out of their way to either get close to her or to avoid her.

David had run a standard background on Cooper and nothing popped up as being suspicious: no criminal record; divorced years ago, remarried; one adult son who was career military and stationed overseas; a stepdaughter in college. His second wife worked at the resort as an accountant—a local girl who was one of Cooper's peers, so he hadn't dumped the first wife for a younger model.

She'd dig around a little more, but didn't expect to find anything odd. Still, she'd do the work because there were times when she'd been wrong about human nature, or she'd misjudged someone.

It was rare, but it did happen.

# Chapter Six

Max had always had a version of insomnia, even when she was young. Over the years it had gone from no big deal to miserable to managable, often related to stress but not always. There were times when she could sleep six hours straight and wake up as if she'd slept twice that long; other times she lasted two hours and then was up for the rest of the night. It didn't matter if she was in her own bed or a hotel or with a lover. The only real benefit of having a lover was that often a bout of early-morning sex helped her doze off for another hour or two. She'd learned that tossing and turning was not her friend, so when she woke up whether it was 2:00 A.M. or 4:00 or 6:00, if she couldn't fall back to sleep in a few minutes, she would start her day.

The clock read 5:13 A.M. Not bad, she thought. She'd slept a solid five hours and felt pretty good. Max didn't like or dislike running, but when home in New York she often ran along the Hudson River, from her place in Greenwich Village down to Battery Park and back. It was more than four miles. The idea of a morning jog on the beach enticed her. She pulled on sweats, a T-shirt, and a windbreaker and ran down the coastline to the end of the resort property, then back and up the coastline to the inlet. All told, she jogged just under three miles. By the time she returned, her skin was cold but her blood was hot. She made coffee, showered, and felt invigorated.

Max stood in the den and looked at her timeline while drinking her second cup of coffee. She needed a conversation with Lipsky first and foremost, and depending on how that went she might question him about Jimmy Truman and the inactive FBI investigation. She'd considered working through her contacts to get the FBI file, but decided she wanted to talk to the investigator herself once she learned his identity. If he found out that she was going around him for the information, that wouldn't bode well if she did need to talk to him.

She read over the police report on the abandoned car in greater detail. Yesterday she'd been focused on the photos and the location; now she wanted to know what exactly had been left in the car. No purse or wallet or luggage had been found, which gave credence to the theory that the car was intentionally abandoned by the owner. There was no registration in the glove box—ownership had been determined based on Florida DMV records, according to Lipsky's notes.

The other personal effects were itemized:

*Receipt from gas station, Norfolk*
*Women's shoes, size 7*
*Women's coat, size 6*
*Vanity case, assorted makeup*
*Earring, diamond*

Was the earring supposed to be *earrings*? Or had one fallen off? Martha had a soft spot for jewelry, and not the cheap stuff.

Very little evidence had been logged. Frankly, the car had been practically empty, and the photos confirmed that. Why? She'd bought it in Florida three months before it was abandoned in Virginia. If she'd been living out of it—Max almost laughed out loud. Her mother living out of a *car*? Never. She'd find someone to manipulate or sleep with to get a roof over her head.

For years, Max had believed that Martha was dead. Now she believed she'd died here, somewhere on this peninsula.

Max had kept journals since she was old enough to write. Her earliest journals were mostly chicken scratch, half of which Max couldn't decipher, even if she could read the words. By the time she was eight, however, she had kept a regular diary. They were stored at her apartment in New York, but she'd brought two with her—along with every postcard her mother had sent between the time she dumped her at her grandparents' house until the last, a belated sixteenth birthday card.

She had written in her journal the day her mother first brought Jimmy Truman to their place.

*Their place?* Hardly. Her mother had rented a condo on the water in Palm Beach. But when her mother settled in a condo or house instead of a hotel, she tended to stay for a month or two, and that made Max happy.

She hated moving.

*October 20*

*Martha and Jimmy went out. I'm here alone, but it's okay. We've been here for two whole weeks and Mom isn't getting that look that she gets when I know leaving is going to happen any day. It's hot and sticky but there's a pool and I love swimming and there's a view of the ocean and I love watching the ocean and waves and the sand except when it gets stuck in my bathing suit and itches.*

*Mom brought Jimmy home last night and he slept in her bedroom. They made noise and I think*

*it's gross, but oh well, Mom said I'll understand
when I grow up. I know what they're doing and it's
still gross and I don't like Jimmy. I still miss Perry,
though it's been so long since we've seen him. He
was my very favorite of all of Martha's boyfriends.
I asked him if he was my dad, but he laughed and
thought that was silly. I asked if it was because
he was black and mommy was white, and he said
no, he doesn't care about that, but they were just
having fun. At least he was nice to me and we
played games.*

*Jimmy is different than Perry. He's different
than a lot of Martha's people and I don't think he's
a nice person. He has a nice smile and everyone
likes him but I don't. I don't know why. Mom says
I'm judgmental. I don't know what that means. She
likes Jimmy and that should be good enough for
me. How does she know I don't like him? I didn't
say anything.*

*She'll get rid of him like she does with all the
others, only it makes me sad because I like this
condo and if she gets rid of him we'll be moving
again. I thought maybe this time I could go to
school, if we stayed long enough. She thinks I'm
stupid for wanting to go to school. She said I should
be happy I can live free, unlike her childhood.*

*November 5*
*Jimmy is an asshole. I called him an asshole to his
face and Martha slapped me and I'm in my room.
I hate them.*

Max alternately called her mother "Martha" or "Mom."
She didn't know why, other than she hadn't really thought
of her mother as one and Martha seemed to prefer being

called by her name. She didn't remember what specifically had happened that led to her calling Jimmy an asshole, but she'd certainly done it. Max had always been blunt and honest—sometimes to a fault, her grandmother used to tell her—and she'd always spoken her mind even as a child.

Though, there were times when she had kept her mouth shut around her mother. There had been a fear in the back of her mind when she was little that Martha would leave her in the middle of nowhere and Max wouldn't know what to do.

In hindsight, Max realized Martha had done her a great favor leaving her in Atherton to be raised by her grandparents. It wasn't a perfect life—Eleanor was strict, she believed in a firm etiquette and propriety and family above all else, even when the family screwed up. How many times had Eleanor covered for one of her children or grandchildren? For Uncle Archer's wild grandson? For Uncle Brooks's infidelity? She detested "dirty laundry" being aired publicly, and worked overtime to ensure that it was sanitized. So when Max announced at the dinner table that Uncle Brooks was cheating on Aunt Joanna, it didn't go over so well.

Max hated lies, especially from people she was supposed to love and trust.

Yet . . . Max had an outstanding education. She had loved school. She loved her grandfather more than anyone, and her great-grandmother Genie. Eleanor? Max respected her . . . most of the time. But when she did things like ensure a killer went to a mental hospital instead of standing trial for murder, Max rebelled. Or when she didn't stand up for Max when the family ganged up against her and contested Genie's will, which had given Max her mother's share of the Sterling estate. It wasn't the money—it was the principle. And while Eleanor hadn't argued *against* her, she hadn't stood up for her. She wanted the family to settle and come to a compromise without the "spectacle" of a public argument. Max put her foot down—her great-grandmother had left her one-fifth of her estate and everything that went with it and dammit, she wasn't going to capitulate and give up the seat on the Sterling Foundation board in order to "keep" money that was rightfully hers.

It didn't matter that she was often the lone dissenting vote on the board, though she had more often than not been Aunt Josie's proxy and on occasion had swayed Uncle Terry and Uncle Emmet—who almost always voted as a block—against Uncle Brooks. With Terry and Emmet she'd learned that if she made a clear, sound argument backed with financial evidence that the decision would be best for the foundation—and that there would be a positive portrayal in the community—they tended to side with her. They were all about image, so it was up to Max to spin it that way. Unfortunately, she didn't always have time to come up with a sound argument for why she opposed Uncle Brooks.

Yes, sometimes she voted against him out of spite. She despised him.

The principle was the point, and that Eleanor hadn't sided with her—clearly, unequivocally—hurt Max more than she'd thought it would.

But Max would rather have been raised by regal Eleanor than her wild, unpredictable mother. In the end, the stability Eleanor provided had given Max something she desperately needed, she just hadn't known it at the time.

Ironic, Max thought as she closed her old journal, that she lived out of hotels and condos and cottages like this half the year. The life she despised as a child she'd reclaimed as an adult.

The difference, however, was that she had a home

base. She'd bought the penthouse in Greenwich Village after she graduated from Columbia. She had a place for her stuff. She had her own bed and clothes and books and a kitchen she'd painstakingly remodeled after she took cooking classes. After every case, she could go home and *be* home. She didn't have to live out of a lone backpack. She had a choice.

And that made all the difference.

At eight in the morning, Max called the Norfolk Police Department. "Detective Marcel Lipsky, please."

Max drove her rental car across the Chesapeake Bay Bridge-Tunnel. She'd never driven the road before, and it was a bit unnerving. The bridge was virtually flush with the ocean, and then dove down to an underwater tunnel. She never considered herself claustrophobic, but she was grateful there was little traffic in the middle of the morning. She didn't want to be stuck waiting under the ocean.

The department Lipsky worked out of was on East Virginia Beach Boulevard, a large, single story, mostly brick structure. She entered and gave her name to the receptionist, and was pleasantly surprised when an officer escorted her immediately to Lipsky's cubicle.

"I'm Maxine Revere. Thank you for agreeing to meet with me," she said and extended her hand.

Lipsky was in his early fifties with a receding hairline and intense dark eyes.

"Bill Bartlett called yesterday afternoon, said you'd been by to see him and that he'd referred you to me. Bill's a good guy, though after talking to him I don't think I'll be able to help you." Lipsky motioned to a metal chair next to his desk. "You're here about the Jane Sterling case?"

"Yes. You investigated the car that was abandoned. The registration indicated D. Jane Sterling."

"I took the liberty of reading the file again this morning,

Bill was kind enough to send it to me. The car was abandoned, found by a local resident. Based on the location, we thought maybe it was a stolen car. It wasn't stripped, and it was older—not the kind that usually gets dumped. There could have been valuables in the car, however, that were taken. Because the registration was in Florida, we reached out to the Miami police and they determined that Ms. Sterling had left Florida in early April. Neighbors indicated that she left one night and never returned, landlord said she hadn't given notice, but had taken all personal items out of the apartment. We put an APB out on her with her driver's license photo, nothing came of it."

"Did you investigate where she might have stayed while she was here?"

He raised his eyebrow. "Bill said he gave you a copy of the report. So you know that no Sterling was registered in any hotel or bed-and-breakfast at the time on the Eastern Shore. We sent a BOLO out to neighboring law enforcement agencies, but there was no indication of foul play. I thought at first an insurance scam, but the vehicle was uninsured. We searched the area for a body—we found nothing. There's a lot of marshes in the area, people have been known to wander and get stuck, especially at night. But we didn't find anything suspicious and no tracks. There was no accident—the vehicle sustained no damage. After a couple of weeks of nothing, my guess was that she wanted to disappear."

He paused, then said, "Bill said she was your mother? That would have made her very young when she had you?"

"She was twenty-one when I was born. The driver's license was under a false identity—and a younger birth year."

"Maybe Jane Sterling isn't who you think she is."

"I saw the photo. Martha Revere, my mother. My great-aunt Delia had her identity stolen eighteen years ago. I didn't know it at the time, her financial advisors and lawyers took care of it. I now believe my mother took her identity. The only reason why she had come here, to Virginia, was because of a boyfriend or ex-boyfriend from Cape Haven." Max went on to explain about how Martha stopped accessing her trust account the month the car was recovered. She was getting tired of having to explain the situation to everyone—they should take her word for it. But they didn't know her, and they hadn't known Martha.

Lipsky absorbed what she told him.

"Your mother's real name is Martha Revere?"

"Correct."

"Did you file a missing person's report?"

"My grandmother did. Nothing came of it, and truthfully, I don't think my grandmother looked all that hard. Seven years after she stopped withdrawing money from her trust fund, my grandmother had her declared legally dead."

"That was what—ten years ago?"

"Sixteen years since she cut off all contact, and nine years since the court hearing."

"And why are you just now following up?"

"I hired a private investigator who uncovered the information."

"Sixteen years later?"

Why did Max feel like she was a criminal being interviewed? She was trying to be forthright with Detective Lipsky because she wanted information, but he wasn't making it easy. Yet, he had agreed to meet with her the same day she'd called him.

He didn't comment further, just looked at her—a common cop tactic in an interview.

"I have always believed my mother is dead," she said, her anger starting to grow, "and while I wanted to know what happened, I didn't begin to seek answers until recently. Hence, I hired a PI who is far better than most. He uncovered the connection between Martha and the Jane Sterling identity, and learned about the abandoned car."

She'd then had to face the truth: that maybe she'd avoided this because she didn't want to know what had happened to her mother. Ironic, perhaps, for a reporter who lived her entire adult life seeking the truth about crimes.

Now that she was ready to know the truth, she feared it was too late.

"I don't have any more information about the case than is in the files."

"You know the area and the people and now that you know she's likely dead—dying on or about the time the car was abandoned—what do you think?"

Cops, especially longtime cops who moved up slowly but steadily like Lipsky, had the best instincts about crime and human nature. They always had a theory—and often, their theory was right or mostly right, because they had worked in the business so long. But proving a theory was often the hardest part. Especially in cold cases.

He leaned back, steepled his fingers, and looked at her. "I don't remember much, to be honest, though some has come back to me after I reviewed the files. The car was off the road, but there was no sign of an accident. I initially thought maybe the driver pulled off because they were tired, get some shut-eye. But there was no purse or suitcase. I concluded that either the car had been stolen and the perp abandoned it for some unknown reason—there was nearly half a tank of gas, so it didn't run out of gas and there was nothing wrong with the engine—or the owner abandoned it because they couldn't afford it or the insurance. It's happened. Don't want to pay for a tow or to junk the car, dump it in a remote place."

"And walk out of there?"

"Someone could have picked her up. There was nothing in or around the vehicle to indicate that the driver had any trouble. No blood, no signs of struggle."

"And now? Assume that Martha's dead. What would you think based on the evidence?"

"Anything I think is unprovable."

"But you're a cop, and you have a theory."

"Not really, but I guess I can play the what-if game. No evidence of foul play, so that tells me the driver pulled over intentionally and attempted to hide the vehicle—it couldn't be seen from the road, but it wasn't crashed or disabled. We determined based on dirt and mud that the car had been parked two, maybe three weeks before it was found. The driver pulled off the road—a dirt road—and parked behind the bushes. The car was locked; we found the keys in the glove box. If the driver was upset about something, depressed maybe, I could see her committing suicide—but how I could only speculate. We didn't find a note or a body. The other option is that she wanted to disappear and had another vehicle nearby."

Max could see that as well, except for the fact that she knew that Martha was dead.

"If there was a crime," Lipsky continued, "the killer could have left the car there, hoping it wouldn't be discovered for a while. But again, we found no unidentified female victims, and no victims in that area. The last major unsolved crime in the county was two male victims, homicide, bullets to the head. That was . . . two and half, nearly three years before this incident. And since? Nothing that would fit this scenario.

"Who was her ex-boyfriend?" Lipsky asked.

"Jimmy Truman. And he might not have been an ex."

"Truman." Lipsky smiled humorlessly. "He was a piece of work."

"You knew him?" It didn't surprise Max, especially after Sheriff Bartlett's reaction.

"I was a deputy in Northampton for nearly fifteen years. Truman was in and out of trouble, but he was slick. Always managed to talk himself out of any situation. Never did any jail time, never violent crimes. Ran a scam on tourists for a time—he was only sixteen. He got probation and his record was expunged when he was eighteen. You said your mother was wealthy?"

"Yes."

"He could have been running a scam on her. Soak her dry. No offense," he added quickly. "Honestly, though, Jimmy was the type of criminal who would run from violence. People can change, but my gut says if he killed anyone, it would have been spontaneous, and probably an accident. And yeah—I could see him covering up an accidental death."

"No one ran a scam on Martha," Max said, surprising herself. She hadn't intended to share this much with the cop, but he made it easy with his what-if scenarios and his breezy conversation style. "Martha . . . she would have been part of it."

"Really?" He sounded suspicious. Or maybe just curious.

"I lived with her for the first ten years of my life. She could con people out of anything. I didn't think of it like that at the time, but in hindsight—of which I've had a lot over the years—I realized she enjoyed people giving her things. She had her own money, she certainly didn't *need* anyone's boat or house or car. But she had a way about her. . . ." Max had thought about it a lot over the years, because understanding her mother had been virtually impossible. In some ways Max didn't care because most of the people Martha scammed could afford to part ways with their stuff. Insurance would pay for it, or they would dismiss it as temporary insanity on their part and walk away.

"She was a con artist," Lipsky said matter-of-factly. "Someone who could convince Scrooge to part with his money."

"Precisely. She had her own money, so people didn't think she *needed* their vacation house, their boat, a ten-thousand-dollar sapphire ring. They just let her borrow whatever she wanted." This was a truth Max hadn't known at the time, but it had become clear through the lens of maturity and a decade of investigating crime and criminals and the people they left behind. "Once, when I was eight, we spent the entire spring in France in a villa because she blackmailed the owner. She'd slept with him and would have told his wife if he couldn't find her a place to *relax*. That's what she said. She just wanted some time to *relax*. And—even though he was so angry about what she'd done—he visited her nearly every weekend."

Sometimes, when Max really thought back into her childhood, she wondered if her mother had other reasons for what she did. But in the end, Max always came back to one thing: Martha was all about having fun, and she thought manipulating people was *fun*.

"Where were you when she disappeared?" Lipsky asked. "You would have still been a minor."

"Living with my grandparents in California. I'd gotten old enough to cramp her style, I suppose, and her boyfriend at the time—Jimmy Truman—didn't like me. The feeling was mutual."

"I'm sorry." He sounded sincere, so Max nodded a thanks. "You might be right," he continued, "and Jane Sterling is your mother. But proving that is going to be difficult."

"Sheriff Bartlett said the state would have kept the

abandoned car. There might be something in there, evidence that would prove it. Even DNA."

"I suppose it's possible. But truthfully? After sixteen years I doubt there's anything usable in the vehicle."

She thought much the same thing, but needed to follow through on it. She shifted gears to the other reason she'd wanted to speak to Lipsky. "I learned through my research that there is an inactive FBI investigation into Jimmy Truman. Do you know about that?"

He was clearly surprised she did. "That's been inactive for years. Yeah, I knew because I'd arrested Jimmy twice when he was a teenager. So the FBI came to talk to me, get my files. But as far as I know, Jimmy has all but disappeared."

There was a fine line about what to share and what not to share when working with the police on a cold case. So far, Lipsky had been exactly what she expected from an experienced cop. He was interested in what she had to say, but didn't want to show it. He didn't know what to make of her theory that Jane Sterling was her mother, but he was open to considering it. And he was intrigued that a local boy might be involved.

She said, "I learned that Jimmy also went by J. J. Sterling. Does that ring any bells?"

"No, but I can run the name, see what pops."

"What was the FBI investigating?"

Lipsky turned to his computer and logged in. A minute later, he wrote a name and number on a slip of paper. "Special Agent Ryan Maguire. Here's his number—you can say I gave it to you. But I can't share anything because it's not my case, and I don't step on my colleagues' toes. It may be inactive, but I don't know how far he got, whether he found something else, or even if the statute of limitations has expired."

"I appreciate this," Max said.

"I'll run the names—Sterling and Martha Revere—and I'll also run any Jane Does found in Virginia, Maryland, or Delaware—from April first of that year up through the present. If her body was recovered after a few years, they may not have had much to work with. Bartlett said he'd run his two counties after he talked to you and nothing showed up, but if she died in the ocean—a boating accident or murder or suicide—currents could take her away."

Max had been thinking about that, but she was pleasantly surprised when Lipsky offered to do it for her. She was running low on resources because other than David, she couldn't use NET employees on this. Not on a personal case she had no intention of writing or hosting a show about.

"Thank you," she said. "If you have anyone who fits her description or age, I'll volunteer my DNA as a sample."

He nodded, jotted some notes. "May I ask what your next step is?"

"This is a cold case for you—and out of your jurisdiction. Sheriff Bartlett was helpful, but unless I can find something solid to bring to him, I don't see that he has the resources to assign a detective to investigate my theory. I have a few people I want to talk to, including Truman's brother."

Lipsky said, "You may want to tread carefully with Gabriel Truman."

"You know him?"

It was clear that he was weighing what to say. "Not well, but Maguire has spoken to him a few times over the years about his brother, and my understanding is that neither Truman brother likes cops all that much."

"I'll take it under advisement. Fortunately, I'm not a cop and if my mother was still involved with Jimmy

Truman when she disappeared, Gabriel may know something about it."

"And if your theory that she's been dead for sixteen years holds true, he probably wasn't involved—he was in the navy. I was still in Northampton back then. If memory holds, Gabriel had a kid and retired from active duty about the same time, though I don't remember the exact dates. I'm not saying he's involved or not—just to be cautious."

"Of course." She already knew that Gabriel Truman had left the navy in September of that year—months after her mother disappeared. He simply hadn't reenlisted, so she didn't think anything was suspicious. Maybe his brother was in trouble or maybe Gabriel wanted to spend more time with his family. Either way, he might have known what Jimmy was up to back then and he may have known Martha.

Max thanked Lipsky for his time, left the police station, and dialed Maguire's cell phone number. It went to voicemail immediately.

"Agent Maguire, my name is Maxine Revere and I'd like to talk to you about your investigation into Jimmy Truman. I have some information you'll want to know." She hung up after leaving her number. If Maguire was still interested in Truman, he would call her sometime today. And if he didn't? Max would come back to Norfolk and arrange for a sit-down with the federal agent.

Her instincts were twitching. There was *something* here . . . she just didn't know what.

Yet.

# Chapter Seven

By the time Max returned to Cape Haven, it was mid-afternoon. She drove straight out to the area bordering Oyster Bay and located the farm still owned by Garrett Henderson, the individual who found her mother's abandoned car sixteen years ago. She had tried calling him on her way back to the Eastern Shore, but he hadn't answered. It took her only a minute to internally debate about showing up without an appointment.

She'd dressed professionally when speaking with Lipsky—gray slacks, heels, and an attractive silk blouse. But she was trekking out again into a quasi-marsh, and figured a farmer like Henderson—soybeans, according to the county maps—would be dressed to work. She didn't want to look like what she was—a New Yorker "roughing it" in rural Virginia. She had no intention of lying to the man, but wanted to make him comfortable enough to speak to her.

She pulled over to the side of the road. There had been no traffic—she hadn't passed one car in the last five minutes—and took off her blouse. She had a button-down plaid shirt that matched her slacks—she should have brought jeans with her today, but she'd been a bit preoccupied. One of the drawbacks of chronic insomnia was forgetting the little things. But with the shirt and changing her heels for sturdy flat boots, she didn't feel completely out of place.

The farm didn't have a website and the only thing she could learn about Henderson was by reading a local agricultural magazine. His family had been growing crops here for two hundred years, and thirty years ago, after his father died, he and his sister got into soybeans and aquaculture—specifically, raising clams in the high saline areas on the Eastern Shore. The photo of him was old—at least ten years based on the caption—but he looked ancient then. However, a basic internet search confirmed he was alive and well.

After her quick change, Max drove the half mile down to the Henderson farm. The entrance to the farm marked the end of the paved road. The dirt and gravel road led to where Martha's car had been found, another quarter of a mile away.

She'd considered that maybe someone on the farm had been involved with Martha's disappearance, but (mostly) ruled out Garrett Henderson. Even sixteen years ago he was old, and if he was involved in something illegal, killing Max wouldn't be his first course of action. He would deny, claim he didn't know anything, or that he didn't remember, and hope she went away. Making Max disappear would be a lot harder than Martha.

Martha had cut everyone out of her life. And while Max wasn't always good at keeping her friends close, she had a few she trusted. There were people who would miss her, who would look for her and ask the right questions.

The Henderson farm wasn't gated or fenced—fences probably would be difficult to maintain because of the winds and storms that blew through here so often. The drive went right through the middle of the land, which had been recently tilled but didn't appear to have anything growing. Max knew next to nothing about agriculture but supposed it was too early to plant soybeans. The large farmhouse sprawled with two distinct add-ons, and a porch that looked recently repaired. It was simple and inviting and appeared well maintained. Two barns were in the back, one that didn't look like it could withstand high winds and the second new and modern. Grain silos and a garage completed the spread, along with land as far as she could see.

She stopped her rental car along the edge of the drive where it ended by the house. She got out, heard machinery in the distance, but didn't see anyone.

She walked up the porch steps and knocked on the wood-framed screen door. Two little dogs came running and barking to the screen followed by an old and slow golden retriever. The wonderful scent of cinnamon drifted out of the door.

"Stop, stop!" a female voice commanded. The dogs continued barking for a moment, then ran around in circles.

A woman about fifty, with wide hips and eyes so bright blue they shined through the screen, smiled at Max. "May I help you?"

"I'm looking for Garrett Henderson."

"My father-in-law or my husband?"

"I suppose I don't know." The police report had Garrett Henderson at this address. "Whoever lives here."

That perplexed the woman, who said, "Come on in, we'll get everything straightened out." She opened the door.

The dogs ran around Max's ankles twice, then ran back into the house.

"Ignore them. They're harmless, just noisy. If you don't mind we'll talk in the kitchen, I'm making dinner and cookies for a bake sale at the high school tomorrow. My youngest had to run for student body president and win, and she has me baking and volunteering and driving every which way. Not that I'm complaining, mind you. She'll be off to college in the fall and I'll officially be an empty nester. By the way, I'm Beth Henderson."

"Maxine Revere. How many kids do you have?"

"Eight. Yes, I know, no one has eight kids anymore, but it was fun, and there are two sets of twins in there. Never a dull moment. Gary and I moved in here with his dad after his mom died a few years back. We only had the youngest two left, and Dad needed the help. Gary has worked for him for thirty years, but Dad just can't keep up the house like he used to, and I was worried about him. He took Mom's death so hard. Having Molly and Wyatt around was good for him." She smiled. "I'm just chattering away. Please sit." She motioned to a large rectangular table that took up the center of the expansive kitchen.

"You could feed an army in here."

Beth laughed. "We have, we have. Thanksgiving is always an adventure. I have fresh coffee—Gary tells me I need to cut back, but I'd never get anything done without coffee. And besides, there are worse habits than coffee—Gary smoked for twenty years before he finally quit."

"Coffee sounds wonderful."

The woman bustled around the kitchen, poured two mugs and put them on the table, then returned with creamer and a sugar bowl. "Help yourself, I need to get the cookies out."

There were already four dozen cookies cooling on metal racks. Beth pulled two trays out of a huge oven, placed them on the stove, and put two more trays in that she'd already prepared. She set a timer, pulled a plate out of the cupboard, and arranged six of the cookies— snickerdoodles, Max suspected—and put them in front of Max before sitting down.

"Now, what do you need with my father-in-law or husband?"

Max sipped the coffee, then explained who she was and why she wanted to talk to the person who found the abandoned car sixteen years ago. She decided telling the truth would get her much further with these people, and it was clear as she revealed her story that Beth was both sympathetic and interested.

"It was my father-in-law, I remember him talking about it, and that was years before we moved in here. I'm sorry that I don't remember the details."

"I wouldn't expect you to, and honestly, I don't know if he would, either. It's been a long time."

"Dad is eighty-one, but there's nothing wrong with his memory, trust me. He refuses to retire, even though Gary has taken over most of the day-to-day production issues. But Dad is the face of Henderson Farms. My son Richard is finishing up a master's program in North Carolina, and he'll start taking over for Gary. Dad is very happy we're keeping the farm in the family."

Max liked Beth, and she already liked the Henderson family. To have such an amazing legacy was uplifting, and Beth seemed genuine. Max had a bad habit of instantly judging people, but most of the time she was accurate in her assessment. Beth was what Max's grandfather would have called, "the salt of the earth," a cliché, perhaps, but there was always some truth behind clichés.

"When will he be back?"

"He's just out in the far field taking soil samples. Dad is very hands-on. We plant in less than four weeks." She looked at an old-fashioned clock above the doorway. "He'll be back in thirty minutes or so, if you'd like to wait. He's the proverbial early to bed, early to rise. You're welcome to stay for dinner—six on the dot."

"I don't want to put you out."

Beth laughed. "Nonsense! I always cook too much. And between Dad, my aunt—she lives in town, but comes out here for dinner more often than not since her husband passed—and Gary, maybe they can help figure out what happened to your poor mother."

Max had never considered Martha a "poor" anything, and certainly not a victim. But the Hendersons had been around for a long time. They probably knew the Trumans, they knew the sheriff, they might have even come across Martha.

"I would like that, thank you very much."

By the time Garrett Henderson walked in with his son Gary, it was nearly two hours later, and Max wondered if Beth just didn't really concern herself about time. Beth chatted with her, had her cutting green beans and then tossing a salad, as if she and Max were lifelong friends. Max had rarely met anyone who didn't either want something from her or didn't trust her. Or both. It usually took her years to get close to someone, her college roommate the one exception to the rule. Even David and she had more than a year of uncertainty before she began to rely on and trust him more than anyone.

She didn't want to leave. This was the type of family she'd dreamed about growing up in, the foolish dreams of a lonely child. It wasn't that the second half of her childhood with her grandparents was bad—it wasn't. She had everything she needed or could want, and in her own way her grandmother loved her.

But the Hendersons were the kind of family Max had coveted: large, extended, full of home cooking, and laughter.

There was certainly plenty of activity, even though most of the kids were out of the house. Molly, the youngest of the clan, had run in, grabbed a cookie, kissed her mom, waved to Max, and said, "Can I miss dinner? Please? Bitsy, Neil, and I need to finish our government project."

"Tonight? When is it due?"

"Friday."

"Molly, can't you meet after dinner?"

Molly frowned. "Okay," she said, "but can I skip the dishes? Please?" She looked at Max. "We wrote a play and each of us is a branch of government. I'm the judiciary."

"That sounds like fun," Max said.

"It is. We just need more rehearsing. Neil is the executive branch and he can't remember *anything*." Suddenly she and Beth burst out laughing.

"You eat, be polite, I'll excuse you early," Beth said as she stifled her giggles. "Wash up."

"Love ya." Molly kissed her mom again and ran upstairs.

"That girl, she gets away with everything. The baby of the family, and she knows it."

"She's full of energy."

"Do you have children?"

"No," Max said.

"You're young, you have time. I had Garth—that's Garrett the fourth—when I was twenty-four. I met Gary in college, we married a month after we graduated, and Garth was born eighteen months later. I know, women are having kids later now, but truly, by the time Molly came, I was *done*." She laughed and Max didn't know what she was laughing about.

"Here," Beth said and handed her a stack of plates with utensils on top, "put these around. We have a dining room, but I prefer eating in the kitchen."

There were six plates. Max put one at the head of the

table, and then three down one side and two down the other. The table could have comfortably sat fourteen people.

Gary came in and kissed his wife, then turned to Max. "I apologize for running in and out earlier, but you wouldn't have wanted to shake my hand after what Pop and I were doing."

He extended his hand.

"Maxine Revere. Your wife was kind enough to invite me to dinner."

"She's not a tourist," Beth said, "she's looking for information, and she's a sweetheart, so I want you and Dad to be on your best behavior."

Sweetheart. Max couldn't wait to tell David that someone had called her a *sweetheart*.

It made her day. Hell, it made her *year*.

"I'm always good," Gary said and slapped his wife lightly on her rear end.

She hit his hand but was smiling. "Please carve the roast."

Gary, also grinning, walked over to the counter where a pot roast was resting on a cutting board. He took out a knife, sharpened it, and sliced proficiently.

Beth left the room. Gary asked Max, "Where do you live?"

"New York," she said.

"Upstate?"

"Manhattan."

"Manhattan." Suspicious, or was that just her paranoia? "Don't get a lot of Manhattanites here."

"I was raised in California."

"Ah."

"You don't like outsiders?"

"No problem with outsiders. But Beth is very . . . kind."

"I'm not here to cause any problems for you or your family. I came to talk to your father about a police report sixteen years ago."

He looked at her oddly. "Sixteen years?"

"My mother disappeared, and I think the last place she came was the Eastern Shore. I'm just trying to put together pieces of a puzzle, but I don't have all the pieces yet."

He shifted, and so did his demeanor. He wasn't suspicious, but he still seemed protective. Of his wife? His family?

She shouldn't read too much into the situation. She wasn't here to cause problems, she was here because she wanted answers, and she would have to convince the Hendersons that they could talk to her.

"All right," Gary said after a moment. He was a surprisingly difficult person to read. Max had no idea what he was really thinking, but suspected it would come out over dinner.

Beth returned with two bottles of wine. Gary took them from her and opened both, one white and one red, and placed them on the table. Beth opened a cabinet and retrieved wineglasses.

Molly ran into the room. She obviously did nothing in slow motion. Max liked the kid. She had never been so carefree. Everything Max had done had been methodical and with purpose. As a child, she didn't run into rooms, but surveyed the situation so she knew what she was walking into. She did so to this day, the only difference being that she was much better at it. She could assess a room almost immediately and without hesitation. That skill came from maturity and lots of practice.

"Grandpop said you're from New York!" Molly sat down and took a roll from a basket that Beth had just set on the table. "I love New York. My mom took me to see

*Hamilton* for my sixteenth birthday. I don't know *how* she got the tickets, but oh, my god, it was amazing. Have you seen it?"

"Yes," Max said. "My producer can get tickets for anything."

"Producer? What do you do? Are you on television?"

"I'm an investigative reporter, though that's not why I'm here. Not exactly."

Gary was still watching her closely, and she didn't want him to think that she was obfuscating or lying. "I host a cable crime show."

"Really? That's cool. I'm going to be a prosecutor."

"Good profession."

Beth said, "The state attorney came to speak at her school last year for her brother's graduation and ever since she's wanted to be a lawyer."

"A prosecutor," Molly corrected.

"Same thing."

"Mom, it's *not*." Molly rolled her eyes. "How'd you decide to be a reporter?"

"It sort of just happened—and I'm not a traditional reporter. I only investigate cold cases."

"Really?" She took a second roll and bit into it.

"Wait until dinner," Gary said.

"Can I have wine?"

"Are you driving to Bitsy's?" Beth asked.

"Yes, but just half a glass?"

"No," Gary and Beth said simultaneously.

Molly rolled her eyes again but she was smiling.

To have two parents who so obviously loved you . . . Molly was comfortable here. Comfortable and confident and loved. Max felt surprisingly emotional, thinking about everything she'd never had growing up.

"White or red?" Gary asked Max.

"Either is fine with me."

"You must have a preference."

"Well, with fish or by itself, I prefer white. But with a roast that smells this rich and delicious, how about red?"

"Red it is," Gary said and poured glasses.

A woman walked in with a man who had to be Garrett Henderson. He looked just like his photo—a full head of white hair. The woman was also recognizable from the agriculture magazine—his sister, Madelyn.

After introductions, they sat at the table and Garrett said grace. It was short and sweet, but clearly heartfelt. The family chattered while dishing up their plates, then Beth said, "Dad, Maxine is looking for her mother who disappeared years ago. She believes the car you found might have belonged to her."

"Oh?" Garrett said.

Max told him—in brief—about how she learned about the abandoned car and about talking to both the sheriff and Detective Lipsky. "You were mentioned in the police report. I know it's been a long time, you might not remember much about it, but anything will help me because I know so little about why she was here and what might have happened."

"I remember," Garrett Henderson said. "We had some folks out of the area dumping their junk off our road. It got to be a problem, so I started patrolling, hoping to catch one of those scoundrels in the act."

"Did you?" Max asked.

"A few people, and word got around to stop dumping over here. They just moved elsewhere. They can go to the dump and do it all legal and proper, but they want to save a few bucks. Well, as soon as they were hit by the fines, word got out. Anyhow, every week or so I'd saddle up one of the horses and stroll about. That's when I found the car."

He cut into his roast, put the piece in his mouth, and chewed while looking at Max. "Your mother's car?"

"Yes. She was using another name. It's a long story, but I'm confident she owned the car under a false name."

"We're in no rush," Garrett said.

Max didn't know how much to tell, but why hold back? None of this was secret. She had her biography on the NET website, including the information about her mother and that she'd abandoned Max a month before her tenth birthday, and disappeared altogether almost six and a half years later. Max had hoped once her show drew an audience that someone would come forward with information about Martha Revere, but it had never happened.

Still, this wasn't about her—this was about Martha, and Max's quest to find the truth. She gave an abbreviated version of the story. All the truth, there was no reason to lie, but as she spoke she was almost, well, *embarrassed* about her mother. These were good people, and she couldn't imagine any of them leaving their children or conning people or frivolously spending money.

"When my private investigator learned that Martha took the name D. Jane Sterling—who is my aunt—I knew it was her car," Max said in conclusion. "That, and the fact that one of her old boyfriends is from Cape Haven."

"Who?" Beth asked.

This, Max realized, knowing that Jimmy didn't have a terrific reputation, was beginning to tread into unknown territory. But if she lied, they would clam up, she was certain of it.

"When my mother left me with my grandparents, she was involved with a man named Jimmy Truman. I knew he was from Virginia, but I didn't know where until I started looking into this abandoned car."

"I am not surprised," Garrett said.

"Pop," Gary said quietly.

"That boy was trouble from the day he was born. Ike and Emily did everything they could. But she also had Gabriel, who made up for Jimmy. One saint for every sinner."

"Dad, that's not true," Beth said. "You have eight grandchildren and not a sinner among them. At least nothing like Jimmy Truman."

Gary cleared his throat. "Just gossip, pay it no mind."

"Well," Beth said, "not *all* gossip. Jimmy was in and out of trouble until he up and left when he was twenty. Good thing, because poor Em had to go back to teaching to pay off the mortgage Jimmy had her take out."

"Elizabeth!" Gary said. "You don't know that for a fact."

Gary clearly didn't like anyone talking about anyone else.

"Well," Beth said, "Sue was Emily's best friend, and Sue is also the organizer for the county fair, has been for twenty-some years. And I run the pie contest. I won ten years in a row and was no longer allowed to enter—which I think is just the dumbest rule I've ever heard—and Sue told me that Jimmy had Em take money out of the house, which was paid off by the insurance when poor Ike's fishing boat went down."

"Enough," Gary said. "I swear, Beth, small-town gossip is only ten percent truth and ninety percent imagination."

Molly was very interested in the conversation and said, "I know Eve Truman pretty well. I mean, we don't really do the same things, she's a sophomore, but she's really smart."

"Molly," Gary said sternly.

Eve Truman? "Who's Eve?"

"Gabriel's daughter," Beth said. "Bless his heart, he's taken care of her since she was a baby."

"Gabriel's a good man," Garrett said. "Gary, I know, you don't like gossip, but hear me out—I'll tell you this as a fact. Gabriel and Jimmy had a falling-out years ago. I won't speculate as to why, that's none of our business. But as far as I know, Jimmy left the Eastern Shore twenty-some years ago and has never returned."

"Amen," Gary said, the final word on Jimmy Truman.

Molly ate quickly and begged to leave, which her parents granted. "It's a school night," Beth said. "Home at ten. Not ten-oh-one, but ten or earlier. And take a plate of cookies for Bitsy and Neil."

Molly kissed her mom. "Thanks. Nice meeting you, Ms. Revere."

"You can call me Max," she said.

"Where are you staying?" Molly asked.

"At Havenly."

Beth sighed and smiled. "I love that restaurant."

"Too expensive," Garrett said.

Gary took Beth's hand and kissed it. "That's why it's for special occasions."

Molly rolled her eyes and ran out of the room.

Madelyn, Garrett's sister, hadn't said much of anything during the conversation. Max said, "I saw in a recent agricultural magazine that you pioneered a new method of raising clams."

Madelyn perked up. "Yes. My son and daughter helped—they did the hard work—but it was really a family vision."

Madelyn was happy to talk about her aquaculture projects, and they enjoyed another glass of wine and seconds. Max found the process interesting—particularly since she loved clams.

When they were done, Max helped Beth clear the table. Beth waved her off. "Look, go talk to Pop. Gary is really the best of us—he's a big believer that we don't talk negatively about anyone. But I understand that you need answers. I couldn't imagine not knowing what happened to my mother. She and my dad retired to Norfolk—my dad has some medical issues, needs to be close to the hospital—but I talk to her several times a week and they come out here for Sunday dinner almost every week. If she just up and vanished—I would raise Cain to find out what happened."

"My mother is nothing like yours. Or you."

"I didn't think it was all wine and roses for you growing up," Beth said. "Considering you call your mother Martha half the time. Did you mean earlier that you haven't seen your mother since you were nine?"

Max nodded. "My childhood wasn't bad. My grandparents are good people, they sent me to private schools and college and never made me feel less simply because my mother was wild and either didn't know or wouldn't tell me who my father was. They were simply . . . reserved, let's say."

"They did right by you," Beth said. "I just can't—well, let's just say my kids know I'll always be here."

"Thank you for dinner. It was delicious."

"Pop is out on the back patio, smoking his pipe. Why don't you take him his cup of decaf? I also made fresh *real* coffee, if you'd like some."

"Thank you."

Max carried Garrett's mug of black decaf and another cup for her and walked out to the back porch as Beth directed. The warm, subtle scent of vanilla and spices mixed with tobacco drew her to the older man sitting in a rocking chair in the far corner. The sun had set, leaving the cloudless sky a brilliant array of indigo, red, and orange.

"Beth asked me to bring out your coffee," Max said. She placed it on the small table between two rocking chairs. "Do you mind if I sit?"

"Are you going to ask more questions?"

"Yes."

"Go ahead."

Max sat, sipped her coffee, and wished she could stay with the Hendersons all night. The peace out here was nothing short of breathtaking. Crickets chirped, owls hooted, and the sound of running water in the house made Max think that *this* was exactly what a home should be like.

"You have a wonderful family," Max said.

"I've got no complaints."

"I want to find out what happened to my mother."

"Over dinner, you didn't sound like there was much love lost between you two."

"There isn't. My mother was beautiful, cunning, and selfish. We moved all over the world at the drop of a hat, based on my mother's whims. I didn't go to school until halfway through fourth grade, when I started living with my grandparents. Martha left me there and didn't come back. Sent me cards on occasion, said she'd come get me, but I suspected she was lying or if she was serious, she changed her mind. After a while, I just didn't care anymore."

"But you do."

Yes, she did. She wanted the truth. She tried to explain.

"My mother hooked up with Jimmy Truman when we were living in Palm Beach. I didn't like him, but that was typical of most of my mother's boyfriends. They found me annoying and said I cramped their style, and I thought there were all jerks who used my mother. Until I realized that my mother used them just as much. I recently hired a private investigator, and we suspect that Martha and Jimmy were together for all or most of the six years between when she left me and when she disappeared."

"Maybe she wanted to disappear. Leaving her car there,

no luggage, nothing to suggest that she was injured—tells me she didn't want anyone knowing where she was."

"It wouldn't surprise me if she did just that. But as I mentioned over dinner, Martha was extremely wealthy. She never accessed her bank account after that April. I believe in my heart—and based on the evidence—that she's dead. That she died around here. Maybe she left the car in order to disappear, but why out *here*? She didn't know this area. The only connection between Martha and Northampton County is Jimmy Truman."

Garrett didn't say anything for a long minute that extended to two and then into three. Max watched the light fade from the sky, and stars begin to appear in the darkness. There was a chill, but Garrett didn't seem to care, and Max wasn't about to get up when she sat next to her single best source of information. Garrett Henderson was a lifelong resident, he'd found Martha's car, and it was clear he knew the Trumans.

"Have you talked to Gabriel?" he finally asked.

"Not yet. I wanted to gather more information before I spoke to him. I have sources in the FBI and learned of an inactive investigation into Jimmy Truman. I want more details about the investigation and my mother and Jimmy's relationship before I approach Gabriel."

"I'll tell you this, Ms. Revere, Gabriel Truman is a good man. I knew his father. Ike wasn't the man Gabriel is, but he tried. One of those things you hear about bad luck following a person, that was poor old Ike. He worked hard, I grant him that, but he never seemed to get on top. Made him bitter. Died young, trawler accident.

"Now Jimmy, he never worked as hard as his dad. I suspect he saw how much Ike labored and figured all that hard work and to get nothing? Well, not nothing, not really—they had a house, they had food, they weren't impoverished. But Emily worked—a teacher—and some people, they always want more, and they want it easy." He took a drag on his pipe and slowly let the smoke out. It blew away from them.

"Gabriel, on the other hand, was a good kid. Much younger than his brother. He was still in high school, I believe, when Jimmy took off—now, my son would say this is gossip, but it's not gossip if it's the truth. And the truth is that Jimmy conned his own mother. The life insurance and accident insurance paid off the mortgage of their home and provided Emily with a nice nest egg so she could retire from teaching. And Jimmy came in and convinced her to mortgage the house again, give him the money for a scheme that never materialized into anything. Might have been a failed investment, might have been an outright lie. I think Gabriel was about fourteen or so then, and Emily had to go back to work. Gabriel worked two jobs, barely graduated from school because he skipped so many classes in order to help his mother. Then he enlisted in the navy and sent most of his paycheck to Emily every month. Gabriel, he's a good man, a good father, and I haven't decided if you're going to be making trouble for him."

"I don't want to make trouble for anyone. I simply want to know what happened to my mother. And if Jimmy Truman had any part of what happened, I will prove it. But I won't hold it against Gabriel Truman if his brother is a criminal or a killer. We don't choose our family."

"What is it you think I can help with?"

"I don't think that Martha's car was left here by accident. I think she was with someone, or that someone else left her car here. Sixteen years is a long time, but can you think of anything that happened back then that gave you pause? Made you suspicious? Did you see someone you didn't recognize or someone you know who was acting odd? It might not be related to the car at all—just anything at the time that was unusual."

Garrett laughed. "Sixteen years—well, I can tell you I remember everything about finding the car because it stood out, but I don't remember anything else that happened that week or that month. It was April, we weren't planting yet. We plant the first week of May. However, your theory that it was likely someone local who brought the car out this way is probably true. We don't get people here. Not even lost folks, because the road ends at my property, and it's just a dirt road. Locals don't come out here because there's better beaches both north and south with easier access. Kids don't come out here to drink because there are easier places to get to without anyone living nearby. My neighbors are all private people. We're the only farm out this way—there used to be more, I bought two adjacent to me years ago. The Scholtens live to the south of us, small spread, not very social. And the spread close to the water, on the small peninsula, is owned by a company. The owner comes out now and again, but never interacts with anyone. There's a caretaker."

Max's instincts hummed. "What company?

"Why?"

"My mother likes powerful men. Money didn't attract her, but power did."

"Couldn't say," Garrett said. "I met one of the owners once—can't say I'd remember him again." He paused. "Boreal. That's the company name, I believe."

Max had never heard of it. She made a mental note to send the name and address to Rogan to follow up. She hoped he had the time. If not, she'd be spending a few days figuring out what Boreal did and who their principals were—specifically, the people who had access to the house near where her mother's car was left.

"Technology company of some sort," Garrett continued. "I was riding Becky—my favorite horse—and ran into the man on a walk. We chatted. I honestly can't remember his name."

"It's been a while."

"He comes and goes."

"Who's the caretaker?"

"Abel Parsons. He's local, but keeps to himself. Lives out at the Boreal spread in a separate cottage, no family."

Max needed to talk to him. He might know something. And she needed to research this business.

"If I may ask, what are you thinking here?"

"Martha was unpredictable in many ways, but the one thing I could count on was that she would find herself with important or powerful people. This community is down-to-earth. I don't know why she'd come here, unless she was with Jimmy—or someone powerful, like whoever runs the Boreal business."

"You think a man you have never met, you don't know, and you just heard about had something to do with your mother's disappearance? That's grasping at straws."

"Perhaps, but I'm going to investigate every thread I find."

Again, silence, and again, not uncomfortable.

"Beth likes you," Garrett said. "I trust my daughter-in-law's instincts."

Max didn't have a response, so simply said, "I like Beth, too."

"I don't think I can help you, but if you want to come out again and talk, we're here. I'll talk to the Scholtens, Abel, too, if you'd like."

That opening, that kindness, twisted Max's heart.

"Thank you, Mr. Henderson."

"Garrett. My friends all call me Garrett."

# Chapter Eight

Gabriel watched Maxine Revere's cottage for nearly an hour before he went inside.

He had never, in the nearly sixteen years that he'd been co-owner of Havenly, gone into a guest's rental without permission.

*Never.*

But this woman could destroy everything he cared about, everyone he loved. He needed to know *why*. He needed to know if his brother was going to destroy him like he'd promised he would.

So he used his master key and walked into the house of one of his guests.

He closed the door and paused.

Silence.

Waves lapping on the beach.

A late call of a seagull.

The sound of distant laughter. The Oldenburgs, who had rented the cottage two over, had a large family, a sort of family reunion, and were picnicking on the beach. It was night, but not completely dark.

He didn't know how much time he had, so he went through quickly.

It was clear Maxine Revere wasn't using the ground floor which had a sitting area, bedroom, and bath.

The middle floor was a large living area that could be converted into more beds, a kitchen and eating area, and a den. The den doors were closed. He opened them and flipped on the light.

At first, Gabriel didn't quite understand what he was looking at. A roll of butcher paper had been tacked to two walls of the den, the artwork had been removed and stacked behind the couch. The furniture had been re-arranged, and the den—meant to be a cozy work space for business travelers—was practically turned into a war room.

He started on the far left of the timeline with a date more than twenty-two years ago: *Atherton*.

He didn't know what that meant, but two months later was another date and notation: *Postcard from Hawaii*.

He stepped closer and removed a postcard that had been tacked to the wall—*Hi, Maxie*—then immediately put it back on the wall, his heart pounding.

He had a shared history with this woman that she didn't know about. Her mother. His brother. The truth overwhelmed him and he wanted to grab Eve and run far, far away.

But he couldn't. Because this was only the beginning.

In the corner of the den was a larger Post-it note and the words: *Martha disappears Northampton County: dead?*

April, sixteen years ago.

He felt physically ill.

The last postcard tacked to the wall was right before Martha Revere's disappearance. Hands shaking, he re-moved it. It had been hand-dated December 31, but the postmark was weeks later.

*Maxine—*

*Sweet baby girl, happy sixteenth. Has Eleanor
driven the spirit out of you or did you wrap her
around your perfect little finger? I thought she'd be
dead by now, but no such luck. Yes, I still read the
society pages and take note. You should, too. So
much to remember.*

*I told you I'd come back but life has plans, baby,
and they'll never bring me west. You are a Revere; I
don't think I ever was. But I certainly have enjoyed
the ride. Live big, Maxie, not small. There's no fun
in being timid.*

 *—Martha*

Gabriel didn't know what to make of the postcard. He
carefully tacked it back up where it had been.

To the right of the corner were many years with very
little information—mostly dates and locations—but he
saw his brother's name.

*Jimmy Truman: FBI investigation opened? Now inactive.*

She knew there was an FBI investigation into his
brother.

The abandoned car.

The police investigation.

Martha Revere leasing an apartment in Miami.

Martha using the name of D. Jane Sterling.

Jimmy using the name of J. J. Sterling.

It made no sense.

Well, *most* of it made no sense to Gabriel, but the parts
he understood could ruin him and destroy his family.

He would never allow that to happen.

Jimmy had broken their mother's heart once, he would
not allow his brother to take from him the only thing that
had made his mother truly happy.

Gabriel painstakingly made sure he hadn't disturbed anything in the den, that each item was exactly as he found it. He turned off the light, closed the door, and walked out.

Maxine Revere had to go. And he would find a way to make her leave, if it was the last thing he ever did.

# Chapter Nine

When Max woke early Thursday morning, she planned her day.

After drinking coffee, eating a banana on toast, and sending off an email to Sean Rogan and David about Boreal and her questions about the ownership of the property adjacent to the Hendersons, she left the cottage.

Time to introduce herself to Gabriel Truman.

He might have all the answers she needed—or at a minimum, a direction for her to pursue.

She showered, dressed, and went to the main hotel for the complimentary continental breakfast, then found the concierge, Reginald Cruthers.

"Ms. Revere, how may I assist you?"

"Do you have Mr. Truman's schedule handy?"

"This isn't our busy season, I can schedule a tour at your convenience. This weekend is booked, but today and tomorrow are mostly clear."

"I just wanted to talk to him for a minute. Where would I find him?"

"He's usually in his office at the boathouse before eight every morning."

"Thank you."

"Would you like me to call him for you?"

"That's not necessary, I'll enjoy the walk."

She left the hotel and walked down to the boathouse, which was the opposite direction from her beach house. Though the skies were clear, there was a brisk wind bringing a chill in from the ocean. She already felt the salt and moisture clinging to her long, thick hair and wisps being pulled out of her loose braid.

The marina at Havenly was moderate in size and impeccably maintained. More than half the slips were rented to locals, and the resort maintained a half-dozen small motorboats to rent and four larger yachts that could be chartered. According to their Web page they had regular tours from May through September, and by appointment during the off-season. Gabriel ran the marina, but he clearly wasn't the only pilot. The Havenly boats were clearly marked with their own insignia and each had Haven as their name. *Haven I*, *Haven II*, and so on.

Gabriel Truman was in his office with the door open. There was no receptionist, but it was still barely eight in the morning. And maybe they weren't fully staffed yet since it was so early in the season.

He looked up when she walked in. Max recognized him from the photo on the resort website. Late thirties, maybe forty. Looked and dressed like a sailor in sturdy, comfortable boat shoes, no socks, khaki pants, and a white polo shirt with the resort insignia on it.

"May I help you?"

"Gabriel Truman?"

"Yes?"

"My name is Maxine Revere, and I was hoping for some of your time."

He stared at her blankly for a second. "I'm in the middle of repairs and maintenance this morning. My staff will be in soon, they'll be able to help with any questions you might have, or you can schedule a tour or charter through the main hotel office."

"I need to talk to you about your brother, Jimmy."

"I have nothing to say about Jimmy," he said flatly. "He's not in my life, and hasn't been for years. Decades."

"Your brother was involved with—"

Gabriel stood and walked around from behind his desk. "I don't care about *anything* my brother has done. As far as I'm concerned, I'm an only child." He now blocked the doorway of his office so she couldn't enter. He was more than a little angry, and obviously fighting to control his temper.

"I'm aware—"

"You are aware of nothing, ma'am. You can leave."

She raised an eyebrow. "I'm a guest here, I'm trying to get information—"

"I honestly don't care. I will talk to you about anything related to our boats or the history of the area or the resort, but I will not talk to you about Jimmy."

"I'm not trying to dig up dirt or hurt your family in any way," Max said, both irritated with Gabriel's reaction and worried that she didn't have a good reason to encourage him to talk. "I'm looking for my mother, Martha Revere, and I think Jimmy may know what happened to her."

"I can't help you. I have work to do, you need to leave."

"I'm not going to leave." Why was he being so belligerent? "You don't like your brother. I don't care. I don't like him, either. I met him when I was nine and after that my mother left me with my grandparents and never returned." The fact that Gabriel hadn't interrupted again emboldened her and she quickly continued. "I'm here because my mother's car was abandoned sixteen years ago and I think Jimmy Truman had something to do with it. If you know—"

This time he did cut her off. "Maybe he did, maybe he didn't, I wouldn't know and I don't care. Good-bye, Ms. Revere."

"Please just listen—"

"I have work to do." He ushered her out of the boat-house offices and locked the door behind him.

"Maybe I didn't—"

But he was already walking away, and Max's words were aimed at his retreating back.

"Well, shit," she mumbled.

Gabriel Truman walked as far as he could get from that nosy woman, until he was at the end of the pier. He needed to regroup, figure out how he was going to get rid of Maxine Revere.

*Revere.*

He was flushed and his heart was beating too fast. He thought for sure when she introduced herself that she was going to accuse him of breaking into her beach house. He hadn't touched much, he hadn't taken anything, but he knew then and he knew now that he should never have walked into that cottage.

But Maxine Revere was going to destroy his life if he couldn't find a way to convince her to leave, that there was nothing here for her, no answers to her questions.

Gabriel jumped in one of his boats and took her out. Being out on the ocean was the only thing that truly calmed him when he was angry. And he was more than angry now. He was furious, deeply worried, and scared.

He had hardly slept the night before when he got home. Instead he'd spent hours online learning everything he could about Maxine Revere. What he learned stunned and terrified him. Maxine Revere was a reporter who had no intention of leaving without answers to her questions.

And there *were* no answers. Gabriel had no idea what happened to Martha Revere sixteen years ago. He hadn't been here, he relied solely on his mother's recollection.

He'd had no idea Martha's car had been found until Bill came over the other night. Her car, but no Martha. He'd never thought she was dead. He tried not to think about Martha and Jimmy at all, but after reading the information Maxine Revere uncovered, it was clear that Martha had been dead for a long time.

He kept the boat close to shore so he could get a cell signal and called the sheriff's office. A minute later he was connected to Sheriff Bill Bartlett.

"Something wrong, son?" Bill said.

"I just had a visit from Maxine Revere. She talked to me about looking for her mother."

"I thought she'd come out and talk to you."

"She thinks Jimmy had something to do with it. Dragging my family through the mud is going to hurt me, hurt Eve, hurt my business."

"I don't think that's her intention, son," Bill said.

"She's a reporter! From New York. She has books published and investigates cold cases."

"Gabriel, I don't think she means harm. She wants to know what happened to her mother, that's it. I've already run Jane Does in the area. Marcel is running a wider search in neighboring states. So far, no one matches her mother's description. Her body hasn't been found, she just disappeared. Maybe there was foul play. Maybe she killed herself. Maybe she took a new identity and is living up in Canada. We don't know, but when Ms. Revere figures out there are no answers here, she'll leave."

Gabriel wasn't certain that was true. Not based on what he'd read last night, but he couldn't admit to that, not to the sheriff. "I don't want her here."

He stared out across the bay. He couldn't see the other

side, and this was how he liked it. There was peace on the water.

"I have no reason to run her out of town, and Garrett's helping her."

"What? Garrett Henderson? Why?"

"Well, I don't know why, but probably because Garrett will do what Garrett wants to do. He's always been that way. She had dinner with his family last night, Garrett called me this morning at the crack of dawn wanting to know about the car and the investigation, thinking maybe I held out on the girl. I didn't—I gave her the file, said as much to him. And honestly, maybe there's some truth to her theory, but it was sixteen years ago. That's a long time to find much of anything."

Gabriel knew exactly when it had been, and he wasn't going to allow a Revere to destroy him. He pictured the attractive, stately woman who stood in his face and demanded that he help her. She didn't look or sound like anyone who would take no for an answer.

"I doubt that, Bill. She clearly thinks there's something to find. She's rented a beach house for the entire month of April."

"Jimmy was a bad apple, everyone knows it—just as certain as they know you're a pillar of the community, Gabriel. If you think that Jimmy's past crimes will come back and damage you, they won't."

Gabriel wasn't as confident as the sheriff.

"Bill, call me if anything happens with Revere, okay? Whatever she digs up, especially about Jimmy, I need to know."

"Of course, you have my word."

Gabriel hung up. He needed to learn everything he could about Maxine Revere, and fast, because the survival of his family depended on getting her out of town before she learned the truth.

# Chapter Ten

Gabriel Truman took family leave from the U.S. Navy as soon as he was able. The letter had come from his mother last month, but he'd been deployed in the middle of the Pacific and after talking to her and her doctor, her death wasn't imminent.

*She has six months to a year.*

Emily Truman could have stopped the cancer years ago, but Emily didn't like doctors and she didn't like complaining about her own problems. Now it was too late, and Gabriel realized he was going to lose the only person he had ever cared about.

It wasn't that his childhood had been perfect. His father was a bitter fisherman who worked hard his entire short life. He was good at his job, and the only time he was happy was when he was on a boat, but the industry had too many downs. Gabriel would never know if the accident that claimed his father's life when he was ten was truly an accident, or if his father had intentionally set the fire. They might never know, but the insurance paid out and because he was working on the job, it paid double—so Emily could pay off the house, retire from teaching, which had become much harder with her worsening arthritis, and have a small monthly income for the rest of her life.

They could have been comfortable, but his older brother Jimmy had practically invented the get-rich-quick scheme. He conned his mother out of money before Gabriel knew what his brother had been doing. Emily went back to work to make ends meet, and they would have lost the house if the banker hadn't been a good friend of the Trumans who restructured the loan so her payments wouldn't put her under. Jimmy had forged Emily's signature on a substantial second mortgage that almost went through. Had Jimmy got ahold of the equity in the house, Emily would never have been able to pay the mortgage.

His fists clenched. Jimmy had finally left town for good and Gabriel hoped never to see him again. What he did to the family was criminal, and he'd burned every bridge in the Chesapeake Bay. He'd found some rich bitch a few years ago, a stupid blonde who doted on him and paid his way. Fine by Gabriel—as long as Jimmy left their mother alone, Gabriel couldn't care less about what happened to him or anyone who was stupid enough to fall for his lies.

The navy had been Gabriel's salvation. He knew everything about sailing and boats because of his childhood, and he loved the ocean. If he didn't see land it never bothered him, there was a peace being at sea that had eluded him his entire life. Between his dad's drinking and his mother's desperation to make everyone happy and his brother's crimes, Gabriel wanted simple.

Six years in the navy and he planned to re-up. What else would he do? But first, he needed to see his mother.

He hitched a ride to the Cape Haven turnoff, then walked the couple miles into town with his pack. The September humidity was tempered only by a sea breeze. Gabriel breathed in, breathed out. The salt air was tinged with oil from the increase in tourist boating. The Chesapeake was losing its vibrancy, the fishing was even worse now than when his father worked on the water, but without the tourists, the towns on the bay would have no income. It was a catch-22. The tourists made the situation worse, but without the tourists the towns would go bankrupt.

*It's not your problem.*

He walked up the brick walk to the two-story Cape Cod–style house on the corner of Main and Elm. The only home he had ever known that didn't float on the water. Bittersweet, perhaps, but it was home, and his mom only had a few more months to enjoy it. He hoped she lived through Christmas, because it was her favorite time of the year. She loved to bake and decorate and sing Christmas carols when she thought no one could hear her. Gabriel loved his mother's singing, but she didn't like her voice, so he would hide on the stairs where he could hear her but she couldn't see him from the kitchen.

He knocked on the screen door so he didn't startle her. "Mom, it's Gabriel," he called as he entered.

The house was exactly as he remembered. The same warm, spicy smells from daily baking—today it was apples, because Gabriel's favorite dessert was apple cobbler. The same furniture, worn but clean and functional. The house was tidy, though there were papers lying on tables and stacks of children's books on the coffee table. Maybe she was babysitting—she loved children, and had often been the go-to house for neighborhood kids. The house where parents didn't mind their kids going for Halloween for fresh-baked cupcakes or caramel apples because everyone trusted and loved sweet Emily Truman.

"Mom?" He walked through the dining room and into the kitchen. There was a high chair in the corner. On the counter a bib. A pink ribbon on the table.

The timer on the oven went off. Gabriel looked

inside—apple cobbler, the juice bubbling through the holes in the crust. Some things never changed. He turned off the oven, pulled the mitt out of the drawer, and retrieved the dessert. He heard footsteps on the stairs.

"Gabriel!"

He put the cobbler on top of the stove and turned to his mom. His face froze in a half smile. There was his mom, white hair and big green eyes, looking far thinner than he'd ever remembered her. She'd never been overweight, but she looked a decade older than her sixty-two years.

But that wasn't the most startling change. Emily held a baby. A girl, dressed in pink, with white-blond curls and the biggest blue eyes he'd seen on an infant. She stared at him as if assessing him, but she couldn't even be a year.

"Mom?"

"I'm so happy to see you." She walked over to the high chair and strapped the baby in, then hugged him tightly.

His arms wrapped around her and he feared he would break her in two. She was all skin and bones. "Mom." His voice cracked. "You should have called me earlier."

"I didn't know until last month that it was cancer."

"You didn't lose all this weight in a month."

She was really dying. Soon, he would have no one. No family. No home.

He could berate her, complain that she should have gone to the doctor sooner, that she should have caught this before it got so far. But none of that would change the fact that his mother had only months to live.

"Are you sure you should be babysitting?" he asked. "Are you feeling okay?"

"You must be starving," she said. "Sit, I'll make us sandwiches."

"I can make them."

"It's my kitchen, Gabriel. I'm not dead yet."

He sat in the chair he'd always sat in growing up.

When his dad was alive they would eat dinner in the dining room—too formal for his taste—but breakfast and lunch were always in the kitchen. His food digested better here, he'd always thought.

The high chair was directly across from him. Emily put a cup with a lid in front of the child. The girl picked it up with chubby hands and drank, still watching him quietly.

"What's her name?" Gabriel asked.

"Genevieve, but that's a mouthful, don't you think? I call her Eve."

*Something* was not right.

His mom had made turkey sandwiches. Not processed turkey meat, but a sliced turkey breast. She used to bake a turkey once a month and they'd have it for dinner one night, then sandwiches, turkey noodle soup, casseroles—whatever struck her fancy. His mom was the best cook in Cape Haven.

"Can I get you something else?"

"Sit, Mom."

She did. She took a small bite of her sandwich. She looked pained as she chewed, but she tried to hide it.

"How are you, Mom? Really."

"I have good days and bad days." She glanced at the baby. "How long were you able to get off?"

"Indefinite," he said. He had a month of emergency family leave, but then he had to either return and reenlist or resign. He'd planned on reenlisting, had already filled out the paperwork, but his commanding officer had put it on hold until he knew what was going on with his mom.

"I didn't want to call, I didn't want to tell you—"

"I wish you'd told me sooner."

"Things became complicated."

"You're my mother. I want to be here."

She glanced again at the baby.

"You can't babysit anymore, Mom. You're tired." Exhausted was more like it. There were dark circles under her eyes.

"Eve is a good baby," Emily said. "I'm a bit worried—well, I overslept yesterday morning and she was crying. She never cries, so I think she was up for a while and I didn't hear her."

He couldn't have heard her correctly. "Where are her parents?"

She glanced down at her hands. "I knew you'd be upset, Gabriel, but none of this is Eve's fault. She's innocent."

His stomach sank. He ran through all the neighbors who could have left their kid with his dying mom. Who would be so cruel? So selfish? Then he knew.

"Jimmy?" He could barely spit out his brother's name.

"Martha came for a few days in April. Eve was only a few months old. She said Jimmy had left them, she didn't know where else to go. I think . . . I think Jimmy got into trouble again. Martha just wanted someone to watch her for a week or two, until she figured things out. But she never came back. I couldn't just turn Eve over to child services. And being sick—I know that's what would happen. They'd take her from me, put her with strangers. She's my granddaughter. I always wanted a little girl, and now I have one."

Tears slid down her weathered cheeks. He'd seen his stoic mother cry only once before, at his father's funeral. Then, too, she'd cried silently.

"Where's Jimmy?" He didn't mean to sound so frustrated, but he couldn't keep his anger inside.

"I don't know. He called once, early July. Right before Independence Day. I asked him about the baby, he said he couldn't come now, but he would. Someday he would, but he was working and couldn't come. I asked about Martha, and he said she had to leave the country, she got into trouble with the law."

Jimmy was a father? Martha left the country? What the *hell* was going on with these people?

Gabriel looked at his niece. "How old is she?"

"Martha left some papers in case I needed them—she was born January twelfth in Miami. That makes her eight and a half months now."

"You have her birth certificate?"

"Yes."

Gabriel had to find Martha and force her to do the right thing, but she's just like Jimmy. She's a con artist, always has been, always will be.

Gabriel had met Martha only once, over Christmas a few years ago when he had a week leave. He hadn't known that Jimmy was coming home as well, and he would have kicked him out of the house except for the fact that his mother was thrilled to have her two sons home for Christmas. Emily was happy, but Gabriel watched Jimmy very closely.

At the time, Martha went by Martha Truman. Jimmy told Emily they'd married, but confided in Gabriel that it was just easier to pretend they were than actually get married. To this day, Gabriel didn't know—or care—about his brother's love life.

But now he had to find Martha, because his mother couldn't raise a baby when she was dying. Gabriel would need to be in Cape Haven in order to help her and to search for the baby's mother. He knew then that he wouldn't return to the navy.

"I love her, Gabriel," Emily said quietly. "She's our family."

Gabriel stared at Eve. She looked right back at him, as if she knew that this conversation was about her, as if she knew that her parents were losers and that he was the only one who might be able to protect her.

"Mom, I have decided not to reenlist in the navy. I'm staying home."

"But you love the navy."

"I've been keeping up on what's going on around town. Brian Cooper is looking for someone to help him renovate the Cape resort and run the tour boats. He talked to me about it last year, when I was here for leave, and tried to get me to buy in. We talk from time to time. He still needs help—he has one investor, but it's not enough. I have a small savings, and the skills he needs."

The Coopers were like the Trumans in Cape Haven— they'd been around for generations. The Coopers were related to Emily by marriage—Emily's sister had married into the family. She and her husband had moved to California years ago, didn't keep in touch with either family, but the Coopers had always watched out for Emily. And Brian, who was more like a brother to Gabriel than Jimmy had ever been, had bought the run-down property with the help of an investor. But he needed help, and he wanted Gabriel to work with him.

It could be an important fixture in the community. Brian had ideas, but it wasn't a one-man job.

"Brian is a good man. He's been wanting to save that property for years." Emily reached out and took Gabriel's hand. "Please, Gabriel, when I go, take care of Eve. Promise me. I know Jimmy hasn't always been . . . responsible. But we're family."

Not *responsible*? Try criminal.

Gabriel looked at Eve and she smiled. She actually smiled at him, revealing two dimples that melted his heart on the spot.

He fell in love, and vowed to do anything—*anything*— to protect her.

"I promise, Mom."

# Chapter Eleven

Max never took "no" or "no comment" as an answer, but Gabriel Truman's over-the-top hostility had her taking a step back and regrouping. She'd clearly missed something.

While Max understood that he might not want to talk about his brother who was an obvious jackass and a criminal, she'd made it clear she wasn't here to damage his reputation or create any problems for him with his business. Was it that simple? Was he concerned that Jimmy Truman might still be in the picture, that he might come in and cause problems for Gabriel or his business? He'd conned his own mother, maybe he had something on Gabriel.

His daughter . . . the Hendersons mentioned his daughter, and she'd also been mentioned in Emily Truman's obituary. But no mention of a mother. He was a single dad. As her ten-month relationship with Detective Nick Santini taught her, custody issues were complicated and emotional. Maybe the mother didn't know about the criminal brother, and if she did she might fight for custody. Maybe she was a troublemaker like Nick's ex-wife. Maybe she was unstable. It honestly could be anything, and Max needed to know exactly *what* in order to convince Gabriel that she wasn't going to do or say anything to put his family at risk. Maybe the fact that she was a reporter made him see red, if he thought she planned on writing about Jimmy Truman, which would embarrass him and his family. She'd assumed he hadn't known about her occupation, but his partner Brian Cooper did, and it was reasonable that so did Gabriel Truman.

Max tried to put herself in Gabriel's shoes. He'd obviously been living with his brother's crimes most of his life, and here she comes in asking about him—yes, he had a family to protect. While she still felt his reaction was uncalled for, she could see why he might not want to discuss Jimmy.

She would make it clear to Gabriel that she wasn't writing a book, an article, or airing a television segment about Martha or Jimmy. Her investigation was solely for her own peace of mind. She wanted the truth; she had no intention of publicly sharing it. Then he might listen. Maybe he still wouldn't trust her, but she would convince him she was telling the truth.

She liked having a game plan. Back at the beach house, she went to the den and looked at her timeline on the wall. She hadn't added the daughter, but it was clear she should have. The kid might not be important to Max's case, but she *was* important to Gabriel. Max respected that—though she wished the man would have just let her explain.

Molly Henderson said that Eve Truman was a sophomore. That made her fifteen or sixteen. Gabriel left the navy in September the year that Max's mother disappeared . . . maybe he left because he fathered a child. Had he been married? A one-night stand? Had his wife died young? A girlfriend who dumped the kid on him because she couldn't take it? He would have only been twenty-three or twenty-four at the time. She had to admire a man who lived up to his responsibilities—it's why she didn't hate her ex-boyfriend for putting his son first.

Max put a sticky note up on the wall by that September: *Eve Truman birth? Who is her mother?*

Birth records weren't generally available online, at least not recent records. Over the last decade county offices had become a lot more private about the information that was available to the public. But Cape Haven was a small town, and if Max asked the right people the right questions, she could learn what had happened to Eve's mother.

Still, she needed more information before she started, and she certainly didn't want her questions to get back to Gabriel when his apparent concern was about how her investigation into Jimmy Truman might impact his family and business.

People were often surprised at the vast amount of information available about them online—all legal and public. Social media, especially among young people, proved to be a proven place to gather data.

She'd already done a basic background check on Gabriel Truman, which was how she knew his discharge date from the navy and that he was part-owner of Havenly—formerly the Haven Resort and Club. He'd served six years in the U.S. Navy, retiring as a petty officer first class. She didn't know much about military rankings, but David had told her after six years that was a pretty high rating.

*"He was likely bumped up right before he put in his papers, if his CO liked him he would give him the promotion. It affects pensions, things like that."*

His profile didn't have anything personal on it—he'd won several racing competitions when he was a teenager, had numerous ratings and licenses from a variety of government and boating agencies. All things that would be important to someone who was hiring him to pilot their charter boat.

Nothing that helped her figure out exactly who Gabriel Truman was.

She then searched for Eve Truman. Teenagers had social media pages, and Eve was no exception. The problem was that every one of her profiles was private. Smart, for a teenager, but very annoying for Max who wanted information.

However, her name *did* come up in several articles on Google News.

Eve Truman was an accomplished sailor herself. She belonged to a junior racing club that had gone from last to first in the three years she had been a member. Max found a photo of Eve from last summer, along with the rest of her team. It was hard to make her out in the group shot, but she had long dark blond hair pulled back with a hair tie and a fresh, clear complexion. The caption read: LED BY CO-CAPTAINS JASON HARRIS AND EVE TRUMAN, THE HAVEN POINT JUNIOR SAILING CLUB TAKES ANOTHER FIRST PLACE TROPHY IN THE SUMMER CLASSIC.

Jason Harris. Co-captain?

Max read the accompanying article in depth. Jason was two years older than Eve and was now a high school senior, which made Eve a sophomore. He might be very interested in talking to Max—especially if she could find an in. Maybe if she was writing an article . . . no, boating was a small, close-knit world. He would likely know all the major magazines and sports reporters by name, if not by sight.

She could go as a philanthropist, perhaps, looking to create a scholarship. And because she loathed lying, even to gain information, she would go ahead and create a scholarship through the Sterling Family Trust. If the board balked, she'd set it up herself.

She had to tread carefully, however—Gabriel was already suspicious of her motives. She didn't want to overstep with his daughter. So she would reach out to the Haven Point director and go from there. Maybe talk to Beth Henderson again.

Max made a to-do list. She felt there was something here, something she could learn from Gabriel Truman if only she was patient and diligent. Fortunately, she was both.

Pleased with herself—she had a meeting with Stephen Galbraith, the president of the Haven Point Sailing Club, first thing Friday morning—Max decided to reward herself with an early dinner. She'd eaten only snack food for lunch and was famished. The wind had picked up through the day, and the skies had turned gray—the forecast indicated rain tonight and on and off in the morning, but it was supposed to be clear by the weekend.

Max didn't mind. She enjoyed the rain, and after her meeting tomorrow morning she would need to regroup and figure out another way to convince Gabriel to talk about his brother. Gabriel Truman was simply a very private person who was protective of his family and angry that his brother was a criminal. At least, that was Max's gut impression. She still felt that Gabriel had overreacted, but she wanted to give him the benefit of the doubt. Family could make everything more complicated and emotional.

She walked to the restaurant, the wind whipping her jacket and hair around her. A few drops of rain fell by the time she arrived five minutes later. She walked into the restaurant, shook off her jacket, and the hostess offered to hang it up for her. "I can get a driver to take you back to your cottage when you're done, Ms. Revere," she said. "The rain is going to be falling hard within the hour."

"Thank you."

Max asked to be seated by a window—it was early enough that there wasn't a crowd, and with this weather she wondered if locals would venture out for dinner. She ordered wine and the crab cake appetizer—she really loved them—while she looked over the menu.

A man in his early forties walked up to her table. He was attractive, with dark hair slightly graying on the sides, and wearing a suit. Based on the way he moved—and the gun in his belt under his jacket—she suspected he was a cop. "Ms. Revere?"

"Yes."

"I'm Agent Ryan Maguire. You left a message for me yesterday. Three messages, in fact—the last one indicated you would be paying me a visit if I didn't return your call."

"And your battery died?"

He smiled, the kind of smile that said, *I know I'm good-looking and smart.* Almost arrogant, but with just enough boyish charm that Max didn't immediately dislike him. "I thought in person was better."

He was blindsiding her—coming to visit on her turf, but when she hadn't expected him. She had to admire the play.

At least, he was *attempting* to blindside her. Maybe he wasn't here to get under her skin, but to get under someone else's skin, namely Gabriel Truman's. More than likely, the feds had talked to Gabriel ten years ago when they opened the investigation into his brother.

She considered having the restaurant box her food and taking Maguire to her cottage, but why should she be forced to change her plans because of this unscheduled visit?

"Please, have a seat."

He did.

"Wine? Beer?"

"I have to drive back to Norfolk, but maybe with a meal."

"Have dinner with me then."

He assessed her. "I know who you are, I know about your cable show, I'm familiar with your articles. Tell me, what are you doing here investigating Jimmy Truman? Do you have information you're withholding from a federal investigation?"

If there was *still* a federal investigation that meant there was a long statute of limitations—or none—or that there were recent crimes they believed Jimmy Truman was responsible for.

"I don't know, but I'm not keeping secrets. You share, I share. I don't bite, Agent Maguire."

"That's not your reputation."

She kept her displeasure at the snide comment to herself as the waitress brought over Max's wine and the crab cake appetizer.

"Drink, sir?"

"Whatever microbrew you have on tap is fine."

"We serve local Blue Mountain, stout or ale."

"Ale, please."

Max said, "So you are joining me for dinner."

"Shall I bring a menu?" the server asked.

"Yes," Maxine said. The waitress left and Max sipped her wine.

"Don't make assumptions about me, and I won't make assumptions about you." But she already had. Maguire wasn't a by the book fed. On the surface he *appeared* to be—he wore a decent, but not too expensive suit and tie; he flashed his badge so he wasn't hiding his identity; and he was straightforward without giving away too much information.

Yet he had a spark that said he liked—*really liked*—

his job. He had tugged at his tie twice since he'd walked in, telling Max he either didn't always wear one, or he wasn't comfortable in it. He'd come here after-hours—unless on call or working a major case, all feds basically worked eight to five. But another signal that he wasn't completely by the book: his haircut. Feds tended to adopt strict dress code standards. Suits and ties, unless undercover, were usually required attire. That also included a neat, trim haircut.

Maguire's dark hair was a bit on the long side. It didn't need a trim, but it was getting close and curled dramatically at the ends.

And he wore Nike running shoes. They were black, didn't completely stand out, but were certainly not shoes most people would wear with a suit.

"Fair enough," Maguire said. "Your messages were a bit cryptic."

"Cryptic? I thought I was excessively clear. My mother had been involved with Jimmy Truman and she disappeared here in Northampton County. I only recently learned this information when a private investigator I hired uncovered a car registered to Jane Sterling, abandoned near Oyster Bay, sixteen years ago this month. When I realized that one of her old boyfriends was from the area, I put two and two together. My PI is very good, learned that there was a federal investigation into Jimmy Truman, so I contacted you."

"That's quite a jump."

"I have other details that led me here, but those are the highlights," Max said.

"You said your mother was Martha Revere."

"She was. She used the name Jane Sterling—Delia Jane Sterling is my great-aunt—and I have proof that her identity had been stolen years ago. It was cleaned up by family lawyers, but that time matches the car registered to D. Jane Sterling, an apartment in Miami, and a few other things."

"Such as?"

"If I choose to work with you, I'll show you everything I have."

"I don't know how you think the FBI operates, but we don't work with civilians on active investigations, especially not reporters."

So there *was* an active investigation into Jimmy Truman. Or was that an intentional information drop? A lie? Feds could be very sneaky.

The waitress returned with Maguire's beer, but Max waved her off before giving her order. "Five minutes, please," she said.

"Of course, Ms. Revere."

When she was out of earshot, Max said, "I don't work with FBI agents on *my* active investigations, either. I called you to set up a meeting; you're the one who chose to 'surprise' me at my hotel. The Norfolk office reopened this investigation just over ten years ago, connected to a Dallas case, so either Jimmy Truman has continued to commit similar crimes, or the statute of limitations is up—unless he killed someone."

"Are you suggesting that he murdered your mother?"

"I haven't gotten that far in my investigation. Those whom I have spoken with indicated that Jimmy Truman was a con man, petty thief, a jerk, but not violent. Still, people change, and I haven't found one person who has claimed to have seen or been in contact with Jimmy Truman in more than ten years. My partner is in Miami following up on the Jane Sterling and J. J. Sterling identities that I believe my mother and Jimmy used there—we have confirmation that J. J. Sterling is in fact Jimmy, and he was last seen in Miami as J. J. Sterling the January before my mother disappeared. According to my PI, he stopped using the Sterling identity about the same time he left Miami. Fast forward nearly six years and your office opens an investigation."

Maguire drank his beer, put the pint back down, never taking his eyes from her.

"If it's still active," Max continued, "that means he's still committing crimes, or that his crime is murder or major art theft."

He laughed. It was a real, hearty laugh.

"Few people know that art theft carries a twenty-year statute of limitations."

"Art history was one of my majors."

"Mine, too."

"Your other?"

"How do you know I had two?"

She simply raised her eyebrow. Few men went to college to major in art history. If they were artists, they went for a BFA. If they were idiots, maybe they would think art history was an easy major or a way to get girls. But Maguire wasn't an idiot.

She didn't say anything. He wanted her to doubt herself, and she didn't.

"Economics. Yours?"

"English lit. I had once upon a time wanted to run a museum."

"I wanted to own an art studio."

"And?"

"I have an exceptional eye, but very little talent."

"We have something in common. College?"

"Notre Dame. You?"

Good school. "Columbia. So now that we've gotten our credentials out of the way, let's order, because I'm starving and the crab cakes only made me hungrier."

Max motioned to the waitress. After she came over, Ryan quickly scanned the menu while Max ordered a shrimp salad. Ryan ordered a burger. "I'm simple," he said when the waitress left.

"I doubt that."

He laughed. "About some things."

"Tell me I'm right about Truman."

"Partly. I did know about his alias, J. J. Sterling, and about the woman, Jane Sterling. I didn't know that Jane Sterling was also an alias. I caught the case only because it was passed to me by the Dallas office. Not every regional office has an art crimes expert."

"Why don't you work out of national headquarters?"

"Norfolk is close enough, and art crime isn't my only area. I'm in the white-collar crimes unit."

Maguire, for all his charm and intelligence, didn't play well with others. He didn't say that, but Max knew enough about the FBI and how they operated to know that most specialists, like those in art crime, operated out of Washington headquarters or one of the major offices like New York or Los Angeles.

"The investigation was opened nearly twenty years ago out of Dallas. Truman's was only one of several names that surfaced. I wasn't even an agent then, still in college, but I spent three years in Dallas after I graduated from Quantico and learned about the case. It went cold fast, and I was transferred to New York to work a major case with Interpol that necessitated me going undercover for two years. Then I was transferred to Norfolk and went about my business. The lead Dallas agent retired, sent me the Truman file because Truman was from Northampton and a piece we believe he stole in Dallas had resurfaced in DC. Because of my familiarity with the original investigation, HQ let me have the case. I reopened it, but couldn't track him down fast enough before he sold the painting and the buyer left the country. Truman slipped away, and I've been looking for him ever since. It's not the only piece he stole."

"Art theft." It seemed far too intelligent a scam for Jimmy Truman.

"You expected what? Drugs? Guns?"

"No, it actually makes perfect sense."

That surprised him. "You know Jimmy?"

"Barely. I met him when I was nine, when he hooked up with my mother. Let's just say, Martha Revere would not win any mother-of-the-year awards. Yet, she loved art and she had talent. More talent than she deserved."

He caught on quick. "A forger?"

"Not to my personal knowledge, and I doubt she was *that* good. But, she *really* knew art. She could look at a piece and know if it was real. She could price art like my grandmother can look at a diamond and know exactly how many carats and the quality of the cut."

"Was your mother a thief?"

She had to respect him for flat-out asking her.

"I don't know. I haven't seen her since I was a kid and she left me with my grandparents. She was declared legally dead nine years ago, seven years after she stopped withdrawing money from her trust fund. The last time I heard from her was a postcard sent sixteen years ago."

He hadn't been expecting that information.

"I didn't know."

"Do you have a photo of Jane Sterling?"

"Only a driver's license picture."

"From Florida."

"You've seen it."

"It's my mother, but she went to great lengths to change her appearance—cut and dyed her hair, lied about her weight—I guarantee you that my mother never weighed 170 pounds in her life, even when she was pregnant with me. First, she was five foot four. Second, she was a bundle of energy. She can't sit still. And the photo—yes, it was a head shot, but she was slender. Too skinny, maybe."

"I see your point."

"I don't know what she was doing with Jimmy Truman, but my mother was all about fun. If Jimmy showed her a good time, she would stick around. As soon as he got boring, she'd leave."

"You must have had an interesting childhood."

She didn't comment. Their food had arrived and she ordered a second glass of wine and started eating.

After several minutes, Maguire said, "You didn't know why the FBI was looking into Truman."

"No."

"I dug around about your mother's disappearance. Called Lipsky, since he gave you my number. Said there's no proof that your mother was Jane Sterling."

"I know it's her."

"Okay."

She almost dropped her fork. "And?"

"And nothing. You saw the photo, you've been tracking your mother, I believe you."

"Well."

"No one else does?"

"The sheriff felt sorry for me—and trust me, I'm not a person anyone should feel sorry for. Lipsky just looked at the facts, and until I can show him unequivocal evidence that Jane Sterling is in fact Martha Revere, he's not going to buy it. Or really care. It's out of his jurisdiction, and there's no evidence that anyone killed her. But it's her, she's dead, and if Jimmy Truman killed her or had something to do with her death, I will prove it. It's what I do."

He nodded. "I looked into your background."

"I would expect nothing less."

"You've reported on some high-profile cases. The

Adam Bachman murder trial. The Blair Caldwell trial. Others."

"Your point?"

"Are you here simply to find out what happened to your mother, or is there a reason I'm not seeing?"

"Does there have to be more?"

"Usually."

Max was comfortable with Maguire, and she wouldn't mind sharing with him some of her more personal thoughts on the matter, but he was still a federal agent and she wasn't certain he would appreciate all of her reasons.

But she didn't really have a choice, because Gabriel Truman walked up to the table. She was about to comment, but he wasn't looking at her. He stared at Maguire, raw anger on his face.

"I told you never to come back," Gabriel said.

Maguire was completely unfazed. "Hello, Gabriel."

"I want you gone. I haven't talked to my brother in years, and I have nothing to say to you."

"I'm not here about your brother," Maguire said calmly. "I'm looking into the disappearance and possible murder of Martha Revere, aka Jane Sterling. Know anything about it?"

Gabriel was nearly red with anger, but his eyes . . . they were far off, almost wild. Max realized he was terrified, but about what she didn't know. Did he know something about what happened to Martha? Why was he so scared?

He turned to Max. He wanted to say something, she could see it in his expression, but he didn't. Instead, he said to Maguire, "Stay away from me unless you have a warrant. I have nothing to say to you."

He strode across the restaurant, so focused on the door he didn't notice that the waiters and patrons were all watching him go. If he wanted to keep a low profile, confronting Max and Maguire and then storming off wasn't the way to do it.

Something was going on with Gabriel Truman, and Max had to figure out what it was.

"I like to ruffle his feathers every so often," Maguire said, completely nonchalant.

She turned her attention back to the fed. "Why? Was he part of Jimmy's schemes?"

"No. If he was, he does a damn good job of hiding it. He doesn't live above his means, he works hard for his living, and all his money is sunk into this business. But he lied to me, and I really hate it when people lie to me."

"We have something else in common." Max took a bite of her salad, but she'd lost her appetite after Gabriel's interruption. She really wanted to know what he was thinking—or what he thought he knew. "And?"

"And . . . it's part of my investigation." He finished the last large bite of his hamburger and washed it down with the rest of his beer.

"You don't share, I don't share."

"The difference is, I don't have to share."

Max leaned back, drained her wine, put the glass down. "Neither do I."

"I beg to differ."

"You're a smart man, Ryan. Don't make me think less of you now."

He stared at her. "You're going to pull the reporter card." But he didn't say it with frustration or anger; he had a laugh to his voice, as if he admired her attitude.

"It's a heavy one, but it always works."

He didn't say anything for a minute. "I had word that Jimmy Truman came to town ten years ago, in January. About the same time he sold one of the paintings he stole in Dallas. I have two witnesses who swore that Jimmy was here at the resort. They didn't see him talking to his brother or anyone else, but one of the maids said he was staying in a cottage on the far end of the property—one that wasn't open to the public yet, they were still renovating. He was there for at least three days, possibly longer. She only knows this because she walked by the cottage on her way home. I came back to talk to her, and she'd left employment and had moved."

"Paid off or killed?"

"Paid off. I tracked her down and she refused to talk to me. Stood her ground. Not so much scared—I think someone lied to her about who I was after. Gabriel Truman is well loved in this town, and I suspect she thought I was investigating him. I don't see anyone lying for Jimmy, unless he had something on them. And this maid, she wasn't a criminal. She was a good church-going woman who had been convinced that I was the bad guy. Yeah, someone paid her off, but she still went willingly."

"And then?"

"Gone. I got a warrant and when I executed it on this club, he was gone. I searched every cottage, but Gabriel refused to let me search his house and because it's not in Jimmy's name, it wasn't covered by the warrant. I don't know why he helped his brother skip town—I don't think Gabriel is one of the bad guys—but he did. Or else he's doing a damn good job of making himself look guilty. Every year or so I come here to the restaurant just to stay on his radar, stir him up, see if he slips."

"He hasn't."

"No, but he's never happy to see me."

"Maybe he really doesn't know what Jimmy was up to."

Maguire shrugged. "Maybe he doesn't. But Jimmy was here for at least seventy-two hours and not for a minute do I think that Gabriel didn't know about it."

"And since?"

"Not a peep. There was some evidence that Jimmy went up to New York, I passed it on to the New York field office, but they couldn't confirm any of the information. So either he went to New York then left the country on a false ID, or he's dead and he died somewhere between here and New York ten years ago. No one claims to have seen him since, and none of the other paintings we believe he stole have surfaced."

Max assessed the fed. She was always cautious about sharing her information, but she'd recently worked with a federal agent on a cold case and had found that sometimes another opinion helped.

"I'll show you my information on one condition."

"I'll need to know the condition," he said.

"Do not shut me out. I'll give you what I have, but I'm not backing down. Don't go around me, don't go through me, don't piss me off. I'll give you room, but I expect information in return."

"Well, that's going to be difficult—I am involved in a federal investigation. But as much as I can, I won't shut you out and I certainly won't shut you down. Fair enough?"

Trust. It was hard for Max to give it, but he looked her in the eye when he spoke and she believed him.

"Fair enough."

# Chapter Twelve

Martha stood in front of the Degas section of the Impressionist exhibit on loan to this small Dallas museum and absorbed the art as one: the color, the lines, the isolation that drew her into his work.

Art was her one true love, and something she couldn't share with Jimmy. He was pedantic in his taste, had no appreciation for the details, the style, the past and future that fine art gave to the world.

The only thing that Martha regretted about her chosen lifestyle was that she had no place to hang art. She couldn't very well pack priceless original pieces of art up in a storage unit or ship them to her mother. Because she spent her trust allowance in full every month, she didn't have the money to buy the pieces she craved.

And most of the pieces she craved weren't for sale.

She loved Degas because of his focus on people. Degas showed more than what was on the canvas. His people were *real*. She could see the dancers thinking, the children contemplating, the woman at the bar regretting. It was heady, to put yourself in one of his paintings. She had no need to lay among Monet's flowers and gaze at the sky; she wanted to understand more than nature, more than contentment.

A hand came around her waist, gently but firmly resting on her hip.

The hand didn't belong to Jimmy.

She glanced up at the man. Forties, devilishly attractive with dark hair and light blue eyes, a hint of five o'clock shadow, and the scent of expensive cologne: a subtle hint of danger that immediately attracted her.

"Watching you absorb this Degas is an erotic vision, one I hope to witness again."

She raised a perfectly arched eyebrow, but didn't say anything. She almost couldn't speak. This man was truly divine. Well-dressed, perfectly groomed, all manner of proper . . . but the way his hand touched her side, the way his mouth said *erotic*, his seductive tone . . . she wanted him.

She was certainly ready for another diversion. Jimmy understood that about her. She'd been with him for nearly three years—which was more than two years longer than any other man. And he catered to her need to break away on occasion.

But she found herself going back to Jimmy because he was the only man she had met who truly understood her. The only man who enjoyed living as she did. He enjoyed the game and the challenge and the sheer joy of doing whatever she wanted whenever she wanted.

She turned back to Degas's work, hyperaware of the man beside her. "He was a master, yet never accepted that moniker. Few, especially in the Impressionist era, could capture the soul like he did."

"I'm having a party on New Year's Eve. I want you there."

"I'm with someone."

"I don't care."

"You don't know me."

"Tell me your name."

Should she? Why not?

"Martha Revere."

"Classically beautiful, like you." He took her hand and kissed it. "Revere. There's a banking family named Revere."

She stiffened. Surprised that he knew of her family, and a little worried.

"I'm the black sheep of the family," she said, trying to sound as if she didn't care that he knew her family name.

He laughed softly. "All the better, as I'm the black sheep of mine."

"Which family would that be?"

"Colter."

"And I've never heard of you."

"Your loss." But he was still smiling and hadn't taken his eyes from hers. "You intrigue me, Martha Revere. Come to my party, bring your boy toy if you insist, but I won't take no for an answer."

He reached into his inside pocket and pulled out a card. "My house, New Year's Eve, nine o'clock. Formal attire."

She took the card: *Phillip Colter.*

Colter. No, she didn't know the name, but that didn't mean much.

"This is my first time in Texas," she said. "At least, for any length of time. I have certainly been missing out, if you're an example of Texas men."

He laughed, a low, sexy laugh.

"I love this great state, but I'm from the East Coast. A small town you've never heard of. My father made a fortune in mining, expected me to follow in his footsteps, but I left that to my brother who wanted it far more than I did."

"Family expectations. They are hard to break from."

A black sheep in the family? The way he looked at her, she thought wolf, and she was more than a little excited.

He smiled, squeezed her waist almost to the point of pain, and walked away.

She could finally breathe.

Jimmy came over. He was drinking champagne and eating hors d'oeuvres.

Jimmy was fun, but he didn't have class. He could fake it with most people, but those like Martha who had been raised in wealth, who knew the difference between Degas and Boudin, who actually liked caviar and wouldn't drink a five-dollar bottle of champagne, could see through him. Most of the time.

Because one thing Jimmy was good at was the show.

"Who were you talking to?"

"Nouveau riche, but interesting." She handed Jimmy his card.

"Colter," Jimmy said flatly.

"Yes. Mining family or something. From the East Coast. Do you know him?"

"Heard of," he said.

"What's with the tone?"

He glanced around, then whispered, "He's a thief."

She laughed so loudly others looked over at her. She covered her mouth. "Really."

"I can prove it. Actually, you can prove it."

"How?"

"We'll have to get into his house."

She smiled. "Well, he did invite me to his New Year's Eve party. Said I could bring my boy toy. Is that what you are, Jimmy? My boy toy?"

He took her away from the art, away from the crowds, and down a back hall into the ladies' room. It was spacious, with private stalls that each had their own private sink and toilet. He pulled her into one, shut and locked the door.

"Jimmy!"

"Shh." He kissed her. Then he put his hands up her dress and touched her. She melted.

The sound of two women talking as they came in had Martha trying to move away from Jimmy's talented fingers as they moved in and out of her body. He pulled her close and whispered directly into her ear, "Don't make a sound." He kept up his attention. She had already been horny from her conversation with Colter; now she was doubly so.

The women were talking about nothing—fashion and art and gossiping about the other women in attendance. And here she, Martha Revere, was being given a hand job in the bathroom stall and they were none the wiser.

It was fabulous.

Even now, Jimmy made her hot. He was the only man who had that effect on her. Others she was thrilled to seduce and sleep with, but sex soon became boring. With Jimmy it was always a thrill. When he sensed she was getting tired with a situation, he was the one who suggested they jump ship. He always had the best plans to take fake people down off their pedestal, people who reminded her of her mother and her stuck-up, arrogant family.

And with Jimmy, sex was always hot. She had sex in public. *That* was a thrill. They'd once broken into a theater in New York, early on a Monday morning, and had sex onstage. It wasn't until after her very loud orgasm that echoed in the vast room that they realized a security guard had watched them. That, too, had been thrilling. So thrilling that they'd participated in some wild parties that she only half remembered. That's when she put an end to some of Jimmy's schemes. While she loved thrills and the unexpected, she didn't like losing control of her body, of not remembering what had happened to her.

Jimmy knew exactly what she liked, how to touch her,

how to seduce her. She orgasmed quick and bit her lip to keep from crying out.

The two women left and they were alone again. She was flushed and wanted more.

"You'll have to wait until we get back to the hotel."

"You promised you'd tell me about Colter."

Jimmy leaned in. "He's stealing a painting tonight."

"Really."

"Yes. One of his crew is an old friend of mine. So on New Year's? I think we should steal it back. And only you will be able to tell what's real and what's fake. This isn't his first time, and it's not like he can report it to the police."

Colter? An art thief? How . . . *interesting.*

"We'll play it by ear," she said.

"Oh, will we?"

"You don't like him."

"He needs to be taken down a peg or two."

"So you *do* know him."

"Yes and no."

"Would he know you?"

"No."

She wasn't certain she believed him. "We should be cautious. Maybe you shouldn't come."

"And leave you to jump into his bed?"

"If that's what it takes for the long game."

He was thinking. "I'll go, I'll let you play."

"And that is one of the many reasons I love you."

"But," Jimmy added, "if we decide to play the long con, we're in it together, understand?"

"I wouldn't have it any other way, darling."

Driving to the party at Colter's estate two weeks later, Martha said, "Colter knows my family. At least by name."

"Are you surprised?"

"What if he contacted my mother? Or my brother?"

Jimmy shot her a look. "You think he'd do that? You're thirty-four. You are hardly a wild teenager anymore. Besides, it's not like we've been hiding for the last three years. If your parents *really* wanted to find you, don't you think they would have tracked you down by now?"

That had bothered Martha, just a bit. When she first walked out she'd been nineteen and her parents let her go because they were fed up with her—and that was fine by her. But after a few months, she knew they were trying to find her, and she liked playing the cat and mouse game. That even with all their money and power they couldn't stop her from doing what she wanted. She used to send her mother postcards just to annoy her.

*Beautiful Paris. By the time you get this, I'll be long gone. Where? I don't know. Madrid? Maybe a cruise.*

*I just spent four months in Australia living with a yummy rancher. You would hate him. He's rich—which you'd love—but he works in the dirt. Not suitable for you.*

*I met a man you would love. A senator, powerful, wealthy, super-uptight conservative. Except, for, you know, in bed. I think you know him. Or maybe you know his wife?*

She always sent them to her mother because she knew that Eleanor would never show her father. And soon, they stopped looking for her. Which was a good thing back then because she didn't want to answer questions about Maxine or her paternity (or, rather, the two men who *could* be her father) or give up her lifestyle. There was nothing Eleanor could do about her trust fund. It was her money, plain and simple, set up by her grandmother who couldn't change it even if she wanted to. And her trust was tied to her brother, sister, and cousins—so if they tried to hold her money, they'd have to hold *their* money.

Like *that* would happen.

But maybe she thought, after she left Maxine with them, that they'd try to find her again. She didn't want to go home . . . but a small part of her wanted them at least to *care*.

Who was she kidding? They had a new young lady to mold into their perfect child. Maxie had always been a thorn in her side—Martha loved her and hated her at the same time. Did that make her a bad mother? Maxie was her *daughter*, her flesh and blood. She loved that she'd grown inside her, that she was part of her, that she'd *created* her. She loved showing the baby around. Maxie had been *gorgeous*. Her red hair was dark and luxurious and wavy—she could have been a child model. Martha had many offers to photograph her, but that wouldn't have been fun, to be mother to a model or actress. As Maxie grew up, Martha thought she'd have a friend, a partner, someone who wanted to do what she did and go where she wanted to go. Someone to have fun with.

But Maxie wasn't fun. She whined and complained and hated moving around. Martha couldn't sit in one place for too long. She'd go back and visit favorite places like Miami and the Caribbean and France and Bora Bora and Vail, but after a month or two she would get bored again and need to move.

"Hey, baby, I'm sorry," Jimmy said. "You look sad. You know I hate it when you look sad."

"Maybe I should go back and take Maxine from them."

"Why? Where did this come from? That kid was nothing but trouble."

"It would make my mother angry." But the truth was,

she didn't really miss Maxine all that much. She *was* a
lot of work, and she was so judgmental, just like Eleanor. Martha didn't need that in her life. And what was
she now? Twelve? Thirteen. Thirteen! It was her birthday
today. Martha had grabbed a postcard at the museum last
week to send off, then forgot. It was going to be late.

Oh, well, it was for the best. Like the kid would
even care. Besides, at thirteen Maxie would be twice as
mouthy as she'd been before. And honestly, Martha didn't
need the kid in her business, and Maxie was the nosiest
kid she'd ever met.

But she didn't like Jimmy telling her what to do.

"If you want—really want her back—after this Colter
thing, we'll go. Okay?"

"Really? You'd do that?"

"Babe, I love you. Whatever makes you happy, we do
it, got it? If you want your kid with us, we'll get your kid."

She smiled. Her decision. That was right. Everything
was *her* choice, *her* desire.

"I'll think about it," she said, though she had already
decided to leave Maxine exactly where she was. Martha
was having far too much fun.


Martha practically salivated over the Degas in front of
her.

Phillip had taken her away from Jimmy, at least for
the night. Jimmy was working one of Colter's friends,
the one who helped him with the thefts. And Martha was
working Phillip.

They were in his bedroom, and the Degas was hung
perfectly over his bed.

"How did you get this Degas? I never heard it was on
sale. It's beautiful." Her voice was breathy, not just because
she was excited, and not just because she had already

identified five very real priceless works of art in Colter's mansion, but because Colter had his hands on her shoulders. He kissed her neck.

"It is beautiful, isn't it? It's a reproduction."

"Really? I know my art, and it's authentic."

He chuckled. "I'm glad you think so."

*With all the other paintings here the real were mixed in with the fake. Good fakes, but her eye was second to none. Here, she was a master.*

"Amazing," she murmured.

"I paid handsomely for the reproduction. Commissioned it myself."

"You have to tell me who."

His tongue trailed from her ear down her neck to her bare shoulder. "You'll have to convince me to share."

She closed her eyes and let Phillip believe he was seducing her. His hands, his mouth, were so very exciting because it was forbidden. He was dangerous and wild and she craved him like nothing else. She leaned back into him, felt how much he wanted her, and smiled.

He whispered, "I don't share. Get rid of your boyfriend and then we can take the world together."

Jimmy loved the plan more than Martha, though if Jimmy knew just how attracted she was to Phillip Colter, he might not love it quite so much. Yet he'd improved upon it, said they were in for the long haul.

And it worked.

For three months, Martha lived with Colter in his mansion. She traveled with him, saw his other paintings—the real and the fake—and never let on that she knew he was lying when he said they were *all* reproductions he'd commissioned.

But Colter grew increasingly dangerous. Possessive and demanding and while the sex was absolutely fabulous, he was pushing her hard outside of her comfort zone. The game was no longer fun. She had to get out before she couldn't, because Phillip Colter wasn't a man who liked to share, and he certainly wasn't a man who liked to lose. But to make this work, she had to take the real paintings and he could never know it was her.

The one benefit she had was that she'd figured out that Colter had many, many paintings copied—and when he stole one from a museum or private collection, he put the fake he had been showcasing in a storage facility. It was Jimmy's job to break in and retrieve the right paintings, and Martha's job to replace the authentic pieces with the reproductions.

Slowly, they moved through Colter's Dallas collection, picking seven of the best paintings, the ones Martha loved above all the others, and replacing them one by one over a five-week period. The last was the Degas over Colter's bed, and replacing that gave her an intense joy. That night she instigated sex because it would be their last time.

And then she started the fight. It was dangerous. He could hurt her. But she had to trust her instincts and her skills.

"That was . . ." She sighed, pulled herself up from the bed.

Phillip pulled her back down. "I'll be ready again soon." He climbed on top of her, pinning her down.

"Phillip, give me five minutes. You wore me out."

She extracted herself, but he held on to her wrist.

"What." He was blunt; it wasn't a question, it was a demand.

"Nothing."

He massaged her naked back. "It's not nothing."

"I want to go to Paris."

"We'll leave next week."

"Alone."

His hands stopped, tight around her upper arms. "Why?"

"This is all . . . just too much. It's too intense. Too . . . intimate."

"I told you that you would love me."

"Maybe I do, but I need time alone."

"No."

She pulled away from him. He didn't release her easily, and it hurt. "If you can't respect that, you don't respect me, and we have nothing."

He stared at her, stunned. "Are you seeing that low-life Truman again?"

"I'm not seeing anyone else."

"He's back in town. That's what this is. You're cheating on me." He rose from the bed, his face red, his body tense. "Don't lie to me."

"I'm not cheating on you," she said. She and Jimmy hadn't slept together since she moved in with Phillip, so that wasn't even a lie.

He slapped her. It came so suddenly, so unexpectedly, that she stood there, stunned.

Then she turned and ran to the closet he'd given her and dressed.

"I'm sorry," Phillip said from the doorway. "I need you so much, I *want* you. I've never wanted anyone like I want you."

"You *slapped* me!"

"I'm sorry. Forgive me."

She didn't have anything she cared about in this house. She walked up to him and slapped him back. His eyes flashed with anger, then he said, "Does that make us even?"

"No. Good-bye."

"Don't you dare walk out."

"I will not be manhandled or manipulated. All I asked

for was a couple weeks *alone* and you go all ape-man on me. It's over, Phillip."

She walked out. He ran after her, begging her, then threatening her. At the front door she turned to him and said, "You come after me or touch me again, I will destroy you."

He stared at her, then laughed. "Oh, you bitch, you think you can threaten *me*?"

"I'm taking your Mercedes. You can pick it up at the airport later."

She ran down the stairs in the dark, worried for the first time that he would come after her. If he really wanted to hurt her—if he wanted to kill her—he could. No one would know or care that she was dead, except Jimmy—and Jimmy would then confront Phillip and get himself killed, because Jimmy didn't know how to keep his mouth shut.

He loved her, really loved her, and he would miss her.

But Phillip didn't come after her, and she drove to the airport where Jimmy was already waiting for her. He looked worried.

He should be. Martha was worried. Phillip wasn't a man to double-cross, and if he ever found out she replaced his stolen paintings with his own reproductions, he would hunt her down to the ends of the earth.

"Baby, are you okay?"

"I will be. Where are the paintings?"

"I did exactly what you said. I drove them to Miami, put them in a temperature- and humidity-controlled storage locker under D. Jane Sterling, and paid for a year up front. I know what I'm doing. Does he suspect?"

"Not about the paintings, but about us."

"Us? We haven't been together. I haven't even talked to Colter, not after his New Year's party."

"He's a jealous man, Jimmy. I think we should lay low for a while. Just in case."

"Whatever you want."

"Where are we going?"

He handed her the tickets he'd bought that morning. "Monte Carlo?"

She smiled. "Perfect."

# Chapter Thirteen

"When did you arrive in town?" Ryan asked, clearly impressed with Max's timeline. "This is extensive."

She smiled. "I'm good," she said simply.

"No argument from me."

"Most of the past information came from my personal journals, postcards my mother sent me, and confirmation—as much as I need, anyway—that Jane Sterling was really Martha Revere."

"I see."

Ryan was focused on a section of Max's timeline from nineteen years ago. "She was in Dallas."

"For approximately three to four months. You'll note that on December first, she withdrew her allowance in New York, then in January through April she withdrew her funds in Dallas. In May she was in Miami. From my own personal experience, my mother always left town right after she received her allowance, so I suspect she left Dallas the first week of April. Also, my private investigator indicated that there may have been some withdrawals that were wired overseas. He's analyzing years' worth of financial data that our family trust accountants have finally shared with me."

"I promised I would tell you what I can. This was the

time frame that a painting was stolen from a museum in Dallas, it's what started the initial FBI investigation."

"And you knew it was Jimmy Truman?"

"No, we suspected someone else, and we still believe that he was working with Jimmy but could never establish a connection. However, we have evidence that Jimmy is the one who moved the painting from Miami to DC. Based on the MO, we determined he—possibly with your mother and another partner—stole more than two dozen paintings from all over the United States."

Max let the information sink in. "Have any of the other paintings turned up? Other than the one Jimmy sold?"

He nodded. "Three. There was a storage locker under the name J. J. Sterling that went into default. The owners auctioned off the contents. The buyer took the paintings to be appraised—he had no idea they had been stolen—and the appraiser notified the FBI. This was a year after Jimmy disappeared. I suspect he took one of the paintings from the locker to sell, but planned to return."

"And he didn't."

"There were no prints on the paintings that could be lifted, but we had his identification from renting the storage space and confirmation he used the J. J. Sterling identity."

"If he has stolen more than two dozen paintings, where are they?"

"That's the million-dollar question. We confirmed he sold one, and then we recovered three. It could be the accomplice has the others." He reached for one of the postcards and asked, "May I?"

Max nodded. Ryan read the postcard.

"Your birthday's this month? April?"

"No, my mother habitually sent me cards late. My birthday is December thirty-first."

He turned the postcard over and stared. Then he laughed.

"She was snide, not funny," Max said flatly.

"This, do you know what this painting is?"

"Degas. One of my mother's favorites."

"It's one of the stolen paintings." Ryan then turned over all the other postcards, one by one. Frowned. Read the messages, then looked at the pictures again.

Finally, ten minutes had passed and Max couldn't stand it anymore. "What? What do you see?"

"There's what"—he quickly counted—"sixteen postcards, and seven of them are of paintings that were stolen. Seven of the nine most recent postcards from April nineteen years ago until January sixteen years ago. The others are more generic. Hawaii. The Caribbean. Eiffel Tower."

"I never found it odd because my mother loved museums and those are her favorite artists. Degas. Boudin. Renoir. Not so much Toulouse-Lautrec, a little too post-Impressionist for her sensibilities, but she appreciated his talent and whimsy."

"Can I take these?"

"No."

He stared at her. "I'll bring them back."

"I have a copier, would copies suffice?"

"For now."

"Fair enough." She took the cards and photocopied both sides on the small portable color copier she had shipped to herself from her office.

Her mother, an art thief. That was not what Max was expecting to hear.

"Who did you initially suspect?" Max asked Ryan. "Who may have worked with Jimmy and Martha all those years ago?"

He didn't say anything. He reached for the copies she had in her hand, but Max pulled them back.

"Max, that is information I can't share. He's not under indictment and if it gets out, it could jeopardize years of work."

"I'm not working this case for the network. I'm working it for me."

"Max—"

"I'm investigating this case, Ryan. I'll find out."

He shook his head. "That would be a neat trick."

"Don't underestimate me." If her mother was involved in something as high stakes as art theft, maybe she stole from the wrong person.

"Time-out," Ryan said. "Let me talk to my boss. These postcards could be huge for us. Where she bought them might give us information about where the other paintings are stored. Or maybe there are clues in her messages to you. Please, Max. I'll ask to bring you in, but this is the first new information I've had in years."

Max handed him the copies, then put the postcards back on her timeline—only this time with the art facing out. Maybe she'd see something different if she looked at the photos rather than the words.

"My mother went to Miami at least once a year, even when I was with her. She loved it there. My assistant located an apartment she'd rented prior to traveling here, also under the name Jane Sterling. He's down there now, tracking down her old landlord and anyone who knew her then. He's also asking about Jimmy—aka J. J. Sterling—and if he learns anything, I'll let you know."

"Max, I don't intend to block you on this, but you have to understand—"

"I do."

"Then why do I think you're giving me the cold shoulder?"

"I just told you that I'll share what I learn."

"It's your tone."

She laughed. "Really. Well, I've shown you all my cards, and you won't tell me one thing I might be able to work with. I'm very good at research. This is the only thing I'm working on, and I'm not leaving until I get every answer I'm seeking. You have other cases you need to work, and something this old can't possibly be a priority for you."

"First, you're wrong—it is a priority because if I want to get a conviction, I need to solve this case, and get an indictment before April of next year because of the statute of limitations, unless I can prove Truman stole more than the three paintings we recovered. So it *is* important to me. Not to mention the missing paintings are virtually priceless, they deserve to be recovered and sent back to their rightful owners—both the individual owners and museums. The insurance companies who paid have a right to the paintings or their money back. And you have a job—you're here on vacation, and I honestly don't think you'll be able to solve in two weeks what two FBI offices haven't been able to solve in nineteen years."

She laughed again. "You really don't know me, Ryan. It's kind of adorable that you think I'm first, here on a vacation, and second, doing this in my spare time. You looked me up, but you didn't really understand what you read, so let me make myself clear.

"I'm not leaving Cape Haven until I know exactly what happened to my mother. It might take two weeks, a month, a year, or the rest of my life. I have a job, but I don't need a job. I took a month off, but I will quit NET before I give up *this* cold case. I have almost unlimited resources and time, and I will use both to find the truth, wherever it takes me. So you can work with me and take advantage of my skills and resources or you can work around me. I guarantee I will learn everything you know and more, and then maybe, when I've solved *your* case, I'll share what I've learned with you."

Ryan opened his mouth, then closed it and cleared his throat. "I don't know whether to admire your self-confidence or criticize your ego."

"My ego can take your criticism." She left her den for the kitchen. Time to cut the fed off. He was clearly cherry-picking what he wanted to share, and she wasn't going to put up with that bullshit. She took a bottle of wine out of her refrigerator and poured herself a glass.

"Were you going to share?" Ryan asked.

"You have a long drive ahead of you." She sipped, stared at Ryan.

He didn't move. "You are something," he said. She couldn't tell what exactly he meant because his tone was neutral.

"Yes, I am."

He held up the copies of the postcards. "I appreciate this, and I'd like to come back this weekend—on my own time—to study the information you compiled during the time the paintings were stolen."

"You're welcome to look at anything I have, but call first. I have my own investigation to run, and now I have twice as much work ahead of me."

"Stubborn," he said.

"Determined," she challenged.

"I'll talk to my boss."

She shrugged. "I don't care. I'll find out what you know whether you tell me or not."

She watched Ryan head for the stairs. He turned back and said, his tone turning serious, "If Jimmy and Martha had an accomplice like I suspect, he may still be around. Be careful."

"Always."

"Why do I not believe that?"

"I'm not reckless," she said. "I'm methodical."

"I'll call."

He walked down the stairs. A moment later, the door closed, and Max stood at the window, the wind howling outside, the rain blowing sideways.

Though Ryan Maguire irritated her because he didn't share *all* his information, he had certainly been more forthcoming than she expected when he first sat down at her table in the restaurant.

She called David, told him everything that had happened that evening, and said, "Can you reach out to Marco and ask him for background on Ryan Maguire?"

"Marco won't like it."

"I don't care. I could call Rogan for help, but it would take longer since I'm not his priority this week. I really need to know what makes Maguire tick."

"You showed him your research, you must trust him. Which surprises me."

"It shouldn't. He was mostly open and honest, so I was mostly open and honest right back. Did you or Rogan get anything on Boreal?"

"Rogan hasn't called, and I can't find much on the company. They are based out of Delaware, however."

"Delaware. I'll bet it's a shell corp." She would be able to get the attorney of record and an address—likely the attorney's business address—and not much more.

"What would a shell corp have to do with Martha's disappearance?"

"I don't know. But Maguire is a white-collar crime agent. He does art crime on the side, it seems, and the white-collar division knows business. Besides, I always get antsy when a business owns property, especially property within two miles of where someone disappears and is never heard from again."

"Don't."

"Don't what?"

"Go over there. You're asking for trouble."

"Nonsense. Everyone in Cape Haven knows why I'm here by now, I'm just going over to ask questions about something that happened sixteen years ago. I promise to be careful."

David was clearly not pleased, but he dropped the subject. "I tracked down the landlord of the condo your mother was leasing. She had it for three years."

"Three years? She lived in the same place for three years?"

"According to the landlord—Annie O'Neill, who's now retired and living in an assisted living facility in Orlando, but seems to have all her faculties—Jane Sterling and her husband J. J. Sterling paid each year up front because they told her they traveled extensively and wouldn't always be around. That much is true, as the place was barely lived in and the landlord only saw them a few times over the years. But there's something you should know: according to Mrs. O'Neill, the last time she saw Jane, she was carrying a baby, two weeks before she left without notice."

Max did not hear that correctly. "You said baby. Like, a child?"

"Yes. An infant."

A baby? That could not be accurate. Or maybe she was wrong and Jane Sterling was not her mother.

She wasn't wrong. She'd seen the DMV photo. She connected Jane Sterling to J. J. Sterling who was Jimmy Truman. She *knew* Jane was Martha.

Martha had a baby? No. Max couldn't see it.

"It wasn't hers," she said flatly.

But she didn't know.

"I couldn't tell you that, Max. Mrs. O'Neill hadn't known Jane was pregnant, and maybe she wasn't—maybe you're right, and the baby wasn't hers. Mrs. O'Neill asked about it, and Jane said she was babysitting for a friend, but something about the exchange stuck out to the landlord, because she remembered it after all these years. She said that was the one thing she thought about when Jane didn't come back, and the police came to ask about her car. That something had happened to Jane and the baby."

"I . . . well." She cleared her throat. "A baby." Max didn't know what to say. "According to the police report, there was no car seat in the car, no diaper bag, or any indication that an infant had been in it."

"Maybe she wasn't lying and she really was babysitting. Watching the kid for a friend."

That was pretty selfless, and Martha was anything but selfless. "If she was an art thief, maybe she moved on to kidnapping."

Even as she said it, she realized it was an even more ridiculous theory than Martha babysitting.

Or having another child.

"Do you really believe that?" David said.

"At this point, I don't know what to believe."

# Chapter Fourteen

Max stayed up far too late for her own good Thursday night looking into Boreal and their business. Garrett Henderson was correct—they were a technology company, of sorts. They didn't actually manufacture or sell a service or product; they bought and sold tech companies. Mostly bought. They didn't appear to dismantle companies, but instead invested in new technologies, then owned the lion's share of the business. Occasionally they sold, possibly when they needed an influx of cash. The lawyer of record was Sharon Proctor-Davis with the law firm of Davis, Orgain, Proctor, and Armentrout. They had a Web page that had virtually nothing on it except a Web form to fill out and a brief about their specialty: contract and tax law. No bios, no street address, only their license number and a PO box.

She sent that information to both David and Rogan, because while David was good on the ground, Rogan was much better in cyberspace.

Her mind was working overtime, however, thinking about Boreal, about her mother being an art thief—of all things!—of why her mother disappeared sixteen years ago and Jimmy was alive and well ten years ago, but hadn't been seen since. Why was Gabriel Truman so angry about her questions? Why wouldn't he listen to her explanation?

She didn't fall to sleep until after two, and woke up before six. She couldn't blame the weather, though the wind and rain had pummeled the cottage all night. The toll of the restless night was evident in the dark circles under her eyes. She showered, carefully applied makeup so she looked less exhausted—no matter how she felt—and ate toast and a banana with her coffee.

Her meeting with the president of the Haven Point Sailing Club, Stephen Galbraith, was set at nine that morning. It was still raining hard when she left the house. If it was a nice day, she could have walked the half mile, but today wasn't that day. She hoped the forecast was accurate and the storm would be over by tomorrow. She drove her rental to the racing club office and parked in the closest available space to the entrance.

When she entered, she shrugged off her raincoat and hung it on a coatrack inside the door.

A young man—thirty at most—came out of an office. He wore a cable-knit sweater, khakis, and an expensive nautical watch. "I wasn't certain you'd venture out in this weather," he said. "I'm Stephen Galbraith. It's a mouthful, I know. You can call me Steve."

"Maxine Revere. Call me Max. Thank you for agreeing to meet with me today."

"We have a friendly race on Sunday in the bay against three other junior clubs—I have a lot of preparation."

"So you agree with the weatherman?"

"By noon tomorrow, it'll be clear, sunny, with winds coming in at twelve miles per hour. I've been doing this for a long time."

She almost laughed.

"You think because of my age I don't know."

"I wouldn't presume."

"I've been racing since I was nine. Helped my father until I could compete on my own. But more than that, I've lived here nearly my entire life."

"In Cape Haven?"

"No, I'm from Westover, Maryland, about an hour and a half north. I live down here now, in Eastville, not far from here. But I spent every summer here—my parents had a little house right on the water outside Eastville."

"Nice place to grow up."

"I have no complaints. My dad was a doctor, a neurosurgeon. My brother followed in his footsteps, but I couldn't imagine doing anything else but boats. Coffee?"

"Great, thanks."

She followed him to his office. It was large, neat, and he had his own coffeepot. He poured two cups and they sat down in comfortable leather chairs facing each other. "So, you said you were researching youth sailing?"

Max had considered all her options in this conversation, and decided to be truthful, though selective, in what she shared.

"I've been staying at the resort while on a working vacation of sorts, and have been reading the local news. When I was young, I loved sailing, so I started reading about your junior club and the success that you've had, especially the last couple of years. The article that particularly intrigued me was where your members volunteer during Thanksgiving and Christmas as a way of raising money for their entrance fees, which I know can be steep."

"Not just entrance fees—we raise money for continuing education, bringing in experts to teach them about boat repair, ecology, oceanography, and even boat building. Our members aren't as affluent as other boating clubs. When people think yacht they think rich, and one of my goals when I came here was to show that boating and competitive racing doesn't have to be just for those who can afford the best boats and expensive clubs. But to do that, the kids have to work hard. We also have a GPA requirement—no competitive boating unless they have a three point oh GPA with nothing less than a C. Our collective GPA is three point six."

"How do you fund this place?"

"The resort donates the office space and boathouse. We have membership fees, though modest, and the kids raise money. I also give private boating lessons in the summer to tourists—truthfully, the money I earn in the summer enables me to live on a small salary here."

"But you love it."

"Without reservation. So you were saying on the phone that you might have a scholarship idea?"

"I was thinking of having my family sponsor a race, or a specific competitor. While I have been sailing many times, I've never competed or belonged to a club, so I'm not exactly sure what you need."

His face lit up. "We have multiple donation opportunities, and some are tax-deductible—such as the continuing education program. I also teach a college-level class in ocean ecology for the University of Virginia, and anyone can take it—high school students receive college credit. Most sponsors for races are in the industry—boat wax, swimsuits, supply companies, the like. Our co-captain Jason Harris is heading off to William and Mary College in the fall on a full-ride scholarship."

Steve walked over to his desk, rummaged through a neat drawer, pulled out a prospectus and handed it to her. It was simple, but professionally printed. "This will give you a good idea about the club and our needs. I create a new one every year with a revised five-year plan. My goal is to ensure that all the kids in the program go to college, if that's their dream."

Max glanced through the prospectus. Steve was passionate about his work and it showed in his presentation.

"I read about Jason in the article about last year's summer classic. He and Eve Truman."

Steve nodded. "Co-captains. Eve is one of those kids that seems like she was born on the water. She joined as soon as she was eligible, on her thirteenth birthday, and for the three years she's been here she's helped us grow and win."

She flipped to the back of the prospectus and there was a photo of Eve and Jason as co-captains for the year. Max stared at the girl. The photo online was small and all she'd gotten from the image was an attractive young girl with dark blond hair and a tan face.

This photo was larger and sharp. Her deep blue eyes looked out with a sparkle, both serious and whimsical. Her hair was sun-streaked, and though in a loose braid, wisps had broken free in the wind.

"Eve would spend every day and night at sea if her dad let her," Steve said. "She's definitely smart enough for college, but probably spends a little too much time sailing instead of doing homework. But she keeps her grades up for the most part. And she is really good with her team. One of those people who can instill confidence in others."

Max barely heard Steve. It was Eve's eyes. She could have been looking into her own. And she knew, without a doubt, that Eve was her sister. Her *half* sister.

Gabriel Truman was a liar. He damn well knew who Martha Revere was—he'd slept with her. She had a daughter with him. And then she disappeared.

Maybe the FBI had opened an investigation into the wrong Truman brother.

Max took the prospectus and promised Steve that she'd look it over and would be discussing a donation with him early next week. She must have hidden her reaction well, because Steve was gracious and thankful, even though she left his office as fast as she could. She wanted to confront Gabriel right then and there, but she was too angry—and not a little bit worried.

Her half sister was living with a man who may have been responsible for her mother's disappearance. Gabriel had already shown Max that he was an angry man—first by not answering her questions, and then at the restaurant when she'd had dinner with Maguire. She'd thought he was mad because his brother was a criminal and he didn't want to be dragged through the mud with Jimmy, but what if his anger came from a more personal reason? What if he feared the FBI would learn the truth about *him*?

But Max wasn't a reporter who went off half-cocked. Well, most of the time. It was true she did confront people with the facts and often compelled them to answer questions, but she couldn't go back to Gabriel without more information.

First, she had no proof that Eve was Martha's daughter. *David found the landlord in Miami. She saw Martha with a baby.*

Second, Gabriel wasn't discharged from the military until September after Martha disappeared. The baby was born before April, before Martha left Miami for good. But Eve could have been born anywhere. She was a sophomore in high school, so most likely was born between October and March. Had Gabriel been on leave? Had he been involved with Martha? If he was on leave nine months before Eve's birth, that would be pretty damning information.

Max went back to her cottage and called David.

"I need Gabriel Truman's official leave information from the navy."

"Good morning."

"I don't have time to play nice, David."

"Those records aren't easy to get."

"But you can get them."

"I know people. Why?"

She didn't want to tell him, but who else could she trust?

"I'm fairly certain that Eve Truman is my half sister."

Silence.

"David?"

"Stand down, Max."

"No."

"Do you realize what you're saying?"

"Yes, Gabriel Truman lied to me about Martha. He was sleeping with her and they had a kid."

"It means he could very well have had something to do with her disappearance. Her murder."

"I know."

"Which makes him dangerous."

"That's why I need his leave schedule. She disappeared in April. If he was on a ship in the middle of some ocean, he didn't kill her."

"Do not confront him, Maxine. I mean it—not until I get there."

"I may not have to if you'll just get me the damn information!" She hung up.

She was losing her temper and at first she didn't know why. She should never have hung up on David or yelled at him.

Her mother had another child. Max had a half sister. Eve Truman was family.

What if Martha had abandoned Eve just like she'd abandoned Maxine? Leaving her with relatives and going off to do God knew what? This time, she left her with her father. Now it made sense why he left the navy, it was to take care of his kid.

She wanted to hate him, but she couldn't. If he gave up his career to raise his illegitimate child, he did it out of love and duty and honor. She respected him for the sacrifice, but she was angry that he'd lied to her face about knowing Martha.

She needed proof that he was nowhere near Northampton County when her mother was here. Then she'd talk to him and demand the truth.

And now, more than anything, she wanted to meet her half sister.

The rain had all but stopped, but the wind brought in moisture from the Chesapeake Bay. Max knew herself, and if she ran into Gabriel Truman, she would tell him what she knew and demand the truth. David didn't say it, but he didn't have to: everything Gabriel had done for the last sixteen years had been to protect either himself or his daughter or both. Which meant he might react violently if he thought she was a threat.

Max checked her email, and responded to inquiries from her staff in New York. Ben had done a terrific job at keeping her out of the loop on projects, and she appreciated it. He'd created a smooth-running operation, and she wasn't his only cable show. He ran programming for the entire NET network, which fully integrated the internet and television and had done so long before most other media companies.

Her phone rang. It was a Virginia area code.

"Revere," she answered.

"Ms. Revere, this is Bill Bartlett."

"Hello, Sheriff."

"I followed up with the evidence locker. I'm sorry it

took so long to get you this information, but I wanted to make sure I had it right."

"I appreciate it. And?"

"Hurricane Sandy caused a lot of damage to the region. It was several years ago, and while the evidence building was secured—and you can go and view the physical items found in Jane Sterling's car—the outside yard flooded. The administrator made a determination of what needed to be scrapped based on the likelihood of foul play or that a victim or suspect would emerge."

"What you're saying is the car was destroyed."

"Yes. I'm sorry. They took photos and a video of the vehicle and put those in the evidence box, but because there was no crime and no one had come forward—it had been many years at that point—they had to make the call."

"Thank you for letting me know." She didn't expect to find anything in Martha's car, but she had wanted to see it—maybe there had been something there, or something only she would understand.

"I talked to the administrator and he agreed to allow you access to the evidence box at your convenience. The building is open regular business hours during the week. I'll email you the address and my contact's name and number."

"I'll do that." When she had the time. Right now, she had something even more important to work on.

"Is there anything else I can help you with?" the sheriff asked.

"No, I'm still working through my notes and theories. But I'll touch base next week, let you know if I've learned anything new."

She thanked him for his time, then hung up. Walked into her den and made a note about the car. She'd looked at the evidence log and there was nothing there that seemed important, but maybe she should take the time to go there in person. Look at the photos.

Max stared at her timeline for more than an hour, willing to see information that wasn't there. She added a string during the months Eve could have been born, and another string nine months back, when she could have been conceived.

The information she'd asked David to get wasn't public. David had been in the army, but he had many friends in all branches of the military. She gave him a fifty-fifty chance of getting the information, but it might take time. It might not be today. And if not today, that meant not until next week.

She wouldn't be able to sit around doing nothing for that long.

The problem was that she didn't know how Agent Maguire's investigation fit with Martha's disappearance, if at all.

*Your mother was an art thief.*

Maybe. If her mother and Jimmy had been stealing art, why? For the thrill? She didn't need the money. Well, maybe she thought she did. Maxine had met people through the years who never seemed to have enough.

If they had stolen more than two dozen paintings over a decade, why had she sent postcards of only seven pieces to Maxine?

Did Gabriel know about the thefts? He didn't live above his means. In fact, he was barely getting by. Havenly was doing well, but it wasn't making him rich, and it took all his time and most of his earnings. Rogan had done a basic background check on him and determined there was nothing unusual or suspicious in his background or his finances.

She opened Rogan's report again. She'd been most interested in Gabriel personally, and anything related to

Jimmy. She hadn't studied the resort. How did Gabriel get the money to buy into the venture in the first place? Tax information was private, but there should be a corporate filing somewhere, and most likely Rogan had included that information.

Brian Cooper had bought Haven Club and Resort seventeen years ago with the help of an investor, and Gabriel joined a year later, becoming a twenty-five percent owner. After initial renovations and a yearlong closure, they reopened the resort as Havenly.

Gabriel and Cooper were hands-on, according to all the news reports and the fact that the resort was their primary source of income. She skimmed the corporate filings, then did a double take. On one required form they had to list all investors in the property. Boreal Inc., was a fifty percent owner. A non-operating partner.

Boreal owned the property near where her mother's car was found.

Maxine didn't wait for David to return her call. She ventured out into the wind and drove back to Oyster Bay.

Abel Parsons, the caretaker of the property owned by Boreal, Inc., clearly didn't want to talk to Max.

"This is private property," he said after answering the door of the caretaker's house. "How did you get through the gate?"

"I left my car there and walked in." Which was clearly obvious since she was soaking wet and freezing cold, even though she wore a lined trench coat. "I'd like to talk to the owner."

"No one's here but me. I manage the property, nothing more, nothing less. Good-bye."

"Who owns this property?"

"None of your business. Go, or I will call the sheriff. You're trespassing. Didn't you see the signs?"

"My name is Maxine Revere," she said. "I would like to talk to the CEO of Boreal about his investment in Havenly, the resort in Cape Haven."

"Ain't going to happen."

"I'll have my producer contact him."

"Go—" He stopped. "What's your name?"

She handed him her business card. "Maxine Revere. I'm with NET, a cable television station. I'm just looking for information."

"I'll pass it along. But if I see you here—anywhere on this property—I'm calling the sheriff. Understand?"

"Thank you, Mr. Parsons," she said, but he had already slammed the door in her face.

Max walked back down the long driveway through the fierce wind. By the time she got back to her car she was shaking from the cold. Yet she considered the excursion a success. Parsons was certainly interested when he found out she was a reporter, and she was confident he would pass on her interest in the resort to someone at Boreal. In the meantime, she would continue asking questions about who might have been at the house the month her mother disappeared.

And she would learn everything she could about both Jimmy Truman and his "saintly" brother Gabriel.

# Chapter Fifteen

Max showered under a stream of hot water but couldn't seem to get herself warm. Served her right, she supposed, for going out in the wet this morning. She decided to stay in for the rest of the day and continue researching Boreal, the paintings from the postcards, and learn everything she could about her half sister.

She couldn't wait to meet her.

*Eve*.

Max wondered if her mother had named her after Martha's grandmother, Genevieve Sterling. She wouldn't be surprised. Though Martha had shunned her family, she had never once said anything negative about her grandmother. Max's middle name was Genevieve, and it wouldn't surprise her to learn Eve was short for Genevieve as well.

All Martha's hostility was directed toward Eleanor. Max often wondered if there was something else going on there, something neither Martha nor Eleanor ever talked about.

Max made herself a sandwich because she had no desire to go back out into the foul weather today. She bundled up in soft, well-worn jeans and a warm, bulky sweater, and sat on the couch by the window, listening to the wind and watching the waves roll violently to the shore, only a hundred feet from her raised cottage.

After she ate, Max read carefully through the Haven Point Junior Sailing Club prospectus again. Everything seemed on the up-and-up. Her quick internet search yielded no red flags, but she sent the information to David and Rogan just in case she'd missed something.

Then she stared at Eve's photo.

Max had never thought about having siblings. She'd idly thought through the years that maybe she had a half sibling—through her unknown father. But Martha had taken the secret of her father's identity to the grave, and Max doubted she'd ever know the truth.

Her family was complicated enough. Her cousin William was the closest to a brother she had, and they had been very close until last year. They were the same age, they'd gone through school together, and Max cared for him. She wished they could mend fences because he, out of everyone in their family, was someone she could talk to about both her mother and her half sister.

She considered calling her grandmother, but until she knew for certain that Eve was a Revere, she wasn't going to involve her family. While she generally knew how her family would react in any given situation—both the good and the bad—she didn't know how they would handle another heir.

The Sterling Family Trust was a thriving, albeit conservative, trust. They didn't invest heavily in anything too risky, and had a checks and balances system that her great-grandfather created to avoid any shenanigans. She'd never met her great-grandfather Sterling—he'd died before she came to live with Eleanor. But he had created his wealth from nearly nothing, partnered with his wife Genie. When he died, she took over his businesses and investments and grew the Sterling family's wealth and reach through her own ideas and ingenuity. Max wanted to laugh when someone said, "I wish I'd invested in IBM or Apple way back when," because Richard and Genevieve Sterling *had* been those visionaries.

Eve deserved her share of the family wealth. Max didn't doubt that her great-grandmother would have insisted, and at a minimum, Eve should receive the same allowance that all board members' offspring received starting on their eighteenth birthday. It would pay for her college and give her a nest egg on which a frugal person could then live on for the rest of their life.

Why would Gabriel deny that to Eve? Max suspected money wasn't important to him, but what about college? Education was critical, especially in this day and age when a degree meant even more than thirty or forty years ago. Did he hate Martha so much that he wouldn't give Eve her rightful inheritance?

She shouldn't read so much into the situation. Maybe Gabriel hadn't known the extent of Martha's wealth. Maybe he thought, because she lived so lavishly, that she had no more money for her child. Maybe Martha lied to him. That certainly wouldn't be unheard of.

A pounding on the door downstairs made Max jump, followed by the buzzing of the doorbell. It stopped, then seconds later started again.

Irritated and a little concerned, she jogged down the stairs and looked through the side window.

Gabriel Truman. Wet, eyes wild, angry.

She shouldn't open the door. But she did.

"You could have called."

He walked in without asking. "What the hell are you up to?" he demanded. He stood inches from her.

She stepped back. David was right—she should have stayed far away from Gabriel. But he'd come here, to her cottage.

Gabriel slammed the door shut and Max said, "You need to go."

"How *dare* you start asking questions about my daughter. How *dare* you pry into my life. I want you gone by tonight. Right now, pack up and leave and never come back."

Though Max was beginning to grow scared—something that was rare and foreign to her—she said quietly but firmly, "No."

He stared at her, obviously confused and highly emotional. "My daughter is a minor and if you talk to her, go near her, I will have you arrested."

"You lied to me about Martha Revere. You said you didn't know her, but I know that Eve is her daughter, which makes Eve *my sister*."

It was clear he hadn't realized she'd figured out the truth. He stared at her—angry and terrified. "You don't know anything."

"I will prove it, Gabriel. Eve is my sister, and she deserves to know the truth about her mother, just like I do."

"You want the truth? I'll tell you the *truth!* Martha Revere was a selfish bitch who left her three-month-old daughter with a dying woman because she was too busy to be bothered. She has no rights to Eve, none, and if you think you can come here and throw your name and money around like you're the fucking Queen of England, you're wrong. Leave it alone. Eve doesn't need to know anything about her mother."

Three months . . . that meant Eve was born in January. Good to know. Max would send that information to David.

"Martha left me as well, Gabriel. I did all right, and it's clear you've gone a great job with Eve." She was trying to appeal to his logical side. "But Martha is dead."

"You don't know that."

"I do know that. Because you're right—Martha was

selfish. She only cared about herself and her money. She was declared legally dead nine years ago this month—because for seven years she didn't touch her money. I think she died here in Northampton County."

He was stunned and thinking—maybe because his emotions were so close to the surface, she could clearly read him.

"Did you kill her?" Max asked bluntly. She didn't think so, he'd been deployed until September, but maybe he had a leave.

He was staring at her with surprise. Surprise that she asked the question? Or surprise that he hadn't thought she'd go down that path?

"Kill Martha?"

He sounded confused.

"You were angry she dumped your baby on your mother. Maybe you tracked her down and lost your temper."

As she spoke, he sank into the love seat next to the door. This room on the bottom floor wasn't as cozy and comfortable as the one upstairs, but she had no intention of inviting him up where he could see her office and all the work she'd been doing. Not yet, at any rate.

"I didn't kill Martha," he said quietly.

"Who did?"

He shook his head. "Until you came here, I had no idea she was dead or missing. I thought she left Eve because she didn't want to be a mother, and while at first I hoped and prayed she'd come back, it wasn't long before I was grateful that she didn't."

Max believed him. Maybe because his emotions were so raw and so real, or maybe because she was good at weeding through the lies to find the truth. But she wasn't going to get too comfortable, because Gabriel Truman was a protector. He would do anything to protect his daughter. He might even kill.

"The month before I turned ten, Martha left me with my grandparents. She never came back. She sent me periodic postcards from all over the world, but she never wanted me with her and while at first I was angry and upset, soon I was relieved. I hated the life she led. No place to call home. No stability. A new boyfriend every month or two. She seduced a lot of men. She was pretty and rich and fun. But I'm learning a lot more about her now, and I don't understand her. I think she and your brother Jimmy got involved in illegal schemes. Why? I don't know. For fun? She didn't need the money. I haven't figured it all out, but I will."

"Leave it alone, Ms. Revere."

"Gabriel, you can call me Max. Okay? And I can't leave it alone. Martha is dead. I need to know why. How. Who."

"If Martha is dead, let her stay dead. You're talking to that FBI agent. He's been around for years, digging into *my* life because Jimmy was a criminal. He thinks I helped my brother, but I didn't. Hell, I don't know, because that damn fed won't tell me anything. I don't even know why he's looking for Jimmy."

Max was surprised Maguire didn't tell Gabriel. "He didn't tell you?"

"The first time he came around, ten years ago, he thought I helped Jimmy escape the country. Harbored a fugitive. I asked what Jimmy was wanted for, and he said questioning. He didn't even have an arrest warrant, how could he be a fugitive? So I told him to take a hike. Every year or so he comes here, to my house, talks to my friends and family. Once he even tried to talk to Eve, two years ago, and I told him if he spoke to her again without a warrant that I would file a report for harassment. She doesn't need to be dragged into Jimmy's life."

"I appreciate that you want to protect her, but Maguire has compelling evidence that Jimmy is a thief."

She left out "art thief" because she didn't want to give too much away, not yet. And Maguire had shared some things that made her want to keep his confidence, at least insofar as he didn't burn her.

"Thief? Sure. No doubt about it. He was a con artist and a bastard. God help me, but I hate my brother, and I never want to see him again. But he *is* a criminal, and I don't want him around Eve. If you dig around in Martha's life, you dig around in Jimmy's because they were two peas in a pod. They deserved each other. Eve doesn't need to be brought into this."

"Eve is my sister."

"Half sister."

"She's family. *My* family. She's entitled to her part of the family trust. We'll have to take a DNA test, but there's no doubt in my mind that she's my half sister. That trust will pay for her college. For her future."

"Money," he spat out. "Is that all you people care about? *Money?*"

"No," she said slowly, but he wasn't listening to her. He'd gone from half reasonable to completely ignoring her.

"I don't want it. I don't want anything to do with Martha's family, and nothing to do with you. If you go near Eve, I will have you arrested. If you tell her any of this, I will destroy you. I don't know how, but trust me, I will find a way. Leave Cape Haven. No one wants you here."

"Gabriel, please—"

But he had already opened the door, and her words were lost in the wind.

And she didn't have the opportunity to ask him about Boreal and their investment in the club.

Maybe the company had nothing to do with Martha's disappearance. Just because they owned property in town, and half the club, and had no principals named on record didn't mean squat. . . .

But it itched in the back of her mind that she needed to find out more about the business.

Gabriel walked into Brian's office and closed the door.

He must have looked like hell, because Brian immediately asked, "What happened? Is Eve okay?"

Gabriel ran his hands through his hair and sat down heavily in the chair across from his best friend and business partner. "I should have told you earlier, but I didn't want to believe it."

"Told me what? You're freaking me out, buddy. What's wrong?"

"Everything. You know the guest here? The reporter? Maxine Revere."

"Yeah, I met her, what?"

"*Revere.*"

Brian sat on the corner of his desk. "It's just a name. It's a coincidence."

"She's Martha's daughter."

"I don't think so."

"She is. And she knows Eve is Martha's daughter, too."

"Well. It's—well, it's not that bad, right? I mean, what can she do? She's not fighting for custody or anything? Dear God, Eve is sixteen!"

Gabriel took a deep breath. "Brian, it's a mess. She thinks Eve is *my* daughter. And if she finds out she's not . . . if she tells Eve. . . ."

"Oh. *Oh, no.* She wouldn't. How could she even think about that?"

"She has this war room in the cottage. I . . . I know I shouldn't have, but I went in when she wasn't there."

"You went into a guest's room? Gabriel, what the *hell* were you thinking?"

"I know! Look, I didn't tell you, but Bartlett came by earlier this week, told me she was in town and what she was doing, and I couldn't help myself. I went in and looked through her stuff. I'm sorry, it was wrong, I know that, but she has this timeline about Martha and Jimmy and she thinks that Martha was killed near Oyster Bay sixteen years ago. If she's right it means that Martha left Eve with my mom and then *died*. Or she was killed. Or hell, I don't know!"

"You need to calm down, Gabriel. First, very few people know that Jimmy is Eve's real father. He didn't want her, you did, end of story. No one needs to know that, least of all a reporter. She'll never find out the truth—me and you, we're the only ones who know. Hell, I didn't even tell Annie."

"You're trying to make me feel better, and I appreciate it, but a lot of people suspect I'm not her dad. They might not *know* she's Jimmy's girl, but sixteen years isn't that long in a small town. They know my mom was taking care of her for months before I showed up."

"No one will mention it, even if they thought Jimmy was her dad. And didn't you tell me that Martha didn't fill out the birth certificate with Jimmy's name?"

"Which makes it worse because she might not even be his. What was that woman thinking? She was insane."

"Calm down, Gabriel. When the reporter doesn't find anything about her mother, she'll leave. Find another story to chase."

"No, she's different, Brian. I feel it in my gut. She says she wants to get to know Eve. I can't—Eve doesn't know anything about Jimmy or Martha. I don't want her to know she came from two despicable people. She's my daughter, Brian. *Mine*. I can't let anything happen to her. What if those people Jimmy said were looking for him knew she was his blood? What if they thought I knew something about whatever the fuck they were looking for? Revere knows that Jimmy was a thief, and so does that federal agent, Maguire. What if Jimmy is still out there and they use Eve as a pawn to get to him? To try to force him to come out of hiding? He wouldn't care about her! He'd let her die! He doesn't care about anyone but himself!"

"Gabriel, you need to calm down."

"This is my daughter, Brian."

"A lot of what-ifs, Gabriel. You still need to be calm, think about things logically."

Gabriel knew that Brian was right, but he couldn't seem to get his head in order. Everything he'd done over the last sixteen years was to protect Eve, his daughter. He loved her as if she were his own child. He couldn't love another child more.

"It's my daughter's life on the line. Your goddaughter, Brian. When Jimmy came here ten years ago he was going to take her away. I was ready to disappear with her to protect her, and he never came back for her. Either the people looking for him found him, or he listened to me and decided to let Eve grow up with a normal life."

"Do you really believe that?" Brian asked.

"No. I think whoever he thought was chasing him found him and killed him. And if they learn he had a daughter, that could put Eve in danger. I don't know what he was into, I don't know what he stole or who he stole it from. But I know that I'm the only one who can protect her. I can't let anyone find out that Eve is not my daughter. Brian, I have to find a way to force Maxine Revere out of town."

His friend, his partner, took a deep breath. "Okay. We'll think of something, Gabriel, but listen to me: don't

# Chapter Sixteen

TEN YEARS AGO

Winter was slow at the resort, and even slower for charter boats. Gabriel spent the morning with his staff securing the boathouse from the pending storm. The cabins had already been shut down for the season, though they kept the lodge open in the winter. They were only at twenty percent capacity and it cost them more to run the place than they were taking in, but Brian was working on turning that around. Gabriel had wanted to shut down for the season, but they managed to break even because of the restaurant. They'd made something special there, thanks to Brian's cousin Jenna Cooper Smith who, with her husband, ran the kitchen like a well-oiled machine.

It had been a dry, cold December, but the first flurries of snow had fallen last week, and they'd be getting two feet between now and the weekend. Gabriel didn't care much for the snow. Maybe because he had always been the one responsible for taking care of the storm windows, of shoveling the walk, and jump-starting his mom's car. It wasn't that his dad was incapable or lazy, he was focused on his job—even when he couldn't go out on the trawler—and nothing else really mattered to him. Gabriel would rather do the work himself than rely on his brother getting around to it, which would be never.

Good riddance. Jimmy had been no good growing up, and he was no good now. Gabriel hoped he never saw him again.

While Gabriel worried about the business, and he was concerned about the pending weather, he pushed everything aside because it was Eve's birthday. The first birthday without her grandmother.

When he returned home five years ago, the doctors told him that his mother had less than a year to live. But she agreed to have surgery to remove the lump in her breast, and that surgery coupled with a complex and expensive drug cocktail had helped prolong her life until last summer.

But those last three months had been hell and had taken their toll on him and Eve. Gabriel was grateful for the extra time he had with his mom, but he wished she hadn't had to suffer in the end.

He wanted to be home for Eve. Mrs. Dodd, their next-door neighbor, met her at the bus stop every afternoon and watched Eve until he got home. Mrs. Dodd was in her seventies, but said walking every day was good for her and the bus stop was only three blocks from their street.

He pulled in to the long narrow driveway that led to the garage in the back of the house. Instead of going inside, he went to the detached garage and retrieved the wrapped box he'd left next to Eve's "doll yacht." He'd spent the better part of the last year building it after Eve informed him she didn't want a *dollhouse* she wanted a doll *boat*. He'd never seen a kid take so naturally to the water as his Eve. She loved going sailing, was a fish in the water, and had no fear. It was the no fear part that worried him.

The doll yacht was too big to effectively wrap, but the smaller box held the two miniature figures—a little blond girl and the tall, dark, and handsome skipper.

Gabriel went inside and heard voices from the kitchen. Eve talking a mile a minute. And a male voice.

His blood ran cold.

*Jimmy.*

He stopped in the doorway. Eve saw him a moment before Jimmy.

"Daddy! It's Uncle Jimmy! He came for my birthday!"

"I see that," Gabriel said calmly. "Pumpkin, can you go upstairs and wash up? I have a surprise, but I need to talk to Uncle Jimmy first."

Eve bounced up the stairs. She did nothing slow.

"Mrs. Dodd, if you'll excuse us. Thank you for bringing Eve home from school."

"No problem, Gabriel," she said, looking from Gabriel to Jimmy, her smile uneasy. "I'll see you Monday." She slipped out the front door.

"Daddy?" Jimmy said with a smirk. "Right."

"Get out."

"She's mine, and I'm taking her."

"You will not touch her. You promised me four and a half years ago that you would never—*never*—come back. You put that kid in danger once, never again. She's safe here."

Jimmy shrugged. "Well, she's my kid, Gabriel."

"You promised." Why had Gabriel even believed his brother? For nearly five years he'd stayed away—why had Gabriel been so stupid as to fall into complacency?

"I need her."

"She's six years old!"

"It's serious, Gabriel."

"Serious? And you want Eve at the center of it? Over my dead body."

"It might come to that, Gabe."

"Do not threaten me."

He laughed. "I'm her father. I have rights."

"You abandoned her years ago. You promised me you would never try to take her back, that she was better off here with me—you know she is!"

"You're barely getting by. I can make something of this mess, I just need my kid."

"Martha put 'unknown' on the birth certificate."

By the expression on Jimmy's face, he hadn't expected this.

"She's mine," Jimmy insisted. "I'll get a paternity test."

"That will take time, and I'll fight you every step of the way."

"Either it'll prove I'm her father or I'm not, but either way *you* have no rights. If Martha didn't put my name on the birth certificate . . ."

What the hell was his brother thinking?

"You want to *use* her?"

"She might not even be mine, and if she's not mine, she's even less yours."

"Get out right now."

"Martha gave Genevieve to Mom *temporarily*."

"Her name is Eve, and she's not going anywhere with you."

"You have no say, Gabe! That kid's a fucking *heir*. She's worth a fortune."

That's when Gabriel saw the desperation in Jimmy's eyes, and took a closer look at him. He'd lost weight, his hair was turning gray, and he wasn't dressed impeccably. Jimmy always looked good. It was one reason so many people fell for his lines. He could play any part, was clean-cut and handsome.

Tonight, he wasn't. Tonight, he was nervous.

"What's going on, Jimmy? Tell me the truth."

"Nothing I can't handle. That kid—*my* kid—is a Revere. She's worth a shitload of money, and Martha's trust fund is just sitting there waiting for her."

"You want her for *money*? Nothing has changed with you, Jimmy. She's your get-rich-quick game now?"

Gabriel had known Martha had money, but he hadn't wanted to know anything about her. He didn't realize how *much* money Martha was worth. And now, Jimmy wanted to cash Eve in like she was a stack of poker chips. Gabriel would never allow it.

"Get off your high horse, Gabriel. You're no saint. You've been lying to that kid for years."

"We agreed, Jimmy. You promised me—"

"Well, things change."

"Do not talk about this to Eve."

"You'd better tell her you're not her father," Jimmy said. "Or I will."

Gabriel felt his entire life crumbling under his feet. Eve was his child. She may not be his blood, but she was his daughter. He had raised her. He'd taught her how to ride a bike and how to swim. He nursed her skinned knees when she fell, and soothed her when she had the flu. He learned how to braid hair and that kisses were just as important as Band-Aids to fix an "owie."

But if he pushed this now with Jimmy, his brother would cause a scene. And while Gabriel had never seen him violent, he could tell that Jimmy was desperate.

"You want money—I can get you money."

"You don't have what I need."

"Shit, Jimmy! She's just a little girl." His voice cracked, and that would do him no good. Jimmy would use his emotions against him.

"If it's any consolation to you, her family is totally loaded. She'll have everything you can't give her."

*But she won't have me. And I won't have her.*

He heard footsteps running down the stairs. "Daddy, can we open presents yet?"

"Two minutes, Eve," Gabriel said, not taking his eyes off Jimmy. He had never wanted to hurt another human being before, not like this.

She must have sensed the tension, because she ran back upstairs and left them.

Jimmy cleared his throat. "I'm staying at your resort."

"*What?*"

"Brian gave me a key to one of the places being renovated. You might really come into some money down the road, I can see it's going to be nice, but right now that resort is a big fat money pit."

He was staying at Havenly? For how long?

"If you skip town, I will hunt you down," Jimmy said. "I'll be back in the morning. Tell her the truth, Gabriel. Tonight."

Gabriel made sure Jimmy drove off. He didn't trust him.

Not. One. Bit.

Eve ran down the stairs. "Where's Uncle Jimmy?"

"He had to go."

"Where's my surprise? You said I had a surprise. It's my birthday! I'm six, Daddy!"

"I know, sweetheart. A big girl."

"Well? Is it about my birthday party tomorrow? Everyone is coming, Daddy! They don't care if there's snow, they're going to come and play games and have cake. Did you get the cake? Is it at Mrs. Dodd's? She said it wasn't, but she was teasing, because it's not here."

"Yes, it is, you little monkey. You're too smart for me."

He handed her the small box. He wasn't going to tell Eve he wasn't her biological father; not on her birthday.

Jimmy didn't deserve her. He didn't deserve anything but a bullet in the back of the head.

Eve ripped open the package, her blue eyes wide and sparkling. "Oh! A skipper and his mate! This is me and you, right? Right?"

"There's a boat that goes with them."

She was so excited she couldn't stop shaking. "A doll boat? You found a doll boat?"

"I made a doll boat."

She wrapped her little arms around his neck and jumped up and down. "I love you, Daddy! Can I see it? Before dinner? Please?"

"Of course. It's your birthday, we can do anything you want."

Gabriel didn't tell Eve he wasn't her father. He had to convince Jimmy that he would break the little girl's heart to take her away from everyone and everything she knew. He would call the sheriff if Jimmy showed up, have him arrested. Buy some time. But he realized that he would have to leave town. Leave Cape Haven and the life he had built for Eve. To protect her, he would do it. But it was the last option.

He couldn't sleep all night. The next day his house was filled with five- and six-year-olds running everywhere. It had snowed overnight, but the afternoon was cold and clear. They had snowball fights, made snow angels, and played push the carrot nose on the snowman.

Jimmy didn't show.

Eve fell to sleep almost as soon as the last child left, and Gabriel cleaned up. And still, Jimmy didn't arrive.

He sat on the cold front porch, waiting, with a shotgun in his lap.

He waited, and still Jimmy didn't show.

Finally, Gabriel went to bed. He didn't sleep more than an hour or two, because every sound, every car, every creak in the house had him wide-awake and alert, expecting Jimmy.

The next morning, he took Eve to the resort and asked Jenna to watch her for a few minutes. He went to the cottage that Jimmy was staying in.

No one was there. *Someone* had been staying here, and he had every reason to believe it was Jimmy, but he wasn't here now, and neither were his things.

Gabriel tracked Brian down in his office. His partner worked seven days a week, without fail.

"Was there someone in the far cottage? The one we're almost done renovating?"

Brian nodded solemnly, got up and closed the door behind Gabriel. "I didn't want to tell you, but Jimmy came by a couple of days ago, said he needed a place to crash."

"Dammit, you should have told me!"

"I'm sure he's mixed up in something again. I made sure he didn't rip us off, if that's what you're worried about."

*I'm only worried about my daughter.*

"Is he still here?"

"I told him he had to clear out yesterday. The work crew is coming in tomorrow to finish painting and laying the floors. I didn't see him yesterday, not since Friday night, but I was going to double-check. I'm sorry I didn't tell you. But—you know—it's Jimmy."

Yeah, it was, and Brian didn't have to explain any further.

"If you see him, let me know, okay?"

"Is everything all right?"

"Yeah. I just—where Jimmy goes, trouble and heartbreak follow."

"I'm sure he's back on the road. But I'll call you first thing if I see him."

"Thanks, buddy."

It took Gabriel months before he was comfortable letting Eve out of his sight for more than two minutes. He'd talked to the school, told them that his brother wasn't allowed to pick her up. He hired a former navy buddy of his who was down on his luck to escort Eve home every afternoon, instead of Mrs. Dodd, when Gabriel couldn't do it himself.

But the fear that Jimmy Truman, his low-life brother, would one day return kept Gabriel diligent.

# Chapter Seventeen

Gabriel was up at dawn, as usual. The sun was already breaking through the thin clouds. The storm was over, and it would be a beautiful weekend. The winds were sporadic, and sailing tomorrow would be a challenge, but Eve loved challenges.

He made coffee and stared at the pot as the dark, caffeinated liquid dripped.

The Christmas before Eve's second birthday Jimmy had come to the house. He looked like shit and he was scared. He'd promised Gabriel, if he gave Jimmy money to disappear, that he'd never return. For one night, Christmas Day dinner, his mother had been happy that her family was under the same roof. She was doing amazing, the cancer was gone (only to return three years later with a vengeance), and Eve was a bundle of toddler activity. Gabriel was surprisingly content, for the first time in his life.

And then Jimmy showed up.

Gabriel gave him every dime in his savings and Jimmy promised never to come back, that he was going to Canada.

*"I think Martha is dead,"* Jimmy had said.

*"Why?"*

*He wouldn't say, not directly. "We screwed up."* *Jimmy must have screwed up big, because never once in his miserable life had he ever admitted to doing anything wrong.*

"Who did you cross?"

"It's complicated. But the kid is better off with you. I heard her call you Daddy."

"I didn't think you were ever coming back."

"It's better this way."

"Is Eve in danger?"

"No."

*But Gabriel didn't believe him.*

"Jimmy, tell me the damn truth for once in your life."

"It's probably best if no one knows I had a kid, you know? Just in case they think I still have everything."

"Still have what?"

"Martha and I had fun for a long time," he said, his old mischievous sparkle shining in his eyes. "We . . . well, let's just say we took something from someone. And he figured out it was us and wants it back. Only Martha was stubborn. She didn't like, um, leave anything with you other than the kid?"

"No."

"Well, okay, just take care of the girl."

When Jimmy left the next day—after Gabriel gave him the money—Gabriel searched the entire house. His mom had her memory intact, she didn't remember Martha leaving anything except Eve's suitcase and diaper bag. But Martha was as sneaky as Jimmy and could easily have hidden something in the old house.

Gabriel hadn't found anything he didn't expect, though he didn't know *what* he was looking for. Now, discovering that Martha's car had been found, that she had been using an assumed name, that people had been after her and Jimmy because they stole something—coupled with the fact that the FBI had been seeking information about Jimmy for nearly ten years—told Gabriel that they had both gotten themselves killed and if anyone knew that Eve was their daughter, she was in danger, too. Gabriel was right to protect her ten years ago, and right to protect her now.

Logically, he couldn't imagine that anyone would think a child would be a threat, but what if they thought Gabriel knew where their goods were? Whatever *it* was.

Would that reporter listen to reason? Could Gabriel trust her enough to tell her about Jimmy's visit and explain that if anyone knew that Eve was not his daughter, that she might be in danger? Did she care enough about a sister she didn't know to walk away?

Eve walked in, her long braid messy from sleep. She yawned, put her arms around Gabriel. "Morning, Dad."

"Morning, monkey."

"Want me to make breakfast?" She reached over and poured herself a cup of coffee.

"I have some errands this morning."

"Breakfast—the most important meal of the day. And I have to go to the boathouse and help Jason prepare for the race tomorrow. He has a problem with one of his sails and can't figure it out."

"I'm sure you will."

He wanted to grab Eve and run away. But that wouldn't solve their problems.

He poured himself a cup of coffee and said, "Breakfast is great. I'll cut up a cantaloupe and you do the cooking, then I'll drop you off at the club."

Max picked up the phone on the first ring. "David?"

"Why am I surprised you're up at six thirty in the morning?"

"So are you. Well?"

"You owe my friend a case of Glenlivet. It's his favorite."

"Order it and charge my account."

"Already did."

"Don't keep me in suspense."

She could hear David sip his coffee. He did it to annoy her, she was pretty certain.

"He wouldn't put anything in writing—might come back to bite him in the ass, he said—but I trust his verbal timeline. You said Eve was born in January?"

"Yes. I'm working on getting the exact date, but sometime that month."

"She would have been conceived between April and maybe July, if she was premature. During those months—in fact, from March fifteenth through September twentieth of that year—Truman was on the USS *Essex* doing maneuvers in the South Pacific. His only leave was three days in Japan and three days in Hawaii, the first in May and the second in early September. He then had a two-week vacation, signed out to home, and returned to base October fourth. He was deployed at sea for another six months on February twenty-fifth, docked August thirty-first in San Diego. Had a family medical leave for thirty days, but put in his papers September tenth. The kid would have been eight or nine months old by then."

"So he wasn't in the States at all the April Martha disappeared?"

"No."

"And he wasn't in the States when Eve was conceived."

"No. Could Martha have gone to Japan? May would be within the window."

"I don't know. It seems . . . odd. She liked traveling to Europe and South America, she'd never seemed interested in Japan, but anything's possible, I suppose."

"That doesn't sound like you."

"What?"

"Confused."

"I *am* confused."

"I'm not."

"What am I missing?"

"He's not her father. Not her biological father, at any rate."

"Now *that* makes no sense."

"Look at the facts that we know. Martha had an infant with her in Miami before she left in early April. Her car was abandoned in Virginia sometime that month, found at the end of April and the police report indicated it had been there for two to three weeks. No sign of the infant, not even a hint that a child was in the car, but Gabriel leaves military service as soon as his tour is up, ostensibly to raise a motherless child. You are confident that Eve is your half sister, which means Martha is certainly her mother. Extrapolate from there."

"Martha left the baby with Gabriel's mother. Then . . . what? She was killed? Tried to disappear? Why? Because of these stolen paintings?"

"I'm only looking at the facts, you need to put them together with your theories. And Gabriel's mother is also Jimmy's mother. Does Gabriel strike you as a man who would be interested in your mother?"

He was asking the question seriously, so Max considered it. She wanted to say, "Every man is interested in my mother," but she didn't. Because that wasn't true. She attracted men who enjoyed fun and adventure, who spent money and liked expensive things. A man like Gabriel— salt of the earth, more comfortable on sea than on land, devoted to his family, not living lavishly—no, she didn't see it. But she didn't really know Gabriel. And people could change. Maybe he had been wild in his youth. Or maybe he got drunk and Martha thought it would be fun to seduce Jimmy's brother. He would have been more than ten years younger than her mother, but that wasn't unheard of. Martha had been a very attractive woman.

"Not at this point in his life," she said carefully. "But why would Gabriel raise a child not his own?"

"She was an innocent child who had no parents. You said that Gabriel and his brother didn't get along."

"True."

"Maybe Gabriel tried to get Jimmy to do the right thing and either couldn't find him, or Jimmy refused to take responsibility. Gabriel lived with his mother and Eve until his mother passed when Eve was five. He took Eve under his wing. She's his niece, he loves her, and the fact that he raised her as his daughter tells me that he loves her like a daughter."

"Yes, I can see that. Okay."

"Tread carefully here, Max. You don't know the whole story, and he's on edge."

Max was glad she hadn't told David about Gabriel's visit yesterday. He would be angry if he found out, but he would insist on coming up, and having him around now—when she was still trying to feel her way around this investigation—would stifle her.

"I'll be good," she said lightly.

"I'm almost done here," David said. "I'm following up on another lead, based on the information Agent Maguire told you about the three recovered paintings."

"What lead?"

"I don't know yet," David said in a sign of frustration. Why, because she was asking questions or because he had a gut feeling?

"Your instincts are getting sharp," she said with a smile.

"I took Rogan's list of possible false identities and am running them against an area in Miami where your fed from Norfolk found the storage locker, and Martha had her storage locker."

"You're thinking there's a third."

"If there is, it probably got shut down. But if I can confirm another fake identity we might be able to trace it. If the contents were auctioned off, there may be a record of who they were sold to."

"Good thinking."

"Don't keep me in the dark, Max—if things heat up, I can be in Virginia fast."

Max drove out to the Hendersons' house Saturday morning. At first, no one appeared to be there, then she saw Beth and her daughter walking back from the barn, each carrying a large basket. Beth waved to Max when she saw her.

"Nothing better than fresh eggs," Beth said as she approached. She handed her basket to Molly and said, "Wash and store them, please. Put a dozen together for the Scholtens."

"Sure, Mom." Molly took the two overloaded baskets to the house. There had to be at least four, five dozen eggs there. "I'll take the eggs to the Scholtens, then I need to go to the boating club and take pictures for the newspaper."

"The race is tomorrow, why do you have to . . . oh."

"*Mom*." Was Molly blushing? Max didn't have the blush gene, she was pretty certain.

Beth laughed. "Go ahead, and invite Jason over to dinner if you'd like. I'm sure Wyatt would love to see him."

"You mean interrogate him. Just what I need, Wyatt *and* Dad *and* Grandpop all giving Jason the third degree."

"You forget that I used to babysit Jason's mother. We go way back."

"Stop, you're killing me!" Molly ran into the house.

Beth was still grinning. "She and Jason are *just friends*, she says, but they've been just friends a lot more this year than ever before. Do you mind coming with me to the garden shed? I have herbs growing in there, I need to trim a few and collect some for dinner tonight. Usually Sunday is our big family dinner, but it's Wyatt's birthday tonight. He and his best friend drove down from college last night, and he needs to turn around and go back to-morrow."

"Where's he going to college?"

"Virginia Tech. He's the smartest of my brood. Of course, I wouldn't say that to him—might go to his head. But he's sharp. Full-ride academic scholarship."

"That's terrific."

She was beaming as she sorted through herbs so lush that it made Max think she'd like to grow her own herbs. The only problem was that she was often gone for weeks at a time.

"Can I help you?"

"Grab that basket over there, on the top shelf. I envy your height." She nodded toward a step stool. "I need one of those in every room."

Max reached up and took down the basket.

"Now, you must have come out here because you have some more questions."

"Your father-in-law said he would talk to the Scholtens and Abel Parsons, the caretaker of the big house on the peninsula, about the time my mother's car was found, to see if they heard or saw anything."

"Well, I know he talked to Edith and Andre Scholten. Spent quite some time over there Thursday night, in fact. But they didn't see anything apparently, and their property line doesn't go down that far. It's a small farm, they run it themselves with only a few part-time hands. And honestly, they wouldn't remember this long, unless it was something really odd."

"I appreciate him trying."

"He hasn't talked to Abel. Abel keeps to himself. Dad

and Gary went over there yesterday afternoon, but they didn't say anything about it. I don't think he was home, but I didn't ask—Wyatt had just come in, and I haven't seen him in a month, since spring break."

"I spoke to Abel briefly yesterday."

"Did you learn anthing?"

"No, just asked him to pass my contact information on to his employer."

"Abel is reclusive."

Max wondered if she should ask about Gabriel and Eve. Max usually went for the bull in the china shop approach. She would annoy someone until they finally talked to her. If she confronted them with the truth, they usually admitted it.

But asking Gabriel flat-out if Eve was Jimmy's daughter—David was right, she had to tread carefully. But not for the reason David thought.

Max wanted a relationship with Eve. Eve was her sister—no matter *who* her father was. If she pushed Gabriel so hard that he vilified her to Eve, she'd never have the kind of relationship she wanted.

She chose her words carefully. "I reached out to Gabriel Truman, hoping that he had information about my mother and her relationship with his brother. He's . . . extremely private."

"Well, his brother is not a nice person. I imagine he doesn't want to bring him back into his life. And for a while, the FBI was around here asking people questions."

"The FBI talked to you?"

"No, but as you can probably tell, we're a small, tight-knit community. One person gets talked to, it gets around. But the FBI talked to several people. Gabriel, of course. The Coopers—Brian and his wife are partners with Gabriel. All the staff at the resort, neighbors, you name it. Seems Jimmy was wanted for theft. That's what we were able to put together, but what the FBI was doing investigating a theft, I don't know. Must have been big. We were thinking bank robbery, but then why not go and say bank robbery?"

Beth had separated the herbs in the basket and put her scissors and a small shovel on a rack with the other hand tools. "Shall we?" she asked. Max opened the door and they walked back to the house.

When they were inside, Max heard raucous laughter from the kitchen. "Wyatt and John are up."

"I won't keep you."

"You're not. Do you need anything else?"

"I was just curious about Eve's mother."

Silence. Dammit, she'd overstepped. The question must have sounded like it was coming from nowhere.

"It's not something Gabriel will talk about, so I wouldn't ask him," Beth said.

"What happened?"

"No one really knows, to be honest. One day Emily had a baby. I don't really remember when—it was in the spring. She said Eve was her granddaughter, and the mother couldn't take care of her. For a while—well, we all thought she was one of Emily's young relatives, a teenage pregnancy and Emily was helping. It was something Emily would do—she was always the nurturer in her family, and a wonderful teacher. She should have had a houseful of kids like me. But we don't always get what we plan, do we?"

"True," Max said, willing Beth to get back on track. "And no one asked her?"

"That would be rude. But we were all open to her talking, and she said Eve was her granddaughter. So we're thinking, why isn't her dad there? Could Jimmy have had a child? Gabriel? When Gabriel left the navy to raise Eve, we put two and two together. That baby, and

Gabriel, gave Emily life—and I mean that literally. She had breast cancer and it was invasive. Gabriel convinced her to have surgery and chemo, and she ended up extending her life another five years. Most of them very good years. Without them? She would never have gotten the treatment. Emily never wanted to bother anyone with her problems, but always helped anyone who needed it."

So everyone simply assumed that Gabriel was Eve's father . . . and he de facto became her father because he never said different.

Beth walked back to the house with Max. "We're having a feast tonight, it'll be a full house, and I would love for you to join us."

"I don't want to intrude on your family."

"Intrude?" Beth laughed. "No one intrudes at our house. A lot of Wyatt's friends are stopping by to catch up, so we're doing it buffet-style and the kids can go do their thing after. Gary is roasting a whole pig—we have a pit we use. Started it at ten last night, it'll be going until three or four this afternoon. We have clam chowder, homemade applesauce I can every year. I picked up snow peas that a neighbor grows in her greenhouse, and they are simply amazing. And, of course, my pies. We eat at six."

"I would love that, and I'll try to make it. Thank you."

Eve Truman had finished checking her sails and was helping Jason untangle a nasty mess on his line.

"How'd you know the block was my problem?" he asked her.

"Just the way the mast was moving. You need to spend more time stowing the lines properly so you don't have to spend so much time preparing before a race."

"I know, I just don't have the patience that you do. You must get it from your dad."

"Look who's here," Eve said with a grin as Molly Henderson walked the dock taking photos of the club members as they worked on their boats.

"Stop it."

She laughed. It was so obvious that Molly and Jason were in love and had been since they hit puberty. Eve used to have a huge crush on Molly's brother Wyatt, but he was a senior when she was a freshman, and her dad would have flipped. If only she was a year or two older. . . . "Molly!" she called out.

"Hey, Eve. Jason." She walked over, all casual. "Do you mind if I take pictures? Alan pays ten dollars for every picture he uses of mine in the paper."

"Sure, we're just doing grunt work now," Jason said. "Tomorrow you should get some great shots. It's going to be amazing. Steady winds, might even get a little choppy, but no rain."

Eve was a little more concerned than Jason about the weather. She'd been tracking the wind patterns and thought the middle of the bay was going to be more unpredictable than Jason did. Fortunately, Steve listened to her, and he would impart any safety concerns to everyone.

Eve was excited because she loved sailing when it was unpredictable, it was far more exciting and challenging. But she worried that some in the club raced more as a hobby rather than taking it seriously. Jason was dedicated, but he had also been preoccupied lately.

Molly shot a bunch of pictures as Eve and Jason finished untangling the lines and then repacking the sails so they would be ready for tomorrow. "Why don't you both come over for dinner tonight," Molly said. "My brother and his roommate are here—it's Wyatt's birthday—and Mom has enough food to feed an army." She was looking at Eve—did she know that Eve had a crush on Wyatt? She'd never said anything.

"Really? That would be fun. Eve, don't you think?" Jason asked.

What, did he want Eve to chaperone?

"Maybe," Eve said.

"My mom invited the New York reporter to come— she is *so* totally cool."

"What New York reporter?" Jason asked.

"Everyone's talking about her—she's staying at Havenly, Eve. Apparently, her mother disappeared here years ago and she's trying to find out what happened to her."

"Here? In Cape Haven?" Eve asked. "Nothing happens here."

"It was a long time ago, and my grandfather found her car, that's why she's been over to the house a couple times. It was abandoned, she like disappeared into thin air. No one has seen her since."

Eve shivered.

"You're not a scaredy-cat," Jason said and hit her in the arm. "And it's probably not true."

"It is," Molly said. "I went to her website to check her out, and it's all there. Her mother left her with family in California when she was nine and never came back." Molly put her hand to her mouth. "Oh my god, I'm sorry, Eve, that was *so* insensitive of me."

She waved it off. "I never knew my mother, it's okay. Seriously." But she felt an odd connection to this woman whose mother had also abandoned her. "Maybe I will come to dinner, so I can meet her. Can I let you know later?"

"Sure, text me."

"I can drive you out there," Jason said. "If you want."

Eve had turned sixteen in January, but she didn't have her license yet. She was taking the class at school one day a week and should be able to get her permit in June, and her license by the end of the year. She couldn't wait, because she hated relying on everyone else for rides.

"Thanks, I just need to make sure my dad doesn't have plans. And it can't be late—we have to be back out here at six tomorrow morning."

Jason groaned. "Don't remind me."

"I'll call my mom and make sure Ms. Revere is going to be there, but even if she's not, I want you to come. It'll be fun." Molly pulled out her phone.

Eve stared at Molly. That name was familiar . . . but Eve had to be wrong. Remembered wrong.

"Eve? Earth to Eve?" Jason said.

"Um . . . I gotta run home for something. We're done here, right?"

"Yeah, thanks for your help, do you want a ride?"

"Nope, nope, I'm good. I'll call you about tonight. Bye."

Eve walked briskly down the pier, then started jogging. Revere was a common name, wasn't it? And she could have remembered wrong. It had been a long time since she'd seen her birth certificate.

Her house wasn't far from the boating club, just over a mile. Her dad wasn't home, which was good, because whenever she asked about her mother he became very quiet and sad. She still didn't quite know what happened between them, and she didn't want her dad to be sad. All that mattered to her was that her mother left and her dad stayed and she loved him for it.

She went up to her dad's bedroom. There was a den downstairs, but he didn't keep the really important papers in the den. He kept them in a locked drawer in the desk in his bedroom. The lock was basic, and she popped it easily enough.

Most of the folders, all of which were neatly arranged, related to the house, insurance, and taxes. She ignored those. She pulled out the folder EVE.

Every one of her report cards was in here. A card she'd given her dad for Father's Day one year with her handprint on it. She barely remembered making it—she'd been in kindergarten. Inside she'd drawn two stick people, one much taller than the other, with big round heads and circle hands with impossibly long fingers. The short figure had long yellow hair. Each had a smile. She'd written in painstaking block letters:

*MY DADDY AND ME*
*BEST FRIENDS FOREVER*

The *i* in *friends* was smaller and sort of above the *r* and *e*, having been added after she wrote the card, probably when her teacher told her she spelled it wrong. Or maybe she'd looked on someone else's card and realized she messed up. She didn't realize her dad had kept this, or the other mementoes, and it made her smile.

Her birth certificate was in a manila envelope. It was a copy, and she didn't find an original. She'd seen this before, when her dad enrolled her in school, and then when she had to provide proof of her age for the boating club. She'd been born in Miami-Dade County in Florida on January 12.

GENEVIEVE NORA TRUMAN
Mother: MARTHA ELEANOR REVERE
Father: GABRIEL JOHN TRUMAN

She glanced down at her mother's birthplace: California. Molly said that the reporter had been left with relatives in California.

Eve's heart was pounding in her chest and she couldn't make it slow down. She almost couldn't think.

She desperately wanted to talk to her dad, but he'd been acting strange all week, ever since the sheriff came to talk to him Tuesday night. He had to know that the reporter was staying at the resort, right? He'd always told her that her mother had problems, that she didn't want to be a mother, and he was sorry about that. Sometimes it made her sad, but not for a long time because her dad was totally cool and he always did stuff with her.

Maybe he didn't know about the reporter. Her dad didn't care much about the resort, only the boats. He spent all his time either working on the boats or sailing the boats. He knew everything about the Chesapeake Bay, took charters out, and the only time she'd seen him truly happy was on the water. He'd even gotten to like the tours he gave every week.

Eve folded her birth certificate and stuffed it in her back pocket, closed the drawer, and left. She needed to find her dad. Something was weird here, and she didn't know what, but she knew he would have the answers.

It took half the morning for Gabriel to work up the courage to go and talk to Maxine Revere, and then she wasn't at her cottage. He waited twenty minutes, staring out at the sea, wishing he knew what to do.

He couldn't tell Eve that he wasn't her father. Eve had often asked about her mother—especially when she was younger. Gabriel had been vague for a while, but when she pushed, he said that their relationship had been brief, they'd been young, and her mother didn't want to be a mother.

*She left you with your grandma and never came back. She had some problems, and I wish I could spare you from the pain and sadness, but know that I love you more than anything, Eve.*

Eve knew that her mother's name was Martha, because when she asked, Gabriel couldn't think of a believable lie. He didn't want Eve to look for her. She'd once asked, when she was twelve, if he had loved her mother. He was honest.

*"No, it wasn't like that."*

*"Was it a mistake?"*

*"No."*

*"But you didn't love her."*

Talking to your preteen daughter about sex was extremely uncomfortable. He'd enlisted the help of Brian's sister to explain female anatomy, and Eve loved Jenna like an aunt. But this wasn't the sex talk, it was even worse.

*"You are the best thing that ever happened to me, Eve. So no, it wasn't a mistake because you are a miracle. Always remember that."*

That seemed to satisfy her, and over time, she stopped asking questions.

But what if this reporter—Eve's sister—talked to her? Eve was a smart kid; if the name Martha came up, she would remember that her mother was named Martha. How could he keep the only family on her mother's side away from Eve? Was that fair to her?

He didn't know, but what wasn't right was that this woman was here stirring up all this shit and threatening him and Eve, using truth as a weapon. This truth could destroy his relationship with his daughter.

When the reporter wasn't back by noon, Gabriel went to the restaurant and looked for her. He told the bartender to call him if she came in.

What if she had gone to find Eve herself? What if that damn woman didn't just give him time to think about what he should do—what he could do.

He grabbed a resort golf cart and drove around to the junior boating club, on the other side of the harbor from the resort. He saw Eve's boat in its slip, perfectly polished, sails down and stowed, her lines expertly tied. She wasn't there. He saw Jason talking to one of the Henderson girls—he knew the Hendersons, of course, two of their kids worked for the resort during the summers while they were in college.

He walked over.

"Hi, Mr. Truman," Jason said.

"Jason, hello. Prepared for tomorrow?"

"Thanks to Eve—I swear, she took one look at my ropes and knew exactly what I'd done wrong."

"Good, the weather should be perfect, with a brisk breeze coming in from the Atlantic."

"First race of the season, even if it doesn't count."

"That's why they're called exhibitions—you can check out your competition. Have you seen Eve? I thought she'd still be here."

"She said she was going home," Jason said.

The Henderson girl said, "I invited her and Jason over for dinner—my dad's roasting a pig. You came over for Labor Day, right? Just like that. There will be plenty. You're more than welcome to join us, too, Mr. Truman."

"Thank you for the invitation, I'll talk to Eve and see what she wants to do. She might not want her dad tagging along."

"There'll be lots of parents," the girl said. "It's Wyatt's birthday, everyone wants to see him." She rolled her eyes. "He just *loves* that he's the most popular person at any party."

Gabriel thanked the kids, but he was thinking about Eve. Why had she gone home? It was Saturday morning, not even lunchtime, and Eve loved being outdoors especially when it was such a nice day—a bit cool and windy, but clear. She should be studying the weather charts, triple-checking her supplies, running through the course in her head. Talking to her team. What she usually did the day before a race.

He called her cell phone. It went to voicemail after four rings.

He drove home, but Eve wasn't there. His heart raced. He didn't want to panic, but he didn't know where she could be. Why she wasn't answering her phone? What if that reporter had tracked her down? Told her that she was her sister? That they had the same mother?

Would it be all that bad? No one knew Eve wasn't his biological daughter, except for Brian. And while some people might suspect it because he hadn't been here when Martha left Eve with Emily, they wouldn't say a word. Or they pushed it out of their minds, forgot about it. Sixteen years wasn't long in a small town, but no one liked Jimmy. He'd hurt a lot of people. Gabriel had always felt the need to clean up Jimmy's messes. Emily would give the shirt off her back to someone less fortunate, not only because she was a good person, but because she felt so guilty about raising a son who had stolen from friends and family.

Gabriel needed to tell Eve the truth himself, before Maxine Revere talked to her. The whole truth—because if that reporter learned that Eve wasn't his biological daughter, and she told Eve, she might never forgive him.

# Chapter Eighteen

Max was missing something.

When she returned to the cottage from the Hendersons' house, she made herself lunch and mixed a mimosa. She sat on the deck and ate, drank, and tried to clear her thoughts. Focusing on the ocean waves was relaxing, and her mind kept drifting back to the postcards.

Why had her mother sent her postcards of art she had stolen—or knew had been stolen? What could she have possibly thought Max could do about it? The six years between abandonment and Martha's death was summed up in sixteen postcards that evidently meant something more than Max had realized.

Everything came back to the postcards.

Max got up, rinsed her plate, mixed a second mimosa, and went back to her den. She removed all sixteen postcards from her timeline. Martha had spent far more time with Jimmy Truman than Max had thought she would. Their relationship was neither simple nor fleeting.

Max took the postcards to the dining table and laid them out on the table in order, message side up. The first card was a belated birthday postcard from Hawaii. That was the only postcard that specifically mentioned Jimmy Truman.

There was a postcard every January—only one came within days of her birthday; most were weeks, sometimes months, late. The birthday postcards had the same theme: happy birthday, have fun, too bad Max didn't know how to have fun, maybe I'll call and chat.

Martha had never called.

Max had twice asked her grandmother Eleanor whether she intentionally kept Martha from her. The first time was when Max and Eleanor had a huge argument. It started after Max informed the rest of the family that her uncle Brooks was cheating on his wife. Eleanor tried the stern lecture, but Max wasn't having it. She was angry— furious, really—that her family were hypocrites, that there was a double standard for them and everyone else. Max tossed back every rule, every lecture, every character trait Eleanor had instilled in her because Eleanor had sided with Brooks. It wasn't until later that Max realized Eleanor hadn't *sided* with her son so much as abhorred Max's method of delivery.

But at the time, Max was angry and upset. She asked Eleanor if she knew where her mother was and maybe now was the time Max should find her.

She'd been fifteen.

Eleanor was hurt, Max realized later, but at the time all Max wanted was to hurt her and she didn't think she'd gotten under her skin at all.

"Your mother does not want to be found. She does not want to return. I've heard on occasion that so-and-so saw her in one place, and another person saw her somewhere else. But never for long. She's still transient, and is truly lost. Yet, no matter how angry I am with you right now, Maxine, I would never want you to leave me."

It took Max a long time before she really understood what her grandmother meant. While she was not sorry she'd exposed Brooks, she ultimately wished she'd exposed him differently. Because she'd hurt people she never wanted to hurt—namely her grandmother and her aunt Joanne, who shortly thereafter filed for divorce.

The second time Max broached the subject was last year, when she asked her grandmother whether the post-cards were, in fact, genuine—or her grandmother's way of protecting Max from her selfish mother. Eleanor said they were all real, but she wished Martha had never sent them.

"You were crushed with each flip, selfish, snide note. I can't help thinking your mother intended to punish not only me, but her own daughter. And I will never begin to understand her. It's taken me years to accept that even if I made mistakes raising Martha, who she became is not a weight I should carry. Nor should you. And yet, you carry the weight for both of us."

Maybe Max did. Because she didn't know what else she was supposed to do.

One by one, Max turned over the postcards and looked at the pictures.

Hawaii was the first, followed by several picture post-cards. A cruise ship. A French vineyard. Other similar scenes.

The first piece of art was a Degas in April, after Max turned thirteen.

Well, not exactly. Her birthday postcard had been from a museum in Dallas and postmarked from Dallas. The Degas was postmarked from Miami. The postcard itself had been perforated, as if it had been in a booklet of postcards. Max studied the fine print on the edge of the postcard. Nothing identified the book it had been clipped from, only identified the painting, the artist, and the year painted. In fact, it was a rather cheaply produced picture postcard.

A Boudin, a Renoir, a Toulouse-Lautrec, and three

lesser-known artists. For Max's fourteenth birthday, a card between the third and fourth painting, Martha sent a generic beach scene from Florida. The back identified it as Key Largo.

The seven pieces of art that Ryan Maguire said were all stolen . . . but there were eight paintings. The next to last postcard Martha sent was of a Caravaggio—a rather violent picture of a beheading.

She studied the card carefully. It was different than the others—first, it had obviously been bought in a gift shop, not torn from a book. Second, it was very specific—a Caravaggio exhibit during that time at a small Parisian museum Max had heard of only because she'd traveled extensively and been an art history major. This postcard had been created to promote the exhibit. It was postmarked from Paris, France, in the middle of May. . . .

Her mother may have been pregnant then.

It might not mean anything. Or it might be the clue to everything.

She read the card carefully.

*Dear Max,*
*I love Paris so much I wish sometimes that we'd stayed here forever. You were seven, we lived in a beautiful villa, remember? This spring has been the most beautiful yet . . . but I'm leaving today. Bittersweet, but no regrets.*
*—Martha*
*P.S. Isn't this painting atrocious? He had talent, but it's so depressing. Some people prefer the dark to the light.*

Was she talking about Jimmy? About someone else? No one? Considering Martha had sent *these* specific postcards, Max suspected there was a double meaning behind most of them. But figuring it out might be impossible.

The last postcard meant nothing to Max at the time, but now that she was here it meant everything.

It was a picture of a shoreline at sunset, and when Max first got it she never considered *where* it was. She might have looked at it at the time, but the small italic print didn't really stand out.

The postcard was a painting of the Chesapeake Bay—which could have been anywhere along the coastline—but it had been purchased at the Cape Haven Museum and Welcome Center. This was printed on the card. There was nothing about the image that stood out, but now Max wanted to find this exact location.

If the seven pictures represented stolen art, maybe this last postcard represented a clue as to where to locate the pieces.

She shook her head. Four of the pieces had already been found—one when Jimmy Truman sold it, and three when a buyer got the pieces appraised in Miami. But Truman had sold the painting in DC, which wasn't far from Chesapeake Bay.

And what about the Caravaggio? What about that piece was so important to Martha?

When Max was younger, the only thing she really cared about, other than swimming and the beach, was reading. If Martha wanted to send postcards that reflected Max's interests, they would be related to books and literature. But these were artworks—paintings, specifically, which was Martha's love.

Max pulled out her computer and researched the Italian artist. Nothing about this painting stood out—it had been on exhibit for two years around Europe and now was back with its owner.

Yet . . .

She called Ryan Maguire's cell phone. It went immediately to voicemail.

"Ryan, it's Maxine Revere. I have a theory I need to run by you. Call me back, please."

While she waited for Ryan, she looked through images from all over the Eastern Shore, looking for the spot where this picture—the last postcard her mother ever sent her—was painted.

Gabriel found Eve an hour later sitting on their personal boat in the Havenly clubhouse. He had bought the twenty-six foot boat when Eve turned ten. Time, weather, and neglect had nearly killed it, but it had a good frame and the engine wasn't completely shot, so together they had restored it.

It was seaworthy now, and they'd taken it out for the first time last summer. There was more detail work to do, and Gabriel loved to work on it. Eve did, too, but she was a teenager with teenage interests. Swimming. Competing. Boys.

Still, they spent a few hours every week out here on the *Emily*. She hadn't wanted to name the yacht after herself, which was Gabriel's idea, but had instead suggested her grandmother. *"I was five and a half when Grandma died, but I still miss her."*

His mother would have said she was embarrassed to have her name on a boat, but secretly be pleased.

Eve was sitting at the stern. The boathouse was closed, the water gently lapping against the hull. They'd taken her out of dry dock just last month for the first voyage of spring, but hadn't had time since.

She looked at him. She'd been crying. Her tear-stained face broke his heart.

He walked down the narrow walkway and climbed on board. He sat across from her. "Hey."

She stared at him. There was no fear in her expression, just sorrow and confusion.

"Eve, what's wrong?"

"I think you know, Dad. You've been acting weird all week."

*Tell her.*

He didn't want to. But if he lied now, she would never trust him again.

"It's about the reporter from New York, isn't it?"

"Is she my sister?"

"Is that what she told you?"

"I haven't talked to her. I almost did—I went to the office and looked up which cottage she was in. I almost went over there to . . . I don't know, just see her. But I didn't. I wanted to talk to you first, but then I didn't know what to say. So I came here."

He was marginally relieved.

"I think she may be your half sister," he said carefully.

She looked at him with such deep trust he let it all come out. At least, most of it.

"I didn't know anything about her until this week. She came here because she learned that her mother had abandoned her car near Oyster Bay sixteen years ago. The same time your mother left you with Grandma."

"Did you know?"

He shook his head. "I always thought Martha just didn't want to be a mother. I didn't understand, but Martha . . . she was selfish, honey. She didn't know how to take care of anyone else. I think the fact that she left her first daughter to be raised by her grandparents shows she never grew up."

"Did you ever try to find her?"

He didn't want to tell her the truth, but he had to. "No, I didn't. I didn't know she left you until I was on leave, months after Grandma took you in. But when I saw you,

I didn't reenlist because you needed me more than the navy."

Tears fell from Eve's eyes, and Gabriel's own eyes burned. He hated this conversation, hated Maxine Revere for forcing it.

"Does . . . does Maxine Revere know about me?"

"I talked to her yesterday and asked that she not say anything until I talked to you. But I didn't know how to bring it up last night. I'm scared."

"Why? Why would you be scared?"

"Because I don't want to lose you."

Her eyes widened. "Dad, you'll never lose me. Never. But I have a sister. I mean, she's older and like, important. I went to her website. She's written books and has a cable news show and she's really, really pretty. I didn't think we were sisters at first, that it was a coincidence."

"Honey, you're beautiful."

She shrugged. "But then I saw a picture of her—it was in this article she'd written about being smart during spring break, you know, like not going out alone and making sure you don't drink things people give you and stuff. Her college roommate was killed by some guy during spring break, I guess. She wrote a whole book about it. Anyway, there was a picture of her when she was in college, with her best friend, and she was much younger . . . and I thought we kind of looked alike. Like our faces, even though she has red hair and I have this mousy mop."

"Stop criticizing yourself. You are beautiful."

"When I saw that picture, I thought, wow, I have a sister and she's pretty and smart and successful. And then I wondered, what was wrong with us that our mother left us?"

"Nothing is wrong with you, Eve. Nothing. Everything was wrong with Martha Revere."

"Why didn't you look for her?"

"I don't know," he said.

Eve didn't say anything.

"I guess—deep down—I was scared."

"You're not scared of anything, Dad."

"I wish that were true. I was scared that if I found her she would come back and take you away. I love you, Eve, I just wanted to protect you from the pain of having an irresponsible mother."

She didn't say anything, and Gabriel didn't know what she was thinking. Then she said, "I want to meet her."

"Your mother? I don't know—"

"Maxine. I want to meet Maxine. You said she knows that I'm her sister, so it's not like I'm going to lay a bombshell on her or anything."

"Are you sure?"

"Yes."

She was certain. He knew that expression, that stubborn streak she had in her.

"Okay, I'll, um, talk to her. Maybe have her over for dinner tomorrow night?" Home turf. Safe ground. His chest constricted. He didn't know what else he could do.

"Actually, Molly Henderson invited me over to her house tonight. She said Maxine might be there, because her mom invited her over."

"Oh."

"You can come with me. I don't mind."

"Are you sure?" He didn't want to go. But he also didn't want Maxine Revere alone with his daughter.

"Yes." Eve got up, walked across the deck, and sat down next to him. She hugged him tight. He immediately hugged her back. They were going to be okay. That was all he cared about, that he and Eve would be okay.

"I love you, Daddy. I know you gave up a lot to raise me, and I will never forget it. I'm not going anywhere, you know that, right?"

"Yeah."

"You still look sad. I just want to know her. To know my sister. Find out more about my mother. Do you think she wants to get to know me?"

"She's seems to be a very smart woman, so yeah, I think she wants to know you, too."

But he hoped and prayed she didn't say too much about Martha Revere.

# Chapter Nineteen

SEVENTEEN YEARS AGO

Martha had always said that life has plans, and she just went along for the ride, but that statement took on a far more ominous meaning when she literally ran into Phillip Colter in Paris on a beautiful spring afternoon.

He was as surprised to see her as she was to see him. And . . . happy?

"Martha."

The way he said her name . . . it was an apology, erotic subtlety, and pleasant surprise all rolled into one.

She studied him. She also assessed her strange reaction to him, because even though she knew she should run, she didn't want to.

"Phillip. You look . . . wonderful."

He kissed first one cheek then the other, then touched his lips to hers, lingering just a moment longer than friendship would call for.

"Dinner. Please. I'm staying at the Le Meurice. Eight o'clock."

She should decline. Phillip was dangerous in so many ways. But he was electric. She had never forgotten him, never forgotten the thrill of sharing his bed, of stealing his art, of holding on to the priceless works, a secret from Phillip and from the world. A secret all her own.

Hers and Jimmy's.

"Is nine too late? I have a previous engagement, but I can slip away by nine."

"I'll send a car for you. Where are you staying?"

"I'll be there," she said, not wanting Phillip to have too much information about her. She might be attracted to him, but she wasn't completely stupid.

He kissed her again and she sighed, unable to keep the sound to herself. She was thirty-six, but felt ten years younger in his arms . . . and ten years more mature. He brought out something in her she didn't know she had, an elegance . . . an idea that maybe, just maybe, she could live the life that her mother had once designed for her. Married to the right man. Living in the proper zip code. Parties and philanthropy and business.

That Phillip Colter was an art thief made the dream even more enticing. Eleanor would find him perfect, and yet Martha would know the truth. That he was dark, dangerous, and criminal.

"I am truly sorry about how I left things between us," Phillip whispered. "I have missed you."

"Nine," was all she could say. She slipped away with a smile.

"We're leaving," Jimmy said.

They were in a villa just outside Paris, the house of some heiress that Jimmy had conned into loaning to them for the spring. People trusted Jimmy. He set up an entire scam that he was a writer and the French government was offering a tax credit to anyone who loaned their property to an artist for three months in exchange for light caretaking duties. The woman was older, and Jimmy wined and dined her—on her money!—until she practically gave him the villa.

It was a beautiful home and the wine cellar was

amazing—Martha was pretty certain they'd opened bottles worth hundreds of dollars. It had been a wonderful stay and they had the entire house to themselves.

"Nonsense. He doesn't know anything. If I don't show up he'll be suspicious."

Jimmy stared at her, angry and worried. Why was he worried? Phillip didn't know they had seven of his paintings, and he never would.

"I don't believe you!" Then he stopped arguing and said, "You're infatuated with him."

"You know I love only you." Which was true. But Jimmy was also right. She *was* infatuated with Phillip Colter. She had followed him in the society pages for the last two years and suspected he'd stolen at least six more pieces from a museum in Montreal. She and Jimmy had traveled to Montreal, too—she didn't tell him why she wanted to go—and she could tell which paintings had been switched. Evidently, Colter had changed his ways. He no longer kept his reproductions hidden away, but hung them in place of the originals.

Had he done that from the beginning, she and Jimmy would never have been able to pull off their scam. Did that mean that he knew what they'd done?

No, he wouldn't have had that warm appraisal of her today. She'd considered that Colter would know his paintings were forgeries as soon as he went to his storage locker and the forgeries were no longer there, but if he had, he hadn't connected the thefts to her.

"It's too dangerous," Jimmy said.

"Jealous?"

"No."

But he was, and that thrilled her on one level and bored her on another. Jealousy was *common*. It was dangerous in itself, because jealousy made men—and women—do stupid things.

"I'll see you tomorrow."

"You're going to sleep with him."

"So? You slept with the old biddy who owns this place."

"That didn't mean anything. It was part of the setup."

"And I don't care, and neither should you."

"He's different."

"Why? Because he's a thief? Because he's attractive and rich?"

"Don't do it."

She finished getting dressed. "Baby, I love you, you know that, but if you start acting like a jealous husband, I'm going to walk. It has no place in our relationship."

"You'd walk after five years?"

"I don't want to," she said honestly. "But I'm going to see Phillip tonight."

"I'm going back to the States."

She frowned. Jimmy had never gone this far before—with a threat to leave. "Without me?"

He seemed to realize they'd reached an impasse. And this time, he relented. "In one week, we leave together. No longer—I don't trust Colter. Agreed?"

She smiled and kissed him. "Thank you."

She didn't give Jimmy a second thought during the days and nights she spent with Phillip Colter. She was on cloud nine, being pampered and romanced. Phillip said he was genuinely sorry about how he treated her when she left two years ago; she let him make it up to her.

On the fifth day, they went to a small museum in the heart of the art district. A special collection of the Italian artist, Caravaggio, was being shown for six weeks.

"I love his use of light and shadows," Phillip said. "Evocative. Real. I recently commissioned a replica of this piece."

The piece in question was the *Beheading of Saint John the Baptist*. Martha had never been a fan of overtly religious artwork, but there was something compelling and violent in Caravaggio's works. This one, however, was the darkest.

She smiled. If he had commissioned a "replica"—which to Phillip meant *forgery*—he planned to steal this painting. She almost wished she could be part of it.

"Too violent for me," she said lightly. "Now this piece . . . this is different."

Called *The Fortune Teller*, Martha was intrigued by the subtle sense of whimsy and cunning. The gypsy girl was clearly putting one over on the boy, and stealing his ring in the process.

"It's a bit more . . . pedestrian." Phillip frowned.

He didn't understand, which made her love of the piece come alive.

"She's smart," Martha said. "I've always loved smart women."

"Hmm."

He was thinking, and she wasn't certain of what, so she diverted his attention to another piece, again with a beheading. "He sure liked violence."

"They were violent times."

Martha had noticed three men following them around. She wasn't positive until they left the museum, and she mentioned it to Phillip.

"Ignore them," he said. "Security."

She didn't believe him. She was a good liar, and clearly Phillip wasn't as good as she.

"Why do you need security?"

"Business. Not important for us." He wrapped his arm around her waist. "I'm leaving for the States next week. Come back with me."

"I'll think about it. I love Paris."

"You can come back anytime you want." He stopped under a fully blooming tree, and said, "Martha, I love you. I have loved you since the day I met you, and have rued the day I chased you away with my overbearing jealousy. I will give you all the time you want, all the space you need, as long as I know that you are mine and no other man can claim you."

Her heart nearly stopped. "You want exclusivity."

"Do not tell me you don't feel the same." He touched the back of her neck lightly and she shivered in response.

He smiled.

"I . . . I will admit that I have been drawn to you for reasons I don't understand."

He kissed her and she melted.

Maybe she could have it all.

The morning of May fifteenth gave Martha three big surprises.

First, she realized that she was pregnant.

Second, Jimmy showed up at Le Meurice and nearly got caught. But it reminded her of what they had—something different than anyone else. He had stayed, he'd said he would leave in a week, but he had stayed for two.

And the third . . .

She came up from the pool house, preoccupied with the home pregnancy test she had just taken as well as seeing Jimmy. She shook him off, told him she'd call him later—she couldn't afford to have Phillip or any of his "security" see her with Jimmy.

She'd been with Phillip for only two weeks. Certainly, this baby was Jimmy's. . . .

She walked in and Phillip was on the balcony, on the phone, and very, very angry.

"Find out who stole from me. Now!"

He threw the cordless phone across the room and it broke into pieces. He stared at her.

And in his eyes, she saw that he suspected.

*Tell him you're pregnant. It'll save your life.*

*If you tell him you're pregnant, he'll never let you go.*

Instead, she said, "Bad business deal?"

"I don't want to talk about it. Where have you been?"

"Swimming. I'm famished. Breakfast?"

"I can't now. Meet me for lunch at one. Don't be late."

He started to walk away, then turned back to her. "I'm sorry if I'm short-tempered, but someone I trusted broke my trust, and I cannot let that stand."

After he left the hotel room, she packed her things and called Jimmy.

"Pick me up in ten minutes out front. We're leaving."

Maybe, if she rode this out, everything would work out and Phillip wouldn't know about the paintings. At least, wouldn't know that *she* had his stolen art.

But she couldn't take that chance. Not after she had seen the violence in his cold blue eyes.

# Chapter Twenty

The buzzer downstairs rang three times. Max went downstairs with her Taser in hand. She wasn't naturally paranoid, but between the incident with Gabriel yesterday, her conversation with David, and her new theory, she thought that a certain amount of caution was warranted. David wanted her to learn how to shoot a gun, and while she had a small revolver in her apartment, and the permit to own it, she didn't feel comfortable carrying it around so had never applied for a concealed carry permit.

Good thing she didn't bring a gun to the door here, because her visitor was Special Agent Ryan Maguire with the FBI.

"A phone call would have sufficed," she said.

He nodded at her Taser. "Expecting trouble?"

She just raised her eyebrows and didn't comment. "You got here fast." She closed the door behind him.

She wasn't certain she could trust the fed, but she needed a second set of eyes on her information, and David was still in Miami. David had checked him out, and on the surface there were no red flags. But mostly, she needed his help because he specialized in art crimes. If anyone could confirm her theory, it would be Maguire.

He followed her upstairs. "I was already on my way

when you left the message. I didn't get it because I was in the tunnel and only listened to it when I was pulling up outside."

"You were coming here? Why?"

"I talked to my boss, and he conditionally cleared you. Meaning, I can loop you in, but he's still concerned because you're a reporter. I assured him that this was a personal matter, and you're more a victim or a witness than someone who's going to stab the FBI in the back."

"Only if you lie to me," she said lightly.

"You're serious, aren't you?"

She didn't answer the question, but it was clear that her tone didn't match her words, and he should listen to her carefully.

"No lies. Either way," he said.

She nodded. "I have a theory and a lot more questions."

She led him to the dining table where she'd laid out all the postcards. "I don't think that there's anything relevant about the first five postcards. Martha sent them either for my birthday or because she was feeling a modicum of guilt for leaving me."

"For what it's worth, you seemed to do all right."

"Better, I think, than if I stayed with her." She stacked those cards to the side. "The one commonality is water—Hawaii, the cruise ship, etcetera. Not unusual—the one thing my mother and I have in common, or that I learned to appreciate from her, was water. I love the ocean, beaches, lakes, bubble baths—give me water and I'm happy."

"I'll keep that in mind," he said with a slight grin.

He was flirting with her. She could ignore it and he would probably stop, but she wasn't certain she wanted to ignore it, not yet anyway. Hadn't cops always been her downfall? She could certainly do worse than Ryan Maguire. At first glance he wasn't her type—hair a little too long, attitude a little too relaxed, attire a bit too casual—but he was smart. She had always been attracted to smart cops. And hair aside, he was attractive. Too attractive.

She hadn't meant to let the silence extend so long as she contemplated her response. She cleared her throat.

"There were sixteen postcards in all," she said. "Seven cards featuring the stolen art you said matched the same MO."

Max showed him the last two postcards. "This is a painting by an Italian artist named Caravaggio. There's one distinct difference between this painting and the other seven."

"It hasn't been stolen."

"Is it true that some thefts aren't reported? For any number of reasons."

"Yes, but a piece like this—I think it would have been."

Max hesitated. "Well, I think it was stolen, but there's another big difference. Two differences, but one you wouldn't know unless I told you, which is that it was post-marked from Paris. But the other difference is the art itself."

Ryan looked at the seven postcards and the last. "It's violent."

She smiled. He did see it. "It's not my mother's style at all. While she might appreciate the art from a talent perspective, she abhorred anything that wasn't whimsical or lively. The Degas is full of light and subtle humor; the Renoir is simply beautiful work. But this Caravaggio is dark and religious. Martha detested religious symbolism in art, considered it patriarchal and conformist."

"Yet it's an incredible masterpiece—Caravaggio's use of light and shadows is original and few artists have come close to capturing his style."

"That's not the question—it's the darkness and the

theme that Martha wouldn't like. What I'm saying is, this painting was stolen. Either she was involved in some way—maybe because she knew the thief—or she simply knew when she saw it that it was a forgery."

Ryan looked at her oddly.

"What?" she asked.

"That's a big leap."

"I said it was a theory. It's like that children's show with the skit 'one of these things is not like the other.' That's this painting."

"When was it sent?"

"The May before she disappeared. From Paris."

"That's seventeen years ago. I wasn't an agent then, but I would have heard if it was missing."

"Maybe they didn't know."

"How?"

"What if the thieves replaced the art?"

"That would be . . . difficult, expensive, and require someone of immense talent."

"And?"

"That's not enough?"

Max waved her hand over the postcards and her notes. "Whoever pulled this off has both money and talent."

"It's not the same MO as the others," Ryan said simply.

"Which is?"

"Each painting was lifted during transport from one exhibit to another. My predecessor determined that at some point between when the paintings were packaged and the transportation company delivered them to the next exhibit or back to their owner, that one or two paintings were replaced with empty boxes. Some of the thefts weren't discovered for weeks or months because the inventory appeared accurate, but the boxes were empty."

"Which also makes it difficult to nail a suspect because you don't have an exact time frame."

"Yes, though we know that the thieves used an inside man."

"You couldn't get anyone to flip?"

"We haven't been able to determine *who* inside. We looked at financials, we interviewed numerous people—particularly the transport companies—and the owners of each painting."

"How are these seven different from the others?"

"That's a good question, and one I've been thinking about since I left here the other night."

Ryan sat down at the table and opened his briefcase. "I have to say it, so don't get mad at me, please. My boss will have my hide if I don't."

"Everything you tell me is off the record."

He grinned, and Max wanted to smile back. Max figured Ryan was forty, or close to it, based on the length of his FBI career and his advanced schooling, but he had a youthful, boyish charm that was contagious.

He took out a laptop and opened it up, typed a long password so fast Max couldn't have stolen it if she tried, and clicked on a folder.

"I couldn't bring my boards—not as extensive as your office, but complete and compact and much easier to store—so I took photos. Plus, I have the file summaries."

"I'm impressed." Max sat next to Ryan as he clicked on two pictures and put them side by side. Each was of a magnetic trifold. One had the seven pieces of art that Martha had sent postcards of to Max, and the other had the remaining eleven pieces.

The differences between the two groups was striking.

"When I saw this, that's when I went to my boss and convinced him to let me talk to you about the case. Use you officially as an expert consultant, just to cover his ass, but he's giving me a lot of leeway."

"Smart man," Max said. She studied the photos.

Though all eighteen paintings that had been stolen were from two distinct periods—Realism and late Impressionism—the seven pieces of art that Martha had been interested in were exactly what Max had said her mother liked. They were beautiful, traditional yet innovative, played with light, and warm, or if dark, they had humor. The other pieces were all extremely traditional or religious. Beautiful, with many exceptional examples of the period, but not cutting edge or standing out for the time. Except for one. A Caravaggio, who was unique both during his time and since. No one had truly emulated his work.

"What are you thinking?" Max asked Ryan. She had some thoughts, but they weren't well formed.

"There's one other clear difference between these paintings." He clicked on another group of photos. The photos had been slightly rearranged. Four were on one side, the rest were on the other. "These four were recovered or we know what happened to them. Jimmy Truman sold the Toulouse-Lautrec and the other three were found in that storage locker, as I said earlier. None of the others have come on the market. The Renoir, the Boudin, and the Degas. They are certainly the more expensive pieces, and those—other than the Toulouse-Lautrec—would be in great demand on the black market."

"You lost me. Why is this important?"

"Art fencing is a very specialized business. It's small, everyone knows everyone else, which is why it's extremely hard to move paintings. Thieves—unless they're hired for a specific job—will sit on pieces for a long time. Often for years. Their goal is to find a private buyer, or move the art out of the country. But until Jimmy sold the Toulouse-Lautrec ten years ago, we had *nothing* on *any* of these pieces. Then, eight years ago, the three in the storage locker practically fell into our laps. We know that Jimmy had that storage locker under the J. J. Sterling alias. It was seized for lack of payment a year after Jimmy sold the Toulouse-Lautrec, the items auctioned off a few months later, and it took the buyer two months before going to the appraiser."

"The same thing happened with Martha's storage under the name Jane Sterling," Max said. "My partner is in Miami investigating that angle. Maybe the other three paintings were in her locker."

"You have a point. I hadn't thought of that. That would be—well, huge. But after all this time whoever bought the contents of the locker would either know they have original art and haven't tried to sell it or they don't realize what they have."

He sounded pained at the prospect. He knew that many priceless works of art had been destroyed or damaged because the people who owned the pieces didn't recognize their value.

"Can you imagine the Degas hanging in someone's guest room?"

"Or over a fireplace. Ugh."

Max contemplated the paintings. "Do you think that Jimmy and Martha stole these seven paintings, rather than your primary suspect? Then sat on them for a few years?"

"Not exactly. The MO is clear and no way I slice it did a different person steal this Degas than this Monet. I'm thinking in a completely different way now. What if they stole the paintings from the thief?"

Max let that sink in. "What on earth for?"

"That's a question for the FBI behavioral scientists," Ryan said. "I just call them as I see them."

"I have someone I could call."

"Is that important?" Ryan didn't seem wholly impressed with criminal psychology. "It's the only thing that makes sense—I might be making a jump here, but come with me. I think we can assume that Jimmy and Martha were together during most of this time."

Max nodded.

"What if she sent you those postcards for a specific reason—namely, she had possession of the actual paintings."

It was something her mother would do—she loved her games.

"What's the time frame? Has your suspect continued?"

"Yes, but he's gotten smarter and taken pieces fewer and farther between. And I suspect—though no one on my team agrees with me at this point—that he changed his MO."

"How so?"

"That I don't know. But most art thieves don't just stop unless they're dead or in prison, and I know my suspect is neither. Maybe because he lost these seven. For example, he stole thirteen pieces in a six-year period, then nothing for four years—then five pieces over the last ten years. Though, nothing is recent. We've also speculated that we don't know about all the pieces. Hence, the change in the MO. That maybe he's found a way to replicate the pieces."

"A forgery."

"Exactly."

"Like the Caravaggio."

He tried to look at her sternly, then laughed out loud. "You made your point. I'll find out about that piece, would that make you happy?"

She smiled. "I learned something else about the art postcards. Most of them are all from the same book. Maybe that book is important? But I can't tell from the card what the fine print means. I searched the internet but came up empty."

"*That* is something I can definitely help with. I'll need to take at least one back with me to Norfolk on Monday."

She nodded, then looked at him oddly. "You're staying all weekend?"

"I wasn't sure how long this was going to take, so I got a room in the hotel. I reserved it under my boss's name because I'm pretty sure Truman has me flagged."

She raised her eyebrow and eyed Ryan carefully. He didn't turn away. In fact, his half smile told him he was going to enjoy this weekend as much as she was.

"You forgot something," she said.

He blinked, confused. "What?"

"The Caravaggio in Paris. Maybe it *was* stolen and my mother knew about it. Who was your other suspect?"

He clicked on his computer and the picture of a very handsome, fiftyish man popped up. "This is the most recent photo I could get of Phillip Colter. It's about five years old. He used to be far more active in the society world, but he's been very reclusive of late. He was on our radar for two reasons: he was the only person to have been photographed at *six* art receptions promoting exhibits that had one or more pieces stolen from it. Not just one city, but cities all over America. My predecessor thought that was far too coincidental, but couldn't get a warrant. He could, however, continue his investigation and learned through his interviews that Colter's primary residence in Dallas, Texas, was filled with masterful reproductions of art from the same era that the thief prefers. Still not enough for a warrant, but enough to keep him on our radar.

"The second primary reason was one I uncovered ten years ago—Colter's name came up when Truman put the Toulouse-Lautrec on the black market. An informant of mine said Colter wanted the piece in the worst way. I didn't understand why, until now."

"You think Jimmy Truman stole it from him."

"I do. And kept it in the storage locker with the others until he needed to sell it for some reason."

"And then Jimmy disappeared," Max said. "Why is this not a murder investigation?"

"We have no body. Colter didn't buy the painting—it was sold to a collector in Russia. We know who has it, but can't get him extradited or the painting returned. That battle is well above my pay grade. But we know that the painting went out through Baltimore; we know Colter was in the area at the time—he's originally from this area— and we know that Jimmy was here, in Cape Haven, for at least three days before he went to Baltimore . . . where he disappeared."

He stared at the painting Jimmy sold to a Russian.

"Half my squad thinks Jimmy left the country," Ryan said. "I don't think he's smart enough to disappear for ten years without a peep. But it's possible."

"I think he's dead," Max said. "And I think Martha is dead, too."

Phillip Colter looked at the photos. With each picture, he grew more angry.

That *bitch*. Not only had she stolen from him, she had bragged about it to her daughter.

Phillip had not known everything about Martha Revere when he first met her. He'd known only that she was the estranged daughter of James and Eleanor Revere, a banking family in California. He knew she lived off her trust fund, so he wasn't overly worried about her sleeping with him for his money. He had learned later that she had a daughter who was being raised by Martha's parents, and for the longest time he chose to believe that Martha had left him not because of his anger, but because of her daughter. It almost made him love her more.

Until he learned that she had betrayed him. She'd seduced him and made him love her and stolen from him, laughing about it with that low-life Jimmy Truman. How they pulled one over on Phillip Colter. How they were smarter than him. Fooled him for years.

One of the pictures crumbled in his hands. Now they were dead and buried, long gone, but not forgotten. Because Phillip was still missing one piece.

Seventeen years ago, when he learned that Martha had made a fool of him, he considered going after her and forcing Martha to return what was his. It didn't take Phillip long to learn that there had been no contact between Martha and her family in years. And he knew enough about the Sterling and Revere families that they wouldn't be party to hiding priceless works of art. He'd walked away from them, considered the seven paintings a loss, until Jimmy Truman put the Toulouse-Lautrec on the market.

He sold one of Phillip's paintings! Sold it as if it were his own. Sold it to a braggart and a foreigner. Took what was Phillip's and degraded it.

He paid for his crime with his life.

Phillip wished he could kill Jimmy Truman all over again.

Yet he still didn't have the Degas.

"Mr. Colter?"

His right hand, Vance DuBois, was right to sound nervous.

"I want this woman. She knows where the Degas is—look at these pictures! She was in on it with Martha."

"If I may?"

Phillip glared at him. "What?"

"She was a child when Martha stole from you. I read the postcards, and her emails—I attached the relevant correspondence to the report—and Martha told her nothing about the paintings or where they are or why they're important. The only reason that reporter is here is because she hired a private investigator and learned that Martha had an alias and her car was abandoned here."

"You don't know that."

"The information was in her emails, sir."

Phillip considered what this all meant. "I need to study these. Keep your eye on her, but don't tip your hand."

"Of course." Vance nodded and walked briskly out of Phillip's home office. He was the only one left in Phillip's circle that he trusted.

Phillip had a lot of studying to do, but he stared at the photo of Maxine Revere.

She looked nothing like her mother. Martha was petite, blond, sparkling. Beautiful, to be sure, but cunning. Shrewd, because she looked nothing like the backstabbing thief that she was.

This woman, Maxine Revere, looked like she could command the world. Serious. Determined. Elegant. Poised. Her eyes—they seemed to be looking right at him. She was downright gorgeous.

Martha had been beautiful as well, but in a completely different way. It was a classic, girl-next-door, effervescent beauty that had completely drawn Phillip in, hook, line, and sinker.

His hand fisted, and the photo of Martha's daughter crumpled.

Martha took many things from him, but the Degas had been his favorite. And he'd only been able to enjoy it for three months before she stole it out from under his nose.

Worse, he hadn't known. She'd made him a fool, flipping the real art with his own perfect forgeries. And he hadn't seen it. He'd slept under that painting every night without knowing. He made love to women believing it was real.

And it was fake. Just like Martha Revere.

He would never have known if his staff hadn't told him the forgeries weren't in his storage locker.

For *two years* she'd fooled him.

She and that pitiful Jimmy Truman had tricked him. Deceived him. Probably laughed over champagne and caviar that he hadn't been able to tell the difference.

But she had known. She knew which were real and which were fake when *no one else* could tell the difference.

He hated her.

*He had loved her.*

Maxine Revere, an investigative reporter no less, would find the Degas. She might not know that she was looking for it, but she would find it. Everything he had learned about this woman over the week, since he'd been informed that she had arrived in Cape Haven, was that she was smart and never gave up.

He wanted the Degas back. And when Maxine Revere found it, he'd take it out of her cold, dead hands.

# Chapter Twenty-one

"I can't believe I missed this."

Max looked up at Ryan. She was tired and crabby from reading and rereading the postcards, rearranging the information and dates every way that she could think. Ryan, on the other hand, seemed to gain energy from the tedious chore.

She was so tired she couldn't even come up with a witty comeback.

"Missed what?" she asked.

"Colter's primary residence is in Dallas, where the Degas was stolen. It was stolen from *this* gallery." He tapped the postcard, which listed the museum. It wasn't even an attractive postcard, one Max had kept shuffling aside because it was so cheap.

"The Degas was stolen from the museum in Dallas?" she asked.

"Yes, at least that was one of the places it was shown. We don't know exactly where it was stolen because it was on a circuit of eight museums across the country. The Dallas museum was the third stop."

"And no one noticed?"

"The fourth stop—Phoenix—had limited space. They only exhibited half the collection. So until it reached San

Francisco, they didn't know the Degas box was empty. We've been looking too broad, it was right under our nose."

"You don't sound happy."

"Because these postcards aren't going to get me a warrant. They might help in a trial, but they're not going to get me what I need first, which is full access to all of Phillip Colter's properties so I can inspect the art."

Max sat up. "Can you tell if something is a forgery?"

"Generally, yes. I have a knack for it. An eye for brushstrokes and subtleties in color and layers that most people don't recognize because they only look at the big picture."

Max was impressed—a rarity.

Ryan winked. "It's why they keep me employed."

"I didn't think it was for your haircut."

"It's regulation," he said.

She laughed. "Is it?"

"Almost."

Max got up and stretched. "I'm starving," Max said. "But I'm trying to play nice with Gabriel Truman for another reason, so maybe we should go someplace else for dinner."

"I'll cook."

"You cook?"

"You surprised?"

"No." She smiled. "Since you're here all weekend, you can cook tomorrow. How about if you join me for dinner over by Oyster Bay?"

"I didn't know there was a restaurant over there."

"It's called the Hendersons' kitchen, and they invited me. I'll call and say I have a guest. And then on our way I'll show you something else of interest and get your take on it." She picked up the last postcard her mother had sent. "I think I found exactly where this was painted, and I want to check it out."

"By all means, let's go."

Max and Ryan had to park on a gravel road and walk over sand dunes and through tall grass a quarter-mile to the spot Max located. As soon as they arrived, she knew she had been right.

She showed him the postcard. It was a painting of the inlet on the eastern coast, with a pristine beach, clear skies, and sparkling water. To the side was a dilapidated fence and a small building, a historical marker proclaiming it was the one-room cabin that a governor two hundred some years ago had been born in. How it had withstood time and weather, Max didn't know, maybe it had been rebuilt. But the scene was breathtaking in its simplicity, beauty, and loneliness.

"This was the last card your mother sent," Ryan said. The wind whipped around both of them. It was growing colder, but the skies were still clear.

"If we assume, and I think we should, that she sent the postcards of the stolen art to me for a reason—even if it was her own personal game—then she sent this to me for a reason as well. Her car was found only a few miles north of here."

"How are you doing? Really?"

"I don't understand."

"You think your mother is dead, Max. And you're investigating this as if she's just another cold case."

How did she respond to that?

"I have to," she said simply. "I personalized my mother's actions for far too long—if I don't distance myself, I won't see things clearly."

She looked around. "Why this place?" she said, mostly

to herself. "On Monday I'll go back to the county offices and find out who owns this land."

"Smart."

She slowly turned in a circle, then stopped. Stared. Was it this easy?

Ryan put his hand on her shoulder and she jumped.

"I'm sorry," he said.

"This is it." She pointed to the property to the north. She could only see the roofline of the Boreal-owned mansion, but she would recognize it from any angle.

"That house?"

"Boreal, Inc., owns that peninsula."

"Don't know that I'd call it a peninsula, but okay."

"It's a hundred acres jutting out into Oyster Bay. It's one of three properties that's accessible from the road where Martha's car was found."

"Not a coincidence?"

"No. Boreal owns fifty percent of Havenly. When I was going through Truman and Cooper's public financial statements, I found the name. Boreal, Inc., invested a small amount when Cooper bought the place seventeen years ago. Gabriel came on board a year later, and then ten years ago Boreal invested heavily in the renovation and expansion of the resort."

"Ten years ago, when Jimmy Truman was here," Ryan said thoughtfully.

"They've owned the property for much longer—long before Martha disappeared," Max said. "I've asked my PI to look into any principals of the company, but I'm not his only client right now and all I've found is the law firm who manages the business. They invest in tech companies and are worth a substantial sum."

"But what does it mean? If it's not a coincidence that your mother sent you this specific postcard, does it have something to do with Boreal? Or that house? Or some-thing else?"

"I don't know," Max admitted. "Yet."

But she wasn't leaving Cape Haven until she figured it out.

They walked back to the car in silence. When Max slid into the passenger seat, she pulled out her phone and started typing a message.

"I'm going to ask a friend of mine to consult."

"What kind of consult?"

"A shrink. Forensic psychiatrist. He's private, but often consults for the FBI and is hired as an expert witness. I met him on the Blair Caldwell trial."

*Dillon,*
*Back in February you offered your expertise when*
*I seriously started to investigate my mother's*
*disappearance. I'm in Cape Haven, and I'm not*
*leaving until I find answers. I could use your brain*
*on this, if you have time to conference tomorrow*
*with me and an FBI agent who's investigating*
*Martha's old boyfriend. If you can, I'll forward*
*you what I've learned.*
*Best, Maxine*

Ryan said, "And we need a shrink why?"

"Because I don't understand Martha. The postcards, the art theft, coming here, and then just disappearing off the face of the earth. But mostly, I think she was sending me bread crumbs. What other explanation is there for the postcards with specific stolen pieces of art? Of this"— she waved her hand in the direction of the beach—"exact scene? One reason I'm so good at my job is because I con-sult with experts when I need to. Dillon Kincaid is one of the smartest people I know and he's familiar with what I'm doing. His brother-in-law is my private investigator."

"You sound like I was going to argue with you."

"Most people do."

"I was just curious. Sounds like a good plan to me." He leaned over and for a split second she thought he was going to kiss her. She wasn't sure what she would think about that. Then he smiled and said, "Don't get so defensive. Sometimes a question is really just a question."

He started the car and headed toward the Hendersons'.

# Chapter Twenty-two

Max and Ryan arrived at the Henderson house at five thirty. There were several older teenagers and young adults playing football in the driveway, and Gary Henderson and three young men were bringing a huge pig around to the back of the house on a piece of plywood.

Max brought Ryan into the house and introduced him to Beth, who was in the kitchen. Organized chaos was the only phrase that came to mind.

"I'm so glad you could make it, Ryan," Beth said with a grin.

"Let me help you with that." Ryan took a large earthenware bowl filled with foil-wrapped potatoes from her.

"You're a doll, just put it over there—the rest of the potatoes have another fifteen minutes or so."

Ryan put it down on a long, low table that already seemed overwhelmed with food.

"You're feeding an army," Ryan said.

"My brood feels like that sometimes, though only half of them are here. And friends, of course."

Beth put Max to work chopping vegetables for the salad, and grabbed a young teen as he passed through. "Jeremy, take Agent Maguire to the basement and help him bring up the ice chest. It's heavy, I don't know what

Wyatt was thinking filling up the water and soda in the basement."

"Yes, Grams," Jeremy said.

"I didn't know you had grandchildren," Max said.

"My goodness, yes. Seven. Jeremy is twelve, the oldest of the young ones, and the only one I get to see with any regularity—my daughter Bridget moved to Boston with her husband and has two daughters, Garth married last year and just had a baby boy, but they live in campus housing. His wife is also in grad school. And then my oldest, Maddie—she's twins with Jeremy's mother—has three kids, and they moved all the way to Arizona. The desert!" She said it as if her daughter had moved to the moon. "Fortunately, Garth and Grace will be moving home when they graduate this summer, and I can dote on that precious baby."

Max wondered what it would be like to be part of a large family. The Hendersons seemed to be a throwback to a simpler time, though their farm was run with the efficiency of the twenty-first century. She had never seriously considered having children—and eight was out of the question—but the clear joy that Beth had was directly related to her kids and grandkids. She loved running this house, which was a full-time job.

There was grunting coming from the basement stairs as Jeremy and Ryan half-carried, half-dragged up a huge ice chest.

A timer went off and Beth moved around to one of two ovens and pulled out two casseroles. Max had no idea what was in them, but they looked cheesy and yummy. Probably thousands of calories, but she didn't care—when was the last time she'd had a meal like this? She cooked for herself on occasion when she was home, but it certainly wasn't this impressive.

Ryan was joking with Jeremy as they wheeled the ice

chest outside. As Ryan backed out the door he winked at Max. He had a big grin on his face, and she imagined that his upbringing had been closer to the Hendersons' than Max's.

"I hope you don't mind that I brought Ryan with me."

Beth waved off her comment before Max even finished talking. "As if you couldn't tell, I love company. And an FBI agent—that's interesting." She raised an eyebrow.

"He's helping me investigate my mother's disappearance."

"So you've made progress."

"Some. I still have questions." A lot of questions. It was as if each answer she'd found led to even *more* questions. Her mother was an art thief. Why? Where was the art? Why had she sent Max postcards of the stolen pieces? Her mother had another daughter. Who was Eve's father? Why didn't Martha tell someone in the family about Eve? And then, of course, the big one: If Martha was in the danger she obviously was in—and she had to know because she left Eve with Emily Truman—why hadn't she contacted her family who had money and connections all over the country?

No matter what Martha had done to the family, and while Eleanor would never forgive her, she would have done *anything* to help. Because to Eleanor Revere, family was the single most important thing.

Maybe Eleanor had something in common with Beth Henderson after all.

Molly ran in with another girl. "Pig is ready! Dad says bring the food out so Grandpop can say a blessing."

"Well, get started carrying the bowls and whatnot. Max," Beth said, "grab that salad bowl, will you?" Beth stuffed three bottles of dressing into her apron pocket and picked up the casserole with an oven mitt, while Molly and her friend carried out potatoes and rolls. It took them only two trips because the second time through, three other people came to help.

Max stepped outside and stood in the back. Thirty people were gathered around the the large back deck. The pig smelled delicious—she had never had a roast pig like this before.

Garrett Henderson said a quick blessing, thanking God for the food raised and grown by the good people of Northampton County, and cooked by his daughter-in-law Beth and son Gary. "The greatest blessing I have received in life is my family, and I hope to never take you all for granted. And to Wyatt, my youngest grandson, who is nineteen today, happy birthday. Now, let's eat."

Ryan came up to Max and whispered in her ear, "I'm glad we came. Don't look so uncomfortable."

"I'm not." Did she really look that awkward? "I like it out here."

"You stand like you're on the outside looking in, Max. They love you here."

"I like them. A lot."

Ryan tensed next to her, and she looked over to where he was staring. Gabriel Truman was standing off to the side, talking to two other men, and apparently both he and Ryan had seen each other at the same time.

"He'd better not cause a scene," Ryan said.

"He won't," Max said, though she wasn't a hundred percent confident.

She looked around and saw Eve standing in the food line with Jason from her sailing club. Eve was looking right at her, frozen, until Jason nudged her and she almost tripped.

"She knows," Max said to Ryan.

"Who?"

"Eve Truman. That she's my sister."

"Sister?"

"I would have told you—it just didn't come up." Maybe she hadn't wanted to talk about it at all, not until she had all the answers. But now that Ryan knew, she didn't intend to keep it from him.

"Gabriel Truman and your mother?"

"I don't honestly know. I think Jimmy's her father, but she doesn't know—she believes it's Gabriel. I'm certainly not going to tell her different—Gabriel has to do that. But either she found out that I'm her sister—maybe through my name alone—or he told her. I just wasn't certain he would do it."

"You have a lot of explaining to do," Ryan said.

"I will later. Let's get some food, then I want to talk to Eve."

She had almost lost her appetite in anticipation.

An hour later, Max found Eve sitting on the front porch swing while most everyone else was still around back. Max asked, "May I sit here?"

Eve nodded. She looked confused, like she didn't know what to say.

"I don't want to make you uncomfortable," Max said. *She* was nervous, and she rarely felt so out of sorts, so this sixteen-year-old had to be anxious as well.

"I'm not," Eve said quickly.

"Is Eve short for Genevieve?" Max asked.

"Yes."

"Our great-grandmother was Genevieve Sterling. She lived a long life, died when I was twenty-one. Really amazing woman. My middle name is Genevieve. It's a mouthful, but I'm proud of it."

She was rambling.

"I'll tell you anything you want to know," Max said.

"I . . . I don't know. My dad—he said it was okay that we talk, but I know he's not really okay with it. Does that make sense?"

"Yes. My arrival threw him for a loop. I didn't know what to expect when I came here, but I didn't expect to find a sister. I'm very happy I did."

"Dad said you think your mother—our mother—disappeared in Oyster Bay."

"I do. I'm generally a blunt person, but this experience—learning that I have a sister—makes me question some of my natural inclinations."

Eve squinched up her nose in confusion. "I don't understand."

"I want to be honest—I'm not someone who talks around things. But I guess I'm walking on eggshells here, and that puts me out of my element." That was an understatement.

Eve glanced at her, then looked away, biting her lip. "I just want to know what's going on. Who my mother was, why she left—I guess she's never coming back?" Doubt and hope all in one baleful tone.

"No, she's not. I believe she's dead. I'm sorry you have to hear that, but better you know it now than to harbor false hope."

"It's sort of easier, I guess—knowing she died, that she didn't just leave me because she didn't want me."

Max's heart twisted. She knew exactly what Eve meant, and it hit her—harder than she expected. Martha had left Max because she didn't want her. And while Max was now thirty-two, and far more self-aware than most people, she would never forget her ten-year-old self, anticipating her mother's return, only to be disappointed every day. Then, every postcard that arrived gave her new hope, only to be destroyed when her mother never called or returned.

It was difficult to reconcile her feelings then with her feelings now. She was better off being raised by her grandparents. She *knew* that, both in her mind and her heart, but the child she'd been was still inside—deeply buried—remembering being abandoned not just at her grandparents, but unwanted long before. The times Martha left her with strangers who didn't want her just so she could go on a "vacation." The times Martha left her alone "just for a little while" that turned into days. When Max begged her mother to take her to Disney World, only to be left at the park for the entire day alone because her mother didn't want to go. Watching families and friends enjoy the amusement part together, creating memories.

Max had never gone to an amusement park again.

"Did I say something wrong?" Eve asked in a quiet voice.

"No, of course not."

"What was she like?"

What did she tell her? Max didn't coddle people. She never had. And she wasn't going to start now.

"I'm still trying to understand her," Max said.

"I read your website. All about your show and your books and what you do. You wrote in your biography that your mom—our mom—left you with your grandparents when you were ten."

"The Thanksgiving before my tenth birthday."

"When's your birthday?"

"December thirty-first." If her mother had told her the truth.

"I'm January twelfth."

"We're sixteen years and two weeks apart," Max said.

"She didn't tell anyone about me? In your family?"

"No. But you were a baby when she disappeared."

"I don't know what happened—I don't think my dad likes her very much."

"Martha was smart, she was worldly, she loved the finer things in life. Especially travel, art museums, good wine. She was manipulative and truly thought she was better than everyone else. No one is all bad or all good, except for maybe Beth Henderson," Max said with a smile.

"Everyone loves Molly's mom."

"Martha was the polar opposite of Beth."

"Do you miss her?"

"I did. Not anymore. She lied to me, Eve, about important things, and I've found it very difficult to muster any forgiveness."

"I'm sorry."

"Don't say that—you have nothing to be sorry for. Nothing, okay?"

"Okay." Eve sighed. It was almost dark out, the sun having gone down, but the lights of the house shined bright, and laughter from the back reminded Max that they weren't really alone.

"I don't have any pictures of her," Eve said suddenly.

"I don't, either."

"Really?" she was surprised. "None?"

"All the pictures of my mother are from when she was younger. My grandmother had them. Martha never shied away from a camera, but back then we didn't have cell phones that could take pictures."

"Why do you call her Martha?"

"Because she doesn't feel like my mother." Max looked out into the dark, beyond the porch. Blocked out the sounds and tried to understand, but realized she might never truly understand Martha. She could, however, understand herself and how Martha's choices—how her life—had created Max. "Martha Revere was wild. She wanted to have fun. She lived off her trust fund and traveled the world because she wanted to. The excitement? The thrill? I don't know. She had me when she was twenty-one and then continued with her jet-setting ways. I didn't go to school at all until I lived with my grandparents."

"Could she do that?"

"Martha would say she could do anything she wanted."

"Was she pretty?"

Max took out her phone. She had her mother's senior picture saved. She'd only scanned it recently, to send to her private investigator to run against Jane Does who might have been found. Rogan had age-enhancing software as well, but Max didn't show Eve those pictures.

She turned her phone to Eve. "This was her senior portrait."

Eve took the phone and looked at it. What did she see? Someone like her? Eve looked far more like Martha than Max did. If Max didn't have her grandmother's eyes, she would have doubted she was even Martha's daughter. But there were some similarities. Their cheekbones, the shape of their face, basic facial features. Eve had Max's eyes—which were different than Martha's—but her hair, her nose, her stature was all their mother.

"She's pretty. Really pretty."

"She was. You look like her. Except you have the Sterling eyes."

"Sterling?"

"Our great-grandmother, and our grandmother, have the same dark blue eyes and the same shape—not quite almond, but not round." Max brought up a picture of Eleanor. "Here's Eleanor."

"You call her Eleanor?"

"Half the time. My great-grandmother wanted everyone to call her Genie, no matter what."

Eve took a deep breath, handed Max her phone back. "Would you send me the pictures?"

"Yes. And maybe someday, I can take you to California to meet everyone."

Eve looked panicked.

"Yeah, if I were in your shoes, it wouldn't sound like fun. And our family is . . . I can't even put it into words."

"What if they hate me?"

"Let me tell you one thing: Eleanor will never hate you. She doesn't know how to show love and affection, but you are blood, and to her that means everything. She's not getting any younger—she'll be eighty in the fall. Maybe that would be a good time to come out, she'll have a big birthday party. I love Eleanor, even though she is difficult and judgmental and stubborn and does things I'll never understand. But she took me in, no questions asked, when Martha left me. She never made me feel unwanted. Now, the other family members—some will welcome you, some will shun you, some will doubt you. I'll have a DNA test done to confirm, but there is no doubt in my mind and my heart that you are my sister. I promise you, Eve—I will protect you. I never thought I'd ever have a sister. I'm thirty-two—how would that even be possible? And now I do, and I hope you give me a chance to really get to know you."

Eve took her hand. The simple gesture brought tears to Max's eyes. She blinked them back.

Eve smiled. "I'd like that."

Max found Ryan talking to a small group of young men about a case of his. She only caught the punch line.

"And they say white-collar crimes are boring."

The others laughed, and Ryan was grinning. He was clearly in his element, and when he looked at Max he smiled in a way that had her thinking of him as something more than a FBI agent.

"Well, my ride looks like she's ready to leave."

"You're not staying for cake?" Wyatt asked.

Max needed to get away from people. The conversation with Eve had drained her, and she wasn't in a social mood.

"Happy birthday, Wyatt. Be good to your mom."

"She's the best," he said honestly.

Ryan walked Max through the house, where they said their good-byes and thanks.

Beth came over with a large disposable plastic bowl. "Here's some pork for sandwiches tomorrow. Slice a bit of apple on top, and it's really good."

Ryan took the bowl happily. "Thank you. Everything was delicious."

"Glad you could join us. Nice to know we have good folk in our local FBI. Are you from here?"

"Iowa."

"I have an aunt in Madison County."

"Hop, skip, and a jump from Des Moines where I was raised."

Evidently that satisfied or impressed Beth.

"Max, please come back before you leave town. You are welcome anytime."

"Thank you." She didn't know why she was suddenly on the verge of tears. She'd met a lot of people in her line of work, though most were victims or victims' families. Why was she so weepy being around the down-to-earth Hendersons?

It wasn't that—it was Eve, and the complex, surprisingly deep emotions she had during their conversation. She felt raw and exposed.

She and Ryan walked out to his car. Gabriel had been waiting for them at the bottom of the porch stairs. He glared at Ryan.

"Gabriel, truce," Max said.

"Why did you bring the cops? What did you tell Eve?"

"Ask Eve. I answered her questions."

"Like what?"

"What you expect. Why did my mother abandon me? Who was she? What did she look like? Those questions." She was trying not to get angry at Gabriel. "I didn't tell her that I don't think you're her father, if that's what you think."

"Shut. *Up.*"

"I think we need to talk, Gabriel—you, me, and Ryan." Ryan cleared his throat.

"I'm serious, Ryan," she said. "We all have information, and we need to share it in order to find out what happened to Martha, what happened to Jimmy, and what happened to—" She stopped herself. She wasn't going to betray Ryan's confidence, not now.

"What?" Gabriel demanded.

Ryan said, "Martha Revere and Jimmy Truman are suspected of stealing a minimum of seven, and possibly up to nearly two dozen, works of art, many virtually priceless. This isn't public—Jimmy's name has been part of my investigation since I first talked to you ten years ago, but only because of information Max had was I able to make great inroads this week."

"Art?" Gabriel almost laughed. "My brother had no expertise in *art*. Theft, sure."

"Martha was the expert," Max said. "Let's talk tomorrow at my cottage. I think it would help everyone."

"Eve has a race tomorrow. I'll think about it. But I need to know, what is going to happen now?"

"I'm going to have a DNA test done, with Eve's permission, to confirm that she is my sister. I know she is, but having the scientific evidence will help ensure that she receives her trust allowance."

"I don't care about that."

"I know you don't. But it'll pay for her college, wherever she wants to go. And beyond that? Well, I just want to get to know her. Gabriel, you've done a great job with her. She's beautiful, she's healthy, she's happy. I'm not going to get between you two. But you need to be honest with her."

"I am."

"No, you're not. I didn't tell her I think Jimmy is her father, and I won't volunteer it. But if she asks me, I'm not going to lie."

"You don't know what you're doing. This isn't your secret to tell."

"Eve is my sister and I care about her. But right now we need to find out what happened to Martha and what happened to your brother."

"Let them both rot in hell," Gabriel said through clenched teeth.

"I wish it were that easy," Max said. She looked at Ryan. Almost pleaded with him to give Gabriel something more.

Ryan said, "Over the course of my investigation, which I took over from a retired agent, I believe that there is a third party involved. And he's still out there."

"Who?"

Ryan was clearly uncomfortable discussing it. "I don't have a warrant, I don't have proof, and I really don't want this information getting out."

Gabriel stared at him. "Ten years ago you came here and asked me about my brother and wouldn't give me shit, so I have a hard time trusting you."

"And I have a hard time trusting you, Truman, because you lied to me."

"I didn't."

"I don't believe that you didn't see your brother ten years ago. He was here for at least three days and stayed at the resort you co-own. So yeah, I think you knew. Maybe you didn't help him, maybe you didn't help him get away, but you knew he was here."

Gabriel didn't say anything for a moment, then said, "I'm not going to admit to anything—but hypothetically, if the brother you hadn't seen in years, who didn't even show up for his mother's funeral, stopped by and said he was taking the girl you raised as your own to family she didn't know because she was an heiress and worth a fortune, then that brother disappeared into thin air—you can see how you might think *you'd* be a suspect."

Max was stunned. She hadn't expected that revelation. Yeah, she could see how the police would think that he had something to do with his brother's disappearance—though not for the reasons they might have initially thought. Fathers often did desperate things to protect their children. She suddenly had a new impression of Gabriel. Whether he killed Jimmy or not didn't really factor into it, though she didn't think he had. He didn't seem to be violent. Angry, maybe, but if he killed Jimmy, Max didn't think that he would have been able to live with himself.

"What happened, Gabriel? Off the record, I won't use it against you," Ryan said. "Having this conversation could get me fired, especially if I'm wrong about you, but it also might help me find out what happened to him."

Gabriel took a deep breath, and in a low voice said, "It was Eve's sixth birthday. January twelfth, a Friday, which is why I remember it so clearly. I didn't know he was staying at the resort until he told me. Brian Cooper, my partner, knew I was angry with Jimmy for not coming to see our mom before she died, a few months earlier. I reached out to him, begged him to give her peace and he said he couldn't. She was dying for three months and he couldn't spare one day."

His fists were tight, as if he wanted to hit his brother.

"So when he showed up, I was angry but also worried. He told me to tell Eve I wasn't her father and that he was taking her to California because she was worth millions. I wanted to kill him—I shouldn't admit that, except that I *didn't* kill him. I couldn't sleep or eat all weekend, waiting for him to return. He never did. Then you came asking questions and I decided to keep my mouth shut. I had motive—he was going to take my daughter. I don't care that I'm not her biological father, she's my daughter. I raised Eve since she was eight months old after she was abandoned by her mother. When I finally talked to Jimmy a year later, asked him what was going on and where Martha was, he said he thought she was dead because she screwed over the wrong person, and he was keeping a low profile. Told me he didn't care about Eve, that she was better off with me and our mother. I agreed, and didn't talk to him again until he showed up when Eve was six."

He looked from Max to Ryan. "Would you have done anything different?"

"I wouldn't have lied to a federal agent, but other than that, probably not," Ryan said. "Jimmy was on our radar because he was looking to sell a painting that had been on our docket for years—stolen, but then silence. No one looking to buy or sell it. Then years later we get chatter about it. We tracked the buyer—a Russian—when he came into this country through Baltimore. It was extremely difficult to pinpoint the exchange, but we know that on January thirteenth—the day after you talked to your brother—the Russian left the country. We confirmed through intelligence sources that he has the painting in question. But we didn't have this information until it was too late to stop him."

"And then what happened to Jimmy?" Gabriel asked. "If he sold the painting, he wouldn't need Eve. Is that why he didn't come back for her?"

"Maybe. The painting was insured for ten million dollars but Truman received only seven hundred thousand cash. More than enough to disappear."

Max said, "Eve is worth substantially more. He may have wanted a larger cushion."

Ryan nodded. "We never found his body or the money. For a time, my team thought he took on a fake identity and left the country through New York, but I was always skeptical. We had no tangible proof, not even a security video—and I scoured tapes from airports and ports for weeks. I still have the recordings, look at them from time to time. Maybe he left through another airport or drove across the border. But, I think he's dead."

"Good. Then he can't hurt my daughter."

Ryan continued, "He had a storage locker with three other stolen paintings. I suspect he intended to sell off the others. But the storage locker went into default, and eventually through a series of events, the FBI was able to recover the three pieces. There are still three more out there, and we now think that Martha Revere may have had them."

"So Martha had the paintings . . . and where did she go? You think she's dead."

"I *know* she's dead, but I can't prove it," Max said.

Ryan continued. "We're not quite sure how Martha and Jimmy hooked up with this man, Phillip Colter, but it's clear that they must have stolen several of his paintings. I use 'his paintings' lightly, because he's been on our radar as an art thief for nineteen years. We just don't have enough evidence to get a warrant to authenticate the art in his homes. It's circumstantial evidence based on his travel and when art was stolen. Colter is originally from Northampton—older than your brother, you may not have known him—and it could be that he figured out that Jimmy was behind the thefts. Remembered him, researched him, I don't know. He doesn't have a history of violence, but then again, maybe no one has stolen from him before. There are still missing paintings, and if Colter thinks you, or your daughter, or Max might have a clue as to where they are, that puts you all in danger."

Gabriel looked from Ryan to Max with a shocked and worried expression. "All because you came here."

"My mother's car was found here."

"You should never have come, Maxine. If Eve is in danger, it's all on you."

He walked away.

And Max stood there, stunned.

Gabriel Truman was right.

# Chapter Twenty-three

Max and Ryan stopped at the resort bar for a drink. Max needed to unwind—there was too much going on inside, and she wasn't used to so much emotion in her life. Eve, Gabriel, she could handle the emotions of other people. But her own? They were making her jumpy.

"Don't let Gabriel get to you," Ryan said after they sat in silence for several minutes after their drinks arrived.

"He's right."

"No, he's a father and he's worried, and said what he thought would get you to back away."

"Maybe."

"I wish you'd told me about Eve earlier."

"I found out yesterday. When you came I was so focused on the art and what Martha and Jimmy were up to—I didn't think about it. But yes, I should have mentioned it."

"How did the conversation with Eve go?"

"Good. I don't know what I expected, to be honest, but Eve is grounded. She was interested in me, in Martha, even a bit in the family. And relieved, I think."

"Relieved?"

"She never knew Martha—she thought her mother

abandoned her. Knowing that she was dead and that's why she didn't return was a relief."

Ryan stared at her. "Not for you."

"I'm a big girl, Ryan."

He ran his fingers over her hand. A very subtle, but surprisingly intimate gesture. Then he withdrew, and she didn't know if she should read anything into it.

Or maybe she would. Maybe she needed a distraction from everything that she'd learned. A way to cleanse her mind, so to speak, so she could refocus her energy into learning the truth about Martha, Jimmy, and the paintings.

Suddenly Ryan tensed. Max was about to ask him what he was thinking, when he said in a low voice, "You have stirred up something big, Ms. Revere. That man cannot keep his eyes off of you."

She didn't know which man he referred to, and asked with a smile, "Jealous?"

He seemed surprised, then leaned closer. "I'm not the jealous type, and you don't seem to be a woman who two-times your lovers."

She was about to come back with an equally sexual comment, when Ryan continued. "Don't look. Phillip Colter is having dinner in this restaurant, at the booth in the corner of the dining room. That was the last thing I expected to see when we walked in here."

"Your suspect? Does he know who you are?"

"I don't know. I haven't interviewed him, or had reason to get in his face, but if I were a successful art thief, I would make it my business to know local FBI agents who might be investigating my activities. However, he appears more interested in you—and I don't think it's for the same reason I'm interested."

Though his words were playful, Ryan's tone had taken on an edge, and he hadn't finished his scotch. Max had been around enough cops to know that Ryan had gone from all-play to all-work in a heartbeat.

"I would think Gabriel had something to do with alerting him but we only told him about Colter less than an hour ago."

"I've been asking a lot of questions about my mother since last week. I made calls before then. I've talked to a lot of people. Anyone could have tipped him off." Max didn't like being a pawn, or being under the eye of anyone, cop or criminal. "Let me rattle his cage."

"I don't know—" Ryan began, but Max was already out of her seat.

"Stay put." She picked up her wineglass, crossed the bar, and walked over to where Colter was dining with another man. She recognized Colter from the photo Ryan showed her earlier, though he was older. He was still attractive, in the way that Paul Newman seemed to keep his good looks even as he aged. Colter was in his late fifties and dressed impeccably, even in what was clearly his "casual" attire of pressed slacks, crisp button-down sans tie, and pricey watch.

Colter watched her all the way over, not giving away anything in his expression—whether he was expecting it or whether he was completely surprised.

"Mr. Colter," she said. "I'm Maxine Revere. May I join you?"

"I would never say no to someone as lovely as you."

"Thank you." She pulled a chair over from a vacant table and sat. Sipped her wine, placed the glass down. She smiled at Colter's associate—taller, broader, younger than Colter. A bodyguard? Hired muscle?

"How do you know me?" Colter said.

"I believe you knew my mother. Martha Revere."

"I did, once upon a time."

Incredible. Colter knew exactly who she was from the beginning. He still showed no sign of surprise.

"I never knew Martha had a child," he continued.

"Most people didn't."

But he did know—maybe not at the time he associated with Martha, but he knew who Max was before he walked into the restaurant. That he lied to her was telling—he wanted information and felt that if he pretended he was in the dark that she would give it to him.

"She kept in touch over the years," Max continued. "Sent me postcards from all over the world. One from Paris nearly seventeen years ago from the time she spent at Le Meurice."

Now she had him. Colter couldn't keep the flash of anger from darkening his pale blue eyes.

"Did she now?"

"You were quite taken by Caravaggio's *The Beheading of Saint John the Baptist,* I believe it was. I'd have to dig through my archives to remember correctly."

"Your memory is just fine," Colter's jaw was tight, his eyes never leaving her.

"I take it you and Martha didn't part on the best of terms. Don't feel bad about that; she tended to burn many bridges."

"I loved her once," he said.

Max hadn't expected that confession. She drained her wine and changed the subject. "Are you on vacation?"

"Business," he said. "And you?"

"Personal." She considered pushing him even further, but right now he'd already given her two truths that would get her far, and she didn't want to tip her hand.

If she was right and Phillip Colter had killed her mother, or had her killed, he might react violently. Not here, not now, but Max wasn't an idiot. Colter was power personified, and he hated her mother.

"I'll get you another wine and we can reminisce."

Max glanced over at Ryan. "I think my boyfriend

would be jealous if I spent any more time in your company."

Colter looked over at Ryan but didn't show any recognition or interest in who he was. Still, she couldn't be sure he didn't know Ryan was an FBI agent. If he didn't know, he would certainly investigate him when they left.

"How long are you staying?"

"Uncertain. You?"

He paused a beat. "As long as I need to finish my business."

"Perhaps we can have lunch this week. Maybe you can give me some insight into my mother."

"I don't know that anyone, child or lover, could understand what made Martha Revere tick."

Max had to agree. She slid over her business card. "Call me if you want to talk."

He stared at the card. "I've seen your show."

"I suspected you had, the way you were looking at me in the bar."

"Your boyfriend is jealous. Possessive."

She was about to say "he's not my boyfriend," but she'd already used Ryan as a crutch. "If he is, he won't last very long."

"Expect my call." He slipped her card into his breast pocket.

Ryan was silent all the way back to Max's cottage. She told him everything she had learned.

"He knows she's dead," she said, waiting for Ryan to say something. "He didn't even ask me about her. He said he loved her, and that may have been true for about five minutes." Still nothing. "He confirmed that they were in Paris together, and he absolutely remembered the Caravaggio. I remember museums, but off the top of my head a painting I hadn't seen in seventeen years? Nope."

They walked inside and immediately Ryan said, "I cannot believe you pushed him."

"I know how to push people's buttons. I only caressed his."

"You're impossible." He walked upstairs.

She followed, irritated. "He never asked how she was, where she was living, *nothing*. He knows she's dead. I must have talked to the right people and they alerted him that I was asking questions. Was it the caretaker? Detective Lipsky? The sheriff? Or maybe—"

"Exactly!" Ryan exclaimed. "He knows you're here to find out what happened to Martha. But if we're right and Martha and Jimmy stole those seven paintings from him, he would want them back, don't you think?"

"He doesn't know you're an FBI agent, though he'll probably figure it out soon."

"Maybe you don't read people as well as you think."

"What is your problem, Ryan?"

"You put a bull's-eye on your back."

"He has no reason to come after me. I don't know where the last three paintings are, if they are anywhere."

"You really think that."

She was confused again. She hadn't drunk that much, she should be able to figure out what Ryan actually meant. Unless he was being intentionally vague to annoy her.

"Spill it, Maguire."

He waved his hand at the postcards on her table. "*This*. Your mother sent you clues. It's the only explanation I can come up with as to why she sent you these specific postcards of these specific paintings. Once we figure out the pattern, I think we'll find the missing paintings. And that Caravaggio—that may just be the proof that Colter was behind all these other thefts. My boss is already in contact with the authorities to track down the painting and have it authenticated. If it's a fake, it could be there's proof that Colter took it."

"Great. And if there are clues here, we should sit down and look at them from a different perspective. Postmarks, word choice—we're two smart people, we'll find answers."

"Don't be obtuse."

She glared at him. "Don't be insulting."

Slowly, Ryan said, "If Colter thinks you'll find your mother's body or dig deep enough to connect him to anything illegal, what do you think he'll do to you?"

"Do not talk to me like I'm a child," she said, equally slowly.

"Stop acting like one."

"You can go."

"No, I can't."

She raised an eyebrow. "First you berate me, insult me, threaten me?"

"Impossible." He took a deep breath. "Your idea was brilliant but your execution was flawed."

"I got the exact information that I wanted to confirm."

"And you put yourself on Colter's radar. You're here in this cottage, the farthest from the hotel, where if he came for you, even if you called for help, no one would get here for at least five minutes. And that cute little Taser of yours isn't going to trump a gun."

"He has no reason to come for me."

"Now he does! Because while you confirmed that he knew your mother, that he was in Paris with her, that he was infatuated with the Caravaggio, and that he knows she's dead—though that's a bit of an assumption—I have no cause for a warrant, no evidence to expand the investigation, and now I have to worry that he's going to come for you."

"But he has no reason!" she repeated, frustrated.

"You invited him to lunch!"

"A public lunch—really, are you always this paranoid?"

He stared at her. "What if he killed your mother? What if he thinks you know where the paintings are? He's here because *you* have been asking questions. There's no other reason for him to be back."

"I've been thinking since we talked to Gabriel—it's just too big of a coincidence that my mother disappears here, Colter is from here, we suspect but can't prove that she stole from him—what if she planned on meeting him here? What if she gave him the paintings to get back into his good graces, or at least not get herself killed."

"But she *did* get killed. And if he had the paintings, why would he be here now? He would know that the FBI recovered three of the seven, and that one is in Russia."

"He shows up today after I started investigating Boreal," Max said. "Yesterday I called the attorney of record for information on the CEO and got nowhere, not even past her assistant. I talked to the caretaker yesterday as well. I think Colter is part of Boreal. It would make sense."

"The company you're researching? It's not on his tax returns. And no, before you ask, I can't show them to you."

"But you can look at his income and maybe his income comes from a company affiliated with Boreal."

Ryan smiled, the tension suddenly leaving his body. "You know, you're pretty smart for a reporter."

"Is that your way of apologizing?"

"Apologizing for what? Pointing out how you put yourself in danger? Highlighting that you're playing games with a suspected art thief and possible killer?"

"I'm not playing games—I was blunt and honest with him, and will continue to be, without giving away your investigation. And second, this won't be the first time

I'm potentially in danger." She blew out a long breath. "Though I guess I'm going to have to call in David."

"David? Boyfriend?"

"Bodyguard."

"Bodyguard?" He looked perplexed.

"Long story short—my producer hired David Kane nearly three years ago when there was a threat against me while I was covering a trial in Chicago. He stuck around. He's smart for hired muscle. Became my assistant."

"So I repeat, boyfriend?"

"No."

"Good."

"Why?"

"Because I really, really want to kiss you."

Heat flared in her stomach from sudden anticipation. These were no tame butterflies.

"Why haven't you?"

He took a step forward. "Because if I kiss you, I will take you to bed."

Max stepped forward, looked Ryan in the eyes, and kissed him.

There was no denying their mutual physical attraction at that point, because if Ryan felt even half the lust she did after one hot kiss, they were both going to be very, very satisfied.

His arms went around her waist and he pulled her close, returning the kiss with equal intensity. He didn't rush; he kissed with the confidence of a man who knew exactly what he was doing and how to please both of them.

Max enjoyed sex; more, she liked to be an active participant. She started backing Ryan up to the staircase that led to the bedroom. She wore low-heeled boots, which made her an inch taller than her five feet ten; Ryan had a good three, maybe four inches on her. She liked that. She liked a lot about him, not the least of which was how he kissed.

He pulled his mouth from hers.

"Don't stop now," she said.

"I have no intention of stopping, sweetheart."

He grinned at her, but it wasn't solely a playful smile. There was an urgency he was holding back, as if he wanted to devour her there, at the base of the staircase, and only because of his maturity was he able to restrain himself.

She would love to see what he would do if she played it slow and easy. Maybe she would find out. She ran her fingers lightly behind his ears, kissed him on his neck. He smelled like sea air and sweat and earth. She breathed in and sighed.

He picked her up, startling her out of all the erotic thoughts running through her head. "You think too much," he said.

"How did you know I was thinking?"

"Damn, you're an open book."

He was the second person this year who had told her that, after she was convinced that no one could read her mind.

"Oh?"

"You're thinking about how to tease me. And someday, I would really love to play sex games with you. But now, we're going to bed." He started up the stairs. She was borderline panicked. No one had ever picked her up like she was nearly weightless. She wasn't overweight, but she was tall and had muscles from running. She couldn't be easy to carry.

He laughed when he got to the top and pretended he was about to drop her. "The look on your face, Max. Have you never been carried before?"

She shook her head because suddenly her mouth was dry and she couldn't speak.

He did drop her then, but onto the bed. Before she could adjust herself, he leaned over and kissed her while unbuttoning her shirt.

She closed her eyes and happily gave up control of their lovemaking.

# Chapter Twenty-four

Gabriel didn't want to leave Eve that night after the Hendersons' party—she had been excited about meeting Maxine, but now was quiet and melancholy. "Do you want to talk about it?" he asked on the drive home.

"Later," she said.

"I'm here whenever you want." He paused. "Did you like her?"

"Yes."

No more, no less. He had a hundred questions, but he, too, was preoccupied. He had been so angry when Maxine had brought that federal agent to the party, but that all disappeared when he heard Phillip Colter's name.

Eve went right up to her room saying she wanted to get a good night's sleep before her race. Gabriel waited for twenty minutes and didn't hear her moving about, so jotted a note that he had to run to Brian's house to talk about business and would be back in an hour. He posted it on the refrigerator in case she woke up and was looking for him.

Gabriel pulled in to Brian's driveway at ten that night. Brian lived in a house on the far edge of the resort property with his wife, Annie. It was a second marriage for both of them, and Gabriel had always considered them family—Brian was a distant cousin—but for the first time, he feared he'd been duped, that Brian had gotten involved in something that would jeopardize everything they had worked so hard for.

He knocked on the door. Brian answered, martini in hand. "Gabriel, what's wrong?"

"We have to talk." He glanced over Brian's shoulder. Annie was sitting on the couch watching television.

"Hi, Gabriel, come in," she called.

"In private," Gabriel said quietly.

Brian looked worried and confused as he took Gabriel to the back of the house where he had a small home office. Gabriel closed the door.

"I need you to be completely honest with me, Brian. I can't help you—I can't help us—if you lie to me."

"You're scaring me, Gabriel. Tell me what's going on."

"Phillip Colter."

Brian stared at him blankly. "What about Colter?"

"Were there strings to his money? When we took the funding from his company, were there strings?"

"I don't know what you are talking about," Brian said. "He invested in the resort because he believed in it and he's been making money every year on his investment."

"That's not what I'm talking about!"

Gabriel couldn't imagine that Brian didn't understand. He'd been so wrapped up in the resort. Every dime Brian had—every dime Gabriel had—had been put into Havenly. They had made something great here. They wouldn't be rich, but neither of them cared about money. What they cared about was providing for their families, providing jobs to local men and women who had been hit hard by the economy. They worked closely with the nearby golf course, cosponsored events, and had just three years ago been listed as one of the top ten golf resorts on the East Coast because the golf club had exploded in popularity after it hosted a tournament that attracted some of the biggest names in the sport. Gabriel and Brian had benefited from that, had been able to expand the hotel, build eight duplex cottages on the edge of the property closest to the golf course, and could charge a premium because of the location.

They had made something for themselves and the community. Yet it was all tainted if Phillip Colter was a criminal.

"Do you want a drink?" Brian asked.

"I want the truth."

"Then you're going to have to explain what you're talking about, because you're making no sense."

Gabriel sat down and took a deep breath. "I think Colter is dirty."

"Like dirty money?"

"I don't know if his money is clean or dirty, but I think *he* is dirty. A criminal. I think Jimmy was into something with him and—"

"Stop. Jimmy? Is this because of that reporter asking questions about Martha?"

"No. Yes. No! It's about the FBI coming in and telling me flat-out that Colter is a suspect in some major art theft or something. I don't know what he did, but he did *something,* and that's why the FBI was all over this place ten years ago. Jimmy was involved. And it's why Agent Maguire is back now."

"Maguire is back?"

Why wasn't Brian listening to him? "Yes! I saw him the other night having dinner with Maxine Revere, and again tonight—only now he finally believes me and knows I didn't help Jimmy."

"Of course you didn't. I told you there was no way he could prove it, and now I really don't see the problem."

"The problem? The problem is that Phillip Colter is the subject of an FBI investigation and Colter's company owns *half* of our resort. We don't have the cash to buy him out."

"Why would we do that?"

"You are not listening. If his money is dirty, the feds can seize all his property—including our resort."

"No."

"Yes!"

"That won't happen."

"Why?"

"It's a company, Colter is only a small part of it. Yeah, he made the deal, but it still went through the company board of directors for approval, and the government can't take over the entire company."

Gabriel rubbed his forehead. What Brian said made sense . . . but he didn't know anything about white-collar crime or what the government could or couldn't do. "I—I don't know."

"I think you're making a mountain out of a molehill."

"I think you're not taking this seriously enough."

"What do you know the investigation?"

"Nothing substantive. Do you think Maguire would just show me everything he had? He basically said he thinks I didn't know what Jimmy was up to, and then explained why they were after him."

"And why were they after him?"

"Because Jimmy stole something—a priceless painting—and sold it. Then disappeared the weekend he came here and wanted to take Eve from me."

"You didn't tell the fed you saw him, did you? That would put you on the hot seat."

Gabriel hesitated. He almost told Brian everything, but there was something about his reaction that was just a little bit off. Gabriel had known Brian his entire life. What was wrong with this conversation?

*He didn't ask about the painting. That it would be odd*

*for Jimmy to steal a priceless work of art. Brian should
think that it was as ludicrous as I do.*

It was as if Brian knew exactly what Jimmy had done.
But that was ridiculous, wasn't it?

Still, he said, "No, I didn't tell the fed anything. I'd
never admit to an FBI agent that I lied to him. Shit, Brian!
I don't care about any of that. I don't care what happened
to Jimmy. But I *am* worried that we're business partners
with a criminal. We have to find a way to get out from
under this."

"Let it die down. It will. If the feds had anything on
Colter, they'd have indicted him. You know how these
law-and-order types work. They throw out a bunch of
shit that scares law-abiding citizens, but when they can't
prove their case, they walk."

Gabriel couldn't believe that Brian was being so lacka-
daisical about the situation, and that further disturbed him.

"Brian, what's going on?"

"Nothing. You have been so intense and paranoid
since that woman came to town. Let it go."

"I can't."

"Stay away from her, Gabriel. You broke into her cottage—do I have to remind you that you're already on
edge? Stay away, and all this will disappear. The feds are
blowing smoke up your ass."

"This is our business, Brian."

"And our business is doing great. We have nothing to
do with Phillip Colter other than he gave us our initial
seed money—through his *company*. Boreal only owns
fifty percent of the resort. We own fifty percent. We're
okay. Don't worry about this."

"I can't help it. It feels like everything is crashing down."

"Nothing is crashing down. Go home, Gabriel. Eve has
a race tomorrow, bright and early. You need to be there to
support her."

Brian was right, but Gabriel couldn't shake the feeling that he'd just been whammied. That Brian was too calm about the whole thing.

Brian walked him to his car. "Gabriel, we're friends and we're family. You know that, right?"

"I'm worried."

"Sleep on it a couple of days. Stay away from the reporter, from the fed. They'll both go away and you'll see that I am right."

"I hope so, Brian."

Gabriel drove off. He glanced in the rearview mirror of his truck and saw Brian standing there in the driveway, watching him leave.

*Brian, what have you done?*

Eve stared at the ceiling, her face wet from tears that had been falling for the better part of an hour. She'd gone downstairs to talk to her dad—demand answers—and saw the note on the fridge that said he went to talk to Uncle Brian.

An omen. A sign that she needed to figure this out on her own.

But she couldn't sleep because she would never forget what she heard at the Hendersons'.

*I had motive—he was going to take my daughter. I don't care that I'm not her biological father, she's my daughter.*

Her dad had lied to her for her entire life. No wonder he wouldn't talk about her mother—he barely knew her.

She loved her dad . . . and that made everything hurt twice as much.

She didn't know what to do. She was no one, nothing, and everyone who had ever said they'd loved her had lied to her.

# Chapter Twenty-five

Eve avoided her dad all morning. It wasn't easy at first—they always ate breakfast together early before a race. But she gave him an excuse that she needed to meet with Jason and left before he could ask any questions, briskly walking in the cold morning toward the sailing club.

She desperately wanted to talk to him, but at the same time what could he say? Would he lie to her again? Would he tell her there was nothing wrong with her birth certificate? Or that she heard wrong last night?

She hadn't heard wrong. Gabriel Truman was not her father, and nothing he said could fix that. She didn't know who she was, who she belonged to. Her whole life was falling apart and she didn't have anyone to talk to.

Eve almost abandoned the race to find Maxine Revere. Max had said she wouldn't lie to her, but Eve didn't know if she could trust her. What a mess! Eve had never had these feelings, these doubts, about anything. Her life had been orderly, both simple and full. She was always busy with sailing, school, and helping her dad at the resort. She realized right then that there was no one she could confide in.

She had friends, that was true—Pamela at school, they went to movies together and hung out and Eve told her about her crush on Wyatt Henderson and Pamela told Eve about her crushes, and her sailing club, she spent more time with them than anyone else, and they did a lot of fun stuff together outside of the club. But Eve had always felt older than her friends. Not like she was all that smarter and wiser, but her dad shared everything with her and she told him everything. Except about her crush on Wyatt. That was not for dads.

At least, she had thought he told her everything. But he hadn't. He'd kept secrets. He'd lied to her. And Eve didn't know how to talk to him about it, what to say, if she could ever trust him again. And this wasn't the kind of thing she could talk about with Pamela or Jason. What would they say? *Oh, Eve, that's awful. Sorry.*

Sorry. Yeah, she was sorry. She almost wished she hadn't overheard any of that stupid conversation.

"Hey, Eve, what's wrong?"

It was Stephen, the head of the club. "Nothing," she said.

"Are you sure?"

"Just tired. I didn't sleep well." She barely slept at all. "Do you have any coffee?"

"Sure, you're early, I just made it."

Stephen started talking about the course for the race, about the wind and what she needed to watch out for, but she was barely paying attention.

Soon the others started coming in. The whole club showed up for the race, but only four of them were competing in the solo competition. Eve left the chatty group to check her boat, but she couldn't focus. She almost wanted to call it off and not race. But then she'd disappoint everyone. This was an exhibition race, there would be a large crowd, potential sponsors, and Stephen had been talking about raising money and how colleges would look at the races when awarding scholarships, and every race should be considered important even if there wasn't a big check or trophy at the end.

She didn't sail for the trophy. She sailed because she loved being out on the water, at one with the boat. For the joy of the sport.

She felt no joy today.

But still, she went out.

It was nearly a fatal mistake.

Gabriel watched the race through binoculars, standing next to Stephen Galbraith. Eve had started out strong, but seemed almost reckless. Eve raced boldly all the time, but today there was a lack of . . . *grace*. She rounded the first buoy far too fast and was lucky she didn't capsize.

"Is Eve okay?" Stephen asked. "She was quiet and preoccupied this morning."

Gabriel didn't answer. What could he say?

His entire body was tense as Eve rounded the second buoy and the boom flew out and around.

She was going to go under. His stomach twisted in knots as he watched her make a daring leap for the boom as it came around. She was listing port side, almost full stop, as she fought the wind and her sails to regain control of her boat. She had been in the lead; now she was almost in last place.

Eve had made mistakes on the water before, but nothing like this—nothing this serious. By the time she rounded the last buoy, she had regained some ground, but it was clear her heart wasn't in the race. She came in eighth out of the fifteen competitors.

Gabriel watched as her teammates came up to talk to her and she brushed them off. She had a cut on her forehead, and a bruise was forming. She didn't go to the reception hall where everyone would meet up, instead she walked down the dock toward the boathouse.

Gabriel rushed up to her. "Eve, are you okay?"

He'd never seen her falter like she had.

"Fine."

"Was something wrong with the sails? What happened? Did a line break? You're bleeding."

"No! I'm *fine*. I messed up, okay? It was my fault! Leave me alone."

She walked away from him.

Gabriel ignored the scene that Eve caused. She didn't have outbursts. Sure, she could get mad and snap at someone, but all day she had been testy, and she didn't have breakfast with him this morning—a ritual they shared before every race.

He followed her up the dock to the boathouse.

"Don't," she said when she saw him. "I don't want to talk to you right now."

Gabriel's stomach churned. "Eve—"

"You lied to me! You've lied to me my entire life! Go away! I *don't* want to talk to you. I don't even want to *see* you!" She absently wiped away tears and walked down to the *Emily*, the boat that they had been working on for the past two years. She stared at it, then walked past to the end of the indoor pier.

His heart broke. She knew. Had Maxine Revere told her? She'd promised she wouldn't . . . had she lied to him last night? He'd known Eve was preoccupied, but she seemed satisfied with the conversation she had with Max. He put her silence on the simple fact that all the new information was overwhelming for her.

Now? What had happened?

He followed her. He couldn't let her stand alone in pain.

"Eve, I'm sorry. Tell me what happened."

She shook her head and kept her back to him.

"Did Maxine say something?"

She spun around and hit him in the chest. "No!"

She had never once—ever—pushed him. It surprised both of them.

"You. I heard you talking to Max and that FBI agent. You told them—you told them that, that, I-I—"

The tears came faster now, and Gabriel's eyes burned. He tried to reach out for his daughter, but she pulled away.

He slumped against a pillar. "You're my daughter," he said, his voice cracking.

"I'm not! You—you had to have faked this!"

She was waving a piece of paper in the air and it took him a moment to realize that it was her birth certificate.

"I . . . I had to. I didn't know what else to do."

"You lied to me. You and Grandma."

"You don't understand."

"Then tell me! *Maybe* I'll believe you. But I don't know if I can believe anything you say anymore. What if you lie to me again? What if you make up something that you think I'll believe just to make me think what you did was okay?"

"You want the truth?"

"Are you going to tell me the truth?"

The tears had stopped and she stood defiant, waiting for answers . . . or waiting for him to lie.

He wanted to lie. Not for him, but to protect Eve. But if he did—he would never have a daughter. She would never trust him again.

"Your mother left you with Grandma when you were three months old. I didn't know. I took family leave when I found out that Grandma had cancer, and she had been taking care of you alone for months. She told me my brother Jimmy had left Martha with a newborn, and Martha had some problems and left you with her. I was so angry—at my brother, at Martha for leaving an infant with a sick old woman—and then I saw you. And you looked at me with such trust and innocence. And I realized at that moment that you needed me and—I, I guess I needed you, too."

How could he explain to a sixteen-year-old what it was like to look into a child's eyes and know that you were destined to be together? It was love—pure, innocent, unconditional love.

"I always thought that Jimmy was your father. I tracked him down a year after Martha left you and he told me he didn't want you, wouldn't know what to do with a child, and I was relieved because I really thought he might take you from me.

"Then you started school and I needed a birth certificate. Grandma gave me the one Martha had left. And she'd named you Genevieve Revere, not Truman. And under father, she'd put 'unknown.' I didn't know what to do, so I paid someone to create a forgery, at least good enough to pass at the school. I don't know why Martha did that—I don't know why she did anything that she did, and that's one thing that I think Maxine and I agree on. That woman—I know she's your mother, but she left Maxine with her other grandparents, and you with Emily. She wasn't fit to raise anyone.

"I never thought you would learn the truth about Jimmy. I love you, you are my daughter, I don't care if you come directly from me or not. I couldn't love you any more than I do now—blood or not. I'm not sorry I didn't tell you—how could I tell a little girl that her parents didn't want her? That they'd abandoned her? *I* wanted you. You're the brightest part of my life, Eve."

"But . . . but Uncle Jimmy came for me. My birthday." Her voice sounded small and confused.

"He said he wanted to take you to California because the Reveres were rich and would pay for you. He wanted to—I don't know, sell you? Leave you with strangers? I couldn't let him—he gave me a day to tell you the truth, and I couldn't. I would have fought for you. I would have sold everything to pay for a lawyer because in no world is Jimmy Truman a decent man or father. But he never came back. I kept waiting and he never returned."

"What happened?"

"I don't know. That FBI agent thinks that he got in trouble with someone—Jimmy was a thief. He stole something, sold it on the black market, I don't know what happened and I honestly do not care because he didn't come back for you. At the time, I thought he found another way to get the money he wanted, so he didn't need you. Eve, I made mistakes. But everything I have ever done since the day I met you, I did to protect you. Please, please, honey, find a way to forgive me."

Eve bit her lip. She felt numb and sad and lost. She wanted to believe her dad—her uncle. If he was her uncle.

But what else did she have? A sister she had just met? A sister almost old enough to be her mother? A family in California she didn't know?

"Don't lie to me, Daddy. Never again, please."

"I won't. Ask me anything, anytime, I will tell you the truth."

Her dad never cried, but he had tears on his face. He had never let her down until last night. Until she'd heard him say that he wasn't her father.

But she had no one else.

She took a step toward him, and he walked briskly to her and hugged her tight. "I love you, Eve."

"I love you, Daddy," she said through her sobs.

She didn't know who she was, but she would figure it out.

# Chapter Twenty-six

Max and Ryan spent Sunday morning going over Max's timeline again in her office.

"I'm investing in a magnetic whiteboard," she said after a sticky note lost its adhesive from being moved one too many times.

"It'll have to be a big one," he said.

"I'll install one on a wall in my office at work and at home."

Ryan looked at the postcards as they were displayed in the order they were sent to Max. "Are these all the postcards your mother sent you?"

"Yes. My grandmother was unhappy—and disappointed—in my mother's chosen lifestyle but she would never have hidden any of them from me. She told me once that Martha had sent her a few postcards through the years, borderline nasty notes about doing things she knew my grandmother wouldn't approve of. They upset her, though, and she never told my grandfather."

"Did she keep them?"

"No. I'm pretty certain she didn't lie about that. She would never have wanted my grandfather to find them because they would break his heart."

"She sounds like an interesting woman."

"Formidable."

"People might use that word with you."

She looked at him with a straight face. "Would you?"

"Sometimes." But he was smiling.

Ryan had certainly made himself at home in her cottage, and surprisingly, Max didn't mind. He wore sweats and a faded Notre Dame T-shirt but was even more attractive that way. Even his hair, which was still a bit too long for Max's taste, fit his persona.

He left the den and went to make another pot of coffee. She followed. She was about to invite him back to bed—it still wasn't noon, and their Skype call with Dr. Dillon Kincaid wasn't until four that afternoon—when he said, "The dates don't match up."

"You had a conversation without me," Max said.

"The postmarks and the handwritten dates."

"Because my mother didn't mail them until long after she wrote them."

"Maybe."

He stared at the coffeepot, clearly thinking. She stepped away, let him contemplate whatever it was he thought he saw, and went back to the den.

It was true that her mother was always late in sending her a birthday postcard, and when Max was ten and eleven, when she really believed her mother would come back one day—for better or worse—it bothered her. How could someone just forget the birthday of their only child?

*The same kind of person who would leave their only child with virtual strangers. The same kind of person who would spend their entire inheritance on fun and games, expensive hotels, two-hundred-dollar dinners, and thousand-dollar bottles of wine.*

At times over Max's early childhood, Martha had spent everything before she received her next allowance payment. There were days when hamburgers were paid for with coins scraped from the bottom of Martha's purse or Max's backpack. But those were few and far between, because inevitably, Martha would find a new "boyfriend" who would carry them over during the lean times.

*Feast or famine.*

She unwrapped a new package of sticky notes, this in a different color than she had been using. Then she realized she needed two new colors, and unwrapped another. On the bright green squares she wrote the postmark of each postcard, just the month and day, not the year. On the bright pink squares she wrote the date that her mother handwrote on the card—the way her mother wrote them, the European way, with the day first and the month second.

She put them not under the postcards but in a row. The cards that related to museums and art, she circled the numbers.

She stared. She didn't see anything unusual or noteworthy about the dates. All but one were mailed between January and July. The lone card that was mailed outside of that window was an "early" birthday card, sent right before Christmas, but dated 01/01, the day *after* her actual birthday. That was also the only card that had a handwritten date *later* than the postmark.

Max was good with numbers—she could figure basic math in her head and she had a fairly solid grasp of accounting principles and patterns. But nothing stood out to her.

Ryan walked in and handed her a cup of coffee—he'd added just the right amount of cream. He leaned over to kiss her, then stopped.

"That's it."

She turned to look at what he was looking at.

"It's a code."

She was skeptical.

"My mother wasn't that clever."

"Numbers are the most common way for people to send codes. But they repeat. Don't you see? It's the days she wrote down, not the postmarks."

He put his coffee mug down and ripped off all the green squares, tossing them aside, only looking at the pink. "She knew from the moment she sent the postcard from the Dallas museum that she was going to hide these paintings somewhere."

Max had always known that her mother was book-smart, but she didn't think she'd be able to come up with an elaborate code over the course of years.

"See?" Ryan said, clearly excited. "The generic Miami beach card came between four sets of art cards. But the two sets of four art cards repeat the pattern."

"That means for *three years* my mother planned this?"

"Too long to be a social security number or an address or a locker combination, so it's not going to be easy. But the code means *something,* and if it means something, it means we can figure it out."

"You're confident."

"About this? Yes, I am. I just need a little time. There could be more clues here."

"Like this." She picked up the Oyster Bay postcard. "It's not a coincidence that when we stood here, we saw the Boreal property."

Ryan was focused on the numbers. He tilted his head, deep in thought.

Max couldn't imagine that her mother had this planned for so long. If she had stolen the paintings from Colter, had she hidden them away and these numbers were a key to their location? It was a long time ago. And four of the paintings had been recovered or their whereabouts known.

"Ryan," she said quietly after their coffee had grown cold.

"Hmm?"

"Put this aside for now. Maybe your FBI code-breakers can see something that we can't."

He rubbed his eyes, nodded. "You're right. But there's something here. Why can't I see it?"

"Maybe you're right. The repeating numbers are certainly odd, and it makes sense considering the postmarks are way off on most of them. But think about it: if we're going with the assumption that Martha and Jimmy stole these seven paintings from Colter nineteen years ago, what could any code mean? How would she know that I would keep the cards for years and even discover that I could put it together?"

"Maybe she planned on retrieving them from you. Or finding a way to tell you there was something on the postcards and to look at them."

"A lot of time has passed."

"Maybe she didn't plan to get killed," Ryan said.

That was a good point.

"You look tired," Ryan said.

"Insomnia is a way of life for me, but I slept pretty well last night." Partly because Ryan was there. She didn't say that to him, however, because she wasn't exactly sure what to make of their mutual attraction. She never overanalyzed her relationships. She took them one day at a time. But after Nick, she found that she was feeling a bit more cautious. She hadn't planned on getting so deeply involved with Nick, and ending it had been bittersweet. Even with Marco, her longtime on-off boyfriend, she hadn't felt so . . . *sad* . . . when she ultimately left him.

"Hungry?" he asked. "I can make some sandwiches from that roast pig the Hendersons cooked. That was amazing. I was very happy when they handed me a to-go bag."

"With all those people, I'm surprised there was any left."

"It was a large pig."

"A sandwich sounds good."

They went to the kitchen and made sandwiches, then sat on the deck to eat. She poured a glass of wine and offered some to Ryan. "I feel like I'm working," he said.

"It's Sunday afternoon."

"Yeah, but I'm not a hundred percent positive that you're safe here."

"You're not going all he-man male chauvinist on me, are you?"

"Only if you want me to."

She shot him a narrowed look.

"I'll take that as you're thinking about it." He smiled and bit into his sandwich.

She couldn't help but like Ryan. He had a natural sense of humor and was confident both professionally and personally. He clearly loved his job, but he wasn't a workaholic—though she saw his potential of getting lost in a case that grabbed him.

"You know everything about me, I know nothing about you—other than you told Beth that you were born in Iowa."

"I doubt I know *everything* about you," Ryan said.

"I used to try to avoid drama, but it follows me around, so I guess I've embraced it. My mother. My family in California. My job."

"And your job is solving cold cases and covering murder trials. I read your website. It was very interesting. I downloaded all four of your books to my e-reader."

She scowled. "I see we're going to have a huge problem."

"You don't like ebooks."

"I like real books."

"They *are* real. Same words."

She shook her head. "I can't touch them. I can't smell them. I have walls of bookshelves in my apartment."

"Big apartment. Maybe I can visit someday."

"Maybe I'll invite you."

He laughed. "I live in a small beach house in Virginia Beach. Small because of my government salary. I have one bookshelf."

"What was the last book you read?"

"A biography about Ulysses S. Grant. My brother gave it to me for Christmas, it won a bunch of awards and I thought it would be stuffy, but it was really good."

"You like history."

"Doesn't everyone?" He winked.

"You went to Notre Dame."

"Full scholarship."

"Smart."

"Smart and poor. But no complaints. Raised by a single mom, my dad was a total deadbeat. My mom raised me and my brother and sister on her own in Des Moines. None of us turned to drugs, excessive drinking, or welfare, so I guess we beat the odds."

"More than good, I'd say."

Ryan nodded. "I go home every Christmas. My mom likes when we're all together. I try to visit in the spring, which is my favorite time of year in Iowa. If you've never been to Des Moines in May, it's absolutely worth the trip. My little brother is a cop there—never left. Married to his high school sweetheart, has three kids, his wife is a teacher. My mom lives less than a mile from them. My little sister is a doctor in Pittsburgh, married to her job, though I think she's seeing someone. She won't tell me because she thinks I'll run a background check on him."

"Would you?"

He just smiled. "Now you know everything about me."

"Allergies?"

"Penicillin."

"Married?"

"If I were married, I wouldn't have been in bed with you last night. And this morning. And tonight."

She laughed. "You know what I meant. Have you ever been?"

"No. You?"

"If you read my bio, you would know I wasn't."

"People lie."

"I don't."

"Really."

"Don't believe me?"

"Don't know yet. Maybe I don't know you well enough."

She leaned on her elbow and said, "My mother lied to me for my entire life. I'm not going down that path."

"What if it was for a good reason? Like Gabriel Truman lying to Eve about her parents."

"Good reason? That remains to be seen."

"He thought he was protecting her."

"It's not to say that a lie is always to hurt someone. Some of the most destructive lies initially had noble motives behind them. But in my experience, eventually that lie will come back and bite someone in the ass."

Ryan stood up. He took his plate and hers in one hand, and pulled her up with his other. He kissed her neck, sending chills up her spine. "How long until your shrink friend calls?"

"Nearly two hours."

"Two hours. What can we possibly do for two hours?" He walked her inside and put the plates next to the sink. "Maybe," he said as he backed her against the wall, "we should try to clear our minds, so we can come at this investigation fresh."

Without waiting for her answer he ran his hand under

her dress and cupped her butt cheeks. She put her hands on his chest and kissed his neck. "You are a very smart man."

"So I've been told."

His hands were on her waist, and she ran hers under his T-shirt, enjoying his warm skin against her fingers.

Ryan heated her up fast. Maybe because this was new, or maybe because she was attracted to him, or maybe because he seemed to know exactly how to touch her without her having to direct traffic. He was intoxicating and sexy.

She was about to pull her dress over her head when the door buzzer rang twice.

"Shit," she said. Ryan laughed.

"What are you laughing about? Think you can turn *this* off that easily?" She ran her hand between his legs.

He groaned and said, "Oh, sweetheart, payback is going to be a bitch."

"I can't wait," she said with a grin.

She started down the stairs, but Ryan whistled. "Stop."

"What?"

"Didn't we have this conversation earlier? That if Colter thinks you have information to lead to his paintings that he'll find a way to get to you?"

"And I told *you* that I plan to have lunch with him, so what's the difference?"

"Preemptive strike," Ryan said.

"I don't get it." She also didn't see him grab his gun— last she saw, it was in his briefcase on the kitchen table.

"You can answer," he said, standing to the side of the door.

She looked through the side window. "Put that away, it's David." She opened the door. "I thought you weren't coming until tomorrow."

"I got the information I needed and took the next flight here." He wasn't looking at her, he was looking at Ryan.

"David, Agent Ryan Maguire. Ryan, my assistant and sometime bodyguard, David Kane."

David extended his hand. He was giving Ryan a solid appraisal. "Good to meet you."

But he didn't sound all that pleased about it.

"Likewise." Ryan glanced at Max with a confused look on his face.

David said to Max, "This place is a goddamn fish bowl. At least you had the sense to close most of the blinds."

"Aren't you in a grumpy mood."

He said, "This the second bedroom?" He walked through the downstairs sitting area to the bedroom, flicked on the light and looked around, then put his small suitcase on the floor.

Why was David acting so weird and making her feel like she had been caught by her grandfather making out with the pool boy?

"Dillon Kincaid is going to call in a bit," Max said.

"Do I have time for a shower?"

"Sure," Max said. "Come upstairs when you're freshened up."

David closed the bedroom door.

Max and Ryan walked upstairs. "You said you weren't involved with anyone." He sounded angry.

"I'm not."

"That guy is jealous."

"David is gay."

"He's—*what?*"

"And yeah, he's acting strange. I don't understand it, either."

"Are you sure he's gay?" Ryan sounded incredulous.

"Well, I haven't watched him in the bedroom, but

we've talked about it, so I'm ninety-nine percent certain he is what he says he is. Most men—especially former Army Rangers—aren't going to confide to their employer that they're gay if they're not. And we're friends." Was that what the odd attitude was? That they were friends and she was sleeping with Ryan? How the hell would he know?

David was one of the sharpest people she knew. He picked up on subtleties better than most. And he went to the bedroom and realized Ryan, who Max had told him was going to stay in the cottage because of the potential threat from Colter, hadn't used the second bedroom.

"Think of David as my overprotective big brother."

"That I can do." Ryan leaned over and kissed her. "I was worried for a minute."

He still looked a bit worried, but probably not that David was jealous. More that David looked exactly like what he was: a tough former Army Ranger who didn't take shit from anyone.

Max smiled. "I told you I wouldn't lie to you."

# Chapter Twenty-seven

Max had plugged her computer into the television so that they could more comfortably Skype with Dr. Dillon Kincaid in the living room, rather than cramming around her laptop in the den. She introduced Ryan.

"I appreciate you fitting me in," Max said. "I wish you'd let me pay you—you're an expert, you should be compensated for your time."

"How about if I spend any more time working on a profile after this call I'll bill you?" Dillon said with a smile.

"As long as you let me take you and your wife to dinner next time you're in New York."

"That would be fun. Kate has been wanting to meet you."

Dillon shifted in his seat, turned a paper over on the desk in front of him, and said, "I read your memo, and the email you sent an hour ago about a possible code in the postcards Martha sent to you over the years. I first want to address your last point, because until you understand *why*, I don't think you'll truly grasp what you're dealing with."

"You mean why my mother, who was independently wealthy, hooked up with a con artist?"

"That's a small part of it. And I need to state the standard disclaimer—I haven't interviewed Martha, of course, so everything I say is based on her actions—and a few of her writings. I can't give you a diagnosis, for example, though I think I can help you with the *why* you need."

"You're not testifying here, Dillon," Max said.

Dillon looked at Ryan. "Agent Maguire? I often consult for the FBI, but this report is private, not to be used in any trial or be included in any case files. If there's a need for my services once you make an arrest, you have my contact information and I would be happy to work with you and your office."

"Off the record," Ryan said. "Got it."

"I was privy to a lot of Martha's background because Max and I talked about her at length during the time we spent together in Scottsdale, during the Blair Caldwell murder trial. Normally, I don't completely trust the recollections of an adult remembering a distant past, but Max is a far better witness than most because she kept journals and she also has a cop-like knack of separating herself from personal trauma. Still, I think you missed a lot of your mother's psychopathy growing up, because as a child you wouldn't know how to frame it. Max, you're okay with me talking about everything you shared with me, right?"

He sounded concerned, and while she appreciated it, she had nothing to hide. "I talk about my upbringing publicly, I have nothing to hide, especially from David and Ryan."

"You have been forthright, but sometimes we forget the pain in our childhood once we look at it through the lens of maturity."

"I'm good." What could she possibly learn that would hurt more than anything that happened in her past?

Dillon shifted his papers. "Martha left home when she was nineteen and lived off an ample trust fund. She moved around extensively, never settling down for longer than a few months. She lived in hotels, in other people's homes, on boats, and occasionally a short-term lease. Many teenagers rebel, especially when brought up in a strict home. The Revere house was not physically abusive, but Martha's parents were strict—especially her mother—and expected very specific behavior and a sense of order, of propriety. They expected their offspring to respect their elders, respect their status in society as being among the upper class, and behave with manners and grace. The Revere home was part of a matriarchal dynasty—Genevieve Sterling was widowed young and grew her husband's wealth at a time when most women didn't have such control over business and finances. Her daughter, Eleanor, saw her mother as the leader in the home, and took it upon herself to lead her own home."

Max had to interrupt. "Eleanor loved my grandfather. And he saw her for who she was, warts and all, and loved her back. He wasn't a weak man."

"I didn't say he was. He was a banker, and the Reveres had some money, but the real wealth—the kind most of us never touch—came from the Sterlings, correct?"

Max hadn't thought of it that way. "True."

"Martha likely was sociopathic from a young age. If I talked to Eleanor—and if she was honest with me—she would tell me that Martha was often in trouble at school because of peer conflicts. I doubt Eleanor would say anything to a stranger—she doesn't sound like she would ever share a personal detail with anyone outside of immediate family."

"True," Max said. "Martha did get in trouble in school—she told me about it—but I never knew the details."

"From what you've said, Max, Eleanor would do whatever it took to make any indiscretions disappear."

"Yes."

"Martha was smart—probably received good grades, even straight As. She would have been capable of it. She likely felt that she was smarter than her peers, and maybe she was in some regard. That sense of superiority grew because she had a strong sense of self. She pushed envelopes because she liked to see what happened. She broke rules because she got a reaction from her proper mother. She did it because of how *other* people reacted, not necessarily because she wanted something she couldn't have. If she was supposed to dress for a formal dinner, she would wear something inappropriate. If she was supposed to be on time for a meeting, she would be late because she could get away with it. Essentially, she was a spoiled brat, but because she was smart, she manipulated the entire house.

"She left when she got control of her trust, on her nineteenth birthday. She was free. There were no strings to the trust, she received her allowance on the first of every month. No requirement to go to school, to get a job. Essentially, free money."

"But it wasn't," Max said. "Grandma Genie worked well into her seventies. In fact, she never really retired, taking an active role in the company she and her husband created. I didn't even meet her until I was nine, but it was clear as anything that she valued what she'd done."

"Max, you know as well I do that even people raised the same way can turn out vastly different. It's why I lean toward the nature side of the nature versus nurture debate. Your mother was, essentially, selfish, but it was more than that—clinically, I don't feel comfortable labelling her at this point, but I suspect she was bipolar, which manifested in her need to constantly be moving around.

But being bipolar doesn't make someone a sociopath. It was simply one more facet to her personality."

Max understood what Dillon was saying on the one hand, but she'd seen how Martha's spendthrift ways had hurt Eleanor and Grandma Genie.

"Did she just want to hurt her family? Is that why she treated the money Grandma Genie earned as if it was her own personal bank?"

"She probably wanted to lash out at her mother, but you can't see it as her desire to *hurt* anyone. The money was hers, she wanted to do what she wanted. And it was, in essence, her personal bank. Certainly it would have been more than enough for the average person to live on, but your mother spent lavishly so found herself short at the end of the month. That's when she fully developed her manipulation skills. She dated wealthy men who would pay for everything because she was young, pretty, and smart. She moved on when she received her allowance, because she was incapable of developing a real romantic attachment to anyone."

Max suddenly felt that she was more like her mother than she'd thought. Had she walked away from Nick too soon? Had she not given him a real chance?

"Max," Dillon said, "I see you thinking, and we'll talk privately later, okay? Just know that you're not your mother. Like I said, I lean to the nature over the nurture side. Why is it that some abused children can grow up and never hurt another human being, while other abused children become abusers? We can debate this topic— believe me, it is not settled in my field. My sister and I have debated this concept extensively, and she leans the other way, that nurture plays a stronger role than nature. But most of my colleagues tend to agree that it's a combination of nature and nurture that creates psychopaths.

"Which bring me to you, Max. The first nearly ten

years of your life you were forced to follow the whims of your mother. Even though you were not what she expected—from her postcards, she never understood why you didn't want to have fun with her, why you were serious all the time—she kept you with her. I'm certainly not saying she was perfect—she clearly abused you."

"She never hit me."

"Maxine," Dillon said sharply, "abuse isn't always physical. She left you for days, all by yourself, when you were still a young child. She berated you because she didn't understand you. You were more of a possession to be kept than a child to be raised. But if someone didn't like you, or didn't want a woman with a child, she didn't care. You were hers, and those people—mostly men— could go jump in a lake for all she cared. Until Jimmy Truman. You said from the beginning that you didn't like him."

"I didn't. The feeling was mutual." She paused, considered what she should say and how she should say it. "Once, when I was seven or eight, one of my mother's boyfriends hit me. Said I mouthed off at him, which I probably did. My mother grabbed me and walked out. When Jimmy slapped me, she said I deserved it."

She had never talked about it, barely remembered it until these last few weeks when she had been rereading her journals and trying to figure things out.

"Jimmy Truman was attractive, charming, and a con artist," Dillon said. "He may have attempted to con her, and she found it exciting. And I think that's the key. Every postcard talks about *fun*. Seizing the day, enjoying the good things in life. Travel. Drink. Food. I talked to my brother-in-law Sean—I know you hired him, so he's covered under our NDA—and asked if she lived above her means. Meaning, that even with the steady allowance, would she need more to live the way she did? Absolutely, he said. I suspect that Truman gave her the permission, so to speak, to go from manipulative to criminal. It wouldn't take a big push—like I said earlier, she didn't respect other people. But with Truman she found her soul mate. The one person who understood who she was and loved her anyway. He fed her psychopathy, helped develop it. Ironically, I don't think he was a psychopath. He was a con artist, plain and simple. Sociopath? Probably. Most con artists have no remorse for their crimes. But generally, they lack the empathy gene—they *may* be violent, but it's not an absolute. With Martha, he met his match, so he brought her into the fold, so to speak."

Max let that sink in. David and Ryan were both quiet—maybe too quiet. She almost felt like she was being the one analyzed.

"You asked me three times, in slightly different ways, *why* Martha stole the paintings. I have two answers. First, because she could get away with it. It was a game to her. Why she was enticed? That's harder to figure out. It may have been Jimmy egging her on or Jimmy may have been the one to steal them in the first place. Perhaps he'd been part of"—he glanced down at his notes—"Phillip Colter? He could have been part of his crew. Maybe Martha wanted the paintings for herself because they attracted her. Max, were these seven paintings to her taste?"

"Yes," Max said without hesitation. "She loved Degas and all those who followed in his style. Not just that, though—it was the era."

"Perhaps Jimmy showed them to her, and they conspired to steal them from Colter—if he's the thief—and he would be hard-pressed to report them stolen."

"Stealing from a thief—oldest trick in the book," Ryan said. "What if I told you that Colter is known for having masterful reproductions in his collection? Some would call them forgeries, except that he commissioned them."

"Interesting," Dillon said. "Would Martha know the difference? If it was a really good reproduction?"

"Yes," Max said. "Martha was a lot of things, stupid wasn't one of them. Though I guess stupidity has a wide range of factors. I would think it's stupid to steal from someone who might kill you to get their stuff back."

"You need to think like Martha. It's a challenge. The adrenaline of taking something that doesn't belong to you—of keeping it, the secret of knowing it. Martha never felt the need to prove she was smarter than anyone. Or prettier. Not even *richer*. Yes, she spent a lot of money, but she didn't throw it around publicly. Nothing that put her in the society pages or under scrutiny. To take and possess a masterpiece would appeal to her, even if she couldn't display it."

David cleared his throat. "So an independently wealthy woman who doesn't need the money steals priceless art because it's fun?"

"Yes, and because she *can*. I think it was a challenge for her, a game, something for her and Jimmy to share, but the pieces they took appealed to her aesthetics."

"How did it take Colter so long to figure out that they stole the art?"

"They used aliases"—Dillon looked down—"Sterling, correct? They may have been in hiding, of sorts. He could have known all along but couldn't find them. He may not have known their real names. And didn't you say, Max, that Jimmy only disappeared after he sold one of the paintings?"

"Yes."

Ryan expounded on that point. "That's how I started investigating Jimmy Truman. I had no idea Martha Revere was involved. I know of the J. J. Sterling alias, but thought it was all on paper. He popped up, sold the Toulouse-Lautrec, then went under again. I came to Cape

Haven to talk to friends and family and no one spoke to me. They didn't like Jimmy, but it's a small town—they're not going to talk to a big city cop." He cleared his throat. "Not that Norfolk is big city anything. But, Doc, why so long? Martha disappeared, and then Jimmy comes out of hiding nearly six years later?"

"You're presuming that Colter knew of Jimmy Truman's involvement. You didn't until he sold the painting, correct?"

"Oh, right. Colter thought Martha was working alone."

"Which makes sense. In fact, she may have been involved with Colter at one point. She may have seen the paintings herself, decided that she should have them."

"So," Max said, "Martha and Jimmy take assumed names—the Sterling identity—and live mostly in Miami, maybe a bit of travel, and it takes Colter years to track them down. I don't see my mother *hiding*. It's not her style."

"This is all speculation. Maybe she used an assumed name when involved with Colter. Maybe he didn't figure out that it was Martha and Jimmy who stole the paintings until later. We can't possibly know the reasons. What we do know is that Colter is a thief, correct, Agent Maguire?"

"Yes, though I can't prove it."

"The seven paintings in the postcards that Max received were stolen using the same MO as paintings you suspect Colter stole?"

"Correct," Ryan said. "None of the other paintings have turned up, and only four of the seven."

"I hesitate to give you any profile of Colter, but if he stole them and they have *never* come to market, that means two things: he was hired to steal them for individuals who didn't intend to sell them—for their private collection, as it were—or he stole them for himself. You said he has masterful reproductions on his property?"

"We interviewed someone in Dallas who worked for his preferred catering company," Ryan said. "She worked at several of his parties and he would give his guests tours of his expansive home and tell stories about his artwork, both why he decided to commission it and about the original. Some people remarked that the paintings looked real—he would say that's the purpose."

David asked, "Why would someone just talk to the FBI?"

David sounded belligerent, but Max didn't comment. She wasn't going to get in the middle of whatever it was that was going on with David.

"Her brother-in-law is a Dallas cop," Ryan said. "He was friendly with my former colleague who has since retired, had the woman talk to him. Colter was on our radar and this was just one more piece of the puzzle— unfortunately, we couldn't get a warrant on the information because there was no physical evidence or actual witness to the crimes."

Dillon said, "He could have been slowly replacing his collection with the real artwork. No one would have suspected, because he had the fakes displayed and he talked about them. But Martha—an art expert—saw the difference. She knew some of his paintings were real."

"Here's a question for you," Max said. "If Colter had these perfect forgeries, why not replace the originals with the forgeries? Then no one would know that they were stolen."

"I can answer that," Ryan said. "The MO gave the thief the best opportunity to grab a painting—while it's en route or in storage. Most of the paintings weren't discovered missing for weeks, some months. To replace a painting means to replace everything, including the frame, which is extremely difficult. And eventually, the con will be discovered. At some point a museum will authenticate the piece, or an insurance company will inspect the physical property that they are insuring. If there is *any* difference, no matter how small, it will open an investigation."

"But he already had these amazing forgeries."

"Security at galleries and museums is generally much higher than security at the loading dock and during transport," Ryan said. "I've consulted with some of the people who lost the paintings and they've made improvements, but nothing is one hundred percent foolproof."

"My brother-in-law would certainly attest to that," Dillon said with a half smile.

"So," Max said, trying to wrap her head around multiple theories at once to figure out what was the most logical, "if Martha realized which paintings in Colter's collection were real, she decided to just take them? Maybe replace them with forgeries of her own so he wouldn't know?"

"I hadn't thought of that, but it would make sense," Dillon said, "since there were years between those thefts and her suspected death."

"And when Colter found out?" David asked.

"He would be furious. He had been conned. This is key: Colter believes that he is intelligent, cultured, a self-made man. From my limited understanding of his background, I suspect he came from a solid middle-class or upper-middle-class background. For Northampton, he would be considered wealthy, but when he went to college—an elite school—he was surrounded by people who had far more than he did. He coveted not just their wealth, but their experience, their luxury. He absorbed everything, and because he was smart, he was able to adopt the attitude, the style, of those around him. He wanted culture, to be seen as cultured. And yet, a woman who never went to college but was born into culture could see the truth on his walls better than he could. He knew which paintings were real because he was the one who stole them; no one else did until Martha."

"He hated her," Max said.

"At that point? Yes. We simply don't have enough information to know when he caught on. Though she used an alias in Miami, she wasn't truly in hiding. She moved around a lot, but she wasn't what Sean would call 'off the grid.' If she used her real name with him, he would know about her family in California, including you, Max, and may have reached out. Now, this is all conjecture. But Colter's psychopathy is not: he wants what he considers his. There are three paintings still missing, Agent Maguire?"

"Yes."

"So either he has them because he killed Martha and took them back, or he killed Martha in a rage because she wouldn't tell him where they were. Either way, he's dangerous. Don't be fooled by his sophistication or charm."

"Colter wants to have lunch with Max," Ryan said.

David looked at Max and raised his eyebrow, but didn't say anything.

"Tread carefully," Dillon said. "He wants to know what you know."

"I don't know anything about these paintings."

"Don't tell him that you have those postcards. He could see it as proof that you were privy to Martha's deception. Everything else—the truth helps you here. You're simply looking to find out what happened to your mother sixteen years ago. Focus on that not the art, and you might be able to get information from him. As soon as he thinks you have information that he does not—information that will lead to his coveted stolen art—he will be in control."

David said, "That would suggest that he *doesn't* have

the art. Otherwise, he wouldn't have come here as soon as Max showed up asking questions about her mother."

"You're likely right."

"Why did she send me the postcards?" she asked bluntly. "I was a teenager. I could have thrown them away. I didn't know what they meant, and there was no way that she'd know I would ever look for her or see the pattern."

"I'm a criminal psychiatrist, Max, not a psychic. There's a lot of complexity in your mother's behavior because it *is* unpredictable. Yet, it's clear she has some sort of personality disorder that prevented her from feeling remorse, from developing emotional attachments to anyone. I suspect Jimmy and Martha fed off each other, and that mutual love of the game, of spontaneity, and conning people—she would have easily seen that as love. She had a soul mate, someone who was just like her. But he wasn't."

"What?" Ryan said. "You just said—"

"I know what it sounds like, but Jimmy is a classic con artist. He may have cared about Martha on the surface, but initially he hooked up with her for his own con. That he learned she was more like him than not kept him around. I looked at his criminal records and what Max sent me about his family. The man conned his own mother out of her life savings. He never paid it back; from what we've learned he never even apologized. He doesn't have the remorse gene at all. And that's why I think Colter didn't know he was involved with the art thefts. Maybe Martha and Jimmy weren't together at the time or maybe they were in it together. Jimmy may have thought Colter might know him or his name, which is why he could have taken another identity. The Eastern Shore is a small place."

Max said, "So when Colter figured out Martha stole from him, Jimmy disappeared. Just walked away because it was dangerous."

"Left his girlfriend and her baby?" David said. "That's his kid and he knew they were in danger, yet he abandoned them?"

David was livid, and his deep sense of loyalty and honor was one of the reasons Max cared for him. He had gotten his high school girlfriend pregnant in an attempt to prove to his football teammates that he wasn't gay, and while he had been messed up as a teen, he had found purpose in the army. He hadn't come out of the closet for a long time, and Max didn't think he was fully out now—only those closest to him knew the truth. David would never put his daughter—or anyone's child—in danger.

"You can't view him through your own eyes, David," Dillon said. "You have to think like he thinks."

"He's a bastard, that's what I think."

"This is one of the reasons forensic psychology is a difficult career—we have to get into the heads of these people in order to not only understand them, but to think like them so we can stop them."

"Does that mean Jimmy walked, Martha panicked, and came here to Cape Haven? Why?" Max was still confused. "Why leave Eve with Jimmy's mother if Jimmy himself bailed on her? Why didn't she call her real family if she was in so much trouble, in danger? She had to know that Eleanor would take them in. Protect her, as much as she could."

Her voice cracked at the end. She would never understand the choices that Martha Revere made. Never. Had she hated Eleanor so much that she wouldn't call her for help?

"Max, I know that—"

She cut him off. "My family has nearly unlimited resources. They could have hired a private security detail to protect her. They would have taken Eve in, no questions, just like they accepted me. But she didn't call. She didn't ask for help. So why send me all these ridiculous postcards to play her own private game and not come to me when everything fell apart?"

She was shouting, and that surprised her. Max was usually very good at controlling her emotions.

"Max," Dillon said quietly, "we don't know her state of mind in that moment. She had a three-month-old daughter, her boyfriend had walked out, and she thought she was in danger. The decision to leave the baby could have been spontaneous, or she thought she could talk her way out of the situation if she confronted Colter herself and left Eve with her grandmother, fully expecting to return for her. But be grateful that she did because that one selfless act may have saved the child's life."

"I guarantee you that Martha Revere never acted selflessly. She had a specific reason for leaving Eve," Max said. "I don't know what, but it wasn't to protect her."

"Max, I'm going to call you privately," Dillon said. "I think we're done here?"

"Yes, thank you, Doc," Ryan said. "We appreciate your time."

Max disconnected the Skype call and walked into her den and closed the door without saying anything to Ryan or David. She didn't know what to say—she had lost her cool. She didn't do things like that.

A minute later, her cell phone rang.

"Hello, Dillon."

"Can you talk?"

"I told you, I don't have secrets from David and Ryan, but yeah, I'm alone."

"This is more sensitive. First, are you okay?"

"Dillon, don't shrink me. I'm not in the mood."

"Being abandoned by your mother when you were nine is one thing—it affects you, how could it not? Yet you created a satisfying and fulfilling life. But all this information you've uncovered in the last two months about your mother—not the least of which is that she had another child—has to affect you on a deeper level. I don't want you to ignore those feelings."

"I'm not," she said. She sat at the desk chair and put her head in her hands. "Yes, I feel like every piece of new information is a kick in the face. The postcards. The art theft. The relationship with Jimmy. I knew him, Dillon. He hated me and I hated him and she picked him over me. That bothered me for a long time, but I always assumed that she dumped him eventually because that's what she did to everyone in her life. I'm not *ignoring* anything. I want to find out what happened to Martha, and if Jimmy—or Phillip Colter—or someone else killed her, I want them to go to prison. I want to find out *why*."

"I wanted to talk to you about your father."

Her stomach tightened. "I told you everything I know."

"And it still bothers you. You want to know why your mother lied to you about his identity. You said something earlier—that your mother has never committed a selfless act. It got me thinking about why she didn't tell you the truth about your own paternity."

She let out a sigh. "Are you sure you're not psychic?"

"I've been accused of it, but no—that question has infused everything you do. It disturbs you. You confronted the man you thought was your biological father, he denied it, even had a paternity test to prove it, and that tore you up. Yet you continued to grow and mature and have already accomplished more in your thirty-two years than most people do in a lifetime. Yet once you knew that she'd lied to you about your father, there was nothing you could do because your mother was gone. She'd stopped sending postcards. You believed that she was dead for years because she stopped collecting her allowance. But I'm going to tell you: The single best thing she ever did for you,

Max, was leave you with your grandparents. It may not have been selfless on her part, but it was the best decision *for you*, even if she didn't think of it that way. I know your childhood wasn't normal or easy. Yet your grandparents took you in and never made you feel less. You said that to me a while back, and it resonated."

"I have thought a lot about this lately, that Martha did me a great favor. And then I thought, why? Why give me to the woman she hated?"

"She thought she was punishing you," Dillon said. "You wouldn't play her game, so she mentally thought, well, let's see how she likes growing up like I did. Another form of manipulation. But—and this is important to understand—she felt she'd found her soul mate in Jimmy Truman. You and he didn't get along, so she got rid of you."

"Why didn't she leave me with my father?" Max asked the question that had been on her mind for years.

"Because I don't think she knows who your father is."

"Well, she must have a list somewhere," she said sarcastically.

"Maybe. She was twenty-one. Young. Wild. Rich. I don't think the thought crossed her mind to figure out who it was. She might have had an idea—this guy or that guy—but it wasn't important to her. That it was important to *you* bothered her, because that made her feel inadequate."

Dillon continued, "When we met I was impressed with you. I reviewed your biography, watched some of your shows, realized that you have made a really good life for yourself. Partly because you had a family who could afford to support your dreams, but at the same time don't assume that just because you came from a privileged family that you have made a life. Like I said earlier—I lean to nature over nurture, at least that nature is going to trump most of what life hands you. I'm not saying that your past—the nurture part of your past—hasn't affected you. It has. It didn't change you, it brought out different parts of your personality. It influenced you and the choices you've made in your career. I don't think that's a bad thing, and I hope you don't, either. Society needs people like you—strong and resilient. I just wanted to make sure that you weren't going to let my analysis of your mother and her behavior impact your choices from here on out—your personal choices."

"Just don't tell me I need a psychotherapist. I tried it once last summer and thought I was going to throw her out the window."

"Formal therapy helps some people and not others, but there's a lot of informal therapy. You have a strong support structure around you. Don't be afraid to keep them close."

"Thank you, Dillon."

"You can call me anytime, Max. I'm serious about that, okay?"

"And I'm serious about dinner."

"Well, you're not far from me. When you wrap up this case, why don't you come by? We live in Georgetown and have plenty of room for you to stay the night."

"I might just take you up on that."

# Chapter Twenty-eight

Ryan grabbed a beer and walked out on the deck, trying to wrap his mind around everything the shrink had said. David followed him out. Ryan tried to give him the benefit of the doubt—he was close to Max, he wasn't involved with her romantically, and clearly Max trusted him. But the guy had been giving him the cold shoulder since he walked in.

"You know Dr. Kincaid?" Ryan asked David.

"Yes."

He didn't expand. "I read the article Max wrote about the Blair Caldwell trial. It was intense." Nothing. "Tragic, really." Again, silence.

Ryan shifted gears. "Kincaid seems to know what he's talking about, though my experience with the FBI's profilers is hit-and-miss. What do you think?"

"Max will find the truth."

"Sure, no doubt, but just mulling this over—if Martha and Jimmy worked together to steal from Colter, he wouldn't give a shit about Max being here if he had all the paintings. He wants the three we haven't recovered."

He waited for David to comment. When he didn't, Ryan was done beating around the bush.

"What's your problem, David?"

"No problem."

"You walked in here with a chip on your shoulder and an attitude like I'm the bad guy."

"Are you?"

"What the hell does that mean?"

David didn't say anything.

Ryan didn't like games. Never had. "Ask me anything."

"I'll just tell you. Leave Max alone."

"Max is a big girl. She can make her own decisions."

David turned to him, looked him straight in the eye. "This is my problem, Maguire. Max has put herself—again—in a dangerous situation. She never realizes it because she is so driven to find the truth that she develops blinders. She is smart, don't get me wrong, but her drive is so strong she dismisses that she's in jeopardy. You were here to watch her back. Instead, you shared her bed. You can't protect her if you're compromised."

"Good thing she has you," Ryan snapped back.

"Damn straight."

This was getting them nowhere.

"I don't get it. Really. Because you say one thing, but you're acting like an overprotective big brother who thinks that no man is good enough for his baby sister."

"There are few men I think are good enough for Maxine."

"And you're going to pass judgment on me like this?" He snapped his fingers.

"We'll say this—the jury is deadlocked. The only thing you have going for you is that Max is—generally—a good judge of character. But even she can be wrong."

Max came out of her den and saw David and Ryan on the deck. By their body language, they weren't just shooting the breeze. Great. She didn't need any more conflict in her life.

She started making dinner and they both came in. David had picked up the phone and was listening. Ryan glanced at her, then went into the den and stared at her timeline. It bothered her that he was looking at the past— before Martha disappeared. Looking at the moments in her childhood that had defined her.

"Thank you, Rogan," David said. "We appreciate— yeah, I know. Gray area." He smiled—as much as David's smiles were—and ended the call. "Your PI went above and beyond. My storage locker theory panned out. Rogan found one that matches all our criteria."

She tilted her head. "Do I sense we can't say where we got the information?"

"We can say that nothing is admissible in court, unless the authorities get a warrant."

"I don't care—we'll uncover the truth and then see what happens."

Ryan stood in the doorway. "Did I just hear that you obtained information illegally?"

David glared at him. "Maybe you should go home now so you don't have to deal with fruit from the poisonous tree."

Ryan was both angry and torn. "This isn't how we do these things."

Max wished she could have talked to David alone. It seemed he wanted to create conflict between her and Ryan, and she just didn't understand it. Yet, she had hired Sean Rogan to get her information she needed to find out what happened to her mother. She would take that information any day of the week, no matter how he obtained it. The truth trumped all else. And if Ryan didn't accept that about her, then they didn't have a future.

Future? What the hell was she thinking? She'd slept with the guy one night, why was she thinking about more?

Because she liked Ryan. It was as simple as that. But

Max had never been one to change to accommodate a boyfriend, which was why she was most likely going to be single her entire life. That didn't bother her. Her confidence and happiness wasn't attached to others. It couldn't be, or she'd implode. For too long she had lived based on the whims of her mother. She tried to be what her mother wanted, but failed. Maybe Dillon was right. At her core, her nature, she couldn't be anything else, and neither could Martha.

"Excuse me, David," she said and, without waiting for a response, went into the den and closed the doors so she and Ryan had privacy.

"Do not tell me that you committed a crime," Ryan said.

"I haven't."

"But—"

"I hired an expert, I don't ask how he gets his information, but I'm not going to burn him. Suffice it to say, he's an expert with computers. We asked him to look at storage lockers in default between the time Martha disappeared and two years after Jimmy last showed his face. Evidently, he found one, and David was about to give me the details. But maybe you should sit this one out. I do understand that it puts you between a rock and a hard place. And I can't for certain say that he obtained the information legally. I'm not going to ask him."

"Gray area," Ryan repeated what David had said.

"Don't be sore. Maybe it's good that you are confronted with these ethical dilemmas now. I'm a reporter, I don't have to follow the same rules you do. I respect your rules—I believe in the system most of the time. But I will break rules when I have to in order to learn the truth. I'm not going to back down."

"And what if it jeopardizes a conviction?"

"And what if towing the line results in someone else getting hurt?"

"What if *you* get hurt?"

"I'm not blind to the danger, but I'm not going to back away. I want to know what my PI found. He wouldn't have called if he didn't think it was important. If you don't want to know it, that's okay. I'm not going to hold it against you. And I just hope you don't hold my rule-breaking inclination against me."

"This is important to you," he said as if he had a major revelation.

"This *is* me," she said simply.

Ryan stepped forward and touched her cheek lightly, then he leaned down and kissed her. "Okay. Talk to David, then just tell me what I need to know and I don't want to know where you got it."

She smiled. "When you first walked into the restaurant Wednesday night, I knew you didn't always play by the rules."

"David doesn't think I'm good enough for you."

"So?"

"I think you listen to him."

"I always listen to him, I just don't always agree."

Max left Ryan in the den and closed the door. "Tell me," she said to David.

"What's with that guy?"

"He's a federal agent. I shouldn't have to explain that to you. We've worked with Marco enough over the years that you get how they think, what they can and can't do. Give him a break, you've been giving him the evil eye since you walked in."

"I don't like him."

"I don't care." She was tired of this. "What did Rogan find?"

David seemed to realize that she was irritated, and he cleared his throat. "Well, Rogan is a smart guy. I gave him the information about Martha's storage locker in Miami under the Sterling identity, and the information about the J. J. Sterling storage locker that the feds learned about. The lockers were both climate-controlled—crucial for papers, books, and art. They were high-end and highly secure. And they were owned by the same chain.

"Rogan went into their system and searched on storage lockers that went into default during our time window under Sterling, Revere, and Truman. And bingo. He found a locker that went into default a year after Jimmy Truman sold the painting. It had been under the name Martha Truman, in Savannah, Georgia. She opened it April second of the year she disappeared. She paid for two years up front. Once it was in default and no one claimed the contents, it was auctioned. A company—Boreal, Inc.—bid and won."

"Boreal. Yet again. They keep popping up."

"Perhaps the other three paintings were in there."

Max considered, then shook her head. "If they were, why would Phillip Colter be here now? And consider this—Jimmy had four of the paintings. They were in his storage locker. What if Martha took three of them and went north? Put them in her own storage locker as insurance."

"Maybe." He sounded skeptical. "You don't know that Colter is connected to Boreal."

"My gut says he is."

"And I trust your instincts. But there is nothing that points to him being part of that shell corp. Rogan couldn't find anything on it—though he said it's difficult to do without either being on-site or breaking into a government database, which he has sworn off since he's married to a fed."

"Consider this: Boreal is the silent investor in Havenly. The company owns property on Oyster Bay only a mile from where Martha's car was found abandoned. And the day after I question the caretaker of the property, Colter shows up here at the resort."

"Maybe Gabriel Truman isn't so squeaky-clean."

"Maybe he knew what his brother was up to, but kept silent to protect his daughter."

"I can believe that," David said. Of course he could, Max thought. David would do anything to protect his own child. He understood a father's love.

But not all fathers are cut from the same cloth. If Jimmy Truman was Eve's biological father, he didn't care about Martha *or* Eve. He abandoned them, left them to face the wrath of Phillip Colter for crimes that Jimmy also committed.

"I need to talk to Gabriel—without you or Ryan around. He knows more than he's saying, but he might not know what he knows, if that makes sense."

"It does. So. What are you going to do about him?" He nodded toward the closed door.

"I like him. I'm going to tell him what he needs to know, and then you're going to be nice."

David grunted.

Phillip was staring at *The Beheading of Saint John the Baptist* that hung on the wall behind his desk. This was his sanctuary, the only place he felt truly comfortable.

That *woman* had taken everything from him. He could no longer show his face in Dallas—sure, no one else knew about the paintings, but *he* did and he couldn't look at the reproductions without feeling the rage simmering.

If he could kill Martha Revere all over again, he would. She lied to him in Dallas, she lied to him in Paris, and she lied to him when he had a gun on her in Cape Haven.

Simply, she betrayed him in the worst way imaginable. She ridiculed him.

It didn't help that Jimmy lied to him and said Martha had taken them all . . . that he'd only had the one he had sold. Now, the FBI had three of his paintings, a Russian asshole had one, and he had only recovered two. The two that his company had bought when Martha's storage locker went into default.

Two out of the seven she stole from him. Two miserable paintings.

And none of them were the Degas.

Vance knocked on the door frame, then entered. Phillip said, "I need good news."

"I have a man on the cottage. We'll know when she leaves." He walked over to Phillip's desk and handed him a key. "This is the master key to every room at Havenly."

Phillip turned it around in his fingers, then handed it back to Vance. "You do it. Get everything she has."

"Sir, the man she was with last night? The one she said was her boyfriend? He's an FBI agent. It's Ryan Maguire."

Phillip tensed. "Maguire? Are you sure?"

"I confirmed it."

Phillip knew Agent Maguire by name only. He'd been sniffing around after the Dallas agent, Roy Porter, retired. Phillip had known Porter by sight—the man was hardly subtle—but he'd never been able to a warrant, and he had never come close to learning the truth about Phillip's hobbies. Maguire's efforts were similar, and Phillip hadn't worried much about him. The only thing Maguire had done that irritated Phillip was when he recovered three of his paintings that Jimmy Truman had hidden from him.

Yet Maguire was here. In Cape Haven. With Martha's daughter. Sleeping with Martha's daughter.

He must have seen the postcards in her office—would he know what they meant? Had he figured out what Martha had done? Was he, too, looking for the Degas?

"Sir?" Vance asked.

"I'm thinking."

"Maybe we should leave, go back to Dallas or better, Montreal."

"No. The Degas is somewhere nearby—I feel it. Martha hid it, and Maxine Revere is going to lead me to it if it's the last thing she does."

"And the fed?"

"It's Sunday, he'll be gone by tomorrow if his interest in Ms. Revere is purely sexual. If he's still here? I have an idea on how to get him out of town and then I'll call her for lunch. I need everyone on board, Vance, and I mean everyone. Meeting here at ten o'clock. No excuses."

"Consider it done."

Vance walked out and Phillip turned back to the Caravaggio. The stark beauty in death calmed him. Reminded him that he could have what he wanted and seek vengeance on those who denied him.

Martha Revere was dead. She was a liar. A whore. A thief.

Jimmy Truman was dead. A traitor, a whiny, sniveling asshole.

Where was the Degas? Why was Maxine Revere screwing the FBI agent who had been investigating him? Maybe . . . maybe they were looking for it together. To share in its bounty. It wouldn't be the first time Phillip encountered a corrupt cop.

He was missing something here. . . .

Everything was in Maxine Revere's cottage. Everything that would give him what he wanted.

He would make it clear in the meeting tonight that Maxine Revere had to be gone from the cottage tomorrow, no questions, so he could learn everything she knew.


Gabriel sat outside Brian's house for two hours. He'd been acting odd all day, and when Gabriel suggested they have dinner, he said Annie had already cooked. That may have been true, but Annie wasn't much of a cook and Brian and Gabriel often dined together, especially when they had so much work going on at the resort.

And then there was how Brian avoided him at Eve's race, and barely acknowledged Eve herself.

Something odd was going on with him, and Gabriel needed to know what.

At quarter to ten, he was just considering leaving when Brian left the house and climbed into his small SUV.

He could be going to work. He could be going for a drink.

Gabriel followed him to Oyster Bay. He thought he lost Brian around a bend, then saw the gates close outside the Boreal mansion.

Boreal, Phillip Colter's company.

He knew last night, and then again this morning when Brian avoided him, that Brian was hiding something. What had he gotten them into? Was the FBI right? Was Colter corrupt? An art thief? A killer?

Had Brian known all along, or did he come out here to confront him?

Was Brian in danger?

Gabriel stared at the house for a good twenty minutes. Two other cars arrived, neither of which he recognized. He wanted to go in, and confront Brian and Colter. But he didn't. Because he had someone he had to protect above all else.

Eve.

Gabriel drove home, checked on his daughter—she was sleeping—and then went downstairs and sat in his chair, his gun in his lap.

Just in case.

# Chapter Twenty-nine

Ryan rolled over in bed and kissed Max before dawn on Monday morning.

"You're not sleeping."

"I've been up awhile," she said. "But I was warm and content and didn't want to leave." She smiled.

"I wish I didn't have to go."

"Duty calls."

"I'm going to follow up on the possible Colter-Boreal connection. If I can make it—and verify the information your PI learned about the storage locker in Georgia—I might be able to parlay that into a warrant. It's iffy, but I think the AUSA will at least listen."

"If I learn anything else, I'll let you know."

"Please be careful." He kissed her bare shoulder. "I've grown quite fond of you—and your body. I don't want either to be hurt."

"I'll take it under advisement." She kissed him again. "How much time do you have?"

"I have to shower—"

"Want company?"

"Do you even have to ask?"

An hour later, Ryan was dressed, fed, and off for the

commute into Norfolk. David came in from his morning run and poured coffee.

Max felt more relaxed and well-rested than she'd been in months. Sex and sleep could do that for her, and she realized that it had been a long time since she'd felt so at peace. Considering that she had even more questions than answers about her mother made that peace feel at odds with her life. Yet Dillon Kincaid had put so much into perspective. Last night she could barely absorb everything; this morning, it had begun to sink in.

"Be careful, Maxine." David sat down across from her.

"How can I not? You're here to watch my back."

"That's not what I meant."

She looked at her half-empty coffee mug. "Maybe I missed something because I'm only on my second cup of coffee?"

"Maguire."

"You don't trust him, got it. But you checked him out, he's clean."

"Are you being deliberately obtuse?"

"That's a million-dollar word," she said. Sometimes, David didn't just say what he thought. It irritated her.

"You just ended a serious relationship and now you're jumping into bed with someone else. And by the look of things, this isn't a casual one-night stand."

Max's head was going to explode. "Could you wait until tonight—or at least this afternoon—when I can have a glass of wine or three before you talk to me about my love life?"

"I get why you ended it with Nick, but he wants to fix things. He cares about you, Max."

"Time-out." Max got up, refilled her coffee mug, and walked outside.

David followed. "I call them as I see them."

"Then you need glasses," she snapped. "You and Nick

are friends, and you're talking to him about me. That's not okay. Could this be any more stereotypical? My gay best friend is trying to fix my love life. Stay out of it, David."

He bristled. Yeah, it was a sensitive subject with him—not the being gay part so much, but that he was involving himself in her life when in the past he had been less friend and more protector. She should apologize, but she was too angry.

"Nick and I were over last September, it just took me a few months to cut ties," she continued. "Because you're right—I cared a lot about him. But I can't wait for him to decide to trust me. And maybe because I can fall into bed with someone else a few months later—maybe I subconsciously knew that it was never going to work. Even if he flew out here today and told me everything his ex-wife was doing to manipulate him and their son and ask for my advice, I wouldn't go back to him. Because deep down, he would think I forced him to share—that it was an ultimatum of sorts." She took a deep breath. "It's over, David. And I'm sorry, because I know that makes things awkward for you. You and Nick hit it off a million times better than you and Marco, or you and any of the other men I've dated. It's nice to have my best friend—my partner—enjoy spending time with my boyfriend."

"Are you that serious about this new guy after a couple days?"

"Serious? Well, I'm not proposing marriage, but I plan on seeing him again. You didn't give him a chance. You glared at him through dinner, grunted out answers to questions, and went to bed early."

"I was tired."

"Ryan is smart. He's fun. We have a lot in common. He's confident and it just *happened*. There was a spark. And I'm going to see where it goes."

"He's not like any of the men you've dated before. Most were wealthy businessmen. A couple of cops that were short-lived. Marco, of course—who still believes you'll go back to him one day. But one thing they all had in common was that they were clean-cut, successful in their chosen field, and serious."

"What makes you think Ryan isn't successful?"

"He's forty. He's been in the FBI for fourteen years and hasn't been promoted. No dings on his record, but he certainly isn't making a lot of friends. By forty with more than a decade of service most agents either leave if they haven't been moved up or they change offices. He did his rookie years in Dallas, then spent nearly twelve years in Norfolk chasing art thieves."

"Where is this disdain coming from?"

"I'm trying to protect you, Max."

"How do you know I'm not just enjoying good sex while I have some time?"

"I know you . . . even though you think you're this cynical woman, you go into every relationship thinking that this is the *one*. But your standards are so high, your expectations so great, that no one can ever live up to them. Then you leave."

"Is that what Nick says? Is that what you think of me?"

"It's what I say after watching you for the last three years."

"If you know me that well, then you know that I have a thick skin. If someone doesn't live up to my expectations? Good riddance. I deserve the best. And I'm not a needy woman, I don't *need* a man in my life."

"You're taking this wrong."

"I don't think I am."

"Nick made you happy," David said quietly. "I want you to be happy."

Her anger dissipated. David *was* a friend. She didn't

have many. They had been through a lot together, and they hadn't always liked each other. But she respected him, and over the last year had learned that he would always have her back. That he would be there for her, as a bodyguard or a partner, when she needed him.

"Thank you."

She stared out at the water.

"He needs a haircut," David said.

"It's kind of cute."

"So you and Nick are over."

"Yes, David, we are. And I'm sorry, if that helps. I tried, but there came a point where I wasn't going to sit back any longer and believe that *one day* he would share. That *someday* we'd be equal partners. I have too much respect for myself to make excuses for Nick. He made the decision to shut me out of the most important part of his life. I realized I couldn't live like that, and I had to leave. And it's okay. *I'm* okay."

"Nick isn't," David said quietly.

"I'm sorry about that, but he'll be fine. He has you, right?"

"You know that's not the same."

"No, it's better. Because you're a friend he can confide in, and I am not."

David shifted his stance, and for the first time Max believed he *really* understood. It wasn't a jealousy issue, but Nick had taken David and Max as a set. With David, he shared his frustrations and battles with his ex-wife over custody of their son. With Max, he wanted to shut that out, have sex, go to the theater, relax. He would talk about his job and her job, but not his son. That would never have worked for the long haul. He couldn't marry both her and David.

Max didn't have a romanticized version of marriage. She didn't believe that there was a soul mate for everyone.

There were couples who worked, and couples who didn't. She recognized that she was selfish on the one hand; she was independent and had definite opinions about most things and generally did what she wanted. But on the other hand, Max accepted that she shouldn't have to give up who she was in order to please someone else. If she could find someone who took her as she was, not only accepted her but *liked* who she was, she would be happy. Part of accepting her meant including her in their life. Marco included her in everything, but had a sneaky way of wanting to change her—he *said* he respected her career, but he criticized so much of what she did. Nick had another way of wanting to change her, namely diminishing her need to be a part of her lover's life in more ways than just sex.

Maybe it was a fine line. Maybe she'd never find someone compatible. But that didn't mean she couldn't enjoy a new relationship. That didn't mean she couldn't date at all.

"You like him," David said.

"Yes, I do."

Max was talking to her producer about edits on her upcoming show when David came into her office. "Eve Truman is here," he said.

"I have to go, Ben."

"Call me back—we're not done with this conversation."

"Send me the proposed voice-over script, okay? I'll look at it."

"You'll edit it," he grumbled.

"Probably. But I'll get it done on time. I really have to go." She hung up and followed David from her office. Eve was standing in the middle of the living room looking lost and forlorn.

"Eve, shouldn't you be in school?"

She shrugged. "I'll be late. I just—I didn't know who to talk to. It's not like I can talk to my friends. And my dad—I know, Max. He's not my dad and I don't know what to do."

David caught Max's eye and motioned that he was going downstairs.

"Do you drink coffee?" Max asked.

Eve nodded. "Cream and sugar."

Max prepared two mugs and sat down on the couch. Eve sat at the opposite end, staring at her coffee, not drinking or talking.

"What happened, Eve?"

"I overheard my dad and you and the FBI agent on Saturday night. I didn't want to believe it so I found my birth certificate. He's on my birth certificate. But he lied. I don't know how, but he lied on my birth certificate and he has lied to me my entire life."

"Lies have a way of coming out," Max said. "They always do."

"I don't know who I am anymore," Eve said, tears in her eyes.

Max felt for her. She'd been there, she'd felt the same way. The only difference was the reason for the lies.

"I'm not excusing Gabriel's deception," she said, carefully choosing her words, "but he loves you. He was scared that whatever Martha and Jimmy were into—and it's clear now that they were involved in something very illegal and very dangerous—would end up hurting you."

"But he could have told me. Because you know what? I don't even know if I'm related to him at all."

Now Max was confused. "What? Related to who?"

"Gabriel," Eve said. "He told me yesterday—he told me that my mother put 'unknown' on my birth certificate. That she didn't put Jimmy Truman down as my father. Dad—Gabriel—altered the birth certificate somehow.

He put his name down. But there was nothing. No one. What if I'm not even his niece? I'm a stranger—a nobody. I don't know anything anymore."

Max had never been more angry at her mother than she was at that moment. She'd lied to two daughters.

"I've been where you are," Max said.

"You don't understand. No one can understand."

"I do. You want blunt? Martha told me who my father was. He was a married man, she'd had an affair with him, and he didn't want anything to do with me. When I was sixteen—same age as you now—I flew from California to New York and confronted him. He didn't deny the affair, but he denied that he was my father. I demanded that he take a paternity test or I would tell his wife. He took the test and he hadn't been lying—he wasn't my father. Martha lied to me either because she didn't know who my father was, or because she didn't want me to know the truth. Or just to keep me tethered to her. I don't really know, and I doubt I'll ever know the truth about my father."

Eve stared at her, eyes wide, and wet, and confused. "Why would she do that?"

"I don't know, and no answer I've come up with satisfies me. But I know who you are. You are Eve Truman. You need to own your name. You're a smart girl, a championship sailor, kind, generous with your time and talents, and beautiful, inside and outside. It doesn't matter who your parents were. All that matters is who *you* are.

"Gabriel did a great job raising you. Don't let his lie destroy your relationship. He loves you so much, he gave up his navy career to raise you. I don't tell you this to make you feel guilty—you have nothing to feel guilty about. It was his choice to leave the military and take care of you and his sick mother. A lot of people wouldn't do that."

"You promised me the other night that you would never lie to me. How can I even believe that when everyone in my life has lied to me?"

"It'll be hard, but it's me. It's who *I* am. The truth is messy, but it's real. People sometimes lie to themselves, and I think Gabriel convinced himself that you were his daughter. But consider everything else he's ever done. Not what he's said, but his actions. He cared for your grandmother. He was by her side, taking care of her until she died. He taught you everything he knew about boats and sailing. I bet he taught you to swim, too."

She nodded. "He's a great swimmer."

"He adopted you—not legally, not formally, but for all intents and purposes, he is your father. Please find a way to accept what he's done, forgive him, because his motives were pure. He loved you and wanted to protect you."

"He apologized a hundred ways but I may never know the whole truth. I don't know who my father is. No one does."

"The odds are, Jimmy Truman is your biological father and Martha put 'unknown' on your birth certificate for a reason only she knows. If you really need to know, tell Gabriel you want a blood test."

"Can they do that? Tell if he's my uncle?"

"Yes. They'll know how closely you're related."

"I don't know." She frowned. "I don't want to hurt him . . . and it won't change anything."

"You don't have to make the decision today." Max knew she would get the test in a heartbeat. It would drive her crazy not knowing when the truth was attainable. She'd learned to live with the fact that she would never know who her father was unless he came forward and claimed her. So far no one had, and after thirty-two years Max doubted anyone would. But Eve had to make her own decision.

"I'll tell you this much," Max said. "I respect you not wanting to hurt your dad, but if not knowing the truth will fester inside you and make you miserable, you need the truth. If you can truly let it go, believe in your heart that Gabriel is your uncle, and continue to call him Dad because he raised you and he loves you, then believe what you want. But it's your decision, okay?"

Eve nodded. "Thank you for, um, listening."

"You want to come back later, come back. Anytime. I'll be here all month, maybe longer."

"I would like that a lot."

"I'm going to ask David to drive you to school, okay? He looks intimidating but he's a good guy."

"That's okay, you don't have to go out of your way, I can grab the bus."

"I insist, you're upset and I'm going to talk to your dad."

She sucked in her breath. "Why?"

"Not about you. I'm not going to betray your confidence. If you want to talk to him about the DNA test or anything else, and you don't want to do it alone, ask me and I'll be there."

"Oh. Thank you." She bit her lip. "Then, um, why talk to my dad?"

"When we spoke on Saturday, I suspected that he was holding back something. Maybe because he didn't know how the information fit with what we were saying, or maybe because he didn't trust me or Ryan Maguire—the FBI agent who was with me. Now that everything is out in the open, I have some questions and I think he has answers—even if he doesn't know it yet."

After David left with Eve, Max walked over to Gabriel's office in the boathouse with a thin folder of the information she wanted to share with him. She found him sitting at his desk staring out the window at the ocean. She knew that feeling—when she was troubled, she often stared at the Hudson River from her penthouse.

"Gabriel," she said.

He turned to face her. It was clear he'd gotten little sleep in the last couple of days. Dark circles framed his eyes and he hadn't shaved.

"I was going to call you."

"Good. May I sit?"

He nodded. "Close the door first."

She did, and sat across from him. "Eve came by this morning."

"She said she would. She's never missed school before."

"I had my assistant, David Kane, take her to school. No need for her to be any later, or have to take the bus. You can trust him—I do, he's a security expert."

"Your bodyguard?"

"If needed, but mostly he's just safety-conscious. He's my assistant—he helps me investigate cold cases."

"I fucked up."

"Yeah, but for the right reasons. So put that all aside, Gabriel. You have to. We have a far more pressing issue right now."

"Phillip Colter."

Now she was surprised. "Yes. What do you know?"

"When Maguire mentioned him, I froze. He is a principal at Boreal, Inc., a company that invested in the resort. Everyone in town knows Colter—at least by reputation. He's a wealthy philanthropist, a recluse. He never comes to town, but I think he's here now."

"He is. I saw him Saturday night at your restaurant."

Gabriel didn't look surprised. "I'm torn about what to do. We can lose everything. But I can't sit by and take money from a criminal. Are you certain he's an art thief?"

"Agent Maguire is, and his evidence is compelling, but he doesn't have enough for a warrant. If you know anything that can help the FBI get that warrant, you need to step up."

"I don't. That's the thing. I've only met Colter once, ten years ago when he was in a meeting with Brian. I didn't even know he was with Boreal until then. Brian introduced us, said they were talking about financing—we'd been hit by a storm the season before and the repairs were killing us, but they had to be done. Colter gave us a short-term loan. And I didn't think much of it. Brian has always handled the finances. After I talked to you and Maguire I went to talk to Brian."

Max cringed. While she liked, as a strategy, confronting people who were lying to her, she always had a plan. An emotional Gabriel went over to his partner's without one.

"He was evasive. I've known Brian my entire life. He's family—a cousin—and he was there for me when my dad died, he helped my mom when I was overseas. He's a good guy. But he was lying to me. Maybe not lying, just avoiding. So I dropped it. Because Brian knows everything. He knows that Martha left Eve with my mom. He knows that Jimmy, not me, is Eve's father, and he knows that Martha put 'unknown' on the birth certificate because he helped me create the forgery. Eve was born Genevieve Nora Revere. We changed Revere to Truman and added my name. And I don't regret it—Jimmy didn't deserve to have her, and after he threatened to take her away, I had to do something to protect her."

"Put the guilt aside for now, we can debate the rightness and wrongness of your actions later. What I need is more information about Martha and Jimmy."

"I don't know anything. I wasn't lying to you about that. I don't know about these stolen paintings or what happened to my brother when he didn't show up when he said he would. And I was on a ship when Martha left Eve with my mom."

"I want to show you something. See if you recognize any of these places. Martha sent me postcards—a total of sixteen—after she left me. The first was from Hawaii, and it's the only one that mentions Jimmy by name." She showed him the card. She quickly went through the others, then put the seven art pieces together. "Maguire and I think that Jimmy and Martha stole these seven paintings from Colter. There is a specific reason Maguire thinks Colter stole them, and I'm inclined to agree with him. It could be that Jimmy and Martha were part of his crew, though the criminal psychiatrist I consult with thinks Martha may have stolen them simply because she could. Either way, they came to be in Jimmy and Martha's possession. This one"—she pulled out the card of the Toulouse-Lautrec—"Jimmy sold ten years ago to a Russian national. It's now out of the country and the FBI hasn't been able to retrieve it. This is the sale that put Jimmy on the FBI's radar, and why Maguire has been hassling you. These three"—she pointed—"were recovered when a storage locker under the name J. J. Sterling—one of Jimmy's aliases—went into default and the individual who bought the contents at auction took them to an art appraiser."

"Jimmy is just not this smart."

"Because it's art? Maybe. But Martha was smart and very knowledgable about art." She paused. "Jimmy was a con artist since he was a kid, wasn't he?"

Gabriel nodded sadly.

"So these last three paintings—two were in a storage locker in Georgia that went into default. The locker was under the name Martha Truman—my mother was certainly not original—and the contents were bought by

Boreal at auction. That means this one, a Degas that is almost priceless, is still missing."

She skipped the Caravaggio because it would be too complicated to explain her theory on that, and went to the last postcard, of the seascape near the Boreal mansion. "This was the last postcard my mother ever sent me."

"Oh, my god." He picked it up, stared at it. "Martha sent this exact same postcard to Eve. My mother kept it as a keepsake. It's in her baby book at home."

"I need to see it."

"Okay."

"And Gabriel, I need to call Agent Maguire and tell him about Brian's relationship with Colter. Maybe it means nothing"—Max didn't think so, but she didn't want to completely spook Gabriel when he was being so helpful—"but it gives us one more connection between Colter and Cape Haven."

"While you're at it, tell him that Brian drove out to Colter's place in Oyster Bay last night. I followed him because he wasn't acting like himself. Whatever is going on, Brian knows exactly what it is."

# Chapter Thirty

In the middle of the night, Martha crept out of Emily Truman's guest bedroom, the Degas in hand. She was not a little bit angry—she was ready to kill someone. Namely, Jimmy, who had gotten her into this mess in the first place. It was his idea to steal the paintings from Phillip. Sure, she went along with it, but she didn't *know* the man, really know him, at the time.

But it wasn't just the paintings. It was that Jimmy had walked out. He'd *walked out* on her and Genevieve. Disappeared.

She'd had a plan—not a bad plan, though it needed a bit of work. They would go back to California. She would explain to her grandmother Genie—who would just *love* that Martha had named her daughter after her—that she had a bit of a problem and needed a loan. One year of her allowance up front. That would give them the money to disappear. Get new identities and go to New Zealand. It was far, far from Phillip and when he got tired of chasing them around, they'd return for the paintings.

Part of the problem was that Jimmy wanted to sell the paintings, and Martha wanted to keep them. She couldn't imagine how they would sell stolen art. They might not have stolen the art from the museums, but the art *was* stolen in the first place. She was pretty confident she could talk her way out of any jail time—she was very smart and good on her feet. But Phillip had time, money, and rage on his side and she was pretty certain he would come after her, even if the police believed her version of the story.

And then the baby. Jimmy wasn't happy about the baby, but what was she supposed to do? Genevieve was his baby too (at least, she was seventy percent certain she was Jimmy's) and he should be helping them figure out the solution.

But like everyone else in her life, Jimmy, too, had let her down. He'd taken four of the paintings from their storage locker and left her a note—a *note*!—that it was time to split up, that she could do what she wanted with her three paintings and he would do what he wanted with his *four*! paintings.

Jerk.

So she had to come up with plan B. Convince Phillip that she could get the paintings back. She still planned on going to California, but Phillip knew who she was and he could easily track her down there. She needed time. Having the baby had really messed her up. She couldn't think straight, she had lost a lot of weight—she wasn't complaining about that part, but she didn't feel well and had no appetite. The difference in having a baby at twenty-one and thirty-seven, she figured. But the biggest problem was that she couldn't seem to make a decision. Everything she thought about doing just . . . well, no decision felt right.

Leaving Genevieve with Jimmy's mother was the only thing that made sense to Martha. Without having to worry about the kid, she could think straight, she figured.

She'd left two of her paintings in a storage facility in the middle of nowhere—neither Jimmy nor Phillip would find them. She paid for two years up front. Jimmy had left two days before she received her April allowance, so she had plenty of money to put her plan into motion.

*Ha-ha, Jimmy, no money for you!*

She shook her head to clear it. Yeah, she wasn't doing well. What she really wanted was to find a spa in the middle of nowhere and spend a month being pampered and recuperating from her pregnancy and birth. She'd have to wait until May when she received her next allowance, but she had a couple of places in mind. She just had to disappear for a couple of weeks, then collect her money, check into a spa and relax. Heal. Come up with a plan. Maybe going to California was not the smart thing to do. Maybe hunting Jimmy Truman down and punishing him would make her Phillip Colter problem go away.

Martha realized she'd been standing in the living room for the last thirty minutes holding the Degas, rolled carefully in a tube. The Degas was her insurance. No one would find it here, unless they sold the house. Maybe not even then. But she wanted to give her baby girl something in case Phillip couldn't be reasoned with. By the time anyone found the painting, it would be so long that they could claim ownership. Martha knew a lot about art and art history, but was a little sketchy on the laws. Still, it had been years since Phillip stole the Degas, and it would be years more before anyone could possibly find it.

Martha took a painting down from the wall, one of those popular paintings by a local artist. She'd found a postcard of exactly this painting in the Cape Haven Museum, where she had originally intended to leave the art, but the volunteer there made her squeamish, watching her much too closely. She'd seen the painting at the Truman house, and when she saw the postcard she realized that she had the perfect plan.

Carefully, she took the backing off the painting of the

Chesapeake Bay. It was ironic, perhaps, that the most iconic picture from the region was only a hop, skip, and a jump from Phillip's house. And she was going to hide "his" Degas there. She giggled, then clamped a hand to her mouth. She certainly didn't want to explain to Emily what she was doing. Though the woman was old, she wasn't stupid. She might believe everything Martha said, but she might talk to someone, too, and if anyone knew that Martha was hiding the Degas here, they might take it for themselves.

The paintings were almost exactly the same size. The Degas was a bit bigger, she realized as she unrolled the old canvas, but she folded the edges under the frame and that provided for a nice, tight fit. No way was it going to slip out. She carefully put the backing back on, then wrote in her perfect handwriting: *Don't Ever Give Away the Seascape.*

She giggled at her own ingenuity. She rehung the painting *just so* and stood back.

No one would know. No one. If that bastard Phillip Colter stood here and stared at the painting, he wouldn't know, either.

The next morning at breakfast, Martha told Emily that she needed to leave. "I hope you can watch Genevieve for a few weeks—I have something I need to do, and I can't bring the baby."

Emily looked conflicted. "Where's Jimmy? Why isn't he helping you?"

Martha burst into tears. It was surprisingly easy to do, maybe because she was already emotional after giving birth. "He left. He walked out, didn't want anything to do with me and Genevieve. We were together for six years, Emily, and now . . . I don't know what to do. I need time to figure things out."

"Oh, honey, I'm so sorry. You can always stay here with me. There's plenty of room."

"I need to think about my options. And, well, I'm thinking if I can just talk to Jimmy, one-on-one, he might do the right thing."

"However long you need," Emily said.

Martha hugged her and thanked her. "Genevieve's suitcase is in the guest room. It has everything she needs—diapers, clothes, baby shampoo. I put a little money in there, too, if you need to buy anything for her. And here's her diaper bag. Her birth certificate is in there and her immunization card, they gave it to me at the hospital, just in case you need all that."

"How can I reach you?"

"I'll call you next week when I get settled, okay? Give you a number and address and let you know when I'll be back."

"All right, if that's what you think is best."

"I do. Thank you *so* much, I don't know what I would do without you."

Martha packed up her lone suitcase—she never traveled heavy. Why, when she could buy anything she wanted when she got to her destination?

She was down to her last thousand dollars, and she still had three weeks in the month. But she had the car and she could probably make it all the way cross-country on a thousand dollars if she slept in the car or rented a cheap motel room.

She shivered. She hated those places. There had been times when she and Maxie were living hand to mouth the last week of a month and no one would take them in and she had to live in one of those ratholes. Ridiculous.

On her way out of town, she dropped the two identical postcards in the mail. One to Maxine in Atherton, the other to Genevieve in Cape Haven.

She stared out at the ocean after she mailed the cards. Maybe she should talk to Phillip. Explain that the entire plan to steal the paintings was on Jimmy. Phillip had loved her, she was certain. He had loved her and he would believe her.

*He's been looking for you since you left Paris. You and Jimmy. He knows the truth.*

He only *thinks* he knows the truth.

She looked at her reflection. She was tired and it showed. She looked older than she ever had before, and last month she'd dyed her hair for the first time ever because she found not one, not two, but *seven* gray hairs.

But Phillip was at least ten years older, he should be happy that someone like her was interested in him.

*Don't go to him. Don't talk to him. Run, Martha. Run away.*

Run? With what money? A thousand dollars was nothing. She could do it, but then what? Keep running? What if Jimmy went to Phillip first? Turned Phillip against her? Jimmy knew her better than anyone. Where she would go, who her friends were. She didn't trust him, not after he walked out. Not after he took the paintings.

The only way to ensure that she came out on top was to talk to Phillip and explain everything. Well, her version of everything.

Jimmy made her do it.

He threatened her.

She told Jimmy she loved Phillip and he flipped out.

Yes, that would do it. Phillip would listen to her because he had always listened to her in the past. And after Paris?

She gained confidence as she drove to Phillip's house outside Oyster Bay. She'd never been here before, but they'd talked about it in Dallas. He'd wanted to bring her here once before, and she'd declined.

She rang the bell on the gate.

"May I help you?" a voice asked.

"Martha Revere for Phillip Colter."

"Mr. Colter is not in town."

"You'll want to tell him I am here."

"Please wait."

Three minutes later, the gate opened. She smiled. Of course Phillip would want to see her.

Emboldened, she drove down the long drive to the roundabout in front of the house. A man, who was short, old, and had beady eyes, walked out to greet her.

"I'm the caretaker. Mr. Colter will be here tomorrow and asked that I prepare a room for you. You can leave your things here; I'll bring them to you."

"Thank you, sir," she said and walked into the house as if she owned it.

Phillip was eating breakfast in the dining room when Martha walked in the next morning. He'd come in the night before—he'd rushed here when Masters called him with the news that Martha had shown up at his vacation house. She'd already been asleep. He let her sleep because he wasn't quite sure what he planned to do.

There was really only one option.

"Phillip, you're here!" She smiled brightly, but he saw her for who she was.

A lying, manipulative, thieving bitch.

He smiled. "Of course I am."

She strode over and kissed him. He tasted nothing but betrayal on her lips.

"Are you hungry?" he asked.

"Famished."

He motioned for her to sit. He asked Masters to bring her a mimosa and a full plate. She reached over for a pastry and started eating.

"I've been looking for you for some time," Phillip said.

"I know, and I'm sorry. I didn't want to leave Paris."

"Oh?"

"It's long and complicated, but finally I left Jimmy. I had to sneak out on him because he hurt me, Phillip."

"He hurt you." For years, Phillip had believed her lies, but he could see right through her now.

"I told him I loved you, that he and I were over for good, and he lost it."

Masters brought out two mimosas. Martha's had a strawberry on the side. She sipped. "Thank you," she said with a smile and took another sip.

"That's all for now," Phillip told Masters. After he left, he said, "Tell me about the paintings, Martha. You know what happened to them."

"Yes, I'm *so* sorry. I never wanted to take them from you—it was Jimmy's idea and I don't know why I went along with it. My feelings for you scared me—I was so used to being on my own, and, well, Jimmy threatened me. I didn't know what to do! But when I saw you in Paris, I knew Jimmy and I were through. I told him and . . . and he said you would never believe the truth. I thought he was right, at first."

"What's the truth, Martha?"

She was looking nervous, as she should be.

"Tell me, darling," he said, his voice calm and reasonable.

"Last month, I retrieved the paintings from the storage locker and I was going to bring them all back to you. Jimmy caught me and he took them."

"Took all my paintings."

"Yes! He took them from me and left. I didn't know

what to do, I was at a loss. But I told myself, Phillip will understand and forgive me. I'll get them back."

"From Jimmy."

"Yes. He wanted to sell them and I refused because I knew, in my heart, they belonged to you. To *us*."

"Where is Jimmy now?"

She swallowed uneasily. Drank more of the mimosa. Coughed. "I don't know. He left me in Miami and I came right here."

"You know you stole from me."

"I didn't want to—"

"You stole from me three years ago. And only now are you coming to make amends."

"I'm sorry, Phillip. Believe me, I'm sorry."

"I do."

She smiled, then coughed again, and drank more of the mimosa. It was nearly gone.

*Good.*

"I'll call Jimmy. Find out where he is."

"Let me tell you what I know, Martha." Phillip stood from the table, walked slowly around the room. Felt Martha's eyes on him. Her fear growing.

She should be scared.

"I've done a lot of research over the last few months once I figured out that you and Jimmy Truman had stolen *my* art from me. *Mine*. I learned that you and Jimmy have been very, very naughty. You're freeloaders. You're con artists. You use and manipulate people for fun and profit and you thought you could use and manipulate me!" His voice rose as he continued.

"At first, but then I fell in love with you."

"You say this now because you know I was close to finding you. I talked to your brother in California. Did you think I didn't remember that you were a Revere from the banking family? He had some interesting things to say. Seems you and Jimmy had blackmailed a friend of his a few years back in Hawaii. Do you recall?"

He could see in her face that she did.

"He told me all about your trust fund. About your games. That you're an art expert. How you abandoned your daughter with your parents six years ago and ran off with Jimmy Truman. He had many stories, and he was more than happy to share, especially after I agreed to fund one of his pet projects."

"Brooks?"

"Your brother hates you, Martha. You are a pathological liar who will say anything to get out of trouble."

"But, I came here on my own to talk to you."

"Where are my paintings?"

"I told you! Jimmy took them. We'll get them back—I promise!"

"I will get them back. And now that I know you don't have them I have no use for you."

Martha jumped up, then collapsed.

"Phillip, please."

"Don't beg. It's pathetic."

Martha tried to pull herself up, but the poison in the mimosa affected her muscles and coordination first.

"You'll never find them without me."

"I will, Martha."

"You won't. Because you're not smart enough." She coughed. "You didn't even know I'd switched the originals!"

Phillip walked over to the mantel, opened the lid on the metal box, and pulled out his gun.

He aimed the gun at her head. "Where is Jimmy?"

"I don't know! I told you I don't know, he left, and you—"

He pulled the trigger twice. Each bullet hit Martha's

body center mass. She collapsed. He didn't need to check her pulse to know that she was dead.

Vance DuBois ran in, gun drawn. "Mr. Colter, are you okay?"

"Double your efforts to find Jimmy Truman. He has my paintings. I want them, I want them now, and then I want Truman to suffer."

# Chapter Thirty-one

Phillip came and sat with the man he had watching Maxine Revere's cottage.

"What's going on?" he demanded.

"The FBI agent left early this morning. At oh-seven-hundred hours."

"And?"

"A teenager came by an hour later. She's still inside."

"Who?"

"I don't know. A girl, blond."

Phillip considered. It was already after nine in the morning. Maybe he should call Ms. Revere and arrange a lunch. Send her far away, then go to her cottage.

Or simply go in and force Ms. Revere to talk.

As he was contemplating his options, the door opened and a man—shorter, stockier than the federal agent—left with the teenager. They drove away in a rental SUV. Almost immediately after that, Maxine Revere left in her rental car.

Good. He had the place to himself.

He told his man to keep watch and alert him if anyone approached, then he used the master key and let himself in.

There was nothing of interest downstairs. The man was staying in the bedroom here, his things neatly put away. He had a suitcase in the closet—the luggage tag read DAVID KANE with a post office box in New York City.

Phillip went upstairs. The cottage was roomy and well designed. The deck faced the ocean and a balcony went all around. The den doors were open and on two walls were charts, sticky notes, and documents.

Phillip walked slowly around the room, at first stunned by the quantity of paper and notes, and then started to feel his blood boil as he came to the corner of the room.

*Martha disappears*
*Car found registered to D. Jane Sterling, Miami*

An enlarged copy of a map of Northampton County was dotted with labels.

*Martha's car found*
*Henderson property*
*Boreal property*
*Truman house*
*Resort*
*Museum*
*Library*
*Sheriff's station*

Why did she have the museum on her list? Was there something there of importance?

Not caring if anyone knew he'd been there, he started going through her papers. He found notes—some things he couldn't make out as she'd written them in her own odd shorthand.

*Postmark?*
*Seascape?*
*When was Eve born?*

Eve? Did she mean Eve Truman, Gabriel's daughter? Why would Maxine Revere care about Gabriel's kid?

Frantic for more information, Phillip tore through notes, files, photos . . . copies of postcards fell from one folder.

His art. The art that had been stolen from him!

He picked up the papers and rifled through. Some of the postcards meant nothing—generic beach shots. But his Boudin! His Degas! One side had a black-and-white copy of the postcard, the other Martha's handwriting.

*Dear Maxie, Happy Birthday—sorry I'm late. Off having fun! I wish you knew how to have fun. I miss you, I'll try to find time to call . . .*

Nothing substantive. Nothing! Except the pictures themselves. . . .

"That bitch!"

There was a prospectus from the Haven Point Junior Sailing Club. In the back was a picture of Eve Truman and her co-captain. And for the first time, Phillip saw the resemblance to Martha.

Eve Truman was Martha's daughter. Martha and Gabriel Truman? That made no sense, but the woman was a slut. Maybe both brothers were in on the scam to steal his art, Gabriel's reputation as a saint notwithstanding.

He scanned Revere's notes for anything else of interest . . . then he saw it.

Eve's birthdate: January 12.

He counted back. She was conceived when Martha was in Paris. In Paris with *him*.

Eve wasn't Gabriel's daughter. She wasn't Jimmy's daughter.

She was *his* daughter.

That *bitch*. She stole his art then stole his daughter!

His phone rang. "What?" he snapped.

"The second man just returned. You're not going to have time to get out—"

"I'll deal with it."

He pulled his gun out.

The door downstairs opened.

The man didn't come up the stairs.

Phillip didn't move. He would come up. He heard him moving around in his bedroom. Then the creak of the stairs.

As soon as the man came into view, Phillip shot him. Hit the man in the shoulder. He stumbled, reached for his own gun, but Phillip shot at him again. He was moving, and he wasn't sure the second bullet hit, but he didn't care. He ran down the stairs. He heard a gun discharge once, twice—

"Shit!" he screamed. The bastard shot him in the arm.

He would have gone back to finish him off, but his bodyguard was at the door. "We gotta go. There are people on the beach. They heard the gunshots."

Phillip left with his bodyguard. He called Vance Du-Bois. "I need Brian Cooper at my house now. I don't care how you do it, if you drag him kicking and screaming, but I want to see him in my office immediately!"

Vance would patch him up, then Phillip would talk to Brian Cooper. Let Cooper explain why he had lied to him for the last ten years.

Then he would kill him for his betrayal and take what was rightfully his.

# Chapter Thirty-two

Ryan had only been in the office for an hour when Max called. She told him everything Gabriel said, and her concern about Brian Cooper.

"I'll go at him hard—I don't have anything on him, though. I don't know how to get a warrant on this. But I'll run it by my boss, see what he thinks."

"You're charming," Max said. "I'm sure you can get Cooper to turn state's evidence."

Ryan laughed. "You have an inflated sense of my talents."

"I don't think so," she teased. "Seriously though, I'm following Gabriel to his house. Martha sent Eve the exact same postcard she sent me—the seascape taken near Boreal's property."

"I'm already running the company—Colter's name isn't popping yet—but I do have a warrant for his tax returns and I'm going through them now. If Boreal shows up, it helps—but getting financial records is a whole lot easier than getting a physical search warrant based on what I have. And we know that Colter hasn't sold the paintings, so we're going to have to dig really deep to find something. Storage lockers with high-end climate control. Insurance payments, looking for any fraud. Unusual expenses. But it's slow going. I've been on this for a while and the guy has no red flags. But now I can look into Boreal and see if I can get him through there."

"I'll send you a copy of the postcard Martha sent to Eve, just in case you see something I don't."

"Be careful, Max. I'm trusting your gut about Gabriel Truman, but there is still a chance that he's involved—considering that he's business partners with Colter through Boreal."

"Eyes wide open," she said.

"David's there, right?"

"He took Eve to school. She visited me this morning and was running late. We're meeting back at the cottage as soon as I get this postcard."

"He should be there with you."

"I'm okay, Ryan, but thank you for your concern. I'll call you shortly." She hung up before he said something that irritated her.

She sent David a text message as soon as she pulled up in front of Gabriel's house.

*I'm at Gabriel Truman's house to pick up a post-card that matches the last one Martha sent to me. I'll be back in an hour, or I'll call.*

She got out of her car and followed Gabriel to the front porch. The house was on the corner, set back, with a long driveway going back behind the house to a small garage. It was two stories with a basement and attic, charming and well maintained. The lawn was trimmed, flowers grew in pots and flower beds, and a huge tree was on one side—a perfect climbing tree, Max thought.

Gabriel let her in. "Um, do you want something? Water? I can make coffee."

"I'm okay."

"I'll get the baby book—it's in my bedroom." He went upstairs.

Max turned in to the living room and stared at the painting over the fireplace.

It was the same seascape that her mother had sent her.

This was not a coincidence.

She walked over to the fireplace, reached up, and carefully lifted the painting. It was heavy, the frame solid, about as wide as her arms. She squatted and lowered it to the floor.

Gabriel came downstairs. "What are you doing?"

"This is the same picture."

"Yeah, my mom loved that picture. She'd met the artist, a local woman. She passed away years ago, not long after my mother, though I think she was twenty years older."

"You said my mother was here—that she came here with Eve and left her with your mother."

"Yes. So?"

"How long was she here?"

"My mother never said."

"I think this is it."

"Is what?"

Max said, "Help me turn this around."

Though Gabriel looked at her skeptically, he helped her turn the heavy picture around and prop it against the couch.

Two things were written on the back.

The first was a stamp of authenticity from a local art gallery, and written in that this piece was number seven of one hundred.

The second was in her mother's perfect handwriting.

*Don't Ever Give Away the Seascape.*

"Whatever painting Colter is looking for is here. But we have to be careful—it's been here for sixteen years, if

I'm right. See?" Max was growing more excited. "Look, you can see that this backing was pulled away and reaffixed."

"I'll be damned."

"Let's pull it back from the same spot, rolling it carefully down."

Gabriel helped her. As soon as they started, she saw the old canvas. It had been folded on the sides and wedged into the frame.

She didn't want to damage the art. Canvas was durable, even after all these years, but the paint itself could flake off or if they scraped it, the texture could be damaged.

"Would you object to me taking the frame apart?"

"No. I just can't believe Martha hid a painting here, in my house."

"I need a hammer. Once I get off one side, the rest should be easier."

It took Max fifteen minutes of painstaking and slow work. She could have done it faster, but she was nervous and excited and most of all didn't want to damage the original. When the frame was finally disassembled, she carefully turned the second canvas over.

It was a beautiful, elegant painting of ballerinas. The light and shadow, the feeling of movement, the details in each women's expression—joy, envy, pain—made Degas one of the leaders of the Impressionist period. Holding this priceless, nearly two-hundred-year-old painting made her heart pound.

"It's the Degas." She was truly awestruck. "It's been here all this time."

"I never knew," Gabriel said. "She put it here? When she left Eve? Now this makes complete sense." He handed Max Eve's baby book. The postcard of the seascape was identical to Max's. On the reverse, Martha had written:

*Sweet Genevieve,*
*I have to go away for a while, and if I don't come*
*back you'll be okay. Look to the bay for answers,*
*look deep, and you'll find true happiness.*
    *Your Mommy*

"I always thought it was just a nothing comment, like a motivational saying. And when Eve fell in love with sailing like me, Eve said her mother was right, that the ocean brings happiness. But it wasn't that—it was about this picture."

"And about as clear as mud," Max said. "I will never understand Martha. You could have sold this at a garage sale and never been the wiser that it was here. I have to call Ryan."

She took a photo of the Degas and sent it to him. He called her back immediately.

"Is that it?"

"Yes. It was behind a picture in the Truman house. A picture that was the same as my last postcard."

"We have to get it secured immediately. I'm on my way. Can you stay there? I can't believe she put it behind another painting. Is it in good condition?"

"It appears to be."

"Take it back to your cottage—no, shit! We don't want to handle it too much. Can you stay there with it? Don't let it out of your sight?"

"Yes."

"I'll be there in an hour. Or less." Ryan hung up.

"Can I stay here?"

"Of course. I still can't believe that was here for six-teen years."

Carefully, Max carried the Degas to the dining table and laid it out. She closed all the blinds—you never knew who could be watching.

Gabriel's cell phone rang. He left the room to answer.

Max took several pictures with her cell phone. She sent one to David, then called him. He didn't answer.

"David, call me when you get this—we found it. I need you to get over to Gabriel's ASAP."

Gabriel stepped back into the dining room. "Maxine, I don't know what happened, but that was the resort. There was a shooting in your cottage. Sheriffs are there now—it looks like your place was robbed or something—and I think your partner was shot. His ID says David Kane."

Max's stomach flipped. "David? He's okay, right?"

"He's heading to Memorial Hospital, it's about thirty minutes away."

"I need to talk to someone, find out if he's okay. I need to get there." She stared at the painting. "Do you have a safe?"

"Not here—at the resort."

But Brian Cooper was at the resort.

"We need to hide this. Someplace absolutely secure. I have to get to the hospital as soon as possible."

David had been shot. He had to be okay. He *had* to. He was *not* going to die on her.

If she had any doubts about Gabriel, they disappeared. He found an ingenious hiding place for the Degas, and then drove her to the hospital. She called Ryan on the way—he would go straight to her cottage and figure out what, if anything, was taken, plus find out what was going on with the local police. Then she called Sheriff Bartlett.

"Sheriff, what happened at the resort? What can you tell me?"

"Ms. Revere, I just got on-site. I was clear on the other side of the county. My two best deputies have secured the scene, and we sent your friend up in a chopper to get him to the hospital right quick. He lost a lot of blood, but they got him stable and he was conscious, that's a good sign. He was hit in the upper-right shoulder and in his right calf."

"Who did it?"

"We're canvassing the area, talking to everyone at the resort, there's a camera at the entrance that takes down the license plate of every vehicle—I have a man going through that right now. We have a solid time frame because when the shots were fired, a witness saw two men leaving in a dark-colored SUV. I may be a small-town sheriff, but I know how to do my job."

Max didn't want to doubt him, but this was her best friend who had been hurt. She sometimes thought David was her only friend. "I have a lot of important papers and research in the den. Do you know if anything was taken?"

"Can't tell—everything is a mess. Someone definitely went through the desk and your files."

"Agent Ryan Maguire of the Norfolk FBI is on his way. He was privy to my investigation into my mother's disappearance, and we have some people of interest we've been working on—he'll know if anything is missing."

"You brought in the FBI? I wish you'd have told me."

"It's a long story, Sheriff. I'm with Gabriel Truman on my way to the hospital now. Please call me, I can be reached at this number."

"I'll call when I have news."

He hung up.

Great. She'd pissed off the sheriff. She hadn't even thought to call him, why would she? He hadn't been sheriff when Martha disappeared, or even when Jimmy returned ten years ago. Small-town politics—she put it aside.

"Emma," she suddenly said.

"What?"

"David's daughter. Emma. She's thirteen. Lives in

Northern California. Oh, God, I'm going to have to call Brittney." David's ex-girlfriend—the mother of his daughter—hated Max. Max was forbidden to have any contact with Emma or Brittney threatened to take away David's visitation rights. It was a long and complicated and ridiculous situation, but Max would never stand between David and his daughter.

She called her producer, Ben Lawson.

He answered on the second ring. "I hope you appreciate that I haven't been nagging you even though you promised to review the script immediately."

"David's been shot."

"What happened? Is he okay?" Ben's voice changed immediately from irritated to concerned.

"I'm on my way to the hospital." She gave Ben the name and location. "I don't know anything. He was stable and conscious when he left in the helicopter."

"Airlifted? Oh, no. I'll call and get information."

"You need to call Brittney. And David's father."

"I'll take care of it. Tell me as soon as you know anything."

"Likewise. Thanks, Ben."

"Is it related to your investigation?"

"It appears that David walked into my cottage when someone was going through my office."

"What did you learn?"

"I think I know what happened to my mother. Oh, and I have a sister."

"A sister? Did you say a *sister*?"

"I have to go." She hung up before Ben could ask any more questions.

Gabriel made excellent time and pulled in to short-term parking. They ran into the emergency room.

Max was good at getting information, and hospitals were notorious for making it difficult. She wasn't a blood relative, a wife, or girlfriend, but she pulled the other card.

"My employee was brought in here by helicopter with a gunshot wound he sustained on the job. I need information. Is he okay? David Kane."

The head trauma nurse came out almost immediately. "You're with Mr. Kane?"

"Yes. I'm his employer."

"Mr. Kane is stable and we're prepping him for surgery. When it's done, the doctor will come out to speak with you."

"How long?"

"I can't estimate that. There is a bullet lodged in his right clavicle. It will be a while."

"Can I see him? Please, just talk to him for one minute?"

"I don't think so, but let me check."

Two minutes later she returned. "You have one minute."

The nurse took Max to where David was being prepped for surgery in a brightly lit room. Two nurses were working on him. His clothes had already been cut off. He was on an IV and there was a mound of gauze on his leg and his shoulder. He had an oxygen mask over his mouth and nose, but his eyes were open.

She took his hand. "David, it's me. It's Max."

He turned his head and winced. He reached to get the oxygen mask off his face. She helped him.

"Ma'am, you can't remove that."

"He saw who shot him," Max said. "David, who did this? Who shot you?"

"Colter."

"Phillip Colter?"

"He took . . . a folder. I don't know what it was. I shot him. I think the arm."

"That's it," the nurse said and put the mask back on his face.

"Do *not* die," Max ordered David. "Do you understand? I will not forgive you if you die on me."

David nodded. Was he smiling under the mask? Probably grimacing in pain.

The nurse injected something into his IV. "You need to leave, we have to get him sedated and the doctor just arrived for surgery."

Max walked out. She slumped against the wall. David was the strongest man she knew. He was tough as nails, her rock. He was indispensable. Not only that, he was her friend. Her best friend. And he was shot working for her.

Gabriel walked over with a bottle of water. "Here."

"Thanks." She drank half.

"Is he going to be okay?"

"I don't know. He's in surgery now. He identified Phillip Colter as his shooter. I have to call Ryan and let him know. He can finally get a damn arrest warrant. Colter is not going to get away with this."

# Chapter Thirty-three

Ryan arrived at Max's cottage just as she called to tell him that David ID'd Phillip Colter. "Stay there, where you're safe," he said.

"For now," she said.

He didn't like that answer, but had a feeling no matter what he said she would do whatever she damn well pleased. It was as annoying as it was endearing.

"Where's the painting?"

"Gabriel has dozens of boat blueprints rolled in the corner of his office. We rolled the painting into one of them."

"Hidden in plain sight. Good. I'm going to send the sheriff out to Colter's place to serve an arrest warrant, and I'll retrieve the painting. We need to get it secured."

"Gabriel wants to talk to you."

"Agent Maguire?" Gabriel said. "My daughter is going to be home in thirty minutes. Can you wait there until she arrives? Get her someplace safe? I don't know what's going on, but I don't want her in that house alone until Colter is caught."

"How about if I take her out to the Henderson spread? They have an army."

"Yes, thank you so much. I would feel better if she was with someone."

"Not a problem. There's a team of FBI agents coming in from my office, and Sheriff Bartlett has called in every available deputy. We'll find Colter."

Ryan hung up. "Bill," he said to the sheriff, "David Kane identified Phillip Colter as his shooter."

"Colter? I'll be damned. I thought that family moved away years ago."

"His company owns the house out on the peninsula off Oyster Bay—the big spread. He's probably there. I have a team of FBI agents coming in, if you need backup."

"I activated our SWAT team, they can be anywhere in the county in twenty minutes."

"Great. Also, Mr. Truman says that Brian Cooper may be working with Colter. I don't know if he had anything to do with the break-in, but he's a person of interest."

"I know Brian. I'll send two deputies to pick him up for questioning."

"Thanks. I promised Gabriel that I would go to his house and wait for his daughter to get home from school."

"Really? Eve is a big girl. Is she in trouble? Danger?" the sheriff asked bluntly.

Ryan needed to tell him a short version. "Colter is a suspect in an art heist, possibly working with Ms. Revere's mother. We suspect that Martha Revere had one of the paintings that Colter has been looking for." Ryan should tell the sheriff that Max found it, but he didn't want to give too much away. Bartlett was solid, but Ryan didn't know everyone else on his staff, and considering that Colter was local and had money, he could have a cop on the payroll. The last thing Ryan needed was for Colter to get to the house before him.

"And?"

"It's recently come out that Eve's mother and Max's mother are the same woman. So if Colter thinks that Max knows something about the painting, he might extrapolate and think Eve knows something about it."

"You know, we've all always wondered about Eve's mother. Gabriel never talked about her."

"Now you know. I'm going to run upstairs, see if I can figure out what Colter took, then go meet Eve." He glanced at his watch. It was two—the Truman house was less than a ten-minute drive. She wouldn't be home until after three.

"I'll go catch up with Mr. Cooper and Mr. Colter and see what they have been up to," Bartlett said.

Ryan went upstairs, showed his badge to the deputy standing watch in the living room, and entered the den. He put on gloves. The room was a mess—Max's timeline hadn't been touched, but her notes were all over the place. He looked at the room, then closed his eyes and visualized the last time he was in here. It was last night, when Max shared information that she hadn't exactly gotten legally. He walked around, looked at the timeline, her desk, notes on the paintings, her mother, Jimmy, Eve—

He opened his eyes. The prospectus from the junior boating club was gone. He looked everywhere, but it wasn't here.

Why would Colter take it?

He had an awful feeling in the pit of his stomach. He ran out to his truck and started driving as he called Eve's high school, identified himself, and was transferred to the principal.

"This is Special Agent Ryan Maguire with the FBI. This is an emergency. I need you to locate a student of yours, Eve Truman, and sequester her in your office until I arrive. Do not let her go with anyone else, only me."

"I'll find out which class she's in and have her removed. Please hold."

Ryan typed in the school and the directions popped up. It was in the next town over—Cape Haven wasn't large enough to warrant their own high school. But it was still less than fifteen minutes away.

He flipped on the grille lights in his truck and drove as fast as he dared through the neighborhood before hitting the two-lane highway. It took four and a half minutes before the principal came on the phone. "Agent Maguire? Eve isn't on campus. At least, she's not in her assigned class. I'm having the vice-principal talk to her friends right now, but Eve isn't someone who has ever cut class before."

"What was the last class she was in?"

"Before lunch she was in math—I confirmed with her teacher that she was there. But no one has seen her since lunch."

Ryan called Bartlett and told him that Eve Truman may be in trouble—no one could find her. "I'm going to check out her house—can you get a trace on her cell phone?"

"I'll take care of it."

Ryan made an illegal U-turn and headed toward the Truman house. He hoped that Eve was playing hooky, because Colter had turned unpredictable and Ryan didn't know what his plan was.

He made the call he dreaded. Max answered on the first ring. "Did you find Colter?" she asked.

"We're looking. But Eve's not at school. I don't know what's going on, I'm on my way to Gabriel's house, but I have a bad feeling."

"We're on our way."

"No, I think you're safer at the hospital."

The phone was already dead. Dammit! He drove faster.

Eve mentally hit herself for the hundredth time over the last hour.

*You are so stupid! You fell for the oldest line in the book!*

She knew Phillip Colter, sort of. He was an investor at the club, friends with her uncle Brian. She'd only seen him around a few times, but you never forget the super-rich.

*There was an accident at the hotel.*

And she'd gone with him. Just like that. It wasn't until she was in the backseat and saw the blood on Colter's arm that she got suspicious.

"You're bleeding," she said. "What happened?"

"A scaffolding fell. It's just a scratch."

Scaffolding? What scaffolding? They weren't doing any renovations this season.

Colter's driver slowed down at a STOP sign and Eve tried to jump out of the back, but the doors were locked and she couldn't budge them.

"Child safety locks," Colter said. "Go, Vance. Just get us to the house as fast as you can."

The house? The driver turned suddenly onto a back road that headed toward the Hendersons' farm. Why were they going out to Oyster Bay?

"Let me out!" she screamed. She tried to grab Colter, she didn't know why, she just wanted out of the car, a sick mix of growing fear and anger and deep dread filling her until she almost couldn't see straight.

Colter pulled a gun on her. "I don't want to hurt you, Eve. Don't make me pull the trigger."

She scrambled as far into the corner of the backseat as she could.

He caught her eye. "Everyone has lied to you, Eve, for your entire life. I am going to tell you the truth. I'm your father, Eve. Your mother lied, that man who you call your dad lied, but I'm not lying. You are mine, and I will prove it. But first, we're leaving this godforsaken town."

Eve didn't believe him, but why would he say something like that?

She sat quietly in the back of the car. She had to find a way to escape. If he thought she'd given up, maybe she could run once they let her out. She wasn't tied up, and she was a fast runner. She slowly pulled her phone from her back pocket. She dialed 911.

"Stop the car," Colter said.

The driver stopped in the middle of the two-lane highway.

Colter reached over and slapped her. "Give it to me," he said. His face was red.

She pressed Send and handed it to him.

He ended the call—had it gone through?—and threw the phone out the window.

"Drive," he told the driver, and didn't look again at Eve.

*Why'd you go with him in the first place?*

Stop. Stop with the regrets. Get out of this mess and then she could feel sorry for herself and her own stupidity.

*You thought something had happened to your dad.*

She didn't care that Gabriel Truman wasn't her father. She was upset that he'd lied to her, but she loved him. She couldn't turn it off. She remembered how he'd cried at his mother's funeral. She'd never seen her dad cry before or since. She'd taken his hand and said, "It's okay, Daddy. She's in heaven. Heaven is a happy place. You still have me."

And he'd hugged her tightly and told her she was the best thing God had given him.

She would never forget when he built her the doll boat for her sixth birthday. She didn't want Barbies or baby dolls, she wanted to play sailor. When she was seven, she wanted to go into the navy like her daddy, and painted her boat gray and put army guys on the deck. She'd made a mess of the beautiful boat, but her dad didn't care. They played naval battles for weeks, and then she cried because she had ruined his beautiful boat. He told her they would strip it and restain it together, which they did.

When she won her first race, he was there cheering her on. When she lost two weeks later and had been so mad because her team had screwed up, he told her the captain is always responsible for his mates, and not to be too hard on them.

*"You are the pilot. They look to you for direction. If you berate them, they won't trust you. Be positive, train together, and take responsibility for your loss. They will respect you more—and perform better—next time."*

When they started talking about colleges when she started high school, she said she wanted to stay close. Maybe not even go to college.

*"I didn't go to college. I won't say I regret it, I wanted to be in the navy. But sometimes I wish I had gone later. There are more opportunities for college graduates."*

*"Is it because I was born that you didn't go?"*

*"No, baby, it's not. It's because I never thought I was smart enough."*

*"You're the smartest person I know."*

*He hugged her. "If you choose not to go to college, you need a plan—and to be able to develop it into a career that is both satisfying and supports you. But you're smart, kid, very smart. You should go to college and at least see all that is available to you."*

*"Molly's brother is at Virginia Tech. He got a scholarship. I don't know if I can get one."*

*"There are lots of ways to fund college, don't worry about that. VT is a great school, and if that's where you want to go, then we'll sit down, figure out what we need to do to get there."*

*"I don't know what I want to do. I love sailing so much, but that's a hobby, you know?"*

*"You love animals. You can be a veterinarian."*

*"Too much math."*

They laughed. Eve was a good student, but had never seemed to master math concepts.

*"Maybe a marine biologist,"* she said. *"Or maybe graphic design. I got an A on my art project, the one where we designed an ad. Uncle Brian let me use his computer at the resort, it has all these programs on it that we have at school. My teacher said I had a good eye."*

*"Honestly, you can do anything, Eve. The world is your oyster."*

*"What does that even mean?"* She giggled.

Tears burned behind Eve's eyes but she held them back. The truck turned in to the gated property down the road from the Hendersons. The gate closed behind them and they drove to the house.

Colter got out and walked up the stairs. The driver opened her door. He tried to grab her arm. She kicked him in the stomach. She was aiming lower, but missed. She kicked again. He grabbed her leg and she kicked up, her tennis shoe hitting him square in the jaw. He grunted and she managed to fall out of the truck. She got up and ran.

He was faster. He had her before she got fifty feet away, and tackled her. Blood filled her mouth and her face scraped against the rocky ground.

She fought, spit at him, tried to scratch him, but he grabbed her from behind and half-carried, half-dragged her to the house.

Colter said, "You're beginning to make me angry. Tie her up, Vance, I won't have any more of this nonsense. Eve, when I explain everything, you'll understand."

She spat in his face.

He slapped her so hard she almost fell from his goon's grip.

The three of them entered the house.

A familiar voice said, "I brought the boat, but why do you . . . oh, my God, Eve!"

"Uncle Brian?" she cried through her swollen mouth. "Help me."

"What have you done, Phillip? Why—"

"You lied to me," Colter said. "You knew that Gabriel wasn't this girl's father."

"What's going on, Uncle Brian?" Eve pleaded.

"Look, Mr. Colter, Jimmy wasn't around. There was no harm in letting Gabriel raise her. Jimmy left. Why do you care? Let her go, please. She's not a part of this."

"She's everything. She's mine!"

Uncle Brian stepped back. "What? I don't think—"

"You're right, you don't think. You didn't tell me about the FBI agent, you didn't tell me that Martha had a child, and you didn't give me everything that was in that reporter's cottage. There was so much more than a few pictures."

"I didn't know what you wanted. I did the best I could—"

Uncle Brian? What was he doing? What had he done? He was helping this man?

"Martha and I were together in Paris when this child was conceived. That was all on the timeline on Maxine Revere's wall. You left that part out."

"I didn't know—I didn't think—"

"You don't think, Cooper."

A gun went off, and Uncle Brian fell to the floor.

Eve screamed. "No! No! I'm not going with you. Uncle Brian! Let me go!" She kicked and thrashed and another man ran in. He pulled her arms back and tied her wrists together.

"Good Lord," Colter said, "shut her up and get her on the damn boat. We're leaving."

# Chapter Thirty-four

Max didn't want to leave David, but he could be in surgery for hours, and Eve was in danger right now.

Gabriel sped back to Cape Haven, his hands tight and white on the steering wheel, and Max was forced to grip the dashboard a couple of times in sheer panic as he erratically passed cars that were going the speed limit.

Her heart was racing as she answered her cell phone when they were only minutes from town.

"Ryan, please tell me you found her."

"The sheriff's department raided Colter's house. Brian Cooper was inside, DOA. Eve's phone was traced to a road leading from the highway to the Colter compound. The caretaker is in custody, but isn't talking. I gave a list of the stolen art to the sheriff and some of it is here, in Cape Haven. I'm going to assume they are the originals but need to wait for authentication. The two pieces that had been bought at auction from Martha's Georgia storage locker are in the master bedroom. And the Caravaggio is in Colter's office. If it's real, you were right."

"I usually am. But this time, I don't feel so good about it."

"I'm heading back to Havenly now—one of the staff

called the sheriff and thinks that Cooper took a boat out from the pier. Said he was acting strange and didn't acknowledge her when she spoke to him. I don't have any other details, but I'm alerting the Coast Guard in case we get confirmation. If he took a boat, he had to have gone around the cape to Oyster Bay. There were vehicles at Colter's house, but no one except the caretaker was found on the property."

"We'll be there in five minutes." Three, with the way Gabriel was driving.

She told him what Ryan had said.

"Why would Colter take her? Why?"

"Leverage, but I couldn't say for certain."

"Brian—I can't believe he betrayed us like this. Why would he bring Colter a boat?"

"Maybe to leverage him? Help Colter escape to save Eve?"

"I don't know him anymore. And now I can't even ask him *why!* Eve is just a little girl. She's innocent. She's not part of this!"

"Focus, Gabriel. You need to calm down. It's hard, but we have to be smart about this."

"He wants that damn painting, he can have it! I just want Eve. I need her safe."

"We'll get her back."

"Why did you have to come in the first place? Why did you have to be here? Everything was fine until you showed up."

Long ago, her grandmother had told her to never apologize if she wasn't sorry. What could she say now? She was sorry on the one hand—she had no idea that her search for the truth about her mother would have present-day repercussions. But at the same time, searching for the truth was part of who she was, and any apology would be a lie. She couldn't think about how she would have done things differently—she didn't have the information ten days ago about Gabriel, Eve, or Colter.

"I am truly sorry that Eve ended up in the middle of this."

"It's my fault. I should never have lied to her."

"No, it's not your fault, Gabriel. It's not yours and it's not mine. Everything you did was to protect her—an innocent child who was being used as a pawn by her biological parents. She understands that."

"Did I do it for her? Or to protect myself?"

"You're too honorable of a man to act so selfishly, to protect himself over others. I believe that, and Eve knows it. So get over the guilt, control your anger and your fear so that we can find Eve and bring her back safe."

Gabriel screeched to a stop at the main entrance of the resort. Several sheriff's cars were there, and a Norfolk police car. Law enforcement had pulled out all the stops and called in neighboring communities to help in the search.

Max jumped out of the truck, wobbling just a bit from the crazy drive. She saw Ryan and strode over to him. He put his hand on her arm, squeezed. "How's David?" he asked quietly.

"Still in surgery."

He nodded, concern in his eyes. "He clipped Colter. Don't know how bad it is, but there was blood spatter and a bullet near the door. Not a lot of blood, but by the location it looks like the bullet went through his arm."

Gabriel was shouting at Sheriff Bartlett who yelled right back at him. Ryan rushed over to mediate. "Truman, you have to calm down."

"We've got this, Gabriel," Bartlett said. "Back off or you'll be sitting in one of my vehicles."

"That's my daughter out there!" Gabriel turned to Ryan. "Where is the boat? Where is Colter?"

"The Coast Guard is standing by and we're waiting for an inventory so we can give them the hull number and description."

"I can tell you. Let me through, one look and I can give you everything."

Ryan nodded to Bartlett, and the four of them rushed down to the docks. Gabriel took thirty seconds and said, "He has *Haven III*. I have all the specs."

Ryan took them down and called the Coast Guard.

Gabriel started walking down the dock. Max was listening to Ryan's conversation, but keeping her eye on Gabriel.

Gabriel was standing a hundred feet away, but she could practically feel the tension and fear rolling off him.

"The hostage is sixteen, blond, five feet four inches tall. Eve Truman," Ryan was saying. "Yes, he's armed and dangerous. Unknown how many hostiles on the boat."

Gabriel untied the ropes of one of the boats, a cruiser that could practically fly across the water. As soon as Max realized what he intended to do, she started running down the docks. "Ryan," she called over her shoulder, but wasn't certain he heard her.

"Gabriel, don't!" she yelled.

He ignored her and jumped into the boat. Max ran as fast as she could, grateful that she was wearing boots and not heels. She slipped once and caught herself, and jumped on the boat just as Gabriel got the engine started and was pulling out of the slip.

"You're coming with me then," Gabriel said and picked up speed. "I am not going to play these games with the cops. That is my daughter out there. She's the only thing that matters to me."

Max could hear Ryan shouting from the dock. She called him and watched him put his phone to his ear.

"What are you doing?" he demanded.

"I can't let him go by himself—tell the Coast Guard."

"Shit, I'm coming after you. He's going to get you and Eve killed."

"I can talk to him."

"I'll track you through your phone for as long as I can."

Max ended the call and said, "Gabriel, think. The Coast Guard is searching for the boat. They have the training for this."

"I'm going to give him that damn painting."

"Let the FBI and Coast Guard negotiate."

"He took my daughter. Why hasn't he called me? He must know something. Or he thinks I know where that damn painting is. Or he found it. Maybe he saw us, I don't know!"

Max considered the possibilities. "He must have known what I was looking for. Found a way into the cottage."

"Brian," Gabriel spat out. "Brian betrayed me. He could have used a master key. Given it to Colter, for all I know."

Max opened the box at the back of the boat and found the life vests. She immediately put one on. With the way Gabriel was driving the boat she didn't want to be tossed overboard. The small yacht was big enough that she didn't think she could fall overboard easily, but she wasn't taking chances.

"It's my fault," Gabriel said again.

"Just stop with that!" Guilt could make people do stupid things.

"I broke into your cottage," Gabriel said. "I saw everything in your office. I told Brian that you were looking into Martha's disappearance, because he's the only one who knew that Eve was Jimmy's daughter. Hell, I don't even know if Eve is Jimmy's daughter! It's not like we can ask Martha! I didn't take anything, but he knew what was there . . . he must have gone in, too, and then reported to Colter. How could he do that to me? To Eve? I don't know what the hell is going on, but I'm going to get her back."

Max considered what Colter could have seen in her office.

*The timeline.*

The postcard from Paris was sent in May. If Martha had been sexually involved with Colter then—at the same time as he appeared to have stolen the Caravaggio—Colter might believe Eve was his daughter.

"Gabriel, we have to be extremely cautious."

"Fuck caution! I need her back. God, if he hurts her I will kill him."

"Listen to me!" She had to shout over the engine as they practically flew over the choppy waves. "Colter might believe that Eve is *his* daughter. I know Martha was in Paris nine months before Eve was born. She probably put 'unknown' on the birth certificate because she didn't know if Jimmy or Colter was Eve's father. That can help. If he thinks she is his flesh and blood, he won't want to hurt her—he'll want to convince her."

"You can't possibly know that. I'm trading that damn Degas. I don't care about a stupid painting, I only care about Eve. I have to protect her, Max. If you can't help, you need to jump out now."

Like she was going to jump out of a fast moving boat into freezing water.

They approached the Chesapeake Bay Bridge and Gabriel navigated expertly. He was also typing on a small computer built into the small pilothouse on the boat.

"What are you doing?"

"All Havenly boats have GPS built in. I'm searching for it."

"You should have told Ryan."

"He's never going to turn over the painting for Eve. It's all he cares about."

"Human life is always more important," she said, but Gabriel wasn't really listening to her.

Max pulled out her phone and sent Ryan a text message.

*Gabriel is tracking Haven III via GPS.*

As soon as Gabriel cleared the bridge, he started working on his radio. "*Haven III*, this is *Haven Scout*. Colter, it's Gabriel Truman. Pick up the radio. Over."

Silence.

"Colter, I swear, if you hurt my daughter I will kill you. I have something you want, and I'm ready to make a trade."

Silence.

"Why isn't he answering me?" Gabriel cried out. "There!" He was looking at an image on his onboard computer. Gabriel adjusted his course and increased his speed, just when Max thought they were traveling at the maximum. "I found you, you fucking bastard. He's heading up the coast, toward Delaware and Jersey."

"You need a plan. He'll see you coming." Max texted Ryan the message. She didn't know if her messages were getting through—she had an intermittent signal on her phone, though she could still see the shore. Gabriel had turned northeast and was parallel, for the most part, to the coastline.

"Gabriel, you have to talk to me," Max said.

"Will you give up the Degas?"

"He's not going to make the trade if he thinks Eve is his daughter."

"Yes, he will! He's a greedy bastard."

"He'll want everything. Eve *and* the painting."

"We just need to get her back." His voice cracked.

"We will. You have to trust Ryan and the Coast Guard. They know what they're doing."

"It'll take too long for them to get up here. They're coming out of Norfolk. We don't have time. I can't leave her alone with that man."

His radio beeped. "Truman?"

"Colter," Gabriel said. "Let her go and I'll give you the Degas."

Silence. Again.

"Dammit, talk to me!"

Gabriel Truman had the Degas. Had he had his painting the entire time hidden away? Had he been in cahoots with his brother? Phillip hated not having all the information he needed to make a decision.

But one decision was easy.

He was not trading away his daughter.

But he wanted the Degas, too.

He picked up the radio again. "Where is it?"

"Safe."

"That isn't good enough."

"Bring Eve to shore and I'll bring you the painting."

He laughed. "So you can send the police to pick me up? I'm safer on the water. I'll send a colleague to retrieve the painting. Then we'll talk about Eve."

"No."

"Some things," Phillip said, "are more important than art. Like family. *My* family."

He turned off the radio and turned to his daughter,

who was tied to the captain's chair because she had tried to get away not once, but twice.

Naughty girl. But she would change.

He had never considered having a family. Maybe once, long ago, when he was younger and virile and had his pick of women. And maybe once, not as long ago, when he was in love with Martha Revere—at least the woman he thought Martha Revere was before she humiliated him.

"Eve," he said calmly, "I knew your mother very well. She stole from me, but I loved her once. A true, real love that I had never felt before in my life, or since. I hate that she kept you from me."

"You're not my father."

"Gabriel has been lying to you for your entire life. Maybe he didn't know the truth, but he knew he was not your father. I am. I spent nearly two weeks in Paris with your mother nine months before you were born. A simple blood test will prove it."

"I don't care, I will never, ever stay with you."

"Child, I don't expect you to understand. I have a yacht waiting for me, and then we will disappear. I have a plan, and even if the FBI sends out the Coast Guard, they are too far away to reach us in time. Then, when we're settled, I'll have all the time in the world to explain to you who I am. You will understand." He would make her understand. It wasn't his fault, or even her fault, that Martha Revere was a lying, cheating, thieving whore.

"You shot Uncle Brian. You killed him!"

"The man lied to me, he lied to you. He knew you weren't Gabriel's daughter yet didn't think it was important enough to tell me? He was a fool. I asked him to get everything from Maxine Revere's cottage, and he brought me photos that meant nothing. Not until I saw for myself. You don't understand yet, but you will. I can give you everything, Eve. Everything."

"I don't want *anything* from you!"

"How can you side with those people? Do you even know who your mother was? Martha Revere, she was beautiful. You look so much like her. So much . . ." He shook his head and cleared his throat. "She should have told me from the beginning that you were mine. I would have taken care of both of you. I would have forgiven her for stealing from me, for *lying* to me, because she gave me something precious. A child." He paused. "I was married once, years ago. We tried for ten years to have a baby. It was her fault we couldn't. Something wrong with her uterus. She tried to say it was me, that *my* sperm wasn't good enough. She was obviously wrong, because it produced *you*. Martha did one thing right in her life, and I'm not going to stand aside and let another man raise you."

"Gabriel *did* raise me. I'm sixteen. Gabriel Truman is my dad, and he always will be."

Phillip scowled. "Enough. Vance, how far out are we?"

Vance went up to the helm and talked to Pete, who was piloting the boat. He called back down, "Six minutes to the rendezvous."

"I need some air. Watch her."


"That is the stupidest plan I've ever heard," Max said.

"It's the only way. I can't do it without you."

Gabriel had sophisticated equipment on the cruiser, and he suspected that Colter was heading toward a larger vessel on the edge of international waters because of the limited fuel capacity of the *Haven III*. While the Coast Guard could board the boat if they knew where it was, he determined that they were still too far out—and they didn't know what kind of weapons the ship had, whether there was a helicopter or another escape plan.

Max didn't want to play decoy, but Gabriel had a point—if they approached the *Haven III*, Colter would likely kill them, or at a minimum, incapacitate the boat. Maybe Gabriel finally realized that Colter would take Eve over the Degas, at least right now. She was his new toy. He would figure he could come back for the Degas, or leverage Gabriel for it once he was safely away.

Gabriel figured out a way he could get to the larger vessel first. He'd already been coming at the boat from a different angle.

"Max, the Coast Guard is twenty minutes away. Colter will be at the ship in two minutes, he could have reinforcements—hell, I don't know!"

Max hated the idea, though Gabriel had a point. Still, they didn't know who these people were, if they were a charter or fully in on Colter's plan. She'd tried to explain as much to Gabriel, but he wasn't listening.

"Please, I need you. Otherwise I'm going to do it alone."

Guilt seeped in. Real guilt. Eve was her sister, but she was Gabriel's daughter, blood or no. And Max had started this ball rolling by coming to town and asking questions.

"Okay," she agreed.

Gabriel maxed out the engine. They saw a ship with a Canadian flag. It was a luxury yacht, one of the nicest Max had ever seen—and she'd been on many pricey yachts. A charter? Did Colter own it? If Colter owned it, they were really screwed. The only thing they had at that point was negotiating with the Degas—and Max might be able to stall Colter long enough for the Coast Guard to arrive.

"You ready?" Gabriel asked. His eyes were half crazy but determined.

*No.*

She nodded.

Gabriel went on the radio. "Mayday, Mayday, Canadian vessel—this is *Haven Scout*. I have an onboard emergency. Mayday."

"*Haven Scout*, what is your emergency? Over."

"My wife just had a seizure. I don't know what's wrong with her, but she's unconscious and I need to get her to shore—you're a faster boat."

"We don't have the authority to go to shore."

"Please, she's going to die."

"We don't have a doctor on board."

"You have a heliport—I contacted the Coast Guard already, but they're too far out to help. Please, she can't die on me."

Silence. So long that Max was certain they were in serious trouble.

"*Haven Scout,* you may board."

"That was too easy," Max said.

"They were probably hired by Colter, a charter. They might not know what he's doing, and they're not going to know me. Lie down. Be boneless. That's the only way this is going to work."

Ryan begged the Coast Guard to let him ride in the rescue chopper. Fortunately, he'd worked with the agency enough over the years that they acquiesced. He hadn't been able to reach Max after sending the ETA, but when the Coast Guard got a call from a Canadian vessel, a sixty-five meter Hessen-built yacht that Ryan knew could go as fast as many of the Coast Guard cutters, that there was an unconscious, unresponsive woman taken from a small U.S. boat, he knew it had to be Max. Was this a trick? Or was she really hurt?

"They called you?"

"Yes, sir."

"Maybe it's a trick. Maybe it's not them."

"The *Haven III* is on a clear trajectory to the Canadian *Infinity*. A boat the size of the *Haven* isn't going to get much farther."

"They said we could board. It's a small pad, but we can make it."

"ETA?"

"Twelve minutes if they remain anchored."

Phillip pulled up alongside the luxury yacht he'd chartered to take them to Nova Scotia, where he had a plane waiting to take him to Paris. He hated to leave the Degas, but he only half believed Truman that he had it. A bird in the hand, he thought, as he turned to his daughter. She had a bruised jaw, but he'd cleaned the blood from her face. Still, she was defiant, and there was no telling what she might do.

"This is for your own good," he said, injected her with a sedative and then untied her.

"I hate you." She tried to hit him, but the drugs already affected her muscles.

"All children go through a phase of hating their parents. You'll get over it."

Rene, the crew member who had been part of Colter's team in the past, helped them with their bags while Vance carried Eve. Pete left with the *Haven III*. He would dock at the first opportunity and go in search of the Degas, in case Truman wasn't lying. But he was also a distraction. If the authorities had learned about the boat, they would track it, not the Canadian vessel.

"We have a problem."

Colter fumed. "What?"

"We encountered a vessel in distress and the captain allowed the occupants on to the boat."

"They'll have to come with us to Nova Scotia."

"He contacted the Coast Guard. The woman is unconscious. He wants to wait for the Guard. I didn't know what to do."

"Where are they?"

"Medical quarters."

"The captain?"

"Pilothouse."

Colter fumed. "Vance, take Eve to the cabins. Secure her. Rene, come with me."

They walked up two flights of stairs to the pilothouse. "You know what has to be done, Rene."

"Yes, sir. I'll take care of it."

They entered the pilothouse. "You must be Mr. Colter," the captain said. "We had a slight emergency, but we'll be on our way shortly."

"We leave now."

"That's not possible, we have a medical emergency, but I can make up the time—we have clear weather all the way to Nova Scotia."

Colter took out his gun. "The boat moves now or you're dead."

When the captain didn't budge, Colter shot him—three times because he didn't like anyone disobeying him.

"Get us out of here, Rene. Now."

"Y-yes, s-s-sir," Rene said and took over for the captain.

As soon as the first mate left them in the small medical bay, Gabriel listened, whispered to Max, "Stay here, play possum. I'm going to look around."

He slipped out. He was familiar with the Hessen-built luxury boat. It was fast, it was sleek, and really a terrific boat that could withstand rough waters.

He heard a ramp being lowered to another boat. He'd anchored the *Scout* on the starboard side, hoping that Colter wouldn't see it. If he saw it, all bets were off.

He walked down the hall to the outer door, but squatted to avoid being seen.

He watched through a portal. He didn't see Colter—sensing two men walking up the metal stairs just out of his line of sight—but a large man was carrying Eve in the opposite direction. She was unconscious or sick. Her hair hung limply around her face. His anger mounted.

But he waited. He had to get to Eve and protect her, wait until the Coast Guard landed. Colter had only one man with him—the other goon left on the *Haven III*. While the captain who had let them board wasn't part of Colter's inner group, Colter didn't know how many on board were involved. A bare-bones crew on a ship this size might be four. How many were here? How many with Colter?

Gabriel couldn't take any chances. He had to get Eve to safety, then he would go after Phillip Colter.

He watched and saw what room Colter's big thug carried Eve into. The man left a minute later. Gabriel was waiting for him to disappear from the outer corridor when he heard a gunshot.

Then two more.

They came from the pilothouse.

Less than a minute later Gabriel heard the engines start.

The boat started moving.

First gunfire, then movement. Something had gone very wrong. Was Gabriel dead? Were they coming for her next? She had to find Eve and some way to get her out of here. Or hide her until the Coast Guard arrived. They should be only minutes away.

*Dammit, Gabriel! What went wrong?*

She sat up and listened. All she heard was the engine,

which seemed to be right beneath her. Max looked at her cell phone—no signal. She cautiously opened the door and didn't see anyone.

The luxury yacht was set up with the crew quarters down below, and the guest quarters on deck, with a second level for the living and the galley, then the pilothouse up top. There were several decks, a lot of open space in the back, but where she was, behind the galley, there wasn't much of anything other than a couple of rooms and two long halls.

Max had been on boats like this in the past, owned by friends of her mother's. Her grandparents had never taken to the seas—her grandmother got severely seasick.

But Max had been on enough yachts as a child and as an adult to figure her way around. She went down the hall, then up the stairs on the aft side. She listened carefully. The boat began to pick up speed so quickly that she almost lost her footing. She regained her balance and continued forward slowly, hoping she wasn't making a fatal mistake.

"It's leaving," Ryan said to the Coast Guard pilot.

The pilot tried to hail the ship. He identified himself then said, "Canadian vessel, we are four minutes out. You need to slow to less than a knot so we can land on your helipad."

There was no answer.

"Canadian vessel *Infinity*, this is the United States Coast Guard. Reduce speed now and prepare to be boarded."

There was no answer.

"You have to land," Ryan said.

"Landing at that speed on that small of a pad is too dangerous, Maguire."

"Drop me."

"You've never trained for this. I'm not dropping you on deck. The cutter is only two minutes behind us."

"That boat is gaining speed—how fast can it go?"

The pilot didn't answer.

"Tell me the truth."

"That model, if customized, goes almost as fast as our cutters. But we'll catch up. It might take a bit longer, but we'll gain on them."

Never had Ryan felt more inadequate. He was a white-collar agent, not SWAT, not a military guy. But dammit, he wasn't leaving Max or Eve with that madman. "We have to get on board."

"We're faster, we're almost there. If they slow down, I'll land."

Gabriel found Eve unconscious in one of the staterooms. He knelt by her side. Her face was bruised and cut up, like a razor burn. "Baby, Eve, honey, wake up."

She moaned, tried to open her eyes. She murmured, "I'm so sleepy."

She was alive. He hugged her close to his chest.

"Daddy."

"I'm here." Eve was lethargic and limp. The bastard had drugged her.

The boat was picking up speed, getting back to the *Scout* was impossible now. The only way they were getting out of this mess was to take Colter down.

"I'm going to take you to Max."

"Max? Max is here?"

"Yes, she came with me to get you. She's in the crew area. Can you walk?"

"Yeah." She got up, but her legs buckled.

Gabriel didn't know what to do. He couldn't take her

out into the unknown, and while the yacht was big, it wasn't *that* big. Someone might see them.

"Okay, okay. Stay put. I'm going to find Max and she'll come here and stay with you. Okay?" He laid Eve back down on the bed. Dammit. He didn't want to leave her. But Colter would be back.

*Colter will come back.*

He had the element of surprise, right? Colter might know that they were on board, he could have tortured or bribed the crew for information, but he didn't know *where*.

"Second thought, I'm going to stay here." He searched the room for a weapon, anything to use, but found nothing.

He clenched his fists. *Nothing* was going to happen to his daughter.

Phillip despised incompetent staff. "You were told to wait for me and then we would leave for Nova Scotia. Why you felt the need to bring on strangers, call the Coast Guard? Now they're pursuing us. Go farther out. Go faster."

"I told you, sir, the captain did it on his own."

"Who else is here."

"Just Johnny. He's solid, I swear. A mechanic. He knows this boat inside and out."

Phillip nodded to Vance. "Find Johnny, stick with him. Rene, I'm counting on you to keep this boat moving, understand?"

"Yes, sir. We're at twenty knots. I can get another four, maybe five knots."

"Do it."

"The helicopter can stay with us."

"Who has more fuel?"

"We do, sir."

"He'll turn back soon. Just keep moving! Whatever you do, do not stop this ship, understood?"

"Yes, sir."

Colter left the pilothouse. He didn't want to panic, but this hadn't gone as he had planned. He considered that maybe he shouldn't have run with Eve—with his daughter—but after he shot the man in Revere's cottage, he feared that someone had identified him. He was right, someone had, and now the police were going to be hunting him like a fucking animal.

He would find a way to get out of this. He was smart, he was successful, and he had money. He would figure it out. He just needed time to *think*!

Ryan listened to the pilot talking to his commander who was on the boat behind them. The Coast Guard was equipped with antimaterial guns that could take out the engine of small, high-speed boats without killing anyone on board. It should, in theory, work on the yacht. Barring that, they wanted permission to rappel on to the deck and board the vessel. Ryan understood bureaucracy—he was in the FBI, the king of bureaucracy—but when they needed to act, they had to have the authority. He knew the Coast Guard was doing everything humanly possible, but they still needed their orders.

"Well?" he finally asked the pilot.

"They're discussing the situation. They know what's at stake and they're coming up with a plan. Just hold on, Maguire. We'll get there, but we need to be smart about this."

Protocols. Ryan's fists clenched.

They were running out of time.

A door opened in the outside hall and Max was ready to bolt.

"Max!" a low voice said.

*Gabriel.*

She slipped through the door and he closed it behind her. All the shades were drawn, no one could see in.

Max immediately was at Eve's side. She looked like she was sleeping, but when Max took her hand she moaned, "Max." Her voice was slurred and almost too quiet to hear.

"What happened to her?" Max asked.

"Colter drugged her. She's in and out of consciousness. What's going on out there?"

"I haven't seen anyone. The Coast Guard helicopter is circling, but they haven't landed—I don't think they can at this speed. I saw their boat a few hundred meters behind. I don't know what the maximum speed is for the Coast Guard or what they're driving out there, but they're not gaining."

"We need help."

"They know. I've been texting Ryan when I could, I just don't know what he got and didn't get."

"If we can take out Colter, we can take back the ship. He has three people for sure—himself, one of the crew, and a big thug."

"Vance DuBois. I met him at the resort. How do we take him out? And there might be more than three people."

"Surprise. But I can't leave Eve alone."

"I'll stay with her."

"I hoped you'd say that. Lock the door behind me."

"Stay here with us. We can hole up here until the Coast Guard can mount a rescue."

"We don't know when that'll be! *If* they can even board before Colter kills someone else. Didn't you hear the gunfire?"

"Yes, but—"

"I'm right."

"Listen to me, Gabriel. If you can get to the pilothouse, you can take over the ship. Slow us down so the Coast Guard can board."

"Or better, go to the engine and sabotage it. I know a thing or two about boats."

She smiled. Good, he was thinking things through, not acting on emotion alone.

"Be careful, your daughter needs you."

Max searched Gabriel's eyes, hoping he wasn't going to do something stupid. But she saw reason and marginally relaxed.

Gabriel kissed Eve on the cheek, then left.

Max locked the door behind him and sat with Eve. She took her hand and squeezed. "It's okay, Eve, help is on its way."

Eve groaned. "Daddy."

"He'll be back soon."

"Max? That man says he's my dad. He's not, is he?"

Max had promised Eve she would never lie to her. She couldn't lie now. "I don't know," she said honestly. "But it doesn't matter who your biological father is. Gabriel is your dad. He always will be."

Eve sighed. "Okay."

"Shh." She heard someone walking by her door, try to open it.

"Eve, you're making this worse for yourself." It was Colter. "Let me in right now or I swear, I'll punish you and you'll never betray me again!"

Eve yelped, then bit her tongue.

"Shh," Max murmured and held her sister tight.

Phillip had not locked the door. That meant someone— Gabriel Truman, the bastard—had found Eve. If he thought a simple lock could keep Phillip from his daughter, he was mistaken.

He walked down to the adjoining suite, but out of the corner of his eye saw something—

A fire extinguisher came at him. Only because he'd seen

the movement was he able to shift, and his shoulder—his injured arm—took the brunt of the blow.

He screamed and discharged his weapon, but it didn't hit his target. He fired again and the bullet hit Gabriel in the arm.

Gabriel lunged at him, knocked him to the deck, wrestling for his gun.

Phillip's self-preservation instincts kicked in. He pinched his fingers into the wound on Gabriel's arm and the man screamed, but didn't let go. Gabriel kneed him in the balls and Phillip saw black for a moment, then felt his head being smacked on to the deck. His gun skittered away. Gabriel went after it.

Dazed, but determined not to let this bastard win, Phillip reached for the fire extinguisher. Gabriel was crawling toward the gun. Phillip hit him on the back of the head with the heavy metal canister. Gabriel collapsed. He tried to get up, then collapsed again.

Phillip spat a wad of bloody spit on him and hit him again, then picked up the gun. He was seeing stars, but he had won.

He shot Gabriel in the back.

"Good riddance."

He didn't see the helicopter until it was too late. A sniper aimed and fired three times, hitting Phillip with each bullet.

The Coast Guard boarded the ship and Colter's accomplices gave up without incident. Ryan searched the boat and found Max and Eve in a stateroom. Eve was unconscious and Max was cradling her like a baby, her body protecting her in case there was a threat.

He was relieved. She was safe. Alive. "Max." His voice cracked.

She looked up at him. "Ryan." Max had been crying.

Her face was wet and red and full of pain. Ryan couldn't imagine this woman, Maxine Revere, ever being vulnerable, but in that moment she was. He knelt next to her. "Eve? Is she—"

"She's okay. Colter sedated her. She didn't see." Fresh tears streamed out.

"Oh, baby, you saw what happened?"

"I heard the fight, barricaded Eve, looked out, hoping to help, but Colter shot him in the back. Is he—?"

Ryan shook his head.

The sobs came then. Ryan sat next to Max and held her and Eve. Held them both close. Grateful that they were safe, that Eve hadn't seen her father murdered in cold blood.

"Max, Eve is going to need you now, more than ever."

# Chapter Thirty-five

Hundreds of people came to Gabriel's funeral—so many, that the church was filled to capacity and dozens of people stood outside. The sky was gray, as if mourning the loss of a good man with occasional fat drops of water hitting the ground as the gods wept.

Max sat in the front with Eve on one side and David on the other. He'd been released from the hospital the day before, but he still looked pale. He would be flying back to New York tomorrow morning, where his ex-girlfriend had surprisingly agreed to come out with their daughter.

Tragedy sometimes had a way of bringing out the best in the worst people.

Ryan sat on the other side of Eve, who sat straight and stared at the picture of Gabriel she had chosen—his military service photo, him decked out in his dress blues. The minister knew Gabriel and his family and said nice things about him. When Eve went up to speak, Ryan took Max's hand.

Eve stood at the pulpit and, after a final look at the photo, turned to the crowd. "I don't know how long I can talk. But my dad was my best friend. He raised me when my mom left me. He took care of my grandma when she got sick. I was five when she died, but he read to her every night, and sometimes I would sit in the door and just listen. Dad had a great voice. It was quiet and deep and even though he didn't talk a lot, he knew how to tell a story.

"Dad taught me everything that is important to me. Sailing. Caring for others. Being a friend. He taught me that doing the right thing is not always easy, and that even when we do something wrong, forgiveness is always waiting for us. I love him. I'm going to miss him."

Tears streamed down her face. She looked at Max and Max nodded. Max couldn't stop crying. She rarely cried, but for some reason this week—almost losing David, losing Gabriel, watching Eve struggle with her grief—had taken a toll on her.

"Thank you for coming to say g-g-good b-b-bye to my dad."

Beth Henderson walked up and wrapped her arms around Eve, led her back to her seat. Max took Eve's hand, and Eve turned to her and sobbed into her shoulder.

Garrett Henderson informed the assembled mourners that the reception would be at the resort restaurant. The minister closed in prayer, then handed Max the urn of ashes. She already knew that Gabriel's will had asked that he be cremated and his ashes taken to sea. Eve had asked Max to take her out to do it. To put her dad at rest.

Max couldn't sleep Friday night. She sat in the kitchen of the Truman home while Eve slept upstairs, playing with a tea bag and hot water. She didn't feel like tea, but she hadn't really known what to do, so had made some. The process relaxed her, as it had years ago when she and Eleanor would make a pot of tea and sit in the garden.

She and Eve had been worn out by all the mourners. Beth Henderson and her husband Gary had cleaned up after all the guests had left. Max didn't know what she would have done without them—probably would have hired a team of people who didn't care about her, about Eve, about what had happened to Gabriel Truman.

David limped in and sat at the table across from Max with a sigh. "I just got off the phone with Brittney. She and Emma will be in New York Sunday morning. They're going to stay for a week."

"That's good. Really good."

"Partly. If Brittney and I don't kill each other."

"You have more restraint than you give yourself credit for." She reached over and took his hand. Max wasn't an affectionate person, but she needed to touch David, confirm that he was okay. "I can't tell you how relieved I am that you're going to be okay. You scared me."

"Now you know how I feel when you go off and put yourself in danger."

"I've never been shot."

He raised an eyebrow.

"Okay, but that was before you started working for me."

"It could have been you."

"I know. It should have been."

"Don't say that."

"I have to rethink some things. My decisions no longer just impact me."

"They never have."

"This is different, David."

"I know it is."

She sipped her tea; it had grown cold. She pushed it away because she didn't really want it.

"I may have to stay," she said.

"You'll do what's right for Eve."

"How do I know what's right?"

"You always do." He let out a chuckle. "Max, you've

always trusted your instincts and your judgment. Don't second guess yourself now—not when it matters the most."

"Staying or going to New York needs to be Eve's decision," Max said after a moment. "And I can live with either one."

"How are you doing knowing what happened with your mother?"

"I don't know *exactly* what happened, but I'm certain Colter killed her. The FBI is bringing in a forensic team to go over Colter's property with a fine-toothed comb. If she's buried there, they'll find her body. If not, I will assume he did something else with the body. But she's not alive."

"I wasn't specifically talking about her death. More generally, everything that she did. It's a lot to take in. If you want to talk—anytime—you know I'm here."

"I know. And I love you for it, David. You've been so supportive of me and this quest to find the truth. Now that I know? Well, I know the facts but I still don't understand why. Maybe I never will."

"You should take Dr. Kincaid up on his offer to visit. He has a knack for putting complex situations into perspective."

"He does. And maybe I will, but I have Eve to think about. Where I go, she goes, at least for a while. I want her to feel safe and comfortable."

"Gabriel Truman did a great job with her," David said. "She'll be okay. Just like you. If there's one thing I have learned about Revere women: you're the most capable people I know. If Eve is half as strong as you, she'll be just fine."

Max and Eve left early Saturday morning to take Gabriel out to sea. Just the two of them. Ryan had offered to join them, but Max told him she needed to do this alone. With her sister.

They hadn't talked much over the last week. There was so much to say, but there had been so much to do. The Hendersons had taken over feeding them, making sure there was enough food for Max and Eve for the rest of the year, it seemed. All day people came by the house, paying their condolences. Telling stories about Gabriel. Confirming to Max that he had been a good man. Eve was quiet, she was humble, and she hadn't cried since the funeral.

Max didn't know where to go from here. She had never faced a situation like this. She prided herself on always knowing what to do and when to do it, but now? Did she stay here, in Cape Haven, and raise Eve? Did she insist that Eve come with her to New York? Did she ask Beth Henderson to care for the sad teenager who had just had her world crushed?

"Here," Eve said and slowed the boat. They were on the *Emily*. Eve had told Max that she and Gabriel had renovated the boat together. One sentence, then nothing.

But that one sentence told Max everything she needed to know about the relationship between Eve and the man who raised her.

"Where are we?" Max asked.

"About a mile past Fisherman Island. Dad and I used to come out here sometimes just to watch the big ships come in under the bridge. Or go a little farther out, to where we couldn't see the land, and sit. It felt like we were the only people in the world. We didn't have to talk—my dad didn't talk a lot. But we didn't have to, you know? And sometimes, he would tell me stories. About his dad, a fisherman. His dad was never happy, except on the water. I think my dad was the same way sometimes."

"There is a true peace out here on the ocean," Max

said. "Especially on a day like today." It was cold but clear, endless blue and green, the waves gentle but constant.

"I miss him," Eve said. She held the urn tight against her chest. "I don't know what to do."

Max didn't know what to do, either. The answers that always seemed to come to her so easily weren't there. She was fumbling around in a world she didn't understand.

"We'll figure it out," she said.

That sounded so stupid. Why couldn't she give Eve reassurance? Hope?

"Are you . . . are you going back to New York?"

"Not right away."

"What . . . what about me? What's going to happen to me?"

She sounded scared, and that was the last thing that Max wanted for her sister.

"You're my sister. We're family. I'm not going anywhere without you." She hesitated. Max couldn't imagine living in Cape Haven. Yes, to visit—it was beautiful and peaceful, even with all the darkness they'd faced these last two weeks. Her life was in New York City, but she was used to traveling. "We'll make it work," she said, feeling more confident as she spoke. "I can work from here, go to New York when I need to be in the studio. I can cut back on travel, focus on cold cases on the East Coast. Maybe I'll quit."

"Quit your job? I thought you liked what you do."

"I do. But I don't need to work."

"What would you do?"

"Take care of you?"

Eve smiled. "You know I'm sixteen."

"Yes, but you still need someone. I mean, I suppose you could be emancipated, but I am your sister. I want to be your sister."

"I'd like that a lot."

Relief flooded through Max. "Okay. Then we'll go from there."

"Do you want to move here?"

Max didn't say anything.

"You promised you would never lie to me."

"I can live here for a while. I might go crazy, but this is your home."

Eve shook her head. She held up the urn. "My dad was my home. Everything I knew about me was wrong. About my mother, my father, Uncle Brian—everything here reminds me of my dad, but it reminds me of what happened, too. I don't know—I think, maybe, I just need to figure out who I am and who I want to be. Does that sound stupid?"

"I think you are very wise."

"Would you . . . would you consider letting me come to New York with you?"

"Do you want to come to New York?"

She nodded. "But I don't want to be trouble."

"You're not trouble. Eve, you are my sister, you are part of me. I never thought I'd have a sister. You're the best thing that I could have found when I started this search. I want you with me. Here or New York, wherever you want to go. We have time to figure it out."

"Okay. Good. I want to go to New York with you. Maybe visit here sometimes?"

"Whenever you want."

"You mean that?"

"Yes, I do. Your house is your house. You have part of Havenly." Max was already talking to her lawyers about buying out Boreal's half of the resort. Considering what their principal Colter had done, she knew she'd get it. But she'd share those details with Eve when they were both not so emotionally on edge.

Eve looked down at the urn. "He died for me."

"Gabriel died a hero. Because he loved you, and because that was the type of man he was."

Eve opened the urn and turned it on its side, letting the wind carry Gabriel's ashes into the waves. She then leaned over and rinsed the urn out, then filled it with water. "Is this silly?"

"No," Max said.

"Can we sit out here a little longer?"

"We'll sit out here as long as you want."

Eve put her head on Max's shoulder. Max held her sister close to her side. Tears fell, silent, as they said good-bye to a hero.

Max was staying at the Truman house with Eve. Ryan had come down for the funeral, but had to go back to Norfolk to wrap up some paperwork. He returned Sunday and Max didn't realize how happy she was to see him.

Max hugged him as soon as he walked in. He hugged her back. "Where's Eve?"

"Sleeping. I don't think she's slept much this week, but after the funeral—and our private burial—she needs it."

"David?"

"Flew back to New York yesterday."

"So it's you and me." He kissed her forehead.

"And Eve. I don't want to leave her alone just yet."

"Of course not."

He kissed her again, this time longer. She felt that familiar heat rise, then he stepped back.

"Wow," she said. "You really missed me."

She was trying to make light of it, but Ryan's expression was serious. "Very much. You okay?"

She nodded. "I'm okay. Eve will be okay, too."

She led him to the living room. She'd put the seascape back into its frame and rehung it. Ryan had taken the Degas to FBI headquarters. The house looked like a home, but it was no longer home to anyone.

"When are you going back to New York?"

"I'm going to take the week and put Gabriel's affairs in order, arrange for a caretaker for the house, then play it by ear. Eve doesn't want to stay in Cape Haven, but she might change her mind."

"You'd move here for her?"

"I would do anything for her. Right now she wants to move with me to New York. I told her okay, but I don't know if that's the right decision."

"Why?"

"Because she's grieving. What if she regrets the move?"

"Then you'll cross that bridge when you come to it."

"Truly? I want her with me in New York. I like it here, but I would go stir-crazy. Still, it's not an impossible commute."

"Spoken like someone who has never commuted in their life." He touched her softly, almost tenderly. "I have to talk to you about something."

"Okay." Her heart thudded. "Anything." She was still trying to keep the conversation light, because this entire week had been filled with darkness. She didn't know if she could handle more sorrow.

Ryan hesitated.

Max said, "Now you have me worried. You're way too serious. Did something happen with the case? With the authentication of the Degas?"

"No, everything is amazing. My colleagues raided Colter's house in Dallas. There were dozens of pieces of art, some exceptional reproductions—we'd call them forgeries if he was trying to sell them—and some originals, most stolen. There are a couple we don't have the provenance for and Colter's accomplice Vance is cooperating, so I'm optimistic we'll find all the answers. And we have thousands of pages of notes, datebooks, and the like that will take time to go through. But I'm working on it."

"That's good news."

"The Degas is the piece stolen from the museum in Dallas. And the Caravaggio was authenticated as well—you were right."

"I usually am."

Now he smiled. "And that's why I'm falling in love with you."

Her heart skipped a beat.

"I have to get it out there in the open. We haven't talked a lot about your past relationships or mine or how open you are to a relationship at all, but I think we're amazing together, and I want more."

"I . . . well, honestly, I don't have a good track record."

"That's clear. You're not married, you're not living with anyone."

"Yes, but it's me."

"Because you're smart? A lot of men don't like smart women. I can assure you, that's not a problem for me. Because you're stubborn? It's sometimes annoying, but mostly charming."

"Charming," she said flatly.

"Because you're independent? Good. That goes hand in hand with being smart. You have a career, you know what you want, you get it. Because you're rich? I don't care about money either way, and I make a good living. I can't fly off to Paris or Edinburgh at the drop of a hat, but I own my house on the beach in Virginia, have no debt, and am already saving up for my retirement. Have been since I was twenty-two because I was an econ major and never believed that Social Security would be around when I hit sixty-five or seventy. Plus I have a pension. So

I certainly don't love you for your money because I get by just fine on my own."

"You don't have to—"

"What? Tell you why you're desirable?"

Max was rarely, if ever, at a loss for words.

Ryan pulled her down onto the couch. "Smart. Stubborn. Damn sexy. Maybe you take too many risks, but I'm okay with that. I haven't stopped thinking about last weekend. I get horny just thinking about when we shared a bed. I have been anticipating making love to you since I left. But it's not fair to you—or to me—to have these feelings and not express them."

She kissed him, her fingers found their way to his hair. "Are you going to cut your hair?"

"No."

She smiled. "What if I told you it was a deal-breaker?"

"I'd still say no. I like my hair. Most men who are forty don't have hair as good as mine. If you want me to cut it, it means you have no taste."

She laughed. She laughed a lot more around Ryan than she had around any of her other boyfriends.

She shouldn't compare Ryan to anyone else. It wasn't fair to Ryan, or to any of the men who came before him. He was an original, one of a kind, and she was definitely interested. More than a little interested.

"And there's something else." He kissed her, then adjusted their position so he was leaning back into the corner of the couch and she was lying right next to him, close. "I was offered a position as SSA of my own white-collar crime squad with an emphasis on art and securities fraud. In the New York City field office. I've wanted it for a while, but because I'm sort of unorthodox in how I approach my job, I've been passed over twice for promotions. This case bumped me to the top of the list. I don't want you to think that I'm taking it just to be closer to you. I mean, if for some ridiculous reason you want to dump me, there're a few million other women in New York who would be very happy and lucky to have me. But this offer came now. I start in three weeks, and I want to see you as much as I can. And being in New York will make that a lot easier." He paused. "Though if you end up staying here, I suppose it's me who will be traveling to see you."

Max rarely feared anything, but suddenly she was scared. "I've only had long-distance relationships."

"Because they're safe," he said. "You'll always have an excuse to walk away, and it's not that hard to leave when you're a thousand miles away from the guy you're sleeping with. This isn't going to be safe, Max. This is going to be fun, it's going to be hot, and it's going to last."

"You can't know that." Was that why she was scared? Because nothing lasted in her life?

"You overthink everything. Sometimes, that's a terrific trait. Other times, not so much. We all have baggage. Some more than others. I was raised in a great home. We had very little, and my mom worked her ass off. She was tired a lot, but she loved us, and we took care of one another. But just because my dad was a jerk who left her and didn't help one iota doesn't mean that I think it's okay to do the same thing, or that I think every relationship is destined to fail. I can see how your rather unusual upbringing clouds your perception of everything."

"I'm clearheaded. I go into situations without any preconceived notions—I go in and look at the evidence, find the truth, and reveal it."

"It's cute that you believe that."

"Now you're insulting me?" She arched her eyebrow. "You aren't perfect, Agent Maguire."

He mock frowned. "Surely, you jest."

"That whole number code theory on the postcards—it meant nothing."

He didn't say anything.

"It didn't," Max insisted. "It had nothing to do with the Degas or Colter or the other paintings."

"Well," he said slowly, "you're right about that. I just don't think that the dates mean nothing. I just haven't figured it out yet."

"But you will," she said with a smile. "And people think *I'm* arrogant."

"Yes, you dig for the truth and you're really good at finding it, so yes, you're a bit arrogant, but very much deserved."

"Glad you see that," Max said. Although Ryan wasn't arrogant, not like she was. He was extremely confident, and she liked that.

"But you're cynical."

"And you're not?" As she said it she realized she had not once thought of Ryan as cynical. Fun, smart, capable, excitable, but certainly not a cynic.

"I don't think just because you've never had a healthy relationship doesn't mean you're damaged goods."

"I wouldn't say *never* had a healthy relationship."

Ryan shrugged, kissed her spontaneously. "Not never. You have one now."

"Do I?"

"I usually get what I want."

"So do I."

"I want you. You good?"

Was she? She'd never met anyone like Ryan before. With all the men she'd been involved with, it was either a game for control—like Marco trying to change her and challenge her all the time, or trust, like Nick, who kept half his life closed off from her. She'd been involved with others, some she liked a lot, some who were good in bed, and some who were simply interesting. But she had never had what Ryan was suggesting they try to have—a healthy relationship. And she realized that not only did she deserve it, she was ready to try.

She smiled slowly. "I'm very good."

"Is that a challenge?"

"Are you up for it?"

"For you? Anytime." He scooped her up.

"You've got to stop carrying me. I'm not a little petite nothing."

"You're perfect, as I'm sure you would agree." He kissed her. "And I like surprising you. I don't think it happens very often."

He walked up the stairs with her and she pointed to the guest room where she was staying, small, but more than adequate.

He closed the door and dropped her to her feet.

"You and me, Max Revere." He kissed her as he backed her toward the bed. "We are going to be great."

# Chapter One

**MONDAY**

FBI Agent Lucy Kincaid reviewed the file on a case she had just finished, to make sure everything was in order for the U.S. Attorney who would be handling the prosecution. She had simply worked on follow-up interviews in a multi-jurisdictional case. Nothing earth-shattering and she'd been home before seven every night this last month. She certainly had no complaints about the mundane paperwork because after two back-to-back complex and dangerous cases, she was happy to have settled into a comfortable routine with her husband and stepson. She'd even taken a three-day weekend to fly to Colorado with Sean to celebrate their one-year wedding anniversary. Her colleague and friend Nate Dunning had stayed with Jesse so Sean and Lucy could have some alone time.

Now, if she could get her family to confirm who was coming over for Thanksgiving, she'd be even happier. She'd wanted everyone here—to avoid traveling with Jesse after he'd been through so much this last year—but no one wanted to commit. She tried not to be down about it, but she missed her brothers and sisters. She sent one last email out to her clan and said she wanted answers by the weekend. Harsh, maybe, but necessary when Thanksgiving was only ten days away. Almost as soon as she hit send, her cell phone rang.

"Patrick!" she exclaimed. She hadn't talked to her brother, who was the youngest of the clan until she came along ten years after him, in weeks, and hadn't seen him since she took hostage rescue training back in May.

"You sound good," he said.

"I am. Sean and I were able to get away for a long weekend for our anniversary."

"So I heard. Terrific. And Jesse is doing well?"

"He's been amazing. Adjusting better than I could have hoped."

"Well, he's Sean's kid, I wouldn't expect anything less."

"So you got my email and you *are* coming to San Antonio for Thanksgiving. You and Elle, of course." She winced that she'd almost forgot to mention Patrick's long-time girlfriend. They'd been living together in DC for nearly two years, but Lucy and Elle butted heads when they were in the same room. Maybe because they didn't always agree on criminal justice issues, and maybe because Patrick was her brother and she didn't think that Elle was quite good enough. Sean had pointed out more than once that Patrick hadn't liked the idea of Sean—his business partner and friend—getting involved with his sister, and yet Patrick had come around.

Lucy tried to explain that this was different, but it wasn't. She knew she was being unreasonable, but she didn't know how to like Elle. However, she'd bent over backwards when she was living out in DC during hostage rescue training. She and Elle had even gone out for coffee a couple of times. Lucy didn't want anything or anyone to come between her and her brother.

"Actually," Patrick said.

And she knew.

"Elle's in the middle of a big case, and we don't know

if it'll be done before Thanksgiving. She can't just walk out in the middle of it. There's three kids at stake. Their dad is nowhere to be found, their mother is in jail for possession with intent, and CPS split them up because the oldest has been in trouble. We're going to try, Luce, I promise, but I can't guarantee."

"I understand," she said but she really didn't. Yes, she understood why Elle couldn't leave. The one thing Lucy admired about Elle was that she fought for those who couldn't fight for themselves. But couldn't Patrick just come out for one night? Would it kill them to be apart for a day?

"Luce, you don't sound like you understand."

"Let me know, I won't force you to give me an answer, okay? I just want to see you. I miss you."

"I miss you too, sis. I promise, we'll really try. How're Sean and Jesse doing?"

"Good," she said, though knew this was just small talk. Sean and Patrick worked together remotely on many projects, and Patrick talked to Sean more than he talked to her.

"Lucy, Nate." Rachel Vaughn, their boss, came down the hall and motioned for them to join her in her office.

"I have to go, my boss just called me in for a meeting."

"I meant what I said, Lucy. I will do everything in my power to come out for Thanksgiving."

"I know you will. Love you." She hung up.

Maybe Rachel had a meaty case that would keep her mind off her family this week.

Nate closed the door behind him and Rachel said, "We have a break in the flood case."

Lucy had been assisting the Bexar and Kerr County Sheriff's offices over the last two months in the case of four unidentified skeletons unearthed during the flash flooding over Labor Day weekend.

"IDs?" Lucy asked.

"Yes, and it's become far more complicated than we thought, which is why I want you to fill Nate in on the case. We're taking lead, working with both Kerr and Bexar, but it's our case."

"Neither of them are going to like it." Until now, Lucy's role had been more logistical as the crime lab was working closely with the FBI lab at Quantico.

"This isn't a Bexar case, though the crime lab is involved. I just got off the phone with the Assistant Sheriff, who is fine with giving this to us and offered assistance as needed. It's Kerr that's raising Cain, so I'm pulling in Nate. This isn't a slight against your competence, Lucy—it's because two FBI agents are going to hold more weight than one and this investigation could be tricky. Cold cases often are."

Cold cases rarely had the resources for multiple agents. They were investigated as time permitted. Now Lucy was more than a little interested in who these people were. All they knew at this point was that the victims were four Caucasians, a male in his forties, a female in her forties, and two teen-age females. The San Antonio ME brought in a forensic anthropologist from the university who said they'd been dead slightly over three years. All four had been shot twice in the back of the head and evidence indicated they'd been killed where they were found, but with the contamination of the burial site, they couldn't confirm.

"And?" Lucy pressed. "A family, right?" That had been the logical assumption, but DNA testing could rarely be done overnight.

Rachel nodded.

"The Albrights. They disappeared just over three years ago, last seen on Friday, September twenty-first. Denise Albright was an accountant suspected of embezzling three million dollars from the construction company she worked for, which had just landed a federal contract for a major public works transportation project. Because federal funds were missing, the AUSA opened an investigation but it was put on hold when they believed she fled to avoid being questioned. The theft had been discovered after she disappeared, but it isn't a stretch to believe that she thought she would be caught. The owner of the company had scheduled an independent audit for the following week."

"No one knew she'd been killed?"

"Her vehicle was tagged crossing the border in Brownsville the day they disappeared. She and her husband both withdrew the maximum they could from their ATMs that afternoon, and used his credit card to fill up with gas in Brownsville and buy supplies at a camping goods store. Security cameras showed a man matching Albright's description at the store, but the gas station didn't keep tape."

"So this wasn't planned—they were running on the fly," Nate said.

Rachel nodded. "So it appears. Her company told her that Friday morning that they were auditing the accounts, and she was told to have all the files together by Monday afternoon."

"They were suspicious of her?" Lucy asked.

"From the minimal information I received from Kerr County, no. The owner wanted the audit before he started on the project. He had multiple projects, but the public works project was eighty percent of his business for the year and he wanted his ducks in a row, I suppose. His contact information is in the file so you can reach out."

Rachel shifted through papers and handed Lucy a business card. "AUSA Shelley Adair handled the case from the beginning, hopefully she has more info about the particulars of the crime. All I know from the database is that it was on hold pending locating Denise Albright. However, we have another issue to deal with—the Albrights also had a son, and his remains weren't found with his family."

"How old?" Nate asked.

"He was nine at the time his family disappeared. He would be twelve if he's still alive, but it's likely that he is buried elsewhere. Ash Dominguez at the crime lab received the same email I did Friday night, from the lab at Quantico, and he's called in cadaver dogs to search the area. Or maybe they left him in Mexico for some reason when they returned."

"They came back with their teenage daughters and not their son?" Lucy said. "That doesn't seem likely."

"We don't know what they were thinking. But someone murdered this family within weeks of their initial disappearance." Rachel handed Lucy a thin file. "That's the report from Quantico. I also forwarded you the email. They can't give us TOD down to the minute, but the tools they have are pretty amazing now and they concur with the forensic anthropologist that the bones were between three years and three years three months old. They narrowed it further with soil samples and put TOD mid-September to end of October. The Albrights were seen crossing the border on Friday, September twenty-first. That's the last sighting of their vehicle. They haven't attempted to access their bank accounts since that Friday, which have been monitored as part of the investigation into the embezzlement. If you need help with the white collar crime angle, you can tap Agent Laura Williams who's been assisting the AUSA, but this week she's wrapped up in a major federal trial. Keep her in the loop, but she might not respond immediately."

Rachel looked from Nate to Lucy.

"Find out who killed this family," Rachel said, "and if Denise Albright was responsible for the missing money. If she's guilty, she had a partner—someone who is capable of killing children. But mostly, find out what happened to Ricky Albright and if there is any chance that he's still alive."

Don't miss the novels in **Allison Brennan**'s
thrilling bestselling **Lucy Kincaid** series

All available from St. Martin's Paperbacks